THE SECRETS
WE KEEP

BOOK 1 OF 7 IN
"The Secret Series"

B. J. STEELE

Spread the Word

While Amazon doesn't require referrals, your personal recommendation is one of the most powerful gifts you can give.
Please share B. J. Steele's books with your friends, family, co-workers, blog readers, and social media followers. Every share, shoutout, and retweet helps us reach new readers and takes us one step closer to making B. J. Steele a #1 Bestselling Author!

✿ Join the VIP List

Want to be the first to know about new releases, sneak peeks, and exclusive content? Join the VIP list today, just click the link below and drop your email:
https://www.bjsteelebooks.com/

DEDICATION

For readers who crave Lucy Score's addictive romance but want Colleen Hoover's emotional punch — this is your next obsession.

CONTENTS

INTRODUCTION

Romance has always thrived on tropes: the billionaire boss, the forbidden office affair, the secret pregnancy that upends everything. Readers love them because they promise drama, heat, and escape. But if you've ever longed for something deeper, something that blends the addictive banter of Lucy Score with the emotional punch of Colleen Hoover, you're holding the right book.

The Secrets We Keep doesn't just give you a billionaire or a baby. It gives you the consequences. What happens when first love doesn't just break you, but leaves you raising a son alone in a town that never forgets? What happens when the man who left returns, not as a fantasy, but as a flawed, exhausted doctor trying to mend more than one kind of heart?

This isn't about a glittering boardroom. It's about a bookstore with creaky floors and a cat who thinks he's in charge. It's about neighbors who gossip as fast as the rain falls, and a small-town fundraiser where paper hearts on a window hold more weight than stock portfolios. It's about secrets, second chances, and the terrifying beauty of telling the truth when timing hates it.

Here, love isn't just an escape; it's a reckoning. Clara Monroe doesn't need rescuing; she needs a partner strong enough to face what was broken and brave enough to build something new. And Ethan Hale isn't a prince with unlimited wealth, he's a man with scars, regrets, and a chance to prove that coming home can be the most daring move of all.

If you're tired of romances that only scratch the surface, this story will take you deeper, into forgiveness, into family, into love that has been tested by years of silence and still finds a way to breathe.

So, settle in. Willow Cove has been waiting for you. And once you start, you'll understand: this isn't just another romance. It's a story about the ones who got away, the lies we told to survive, and the hope that even broken hearts can still come home.

***What Secrets* do you Keep?**

(Book 2 of the "Secret Series" Coming Soon). Read all the books. Join the VIP list and help choose a Character for Book 2 in "The Secret Series." Look at our Movie Trailers on our website.

SUMMARY

In Willow Cove, gossip spreads faster than a summer storm, and Clara Monroe is about to be the headline.

Twelve years ago, Ethan Hale was the boy who stole her heart, then broke it. Now he's back, no longer the small-town golden boy, but a billionaire doctor burned out from city life. He returns with swagger, charm, and the same devastating smile… only this time, he has no idea he's the father of Clara's twelve-year-old son.

As the town's newest physician, Ethan is determined to rebuild his life in the very place he once left behind. But between small-town gossip, meddling neighbors, and a fundraiser that throws him into forced proximity with Clara, he quickly learns two things:

Willow Cove never forgets.

Neither does Clara.

Every stolen glance reignites old passion. Every brush of his hand tempts Clara to trust again. But secrets this big don't stay buried, and Ethan is about to discover that fatherhood is messier and more rewarding than he ever imagined.

With a protective single mom guarding her heart, a secret son with a sketchbook full of surprises, and a town that thrives on second chances, Ethan must prove he's not the boy who left… but the man who's here to stay.

A swoony, slow-burning small-town, second-chance romance with a secret baby twist, perfect for fans of steamy love stories, meddling townsfolk, and happily-ever-afters that are worth the wait.

CHAPTER ONE

The Secrets We Keep

CLARA

The bell over my bookstore door is a chronic overachiever. It dings for breezes, sighs for moths, and once rang a full requiem for Henry Parker's scarf. But that morning, it yelped, one sharp, surprised yip that yanked my head up from the stack of romances I was pretending wasn't a therapy session.

The bell doesn't false-alarm. It's an omen machine, and somewhere under my ribs, a smaller bell answers. Today, its ring doesn't say trouble. It says *brace*.

"Emergency?" I asked the room.

Midnight, my sleek black cat and benevolent tyrant, blinked from the counter. He is pro-drama only when he causes it.

"Not an emergency," Maya announced, barreling in on a gust that smelled like cinnamon and weather decisions. My best friend carried two to-go coffees like trophies and her hair like a warning. "But you're going to want caffeine."

You look like you just saw a ghost, or worse, good forearms. This town's gossip mill doesn't need lube; they've got you two.

"I'm in a committed relationship with caffeine." I took the lid off and moaned. "Did you sweet-talk the foam into a heart?"

Save those noises for after-hours, Clara. My latte can't compete with your love life, or the lack of one.

"I bribed it with hope." She leaned on the counter and lowered her voice. "Also, rumor has it the clinic board found a new doc."

Clara's pulse skipped. The town loved new arrivals, but she hated that every whisper still tugged the old wound open. Every secret here traveled faster than the weather, and hers wasn't built for storms.

Midnight turned his head very slowly, which is his version of a gasp.

"Willow Cove has twelve thousand opinions and three stoplights," I said. "We'll make him a casserole and a conspiracy theory and call it civic engagement."

"Clara." Maya's eyes did the earnest thing. "It's him."

I school my face into the expression I reserve for unreliable weather and men with jawlines, polite, cautious. My hands, traitors, practice hope on the countertop.

The stack of paperbacks slid: bared abs and promises skittering toward the floor. I saved the books and lost my pulse.

"Lots of men are named 'him,'" I said. "It's biblical."

"Lots of men are named Ethan Hale?" she asked gently.

Midnight's tail flicked. Traitor.

"I don't care if it's Ethan Hale." I absolutely cared. "We have a fundraiser to run. I have a cat to impress. Also, I'm immune to men with jawlines."

"Uh-huh. Tell your eyebrows." She lifted a brow and offered me a napkin. "You're doing that thing where you hold your breath. Stop."

The bell yelped again.

"Not him," Maya whispered, reading the bell like scripture.

It was Mayor Tom with two fistfuls of flyers, a tie at half-mast, and the buoyant catastrophism of a golden retriever who ran for office. "Books & Hearts Gala, people!" he boomed. "Lanterns, not pirates!"

"We are not revisiting the pirate year," I said, grabbing his stack.

"The parents still talk about it," he said, misty. "The eye patches. The litigation." He clapped his hands once. "Okay, Clara, I need your windows, your charm, and your paper-cutting fingers. We're making a donor wall: gold hearts for fifty, silver for a hundred, one big red book for the generous souls who make angels weep."

Midnight peered into Tom's tote and smacked a roll of tape with a paw. Approved.

"Gala HQ is here," Maya said. "Cinnamon bribes will be deployed. We will fund a clinic so that good people can fake symptoms to visit."

"Minimalist glitter," Tom breathed.

"Boundaries," I corrected, because Tom needs words like seatbelts.

Boundaries," I corrected, because Tom needs words like seatbelts.

Behind him, Mrs. Donnelly leaned in from the bakery stall, stage-whispering: "If you two don't kiss by chapter twenty, I'm demanding a refund." The whole shop laughed. Midnight rolled his eyes like a cat used to plotlines.

The bell yelped a third time, suspiciously like a drumroll.

"Not him," Maya mouthed.

It was Mr. Pierce with Ace, the Dalmatian, who does weekly therapy rounds at the clinic and has more emotional intelligence than anyone on the town council. Ace sat, accepted a pat, and scanned the premises. Midnight narrowed his eyes. A détente was reached.

"You look like a woman who's about to pretend she's fine," Mr. Pierce said kindly.

"I am fine," I said, and then remembered I'd promised myself to stop lying to the retired firefighter who sees through weather and women. "I am… hydrated."

"Hydration is courage," he said. "Ace agrees." Ace thumped his tail once.

Midnight disdain-blinked. Courage is canned tuna, his face said.

The gust that came next wasn't so much weather, as it was timing.

The bell didn't yelp. It sang, one clear, surprised note that landed somewhere under my breastbone. The doorway seemed to shrink to fit him, rain-dark hair dripping, scrubs clinging like memory had dressed him, not fabric. Even the air smelled the same, cedar soap and trouble.

I turned.

Ethan Hale looked exactly like a memory I'd sworn I'd refiled: tall, rain-damp hair, scrubs under a jacket, eyes I used to think in. His mouth did a quick flicker of a smile I didn't believe in anymore, until I did.

"Hey," he said. It came out like a question he wanted me to grade.

The room remembers him before I do. The bell hushes. The wood underfoot shifts. Even Midnight sits taller, like we've all been caught telling the truth at last.

"Hi," I said. If my voice was steady, it was because my knees were polite.

He took us in: the bell still humming, Tom already plotting, Maya gripping a cinnamon knot like a weapon, Ace dignified, Midnight ready to file a complaint.

"Did I miss the heist?" Ethan asked. "Because this looks like a planning meeting."

"Gala," Tom announced. "Lanterns, not pirates. You're late; please donate."

Ethan's mouth tilted. "I can do lanterns." He looked back at me. "Can I do lanterns?"

"You can do donations," I said. "Lanterns must be earned."

Maya gave a low whistle. "We're doing banter."

Ace wagged once, promising.

Midnight yawned: derivative.

"Welcome back to Willow Cove," Mr. Pierce said, saving me from having to choose between civility and history. "You look like a man who intends to stay put."

Ethan's gaze flicked to me and away. "That's the plan."

My chest made a sound only I could hear. It was either hope or heartburn. I set the red paper book in the center of the window and pressed it flat against the glass.

"Clara runs gala HQ," Maya said briskly, because she learned first aid for conversational hemorrhages. "We are building a donor wall of hearts and a program that makes people ugly-cry in public."

Tom nodded. "Tasteful crying," he said. "PG-13 tears."

"I came to buy hearts," Ethan said, sliding his card across the counter, "and offer a storage closet I already apologized to."

I raised a brow. "The closet that ate the AED?"

"Evicted," he said. "Joan runs the place like weather with bangs."

"Good. We're allergic to chaos." I slid the first gold heart toward him and held out a Sharpie. We're allergic to chaos." I slid the first gold heart toward him and held out a Sharpie.

"Sharpies I can afford," he muttered. "The town's probably still googling my net worth, but nobody tells you how stupid money looks when you're buying tape. "Who's your first name?"

He didn't answer me. He looked past me to the window. A woman in a yellow raincoat hovered on the sidewalk, clutching an envelope like it might fly away. She caught my eye. Her relief made my throat tight.

"For my dad," she said when she came in. "He used to say Dr. Hale… your Dr. Hale… bought him six months he didn't deserve. I wanted to give something."

"Name?" I asked because my job today was paper and permission.

"Daniel Ortiz," she said. "Silver heart."

Ace sidled closer and leaned against her leg. The woman pressed her lips together and nodded like the room had signed a pact.

I wrote Daniel Ortiz slowly, carefully, and pressed the silver heart to the glass. The tape made a small, satisfying sound; I could have sworn the old bell tried to harmonize with it.

When the woman left, the door made a soft kiss against the jamb. The quiet that followed wasn't awkward. It was… wide.

"Thank you," Ethan said, low. I didn't look at him. I didn't have to. He was looking at the silver heart like a man who knew what extra time costs.

"Donor hearts will make people slow down," Noah said from the front window.

He'd arrived without fanfare the way twelve-year-old boys do: a sketchbook, a curated aloofness, hair that no comb can convince of anything. His sneakers squeaked when he shifted his weight; Midnight materialized beside him like a shadow with opinions.

"Slow down to look?" Ethan asked, careful.

"Slow down to care." Noah flipped his sketchbook around. Crosswalk concept: open books, pages becoming waves, tiny foxes hidden where only the curious would see. "You can't speed when you're hunting Easter eggs."

Ethan grinned, surprise and awe tangled. "You just solved traffic."

"Mayor Tom's problem," Noah said, deadpan. "I take cookies."

Tom slapped a hand over his heart. "Consider the cookie fund appropriated."

Ace made a noble sound that suggested competence. Midnight leaped onto the sketchbook and sat on the foxes. Editorial approval.

"Okay," I said, clapping once, because we were about three seconds from me flinging myself into a wall to avoid eye contact. "Assignments. Tom, copy shop. Maya, cinnamon bribes. Mr. Pierce, Ace morale rounds. Noah, sketch revisions. Midnight, supervisory glare."

"And me?" Ethan asked.

"You are a volunteer with good handwriting," I said, and handed him a stack of blank hearts. "There are rules."

"Do they involve glitter?"

"Minimalist glitter," I said. "Boundaries are beautiful."

"Copy that," he said, and smiled in a way that made the bell do that quiet hum again.

For a flicker, the grin slipped, his eyes dark, bare, like he was begging me not to send him away again. Then he masked it with humor, but the honesty had already landed in my ribs.

By afternoon, the window glittered with names: grandparents, high school English teachers, lake walkers, a mysterious "Anonymous" with a goose doodle I chose not to interrogate. People slowed outside. That was the secret pleasure of paper hearts, the way they turned the world into a better driver.

"Cinnamon intervention," Maya said, sliding a plate across the counter. "Also, the clinic board wants you to MC the gala. You own a microphone and a spine."

"MC," I repeated, like an acronym might help me forget that public speaking makes my palms perform an interpretive dance.

"You'll be brilliant," she said. "You'll say words, and people will make money." She peered at the window. "That red book is lonely."

"Big donor will come," I said, and tried not to glance at the man who already knew where the big donors kept their pens.

As if summoned by a character arc, the wind decided it lived here. The bell did a tiny, frightened clink. Rain began politely, then remembered who it was and came sideways.

"Window," I said. "Midnight, do not assist."

I grabbed painter's tape. Midnight followed because disobedience is his love language. I anchored the top seam while the pane complained in a language I'm fluent in, a glass language.

"Left edge," Ethan said, already at my elbow with a steadying hand on the ladder like he'd never unlearned me. "Top seam."

"I make the plans in this store," I said out of habit, but my fingers were grateful for the help. The bead of water nosing the corner thought about its choices and retreated.

"Stable," Maya called from the counter. "Improving. Ace, morale."

But when his hand skimmed her hip to steady the ladder, heat licked sharper than lightning. She almost told him to let go, except her body leaned, reckless traitor, into the press of him.

Ace did a lap and collected three pats, while Midnight leapt onto the sketchbook and sat on the foxes like a literary critic who disapproved of joy. The whole room laughed, relief messy and needed.

Ace did a lap and collected three pats and a promise of a later hot dog. Midnight supervised from a coil of twine and made a face that translated to amateurs.

The pane gave a single high, thin ping, like a chaperone clearing its throat. *For a flicker, I imagined him gone again, like the storm would take him back to the city and leave me with only tape and silence. The thought bit deeper than the rain.* We climbed down at the same time and turned into each other because timing is a prankster.

A **short body-memory flash**

CLARA

The way his touch recalls senior prom under the bleachers, when they nearly went further but didn't.

His hand rises, then pauses. I nod before I know I've done it. Fingers bracket my jaw, steady, asking. The kiss lands like current through copper: quiet, exact, inevitable. His chest pressed mine against the ladder rung, heat threading through restraint. The storm outside cracked, but inside the crackle was only us, wanting, bottled, dangerous, patient. His thumb brushed the edge of my lower lip as if memorizing what he didn't yet dare take.   For one suspended breath, my body leaned anyway, ribs rising to meet a mouth that wasn't supposed to be mine anymore. Heat crackled down my spine like copper wire daring me to misbehave. The ache of twelve years pooled in the inch between us, hotter than a kiss would have been. When we part, the window sighs, and the bell, smug thing, rings once.

We don't kiss. We decide not to. The decision itself hums between us. Noah sketches them without realizing, drawing foxes hiding between their outlines. He tells himself it's "for the gala," but it's really his first subconscious acceptance.

"Okay," I said, to the tape, to the bell, to my body. "Okay."

"Okay," Ethan echoed, because he was kind enough not to call my okay a prayer.

We lasted forty-seven minutes without saying anything dangerous. That's a personal record.

"Mayor," I said, "we need your bench for a poetry reading at the gala. And your microphone. And a speech with no pirate jokes."

Tom saluted. "I can give you two of those things." Lanterns, not pirates," I remind him. He beams, scribbles it on his notepad, and later we'll find the words on mugs, stickers, and at least one child's drawing taped to the town hall wall.

He flapped toward the square with a packet of flyers and a dangerous optimism.

"Clara," Maya said in the voice that gets me to look at the thing I'm trying to pretend isn't in the room. "He's here."

"I noticed," I said. "So did my endocrine system."

"You're going to be nice," she said. "And firm. And witty. You are not going to stand in your own way and call it caution."

I narrowed my eyes. "Has anyone ever told you you'd make a fantastic villain?"

"Yes," she said, pleased. "They were right."

I had just decided to be exactly as brave as my cat thinks he is when the door swung open again.

A woman in a sunshine-yellow raincoat stood there, drops beading on her lashes, envelope trembling in her hands. "I; Is this where; I heard; the hearts, " She broke off, embarrassed by her own trying.

"You're in the right place," I said. "What name would you like to honor?"

She swallowed. "My dad. Daniel Ortiz."

"We have him," I said quietly. The silver heart gleamed like it had been waiting. "We'll put yours next to his."

The woman pressed her lips together. "He always said this town saved him three times: once when the dock didn't break, once when the church bell rang, and once when a doctor remembered his wife's name."

"Doctors who remember names should get cinnamon knots," Maya said. "That's my policy."

Ethan didn't say anything. He was looking at the window like a man being allowed to stay for once.

When the woman left, Noah drifted in from the side aisle like a shadow that remembered birthdays.

"Donor list is long," he said, practical and soft. "We're going to need more hearts."

"Good," I said. My voice cracked. "Great."

"Mom," he said, like he could read the weather in my posture. "Breathe."

I did. The bell made a small, approving sound.

At four o'clock, the rain decided it had a personality. The bell tried to hide in its own bracket. Lightning took a very dramatic photo of the lake.

"Close up early?" Maya asked.

"Weather is a suggestion," I said, and then the pane pinged again.

"Left edge," Ethan said, already there. "Top seam."

"I make the plans," I said, smiling this time.

"I take direction," he said, and smiled back. It hit me in a place I thought I'd locked.

We smoothed the tape. The pane held. The storm breathed. So did I.

The bell rang once. Not nervous. Not loud. A note that sounded a lot like stay.

I was alphabetizing romances I didn't intend to buy when he came to the counter with the stack of blank hearts I'd given him, each one filled in with patient black letters: the name of a librarian who'd bought cookies for kids' reading hour, the high school shop teacher who fixed the broken step in front of the diner, the woman who left notes on park benches that said You're doing fine. Keep going.

"You have nice handwriting," I said.

"I learned from a nurse with standards and threats," he said. "You have nice windows."

"You should donate to them," I said. "It would be very attractive of you."

He laughed, quiet. "I can do attractive." He slid his card across the counter. "Start with three silver, two gold."

"For who?" I asked, pen hovering.

"For the ones who slowed me down enough to notice things," he said. "And for the ones who taught me to keep moving when I wanted to stop."

"Specific," I said, because if I said thank you, I might cry in a store where I am the boss.

He tilted his head. "You okay?"

I considered lying. I considered telling the whole town the truth because they were all standing here under the skin of my life anyway. Then I did the thing I tell my son: name a weather pattern, don't become it.

"I'm okay," I said. "Today has… a lot of nouns."

"Verbs help," he said, and tapped the stack of hearts. "Let's go make some."

We did.

By closing, the window glowed. Cars slowed. People slowed. The storm decided to take a lap around the lake and mind its own business. Maya scribbled a list for the gala. Tom promised a microphone and no pirates, which means I will write cue cards that say no pirates in all caps. Ace collected a payment in pats. Midnight permitted nothing and was paid in nothing.

Ethan shoved his hands into his jacket pockets and looked at me like a promise he wasn't allowed to say yet. "Can I?" He stopped. Tried again. "Do you need anything?"

I wanted to say yes. I wanted to say bring soup, bring patience, bring a new verb for love. Instead, I write the truth on my ribs where only I can read it: *Not yet. Not never. Just not yet.*

"Can you come back tomorrow?" I asked instead. "Lanterns don't hang themselves."

His relief was so loud the bell blushed. "I can do tomorrow."

"Good," I said, and locked the door. "Tomorrow, then."

The bell gave one last satisfied ring, and somewhere inside my chest, something answered it.

Maybe tomorrow still carried work, gossip, and ghosts. But tonight, the window glowed, the boy slept safe, and the man who had left once was still standing here, willing to stay. And for once, that was enough.

When I got home, Midnight did a perimeter check and then forgave me for being a person. Noah set the sketchbook on the table and leaned his head on my shoulder with the kind of trust that makes the world quieter.

"Hey, Mom?" he said into my sweater.

"Mm?"

"You know how you always say we can do hard things?"

"I was hoping you hadn't noticed."

He snorted. "You breathed."

"I did." I kissed his hair. "You did too."

"Yeah," he said. "We did." He pretended not to smile, and then he actually smiled.

In the bathroom mirror, I looked like a woman who did not drown today.

I brushed my teeth. I turned off the light. I let the house be dark and soft. When the wind lifted off the lake and pressed its hand to the windows again, I put my palm to the glass and said the word I'd practiced all day.

Stay.

The pane held.

So did I.

CHAPTER TWO

When Doors Begin To Creak

COLD OPEN — DREAM SEQUENCE
CLARA

The storm in my bones starts first. Clouds press low, the lake tilts into silver, and I'm barefoot on the dock again, breath loud in my chest. He's there, Ethan, older, sharper, the lines of his body carved by time and work. Rain glosses his shoulders, his shirt clinging as if it were sewn from my memory.

"Clara," he says, not as a question, but as a summons.

I go. My feet slap boards that should break but don't. Lightning makes a photograph of us in black and white. When I reach him, he doesn't kiss me first; he lifts my face, thumbs my jaw like I'm something he can memorize again. And then his mouth claims mine.

It isn't the sweet, careful thing I used to dream. It's heat. Urgent, soaked, a decade of starving tucked into seconds. My hands find his chest, then his wet scrubs, then his waistband, tugging him closer until there's no air, no space. His mouth moves down my neck, tasting salt and rain. I gasp, arch, press into him.

The dock groans but holds as he presses me back against the post. One hand fists my hair, the other braces my thigh, lifting. My body remembers him like no time has passed. My dream self is shameless, wrapping legs around his hips, pulling him inside me like the storm demanded tribute. It's open, raw, a claiming. The thunder drowns my moan, but I feel it in my bones.

"Terms," I gasp, because even in a dream, I need the word.

He stills. "Signed," he breathes, and the word is a heat I feel in my throat, promise, not pressure.

"Signed," he growls against my ear, moving with me, in me, until the dock, the rain, and my pulse collapse into one long shudder.

The bell rings once, sharp, smug, and the dream dissolves. I wake sweaty, tangled, clutching a pillow like a confession.

REALITY (WHICH NEEDS COFFEE)

Willow Cove doesn't do whispers. We do bulletins. And my bookstore is the unofficial headquarters of both.

By the time the church bell clanged three lazy notes, the rumor had already bought a latte, borrowed my stapler, and settled into Rose and Henry's favorite armchairs.

"Clara, darling," Rose called, patting the arm of her throne like I was a cat she could summon. "Do you think cardiologists prefer Earl Grey or rooibos? I'm only asking to avoid… irony."

Henry lowered his newspaper. "I thought the new fellow was an emergency physician. Or a neurosurgeon. Or a, what's the one with robots? Do we have robots?"

"Do not put robots in my shop," I said. "I have a cat. He is barely tolerating the espresso machine." Midnight, the aforementioned espresso-machine hater, stretched along the counter like he'd invented black velvet, flicked his tail once, and judged us all.

"Mom." Noah didn't look up from the window seat where his sketchbook lived and breathed. "If he's a cardiologist, does he come with a defibrillator? Can I borrow it for Algebra?"

"Finish your math," I said. "You may not befriend medical equipment."

He held up his sketch. A cartoon heart in sunglasses, with a stethoscope slung like a swagger. Midnight sat on it immediately. Artistic notes: denied.

The bell above the door jingled once and then regretted it. Maya blew in, curls damp from the flirtatious drizzle, and two lattes balanced on a tray like she was smuggling joy. She set one in front of me and one in front of Midnight on principle. Midnight sniffed the steam, offended, and turned his back.

"Good morning to everyone except cardiology," she said. "Also, your eyebrows are doing the thing."

"My eyebrows are fine," I said, taking a life-sustaining sip. "My eyebrows took a vow of composure."

"Your eyebrows are texting me 'panic' in Morse code." She leaned on the counter and lowered her voice. "Clinic board says the new doc arrives today."

Henry perked. "Does he play cribbage?"

"Does he have hands?" Rose countered. "We need hands. And a face that says, 'I remember prescriptions and birthdays.'" She turned the benevolent laser of her attention on me. "We also need forgiveness. And tea."

"Y'all need boundaries," I said.

"We have boundaries," Maya said cheerfully. "We're about to tape them to your window in gold."

The bell offered a half-hearted ding to flapped Mayor Tom, who, already considering retirement, clutched a tote and a vision.

"Citizens!" he announced to the twelve people within earshot and one dog-shaped shadow on the sidewalk. "Behold: The Books & Hearts Gala. Lanterns, not pirates." He squinted at me, preemptively scolded. "I am rebranding."

"No eye patches," I said, pointing. "No parrots. No litigation."

Tom sighed like a man haunted by fond liability. "Fine. This year, we have elegance, dignity, and gold paper hearts. We need your windows, your tape gun, your moral authority." He spilled flyers across my counter like confetti with paperwork.

Midnight peered into his tote, smacked a roll of painter's tape with a paw, and deigned to approve one (1) strip of minimalist glitter.

"Gala HQ is here," Maya said, dragging a whiteboard out from the back with the kind of flourish that scares donors into being generous. "We will deploy cinnamon bribes, tasteful string lights, and the full weight of my spreadsheet wrath."

"We're creating a donor wall," Tom said, bouncing. "Gold hearts for fifty. Silver for one hundred." He held up a deep red paper book like Simba on Pride Rock. "The big donor. The One Book to Rule Them All."

"Paper rings," I muttered, taking the red book and smoothing its crease. "We'll tape hope to glass and call it fundraising."

"Minimalist glitter," Tom whispered reverently.

"Boundaries," I corrected, because he is married to slogans and I am married to tape.

The bell dinged again, more confident. Mr. Pierce, retired firefighter and town oracle, stepped in with Ace, the Dalmatian who does therapy rounds at the clinic and gives better hugs than therapy covered by insurance.

Ace sat. Ace always sits. He blinked once at Midnight. Midnight blinked back. Treaty sustained.

"You look like a woman bracing for weather," Mr. Pierce said, eyes warm. "Inside and out."

"I am perfectly calm," I said. "I am a human duct tape dispenser."

"Hydration," he said, and handed me a water bottle that said YOU'RE DOING GREAT in cheerful font. "Ace concurs." Ace thumped his tail. Mr. Pierce added, "We'll be at the clinic. The new doc requested therapy mornings. He wants the place to feel like home."

My stomach did an elevator. "Home is political."

"Home is also chairs," Henry said, folding his paper. "And tea. And advice."

Rose patted his knee. "We should embroider that. On an apron."

"Put it on a sign," Maya said. "Put everything on a sign."

"Put nothing on a sign," I said. "We are not becoming a farmhouse."

The door popped again, and the drizzle intensified to a purposeful downpour. A woman in a sunshine-yellow raincoat hovered at the threshold, envelope clutched in a white-knuckled grip. Her eyes flicked from the donor hearts stacked on my counter to me to the brave part of herself that had dragged her inside.

"I, hi, " she stammered. "The hearts… Is this where…?"

"You're in the right place," I said, softening. "What name would you like to honor?"

She swallowed. "My dad. Daniel Ortiz. He… he said once that Dr. Hale bought him six months and remembered my mother's name when he didn't deserve either." Her laugh was a wet hiccup. "I wanted to… I mean, it's not much…"

"Names are everything," I said, because today they were. "Silver heart?"

She nodded. Ace sidled close and put his chin on her calf. She pressed her lips together, breathed, and smiled down at him as if prayer came in spots.

I wrote Daniel Ortiz in my neatest script and pressed the silver heart to the front window. The tape made a small hush-click, my favorite sound after "I'll bring snacks." For a second, the old bell tried to harmonize.

The woman touched the glass, then her chest, then Ace's head, and left with her shoulders one inch lower.

Silence settled for the half beat reality gives you when it knows it's about to be dramatic again.

"Hey, Mom?" Noah's voice arrowed from the window. "Minimalist glitter is trending." He held up his sketch. "Also, crosswalk draft three. Hidden fox here. Goose here." He tapped the margin. "Drivers will slow down so they don't miss the Easter eggs."

Tom leaned over the page and made a noise like civic ecstasy. "Genius! Traffic calming via whimsy! A boy after my own infrastructure heart."

"Cookies," Noah said without making eye contact.

"Appropriated," Tom vowed.

Midnight hopped down and sat directly on the fox, which was his version of a blurb. Ace gave a professional nod. Maya took a picture for the gala page and captioned it #GlitterButMakeItCharitable.

"You know," Rose said, "if the new doctor is a cardiologist, I'll brew peppermint. It feels less… indicting."

Henry nodded sagely. "We shouldn't taunt arteries."

"You can't taunt arteries," I said, ripping another heart. "They don't have ears."

"Tell that to my left anterior descending," Henry muttered.

"Okay," Maya clapped, then pointed at me. "You: emcee the gala. You have excellent eyebrows and a voice that bossed me into braces when I was twelve. The mic will obey."

"Public speaking," I said, feeling my palms try out new choreography. "My favorite adrenaline."

"You'll say words, people will do money," she said. "Then we'll hide in the pantry and cry from efficiency."

"I can cry from efficiency," I admitted.

"Put that on a sign," Tom said.

"No," I said.

"Fine," he pouted. "On a sticker?"

"Maybe," I said, because I am weak when stickered.

The bell rang again. The breeze brought in the smell of rain deciding. Midnight's ear flicked. My instincts sat up.

"Not him," Maya whispered, reading the bell like astrology.

It was Mrs. Donnelly, clutching three romances like a life raft and vowing to wage war on the goose who keeps eating her hemlines. I rang her up with discounts for avian trauma, watched her march out into the drizzle, and felt my ribcage do that thing it does when a decision I can't make is about to arrive anyway.

"Clara," Rose said gently, the way you talk to someone standing on a dock, remembering how to bend. "Sometimes doors creak before they open."

"And sometimes they're stuck," I said, because a girl can be pragmatic.

"And sometimes," Henry added, "they need a dab of oil and a bribe."

"Bribes," Maya said brightly, sliding a cinnamon knot toward me. "I come prepared."

I bit the gratitude and sugar at the same time. Rain stubbed its toe on the awning. The bell inhaled, thought about its choices, and let go, one bright, sure ring that landed under my sternum like a thumbprint.

Maya's eyes went wide. "Brace."

I pressed a gold heart to the glass and smoothed the tape with a palm that suddenly felt like an altar. My reflection looked like a woman who had learned how to stand up inside her own skin. The red paper book waited in the center like a dare.

The door swung.

He stepped in as if the lake had pushed him.

Ethan Hale in scrubs and rain and a smile that had done too much work in my memories. He took my store in with one glance: the donor wall, the cat monarchy, the mayor's zeal, my hands still inked from names.

"Hey," he said, quiet enough that the word stayed where it landed.

"Hi," I managed. If my voice was steady, it's because my knees were raised right.

Maya made the shape of a cross with two cinnamon knots for me. Tom made the shape of a donation request with his whole body. Mr. Pierce took Ace's badge out of his pocket and clipped it to the dog, like a reassurance that he had a uniform.

"Did I miss the heist?" Ethan asked, dripping on my mat. "Looks like planning."

"Gala," Tom chirped. "Lanterns, not pirates."

Ethan's mouth tilted. "I can do lanterns." His eyes came back to me. "Can I do lanterns?"

"You can do donations," I said, grabbing my tape gun because my hands needed a job. "Lanterns are a privilege."

"Banter," Maya breathed, blissed out. "We have banter."

"Welcome back, Dr. Hale," Mr. Pierce said. "We're a town that still knows how to clap for people."

Ethan's gaze flicked to me and away so fast I could pretend I didn't notice. "I heard." He lifted his brows at the window. "You're doing this."

"Minimalist glitter," I said. "Boundaries are beautiful."

He blew out a breath that sounded like a man remembering he had a ribcage. "They are." He slid a card across the counter. "Three gold. Two silver. The red one when I deserve it."

Maya made a sound that might get us banned from respectable churches.

Tom whispered to Ace, "Are we witnessing a metaphor?" Ace wagged once: possibly.

I wrote the names he gave me in my neatest script. He didn't look at the glass. He looked at my hand, as if he were memorizing where I put the pressure.

"Thank you," he said when I pressed the hearts to the pane. "For… everything." He didn't say what everything was. That was considerate of him.

Behind me, Noah shuffled. The acoustics changed; that's how you know when your son is about to throw a truth grenade and hide behind sarcasm.

"We're designing a crosswalk," he told Ethan, tone a solid mix of bored and feral. He lifted the sketchbook half an inch. "It's interactive. Only for people with eyes."

Ethan's smile got honest around the edges. "People slow down for wonder," he said.

Noah blinked like he'd heard a new word he might like. He put the sketchbook down. Midnight sat on it. Contract signed.

"Clara runs Gala HQ," Maya announced to break the spell before I floated away on it. "We're creating tasteful crying and a donor wall that looks like hope with tape."

"Tasteful crying," Tom repeated, starry. "PG-13 tears."

"In the interest of public safety," Henry said, "we should brew peppermint."

"And maybe decaf," Rose added.

"Also snacks," Noah said. "For artists. Me."

"Appropriated," Tom said again, because once he finds a word, he wears it out.

The bell flirted with a new draft of itself. Rain leveled up to A Mood. The big front pane gave a tiny, strained ping like a glass throat deciding whether to sing or scream.

"Window," I told the room. "Midnight, do not assist."

Midnight followed. He only disobeys commands.

I anchored the top seam with tape while the pane whined, 'What if, what if, what if.' A bead nosed the corner, considered a career in puddle-making, and slunk off under my glare.

"Left edge," Ethan said from behind me like he'd never forgotten the language of my shop. His voice was low, deliberate, and close enough to warm the back of my neck. His hands braced the ladder, and I let myself notice: strong forearms, veins like calligraphy, scrubs stretched just enough to remind me of muscles earned by work, not vanity.

"Top seam," he added. The timbre of it went straight down my spine.

Maya coughed behind us. "Pent-up chemistry aisle three. Somebody grab a mop."

I flushed but held my line. "I make the plans in this store," I said, because armor is just a habit.

"Make this one with me," he said, steady. And I did.

When I pressed the last strip, the pane sighed and decided to be brave. Ace did a lap and collected three pats and a promise. Maya yelled, "Stable. Improving," like a nurse with pastry certifications. Tom asked if the tape was deductible, and I pretended not to hear him.

We climbed down and turned simultaneously. The inches between us became math I didn't want to solve. His gaze caught mine, hot and searching, and for a moment I wondered if the storm outside was jealous.

"Okay," I said to the tape, the window, the part of me that was still seventeen.

"Okay," he echoed, but his voice made it sound like a vow.

The afternoon fell into its Willow Cove cadence: rain light on the glass, customers breezing in with damp cheeks and gossip, a farmer asking for "books about goats that do not end in tragedy," Rose requesting a romance "with a doctor who repents," Henry telling a pun about anesthesia so bad even the geese left town briefly.

And then the door opened on sunshine-yellow again. The woman with the envelope. Relief steadied her voice this time. "I, can I add one for my mom? Luz."

"Of course," I said. I wrote "LUZ" and placed it beside Daniel's. The tape whispered. The bell agreed. The window glowed like it.

CHAPTER THREE

Rain, Deer, Bell

The deer's eyes flash like twin coins just beyond my headlights, and the world squeezes into a tunnel of rain.

"Easy," I tell the wheel, as if it will listen. I pump the brakes once, twice, the rear fishtails, and for one long breath, there's nothing but water and the slap of my heartbeat in my throat. The lake to my left is a black sheet tugging at its moorings; on my right, Maple Street blurs into streaks of amber. I correct, the car straightens, the deer vanishes as if the town swallowed it whole, and a laugh I don't mean to make tears out of me. The kind you hear after a code when the patient lives. The kind you hate yourself for needing.

It's not the city. There are no sirens to tuck yourself inside. Here, the rain has a voice. Here, the church bell counts time like an old friend with a pocket watch.

Three bongs. The old rope knows my name.

I pull to the curb in front of Monroe Books & More and kill the engine. The sign in the window bleeds gold through the rain. Warm light, a cat silhouette, a crooked display of paper hearts. I sit there with my hands on ten and two and try to breathe like a normal man who just made a normal drive in a normal storm toward a normal door that belongs to the woman he never stopped loving.

I'm not eighteen anymore. I don't run on adrenaline and promises. I've learned how to let the heart settle by counting a pulse at the wrist and staring at the second hand. But tonight, the second hand keeps stuttering, and every stutter is her name.

Clara, Clara, Clara.

A gust tilts rain off the lake and slaps it against my windshield. I grab the umbrella, fail to open it, classic, and bolt. The air is cold enough to bite, the kind that sharpens you. The bell over the door gives one uncertain breath and then a full jangle that feels like a verdict. I step inside, drenching the mat, trying not to track storm water onto the old wood floors, and fail at that, too.

She's there.

At the window, palm flat to glass, pressing a gold paper heart into place like it's a seal on a letter she's sending out into the world. Her hair is damp around her temples. There's ink smudged on the side of her hand. She turns, slow, as if her bones negotiated this with time, and my body remembers every language we used to speak. The bookstore's warm, but I go colder first, the way you do when a wound breaks the surface and the night air finds it.

"Hey," I say. The word scrapes. I'm still out of breath from the near miss; the rain puts a shine on everything, my jacket, her lashes, the cat who's staring at me like security.

"Hi," she answers, and her voice is steadier than I deserve. Something in my chest settles and shatters at once.

Behind her, a boy with a sketchbook looks up; his pencil is midstroke over a drawing of open books that become a crosswalk. He's taller than I expected. Older than I can think about yet. There's a smear of graphite along his thumb. His gaze flicks to my face, curious, then wary, then back to the page. A friend once told me that every first meeting is a negotiation. This one feels like a treaty with a dozen clauses I can't read yet.

"Sorry for the… entrance," I say, lifting a hand in what I hope is a universal sign for I come in peace and also water. "Road's slick."

Maya appears at Clara's elbow like she's been braced for this moment for years. "We've had deer training since kindergarten," she says. "Welcome back to Willow Cove." Her tone is flippant; her eyes are measuring. I don't blame her.

"Ethan," Clara says, saying my name like a test she already passed. It puts a crack right through me.

A display near the door wobbles on its spindle, wind, old floors, bad karma, and I move without thinking, catching the teetering tower of books in both hands before it tips. Two hardcovers slide, and a paperback flutters loose like a bird before landing against my chest. The cover kisses wet cloth. Reflex: I hold it there for a beat. It's a romance, city skyline, rain on glass, a couple on a fire escape leaning toward each other like gravity made new rules just for them. I'm soaked, she's dry, and the space between us feels like a live wire.

"Still good with emergencies," Maya says, mild.

"Occupational hazard," I answer. "I have a lot of practice not letting things fall."

Clara's mouth lifts at one corner. It does things to my equilibrium that should require a consult. The cat, Midnight, right?, launches to the counter and sits tall, tail wrapped, yellow eyes flatly judging. I get it, man.

I set the books back and aligned the corners. I used to alphabetize Clara's locker door poetry magnets when she wasn't looking; she'd threaten to break my fingers and then kiss the threat right off my mouth. The memory hits me low and hot, and I tamp it down where decent men keep things they have no right to want yet.

"Hi," I say again, because the first one didn't carry everything I needed it to. "You look, " Alive. Fierce. Like home after a long winter. "Busy."

"We're doing the donor wall," she says, motioning to the window. Gold, silver, one a red book cutout that glows deeper in the lamplight. "For the clinic fundraiser."

"Good," I say. "It'll help." I hear the strain in my own voice. The clinic needs a lot. So do I.

The boy's pencil stills. Maya clears her throat pointedly. The bell over the door settles back into its bracket with a tiny click that somehow sounds like: Behave.

"Let me buy some paper hearts," I say. "To start."

"You can donate at the register," Maya says. "Cash, card, case of cinnamon rolls, all accepted."

"Card," I answer, and my hand is steadier than I expect when I pass it over. I don't look away from Clara while Maya taps the amount. You can build a life out of the moments you don't look away. You can lose one that way, too.

"Thank you," Clara says, and her eyes meet mine properly now. In them: the girl by the lake I left, the woman inside this window light who learned to hold a town together with tape and hope. The clock somewhere behind the counter ticks, a sound so small it feels like a spell.

I sign the receipt. The ink bleeds; my hand is still rain. "I heard you needed therapy mornings," I say lightly, because it's a safe bridge. "I'm… planning to bring a Dalmatian bribe."

Clara's mouth curves. "Ace is incorruptible."

"We'll see." I don't mean the dog.

First Sight, Second Breath

I strip off the jacket, wring it discreetly by the door, and hang it on the old coat tree that's been by this threshold as long as the town has had opinions. I step closer to the window without fully stepping closer to her, which is a thing I didn't know was possible until right now.

"Minimalist glitter," Maya says, gesturing to the gold hearts. "Clara's superpower."

Clara elbows her. "It's called tape."

"Hope," Maya counters, then to me: "You can help by not ruining the aesthetic with your puddle."

"On it," I say, sliding a mat with my foot, mindlessly ready to be bossed. It's easier than thinking about the way Clara's gaze keeps catching on my mouth and darting away like it touched a hot lightbulb. Or the way my own gaze keeps cataloging what the years did: the new steadiness in her shoulders; the softness she has to stretch to fit the days; the quiet confidence of a woman who has been scared and walked through it, anyway.

The boy stands, sketchbook tucked reflexively to his chest. I offer a small nod. "Hey."

"Hi," he says. His voice is still climbing into itself. "We're designing a crosswalk." He lifts the book half an inch, as if the art can be a shield and a gift at once.

"It's good," I say, and mean it. "People slow down for wonder."

He blinks like I've said something unexpected and then pretends he didn't hear me at all. I respect that. My chest does something I can't name. I don't try to yet.

Maya goes mercifully busy counting hearts and clacking keys. The cat leaps down and patrols the baseboards like a general inspecting fortifications. The rain turns the window into a mirror for a second, and I catch us: me beside her, the paper heart between our shoulders, names written in careful ink. A future inside a pane of glass that hasn't decided whether to fog or clear.

"You're really here," Clara says. Not a question.

"I am."

"For how long?"

"As long as it takes," I say, and I can feel how that sounds. I adjust. "As long as we need."

"We?" Her brows lift.

"The town," I answer quickly, and then don't run from the thing that brought me through rain and years and a deer with a death wish. "Me. You. The clinic. Whoever needs me."

Her throat moves. The paper heart in her hand sticks to her finger for a beat before it gives. "We're fine," she says. "Willow Cove has a way of figuring itself out."

"I heard."

Silence. The good kind and the terrible kind. The clock ticks. The bell trembles faintly with some draft and then settles. I feel ungainly in my own skin, like a man who left a part of himself somewhere and has to relearn the weight of walking.

"Do you remember?" I say, and then stop, because too many answers to that question exist.

Her smile this time is small and sharper. "Which part?"

"The dock," I say. "That storm senior spring. The way you put your weight in your knees so you wouldn't slip, and I thought you were braver than me."

"You were stubborn," she says softly.

"I still am."

"Some things don't need to be reclaimed," she says, and I take the hit because I deserve it and because there's something under the sting, a door not closed, maybe, only latched.

I move two inches closer, instinct pulling like a tide. The rain outside hushes into a steadier curtain. Her breath catches. Mine does worse things. If I touched her, even just the line of her wrist where the ink smudge dims to skin, I would forget everything I learned about being careful.

"Coffee?" I ask, voice lower than intended. "At Maya's. Not now," I add quickly, because that is not the order of operations, and the boy with the sketchbook is still watching, and my heart is making terrible decisions on my behalf. "When you want. Or never. You set the terms."

The corners of her eyes soften. "Terms," she repeats, like the syllables themselves are something she can measure and find acceptable. "I'll… think about it."

"I can wait," I say, and it's the truest thing I've said in a decade.

"Good," Maya murmurs without looking up. "Because she's busy and you're dripping."

I swallow a laugh. It makes room in my chest for air.

Flashback: The Locker and the Lake

I used to slide notes into the vent of her locker because she liked words that had to find their way out of small spaces. She'd read them like spells, lips moving, eyebrows doing that tilt that meant I'd landed the joke or the heart or missed both. She kept one folded in her wallet the year I left; I know because I watched her tuck it there at graduation and did not ask her to show me again, because some things you can't endure twice.

In the ER, when the night stretched thin and the fluorescents made everything look like a bad decision, I'd take my break and open my phone and type messages to a number that didn't exist.

Clara, the subway stalled, and a stranger started singing; for three minutes, the city seemed to hum in the same key.

Clara, today a patient brought me a drawing his daughter made of the moon. It looks like a cookie. I wanted to eat it.

Clara, I bought cedar soap because it smelled like home, and then stopped using it because it hurt.

I never hit send on any of them. I did not know that restraint can cause bruising in the same way as impact.

On the dock senior year, the storm made the lake into hammered tin, and she told me with her chin up and her voice steady that she wouldn't beg me to stay. "Bridges need maintenance," she said, and it sounded like a thesis. "You can't just sprint across them and expect them to hold when you come back," I promised I'd be better than every boy who left. She kissed me like the future was a thing we could bite into and save for later. I left anyway. The bridge held for a while, because she's a builder. Eventually, all that neglect did what neglect always does. And here we are, at the footings, checking the bolts.

I look at her now in this soft light, paper hearts like scales on the window, a boy whose outline I don't know yet, and the ache rearranges itself into something I can use: resolve.

Terms and Tells

"Mayor Tom wants weekly planning meetings," Clara says, flipping her clipboard to a fresh page. Practical. "If you're joining the committee, you'll need to endure his brainstorms."

"I've survived attending surgeons at two a.m.," I say. "I can survive, Tom."

"Don't be cocky," Maya warns. "He once attempted piratethemed crosswalks."

"I've heard the legend."

"We meet here on Thursday at seven," Clara says, pen poised. "Committee is small: me, Maya, Tom, Rose, Henry, Mr. Pierce. You."

"Me," I echo, and it feels like adding my name to the glass.

My phone buzzes in my pocket. My body recognizes the haptic pattern before my brain does; I ignored this same number twice on the drive. I don't pull it out. The part of me that still calculates risk even in rooms with lullaby light has already read the message: Board call moved up. Package sweetened. We can make this worth your while, Dr. Hale.

Clara's gaze flicks to my pocket and back to my eyes, quick as a sparrow. "If you need to—"

"No," I say, maybe too fast. "Not now."

She nods, like I've passed a test I didn't know she was giving.

The boy sidles closer to the counter and sets his sketchbook down, not open, just there. Midnight steps onto it immediately and sits. "You're not helping," the boy tells the cat.

Midnight blinks, then allows his tail to drape off the sketchbook like a ribbon.

"What's your name?" I ask the boy gently.

He hesitates, measuring, then: "Noah."

Something tightens under my ribs in a way I do not let show. Noah. It's a good name. It holds. I say it once in my head to hear the shape of it and put it away for now with the other delicate things I can't take out in public.

"It's nice to meet you, Noah," I say aloud. "That crosswalk is going to save lives."

He shrugs like maybe, maybe not, and then his eyes catch on my sleeve. "You're soaked."

"I lost a fight with an umbrella."

"You should borrow the one in lost and found," he says, deadpan. "Ms. Clara will charge you late fees if you return it wet."

"Accurate," Maya says.

Clara rolls her eyes, but there's pride tucked in it like a secret.

For a second, the three of us are arranged around the counter like a family in a staged photo, accidentally capturing something real. It's too much and just enough, and I feel a step inside my chest that could be the first one toward everything we're going to try to build.

"Thursday at seven," I repeat. "I'll bring Ace. Not into the store," I add, at Midnight's glare. "For a premeeting lap. Therapy morale."

"We like morale," Clara says softly.

"Good." I reach for my jacket. My fingers brush hers where the cuff is still dark with rain. Electricity is a lazy metaphor, but it's the only one that fits: the spark has patience; it takes its time crossing the gap. She inhales; I do something worse. The room narrows and goes brighter at the edges, and if I leaned an inch, just one, we'd be history meeting present in the only language that ever-made sense to us.

"Terms," she whispers.

"I remember," I whisper back. I let the cuff go. The spark, somehow, stays.

At the door, the bell seems to want to bless or warn; I can't tell which. I push it gently and step into rain that already knows my name. Across the street, Mr. Pierce waves from beneath a wide-brimmed hat; Ace sits at perfect attention, head cocked like he smells the shape of the future. The church bell wakes me out and then, with a kind of smugness only old wood earns, rings once, clean, bright, like a promise signed.

My phone buzzes again. I fish it out, open the message because men who ghost the past don't get to ghost anything else, and type four words that feel like home: I'm no longer interested. I hit send. The rain takes a step back, or maybe I do.

When I glance through the window again, Clara is looking at the new heart I bought, the ink still wet on the name, Daniel Ortiz, and then she looks at me. Not the boy I was, not the man on magazine covers, just me. For the first time in thirteen years, I can stand that kind of looking.

Behind her, Noah flips open his sketchbook, and even from across the street, through rain and glass and the cat who insists on being a punctuation mark, I recognize the curve of a line I've drawn a thousand times on blank forms and whiteboards and a life that kept refusing to balance.

It's a jawline. Mine.

The bell rings again somewhere inside my chest, one, two, three, and I press my palm against the cold window from outside like a man testing glass. It holds. For now, that's everything.

CHAPTER FOUR

The Night The Lake Listened

DREAM: EDGE OF THE STORM

The storm begins like a rumor: soft, then it spreads everywhere.

Wind lifts the lake in shivers, the surface going from glass to hammered tin in a heartbeat. Petrichor swells in the air, the wind pushes from the west, and spray flecks my lips with brine. Streetlamps smudge into halos; the rope bell at the church counts time like an old friend with a pocket watch, one… two… three, each sound a pulse in my throat. I'm running, not away or toward, just running, breath burning in my chest, rain stinging my cheeks. The dock arrows out into dark water, and I hit the boards at speed, soles sliding, arms windmilling, and, somehow, my weight finds balance. Knees soft. Toes spread. Don't slip. Don't drown. Don't look down.

A figure stands at the far end; a silhouette caught between lightning and the lake. A ghost of cedar soap clings to my senses; Ethan's scent, memory made flesh. I don't need to see his face to know him. Recognition isn't sight; it's muscle memory. He lifts a hand like a promise. He's older this time, lines around the eyes, steadier shoulders, a kind of gravity people earn by touching too much at night. But he's also still the boy who kissed me under the bleachers and whispered that the universe had been showing off the day it made me.

"Clara," he says, thunder from far away. The dock shudders.

A cat yowls from shore, imperious, warning. I don't see Midnight, but I feel the shape of him in the sound, like punctuation.

"Terms," I say to the wind, though I haven't said the word out loud in thirteen years. This time, terms mean boundaries: no more sudden exits, no more silence turned into punishment, transparency above all. The boards hold. The rain thickens. My palm opens like I'm pressing a paper heart to an invisible pane of glass.

His hand appears in the dream, older, steadier. Not to grab, but to ask. Even asleep, my body answers.

I wake with my hand fisted in the sheets, heart thrashing, the taste of rain clean and metallic on my tongue.

I'm not eighteen anymore. I don't run. I choose.

But when the bell in my bones rings three times, I sit up and listen.

PRESENT: WINDOWLIGHT

Morning in Willow Cove is always honest. The lake wears whatever sky it's given; the town answers with coffee and opinions. Willow Cove likes to nudge fate with gentle hands. At Monroe Books & More, the day begins with the usual chorus, floorboards creaking, pages whispering, the heater humming, the bell above the door practicing its jingle like a singer clearing her throat.

"Minimalist glitter," Maya says, sliding a tray of cinnamon knots onto my counter and fogging the window with a theatrical sigh. "Say it with me."

"Minimalist glitter," I echo, because I'm a good friend and because the donor wall for the clinic fundraiser will live and die by tape and hope.

She smirks. "#GlitterButMakeItCharitable. We'll trend by noon."

I hold a gold paper heart to the glass. Outside, mist hangs low over the water, as if the lake has decided to keep a secret. I press the tape; the heart adheres. Names glow in neat black script. Daniel Ortiz. Rose & Henry. Anonymous with a drawn goose because of course. The Crossword Crew. Lakewalk Moms. Our little town universe taped in gold.

"Tell me you slept," Maya says.

"Define sleep."

"Clara."

I tell her about the storm dream, the dock, the hand raised like a promise. I don't say his name. I don't have to.

"Your brain is a screenwriter with too much budget," she says softly, bumping my shoulder.

Before I can reply, Noah slouches out from the back with a sketchbook under his arm and crumbs at the corner of his mouth. "Morning."

"Teeth?" I ask.

"Brushed. Mostly." He flips open the book and reveals a new version of his crosswalk design, open books flowing into each other, tiny foxes and geese hidden in the pages so drivers will slow down just to look. "Mayor Tom wants to see this after school."

"He will faint in public," Maya says. "We'll need smelling salts and a press release."

Noah grins, but the smile tugs shy around the edges, like he doesn't quite trust good things yet. His shoulders have stretched again, another growth spurt, and for a flicker, I see Ethan's jawline shadowing his. I recognize the shape of that skepticism. I taught it to both of us.

The bell above the door clears its courage and then offers a polite jingle. Rose and Henry arrive with hand-knit scarves and weather reports ("It's a flirtatious drizzle," Rose declares). Mr. Pierce follows with Ace, the Dalmatian, for a quick lap to practice therapy manners. Ace sits primly at the threshold until I nod; Midnight appears on the history shelf and pretends not to care.

"These are perfect," Mr. Pierce says, reading the names on the donor wall like scripture. "Tasteful. Hopeful. What's the word, Ace?"

Ace thumps his tail. He's already promised to serve as photo booth greeter at the gala, where children will pose with him like he's the town's celebrity. Midnight blinks once, which is a cat for you, may continue.

"Tell Tom I'm donating a walk with the gentleman here," Mr. Pierce says. "One hour of dog joy. Good for what ails a soul."

"Put it on the list," I say, as if I haven't already written it three times in different pens because writing is how I make things real.

The bell clears its courage again. The storm in my dream is long gone, but the air in the store feels barometric, about to change.

FLASHBACK: BLEACHERS

The first time Ethan kissed me, the world was sticky with summer, and the stadium lights made the night look borrowed from a bigger city. We were seventeen and invincible in the exact way that makes adults nervous. It was homecoming week, which made everyone a little more reckless with hope.

We'd lost the game, but the boys didn't care. They were all neon Gatorade tongues and laughter that smelled like someone's older brother's cologne. I wasn't there for football. I was there because I worked the concession stand for the library's fundraiser and because Ethan, who moved through the halls like he had a map no one else could see, had stopped by earlier to buy a hot chocolate and memorize my mouth.

He found me after, beneath the bleachers, where the air tasted like rust and clover. His thumb brushed my lower lip; his breath skated my collarbone. "Do you ever feel like the stars are listening?" he asked, and it was such a ridiculous, beautiful thing that my heart decided without consulting me.

"Only when they're rooting for me," I said.

He laughed with his whole body. Even then, I loved that, how his joy started in his eyes and then got away from him. "They are, you know," he said, stepping closer. "I asked them."

"About what?" I could feel his breath now, warm and mint-sweet.

"About you." He tucked a strand of hair behind my ear the way boys do before they know that gesture belongs to something bigger than a gesture. "I told them I was going to fall so hard, and they should probably brace."

Then he kissed me.

Not careful. Not careless. Just… us. A hello and a yes, and a please. The metal of the bleachers was cool against my back; his palms were warm on my waist. Somewhere up in the stands, someone whooped; somewhere on the field, a whistle blew; here, the night went quiet because it wanted to watch. When we finally came up for air, we were both a little stunned. Not at the kiss. At the clarity.

"You're trouble," I told him.

"I'm a solution," he said, and grinned like the future was a thing we could borrow and return in perfect condition.

We made rules under those bleachers, because we were children and rules made us feel like adults: no lying, no cheating, no ghosting, no running without a goodbye, no turning silence into punishment. We wrote them in pen on the back of a napkin from the concession stand. Midnight wasn't my cat yet, I didn't know him, but a stray tabby slinked past with a sardonic meow, and Ethan swore she winked at us as if the universe had sent a witness.

We walked to the lake after, fingers laced, the whole town a set behind which we whispered our lines. I told him I wanted a bookstore because books had been fixing me since before I knew I was broken. Someday, I said, I'd raise money with paper hearts. He told me he wanted to be a doctor because fixing things felt like oxygen to him. We lay back on the dock and picked a star to name after each other, like you can just do that. We were seventeen. Of course, we could.

When he walked me home, he asked if he could come inside. I told him no, but I cupped his face at the bottom of the porch steps and kissed him again, longer, until he said my name like a promise and a plea.

I kept the napkin in my jewelry box. For weeks, the paper smelled faintly like hot chocolate and metal.

FLASHBACK: THE DINER

October came with its annual cinnamon agenda. The Lakeside Diner was filled with fishermen, teenagers, and women who called everyone "hon." Checkered floors, booth 3 with a view of the lake, and a lemon meringue pie crowned with peaks like royalty. We slid into the booth wearing a sky the color of denim.

"Two pancakes with extra blueberries, one hot chocolate with a mountain of whipped cream, and…?"

Ethan looked at me instead of the menu. "Same."

"You can't both eat that," Dale, the waiter, said. "This town has only so much insulin."

"We're growing," Ethan deadpanned.

I snorted. Dale shook his head like he didn't know what to do with kids who laughed like this, then left us to our conspiracy of tenderness.

"Tell me something true," Ethan said when we were alone.

"I used to hide in the non-fiction stacks when my parents fought." I hadn't meant to say that, not then, not like that. The honesty landed between us like a stone in water, concentric circles of new understanding. "Tell me something true." Books were shelter; someday they'd become walls and windows and a roof of their own.

He didn't hesitate. "When I'm scrubbed in, I feel like my body remembers a different language. Like I'm built for it."

"You're seventeen," I teased, because I could feel the way the confession scared him. "You've scrubbed… in the kitchen?"

"Metaphorically." He toyed with the paper-wrapped straw like it held codes. "I don't know. I can't explain it. I just… know."

"You will," I said, and I meant it.

Our pancakes arrived like a dare, and we met it like champions. Syrup on his knuckle; I licked it off before my brain caught up to my mouth; his inhale went ragged; I hid my face in my hands and then peeked through my fingers to find him looking at me like I was the answer to the question he hadn't known how to ask.

"Round two's mine. Winner buys the pie," I whispered.

We paid in crumpled bills and coins and left Dale a tip so embarrassing that he came after us to return the quarters. We ran instead, giddy and damp with autumn air, down to the dock.

We kissed in a way that made promises brave. Not for the first time. Never like the last. The lake watched and didn't tell.

FLASHBACK: THE LETTER

The day the letter came from Columbia, Ethan climbed the fire escape behind my house because knocking on my front door felt like tempting fate. I met him at my window in an oversized sweatshirt with a bookstore logo I didn't own yet. Lila had scribbled a joke on my homework about running away to Paris; I thought of it even then, her restless spirit a catalyst to come.

He didn't speak. He just held out the envelope with hands that shook, sharp, official, heavy with a future that had already started.

"You knew you'd get in," I said, trying for light.

"Knowing and opening aren't the same." He laughed without humor. "Come with me?" The words were soft, reckless, everything.

"And live in a shoebox in New York while you learn a new language in a different skin?" I swallowed. "I can't. Not now."

He nodded like he'd known the answer and still needed to hear it. "Then I'll come back to you," he said fiercely, and it was so earnest my eyes stung. "I'll build bridges between everything I want until the path is clear. Winter break; I'll come home, we'll start again."

"We have rules," I reminded him, fishing the napkin out of my desk drawer like a talisman. "No ghosting. No running without a goodbye."

He pressed his mouth to each line like a vow, then to my palm, then to my mouth. "No running," he whispered against my lip. "You're my constant, Monroe. I'll make sure the math loves us."

Except life isn't math. Or if it is, the variables win sometimes.

FLASHBACK: THE GOODBYE

He left in June on a morning when the town smelled like cut grass and hope. We kissed at dawn on the dock while the lake pretended to be made of silver. He said goodbye as if he thought the word could be shaped into 'come back'. I opened my mouth, almost told him about the second line on the test, but swallowed the words until they burned.

He did, small and quick at first; Thanksgiving, a weekend in March when the city ate him and spit him back out for two days, a summer that tasted like peaches and salt. Then the visits thinned as rotations started and ambition required blood. Calls turned into texts turned into voicemails turned into silence. Once, he sent me a photo of a moon that looked like a cookie and wrote, Wish you were here. I held my phone and built a life while I waited.

I didn't tell him about the second line on the test. At the clinic, the nurse pressed my hand and told me I wasn't alone, even if I felt like it. I wasn't brave enough to share that truth with Ethan then.

I didn't know how to say I need you when the only language we'd been fluent in was we can do this from anywhere.

I told myself I'd tell him later, when he wasn't on nights, when he wasn't on fire. Later stretched out like the lake in August, wide, warm, deceptively safe. I learned to hold joy in one hand and fear in the other without letting either spill.

PRESENT: ECHOES

"Clara?" Maya's voice is careful, the way you hold a glass you don't want to drop. "You went somewhere."

"I just… remembered." I rub at the ink smudge on my thumb that won't come off, the kind you only earn by writing names you're afraid to forget. "He used to say the math would love us."

"Math can be convinced," she says. "Especially with baked goods. And page counts. Sixty to eighty thousand words, bingeable in a weekend, perfect for KU."

Noah leans a hip against the counter, watching us with that old-soul focus that makes my breath catch. "Is this about the doctor?" His tone is dry, protective, curious all at once, the kind of joke you make when you want the answer but can't quite admit it.

The room does a trick I hate, gets too quiet in a way that amplifies breath and heartbeat, as well as the tiny sound the heater makes when it decides to start working again.

"Yes," I say, because I refuse to teach my son to be afraid of honesty. "I knew him when I was your age. We… cared about each other."

Noah's gaze flicks to the window, to the donor wall, to the rain, thinking about committing. "And now?"

"And now I'm making paper hearts and choosing what to give the town, and when to give the rest."

He nods, as if this is a lesson he suspected was coming. "I can help with the hearts. Payment accepted in pie."

"You already are," I say, touching his crown with my palm. He leans in, brief and warm, then straightens like the man he is becoming.

The bell makes a sound that isn't quite a ring. It's the intake of breath before one. My hands find the next gold heart. The shop smells like cinnamon and pages and the faint metallic promise of weather.

"Terms," I tell the window. The word fogs the glass. Boundaries before gravity. This time. On the other side, somewhere, soon, someone I used to know is learning how to breathe in the same key as this town again.

If he's learned anything at all, he'll wait.

If I have

If I have, I'll let him.

PRESENT: MARKET DAY

By noon, the drizzle turns decisive, and Willow Cove answers with umbrellas the color of candy. Stalls pop up along Harbor Street, honey, candles, watercolor postcards that make the lake look like it practices being beautiful. I carry a box of donor hearts under one arm and a stack of gala flyers under the other while Maya flanks me with a tray of sample knots like a pastry bodyguard.

"Fundraiser committee meets in the library room at four," she announces to anyone with ears. "There will be agendas. And sugar."

"Both essential," I say.

Mr. Pierce demonstrates Ace's handshake to a ring of children. Rose bargains for peonies that are obviously not in season. Henry pretends not to eavesdrop while perfectly arranging his scarf, which is to say he is absolutely eavesdropping. The town hums with that Willow Cove magic, the kind that feels like someone ironed the day and laid it warm over our shoulders.

"Clara?" Mayor Tom materializes, tie slightly askew, enthusiasm perfectly intact. "Your son's crosswalk sketch… I had to sit down. A bench is fainting. Not embarrassing."

"He'll bring the portfolio after school," I say. "We'll bring smelling salts in case the bench is busy."

Tom grins. "Also, small request for the gala: can you emcee? Poise, humor, zero nonsense, three things I do not possess."

Maya arches a brow. "She can. And she will."

I set the donor box on the community board table and begin pinning. People line up to sign hearts. The Crossword Crew arrives en masse, pencils behind their ears. The Lakewalk Moms insist we add QR codes to drive last-minute pledges. Every name feels like an oar in water, rowing us somewhere gentler.

I'm taping the last heart when my phone buzzes with a number I don't recognize. I don't move to answer it. Not yet. Rain tongues the canvas of the honey tent. The bell from the church carries over the square, once, twice, like it's reminding me there are clocks and then there are choices.

FLASHBACK: PROM NIGHT

Prom smelled like hairspray, eucalyptus, and moonlight borrowed from someone wealthier. Lila pinned my hair and called me a goddess until I believed her. Ethan arrived with a gardenia and a look that made the hallway seem smaller. We took pictures on the porch while my mother told us to be saints and my father pretended he didn't remember ever being young.

The gym was a chandelier of paper, a galaxy of streamers. We danced like people who had been practicing in our ribs for months. When the slow song threatened to tip me into tears, Ethan tugged my hand and we slipped out the side door into the night.

"Dock?" he asked.

"Always."

The lake took us in. We walked the boards, shoes in hands, wood cool under our feet. We didn't talk at first. We didn't have to. Wind stitched goosebumps into my arms; he draped his jacket over my shoulders like a benediction.

"I'm scared," he said finally. He said it to the water but gave it to me. "Of wanting everything."

"You get to," I told him. "You just have to learn how not to burn while you're shining."

He kissed me like agreement, like prayer, like we were inventing permission. My back pressed to a piling; his palm cradled my jaw; my fingers found the nape of his neck where his hair curled when he forgot to get it cut. Kissing turned into that quiet that hums behind a door you're not sure you're allowed to open yet. We did not open it. We explored the threshold and promised to do so someday.

He took out a folded sheet, our rules, copied in his handwriting. "Add one more?" he asked.

"What?"

"Tell the truth even when timing hates it."

"Deal." I signed my name next to it, ink skipping because the dock boards weren't level, and also because my hand shook.

Back in the gym, the DJ played a song so cheesy even the stars rolled their eyes. We laughed until a teacher shushed us, then laughed at being shushed, then kissed in the shadow of the bleachers with the kind of tenderness that always makes time look away.

PRESENT: TOM'S OFFICE

By four, I'm in Mayor Tom's office with Noah and Maya, the room smelling faintly of lemon cleaner and civic pride. The crosswalk sketch sprawls across the desk, pages tiled like an origami secret. Books streaming into one another, a little fox trotting along the spine, geese flying where drivers will glance and slow.

Tom presses his fingertips together like a cartoon mastermind. "This is art. This is traffic calming. This is, someone hold me."

"No fainting," I say, because I'm emceeing now and therefore in charge. "We have permits to discuss."

Noah speaks clearly and steadily about sightlines, non-slip paint, and how stories make people better at being cautious. Watching him, I feel that ache that is joy grown too big for its container.

Tom nods. "We'll start with a pilot at the library. Unveil at the gala. I'm texting the public works team now."

My phone vibrates again, the unknown number. This time, I pick it up and step to the window.

"Hello?"

There's a pause. Then a voice I know in my marrow. "Monroe."

My name in his mouth empties my lungs. I look down at the square. Ace is teaching a toddler how to give a high five. The honey tent has a line. The lake wears the afternoon like silk.

"I'm back," Ethan says. Simple. Just that.

I close my eyes. "Willow Cove has rules," I say, buying myself breath. "Mine, too."

"I know," he says, and the way he says it tells me he's learned a few new languages and forgotten none of ours. "Tell me where to start."

"Start with time," I say. "Not a scene. Not an ambush. Time."

"I can do that." A rustle, a faint hospital intercom somewhere behind him, or maybe a memory making noise. "I'll come by when you say."

"Tomorrow," I tell him, because I need a night to remember how to stand on the dock with my knees soft. "After the committee meeting. Six."

We hang up. I breathe. My ribcage behaves, eventually.

"Everything okay?" Maya asks.

"Everything is… scheduled," I say, and realize I'm shaking a little. She takes my elbow like we're crossing a street we've crossed a thousand times and still look both ways.

DREAM: THE LAKE LISTS

That night, the storm dream returns, but the lake is calmer. The dock holds like a sentence that knows where it's going. I walk to the end and find no one waiting. Instead, there's a small tin box, dented and familiar, the kind nurses use for bandages and secrets. Inside, our napkin of rules, the ink is darker than it should be. A note in Ethan's blocky print: Tell the truth even when timing hates it.

The bell rings three times. I turn. The figure at the shoreline is me, a year from now, hair a little longer, eyes a little rested. She raises a hand. Not goodbye. Permission.

I wake smiling, mistaking it for bravery, until the smile shakes.

PRESENT: LIBRARY ROOM

Committee meetings in Willow Cove are theater with agendas. We gather at a long table between stacks that smell like time. Rose claims the head like a benevolent monarch. Henry distributes spreadsheets as if they're party favors. Mr. Pierce has Ace stretch in the corner while children pretend they're not watching him be perfect. Mayor Tom sets a timer on his phone labeled brevity and forgets to press start.

"Key items," I say, tapping my list. "Permits, pledges, program."

Maya slides mockups to the center. "Minimalist glitter achieved."

We slot in a poetry reading, the unveiling of Noah's crosswalk, and a silent auction basket filled with experiences (Ace's walk, Rose's red scarf lesson, Tom's promise to assemble IKEA furniture without cursing). I pencil my name next to the emcee and feel my stomach do a careful cartwheel.

"Any new sponsors?" Rose asks.

"The Lakewalk Moms added a matching hour," I say. "And The Crossword Crew wants the puzzle at the gala to hide a clue only visible under blue light. Because of course."

We laugh, we plan, we promise. By the end, pages are taped and clipped, and the program is a skeleton that will happily grow muscle. When everyone disperses, I linger with my hand on the donor box, the weight of names a comfort.

"Six?" Maya asks softly.

"Six," I say.

EVENING: THE CAFÉ AFTER HOURS

We keep the café open late for the quilting circle once a month, which means the lights are warm and the room smells like vanilla and cinnamon after the rush. I brew chamomile and pretend it's courage. The bell over the door gathers itself, then rings.

He steps in, damp at the edges from mist, hair shorter, eyes the same. Gravity in a person. The kind you get from holding hands in rooms where hands shake.

"Clara." My name again, a careful offering.

"Ethan." I stand straighter without deciding to. My palms remember his jawline; my mouth remembers gardenia and mint and promises. My spine remembers rules.

Maya, genius that she is, slides two plates across the counter. "Chef's special: truce pie. I'll be in the kitchen pretending the dishwasher requires focused supervision." She disappears with the grace of someone who knows when to vanish.

We sit by the window where the rain stitches fine lines across the glass. For a minute, we let the room make small noises around us. Cups. Clock. A laugh from the kitchen. The town is moving on, as towns do.

"I'm sorry," he says. Not a prologue to an excuse. An entire sentence.

"For which part?" I keep my voice even. Boundaries before gravity.

"All the parts that sound like I loved you and still made you carry the quiet alone." His eyes don't look away. "I thought I was building a life for us. Turns out I was building a life and assuming you could live in the blueprints."

The breath I hadn't realized I was holding exits like relief, deciding to behave. "We were young," I say. "And you were on fire."

"I should have learned to warm without burning."

Silence again, but this one is companionable. I slide the plate toward him. "Truce pie has rules."

"I'm listening."

"One: no rewriting history to make it prettier. Two: No asking questions you don't want honest answers to. Three: we tell the truth even when timing hates it."

He smiles ruefully and proudly at once. "You kept the list."

"In my bones," I say. "And in a jewelry box."

We eat pie and talk like people who remember each other's first languages but need to learn accents. He tells me about residency nights that stretched a human into a wire, about the way he started measuring time not in hours but in patients who kept breathing. I tell him about buying the store, about how a town holds you up and also holds you accountable. He says he has taken a part-time position at the clinic here, with plans to expand services. The clinic that will benefit from the gala. The circle closes with a click, and I feel it in my knees.

"You're staying?" I ask.

"I am." A beat. "Unless you tell me the math hates it."

"The math wants more data," I say, and he laughs, quiet and relieved.

He doesn't reach for my hand. I don't reach for his. The air between us is busy with could, would, and maybe. When we finally stand, our shoulders do that near-miss that used to undo me. It still could. I let it not.

"Tomorrow," he says. "I'll be at the clinic at eight. If you need any-thing for the gala, medical stuff, first-aid station, whatever, tell me."

"I will," I say. And I mean it.

Outside, rain has polished the street into a mirror. We walk to the door together and stop beneath the awning where the wind can't find us. He looks at me, as if we are both trying to see the same future with-out speaking it into a shape that can shatter.

"Good night, Clara."

"Good night."

He steps into the drizzle. The bell notes his exit without drama. I lock up, breathing like the first page of a new chapter, then head home beneath my umbrella while the lake rehearses its calm.

NIGHT: HOME

Noah's light is on. Midnight supervises from the back of the couch with the disdain of a small god. I set my keys in the dish shaped like a book and exhale the second half of the breath I've been holding since he called.

"How'd it go?" Noah asks without looking up from his sketch, now a cityscape of books that looks suspiciously like our street.

"We agreed on truce pie."

"Solid first step." He glances up. "You okay?"

"I am," I say, and it surprises me to mean it. "Tomorrow's busy. Library at nine, vendor calls at ten, dress fitting at noon, want to come be honest about hemming?"

"I can be brutally supportive," he says, dimples hiding in his cheeks.

I kiss the crown of his head. "I know."

In bed, the house nestles around me. The storm keeps its distance. Sleep comes like a tide.

CODA: A SMALL OMEN

At dawn, a gull drops a silver candy wrapper on the bookstore step like tribute. I pick it up and laugh because Willow Cove is never subtle. On the window, our gold hearts shine, anchored, not pressed, each name a promise. Somewhere downtown, a phone vibrates with a new email bearing an out-of-state subject line I will overhear next week in the most inconvenient hallway. Future-me can lift that weight. Present-me straightens the hearts and opens the door to the bell's clear hello.

CHAPTER FIVE

Stormlight, Tape, And Truth

CLARA

The thunder doesn't knock, it barges in.

One second, the bookstore hums like it always does, the heater purring, pages whispering, Midnight performing surveillance from the history shelf, and the next, the sky tears open. Rain slams the lake into hammered tin; wind leans its full weight into Harbor Street. The bell above my door jangles a warning as the lights flicker, steady, then flicker again.

"Mom?" Noah's voice arrows from the back room.

"Front!" I call. "We're good, just weather showing off."

Liar, my pulse says. My pulse has opinions.

The power hiccups. A pane in the big window gives a sound I've never heard before, like a glass throat deciding whether to sing or scream. I move on instinct: take the step stool down from the display, slide the donor box to the ground, palm the taped gold hearts to make sure they hold. Names shimmer under my hand: Daniel Ortiz, Rose & Henry, The Crossword Crew. The town, glued together by hope and tape.

The pane decides: a starburst crack blooms in the corner. "Noah," I say, too calm. "We're closing for an hour."

He appears lanky and pale with that brave face he wears when pretending not to worry. A drop blooms on the inside of the glass like a tear. Then another. The rain has found a seam.

"Go grab the towels," I say. "And Midnight's carrier."

Midnight jumps down, offended that the weather didn't clear its plans with him. He stalks to the counter, tail high, as if he will personally file a complaint with management (the universe).

The front door blows inward on a gust, and Mayor Tom stumbles in, hair wind-swept, tie at half-mast. "Clara! The street," He points behind him. Harbor looks like someone poured a river into it.

"We're okay," I say. "Help me shift the display."

Noah skids back with towels; we wedge them at the baseboards while Tom hauls the romance spinner three feet from the window. It's not enough. Wind shoves; the cracked pane pings again, a tiny desperate song.

"Back room," I tell Noah. "Now."

He hesitates. I put command into my voice, the kind you learn when your heart walks around in someone else's body. "Go."

He goes.

Another gust. The starburst threads expand. My mouth goes metallic with the memory of a storm on the dock years ago, knees soft, weight centered, breath held. Don't slip. Don't drown. Choose.

"Clara!" Maya barrels in with a tray of cinnamon knots and zero respect for danger. "I brought sugar as a personality stabilizer" She says in the window. "New plan. I brought morale for triage."

"Midnight's carrier," I say. She's already on it, shoving aside a box of signed bookplates to fish out the blue plastic crate.

The pane lets go with a noise like a high note breaking. It doesn't shatter; it sighs. A hairline fracture snakes down, and the rain becomes a thin sheet on the inside of the glass. I throw a towel against it. Water laughs and slips around the terry, pooling for the books like a thief who's cased the joint.

"Out," I tell Tom. "Get people to steer clear of the storefront. We'll be right behind you."

He nods, surprisingly competent, and bolts. Maya kneels to corral the water. Midnight steps into the carrier with the forbearance of a king, allowing exile.

A shape flickers in the doorway; the bell catches its breath and then rings like a clean strike of silver.

Ethan.

He's rain-damp and breathing a little fast, like he ran the last block. His eyes go to the pane, to the puddle, to my face. In that order. "You okay?"

"We're improvising," I say. "It's fine."

He shrugs out of his jacket on the move and drops to his knees beside Maya, shoulders bumping. "Tom said the glass gave." He glances at me. "Back room's drier?"

"Mostly."

"Then we stage triage there. Towels, books, people."

"I make the plans in this store," I say, because habits are armor.

"Excellent," he says, unfazed. "Make this one with me."

"Terms," Maya mutters without looking up. "Also, I'm commandeering your cinnamon knots, Clara. For morale."

We move. I'm a woman made of tape and lists; he's a man built for emergencies; together we become efficient. We box the bottom shelf paperbacks with the speed of thieves and the reverence of priests. He lifts stacks like they weigh nothing; I throw towels like spells. Noah reappears with Ace in tow; Mr. Pierce just behind them, rain glossing his hat brim. Ace sits at once, noble and alert, as if auditioning for the role of the town's therapy metronome.

"You, sir," Mr. Pierce tells him, "are here for emotional regulation."

Midnight, safely crated, blinks at us like we clearly deserve whatever happens next. The crack threads downward another inch.

"Back," Ethan says quietly to me, chin indicating the office. It's not a question; it's a request. I nod, shoulders tight, and carry a box toward safety. He follows with two.

In the office, the sound of rain becomes a steadier drum. The room smells like paper and cedar soap, and the adrenaline sweat I pretend I don't make. We stack boxes on the desk, and I reach for another towel. My hand slips; he catches my wrist.

Not romantic. Reflex. Skin to skin, though, and my body makes a list of reasons it remembers him.

"You're bleeding," he says.

I look. I've scraped the inside of my forearm on a staple; it's thin but dramatic, the kind of cut that looks worse than it is. "Occupational hazard."

"Sit." He guides me onto the stool like I'm a patient who might bolt. "Do not argue with the person holding the gauze."

"Are you holding gauze or just manifesting it with your ego?"

He grins despite himself and plucks the first-aid tin from the shelf, a white cross with a dented lid. "Manifested."

His hands are warm and sure. He cleans the cut with practiced tenderness, mouth set, eyes steady. I focus on the sound of rain on the roof, on the way the thunder has moved farther off, on the little crease that appears between his brows when he concentrates. I used to kiss that crease like a job.

"Still good with emergencies," I say lightly.

"Occupational hazard," he echoes. "Also, a hobby." His gaze flicks up. "You're shaking."

"I'm fine."

He doesn't argue. He just tapes the gauze down and lets his thumb rest a second longer than necessary. My breath does the thing where it forgets its job, then remembers too much at once.

Noah's voice carries down the hall. "We got the display off the floor. Ace says he helped."

"Good," I call, and the steadiness in my voice surprises me. I'm fine. I'm fine. I'm.

Ethan's hand drops. His attention shifts past my shoulder, goes very still. I follow his gaze.

On the corkboard above my desk: a photo I stopped seeing years ago because grief taught me how to blur. Noah at six months, cheeks like apples, eyes so bright they look invented. Lila took it; Ethan's sister, all glitter and mischief, sending me a print with a Post-it that said, For the Monroe Museum, xo.

Ethan steps closer like the picture has gravity. He doesn't touch it. He looks, and I watch a dozen realizations move across his face in quiet succession. The math, as he used to say, starts counting itself. The time-stamp in the corner. The tilt of the baby's chin. The color of his eyes.

He turns to me. The room rearranges around the axis of his voice when he says, low and even, "He's mine, isn't he?"

The world rushes in and out like a wave that can't decide which shore to love.

"Yes," I say. The word lands between us like a book you need two hands for.

He closes his eyes. Opens them. There's no shouting in him, no drama. Only a quiet that makes more noise than thunder. "How old is he now?"

"Twelve." My mouth is dry. "He likes foxes and hidden drawings and pretending he doesn't care what people think of him. He does."

Ethan swallows around a thousand unsaid things. "Why didn't you?" He stops himself, jaw working. "No. That's not... We were kids. I was... gone." He shakes his head once, as if the word isn't big enough to carry the shape of those years. "Does he know?"

"Not yet," I say, and I hate that the answer can bruise a mouth. "He knows his father was someone who loved me when I was his age. He knows that person didn't stay." I hold his gaze because I refuse to teach my son to be afraid of honesty. "I wanted to tell you a hundred times. I didn't know how to ask you to choose us when you were choosing survival."

He flinches, not at the accusation, there isn't one, but at the truth inside it. "I should have come back," he says. "I told you I would."

"You told me a lot of beautiful things," I say softly. "Some of them broke on the way here."

"Clara." My name in his mouth is a careful offering. He presses his fingers to his eyes like he can rub the last thirteen years into a shape he recognizes. "I missed," He gestures helplessly, like the air might fill in the rest. First words. First steps. First, everything.

"You missed heartbreak, too," I say, because I won't sanctify the past. "Screaming at two a.m. Fevers that laugh at medicine. The way a person can be a miracle and also a hurricane. You missed joy like oxygen." The last part comes out bare. I don't look away.

He nods slowly. "I want to do better with the part that isn't missing."

Before I can answer, a crash from the front yanks us both back into now. We're moving on the same beat, down the hall, around the counter, where the romance spinner has finally surrendered to gravity. Books everywhere like a flock of startled birds. Ace shifts, attentive. Midnight meows acidly from his crate as if to say I warned you.

"Everyone okay?" Ethan asks.

"Fine," Maya says, winded. "One paperback tried to take me out. I told them to respect women."

"Language," Rose chides cheerfully from the doorway as she and Henry splash in, raincoats shining. "Oh, my. It's wet in here. And dramatic."

"Go home," I tell her. "We're closing."

"Nonsense," she says, beaming at Ethan with grandmotherly impertinence that sees through time. "We came to help."

Henry's gaze swings between us, then stops on the paper hearts. "I like the new gold ones. They glow like promises that kept themselves."

Ethan stoops to lift the spinner like it weighs air. His face is composed, but I can feel the ripple of new knowledge like a weather front moving through the room. He looks at Noah, who is wrestling a stack of damp romances into a box with more determination than method.

"Noah," Ethan says, and somehow manages to tuck warmth into two syllables without terrifying me. "Nice teamwork."

"Thanks," Noah mutters, wary as a fox. He glances up, eyes catching on Ethan's for a beat too long. Something unspoken crosses between them, a question neither can form yet. Noah looks away first, cheeks flushing like betrayal. Of what, I don't know.

"Let's get the rest into the office," I say briskly. "Then I'm taking everyone to Maya's for chamomile and bribery pastry."

"Bribery accepted," Maya says. "My kitchen is the only dry thing left on this street."

We move through water and paper until motion drains the adrenaline, leaving only tired human beings with wet socks. When the last box is high and dry, I lock the office and flip the sign to CLOSED. The bell sighs.

Outside, the storm decides it's had enough. The rain falls softly, like the sky has just remembered its manners. We step into the mist: Noah with the cat carrier, Mr. Pierce with Ace, Rose and Henry arm in arm, Maya prescribing sugar for everyone like a priest with wafers.

Ethan falls into step beside me under the awning. The street reflects our feet in little broken mirrors. He keeps his voice low. "Thank you. For… not lying."

"I don't lie," I say. "I edit."

The corner of his mouth lifts. "You'll tell him when you're ready." He glances at Noah. "I'll be here when you are."

"Terms," I say. The word tastes like electricity and sandbag.

"I remember," he says. "No running without a goodbye. No silence as punishment. Tell the truth even when timing hates it."

The list slices me open and stitches me back in the same breath. "We wrote that on a napkin under the bleachers," I say. "It smelled like hot chocolate and bad choices."

He huffs a laugh that sounds like a first step. "I'm not asking you to forgive me for all of it in a storm with wet socks." He tips his head, rain dotting his lashes. "I'm asking for time."

"Time," I repeat, because this is my life and I get to say it twice.

Noah turns, reading us like a book he pretends is boring. "Are we going or are we doing the thing where adults stare at each other until the weather changes?"

"We're going," I say. I lead the way toward the café. Behind me, the bell over my door rings three times, clean, clean, clean, like it's decided to be on our side.

ETHAN

It's remarkable what the body can do with shock when it's given a job. It can carry boxes through water, smile at neighbors, and lift a spinner that wants to pretend it's a trebuchet. It can keep your hands busy until your heart catches up.

Mine does in the doorway of Maya's café.

The room is warm and cinnamon-sweet; the windows fog at the corners, as if the night is leaning in to eavesdrop. Clara shakes rain from her sleeves; Noah sets the carrier on a chair and negotiates with Midnight, who has decided captivity is a social experiment beneath him. I take a breath that isn't emergency shallow and let the reality unfurl: I have a son. He is twelve. He has eyes I've seen in a mirror and an artist's hands and a protective streak I recognize from somewhere under my ribs.

"Sit," Maya orders like a benevolent dictator. "Tea first, existential crises second."

"Third," Tom says, bursting in and then stopping fast when he sees our faces. "Right. Fourth." He backs out. The bell forgives him.

Clara wraps her hands around a mug like she's coaxing heat into bone. I sit across from her because I don't trust my hands if I sit beside her. Mr. Pierce gives Ace a down command that would make a drill sergeant weep. Rose and Henry hold court at the next table like kindness royalty.

Maya deposits a plate between us. "Truce pie," she says. "Rules apply. No editing the past into a prettier lie." She jabs a fork in my direction. "Also, if you mess with her heart again, I will salt your coffee."

"Understood." My voice is hoarse. I look at Clara and try to fit thirteen years into a handful of words that can't possibly hold them. "I'm sorry," I say.

"For which part?" she asks, gentle and surgical.

"For the kind where love isn't enough to make a boy brave the right way." I steady my breath. "For missing the parts that mattered most. For assuming you could live inside my blueprints."

Her mouth softens, not a smile, exactly. A recognition. "We were young."

"We aren't now." I close my hand around the mug and feel the heat annotate my bones. "I don't expect you to open the door to him and say 'this is your father' because I think the syllables will fix everything." I glance at Noah. He and Midnight are in negotiation; the cat is winning. "I'm asking to earn it."

Her eyes shine, and to my shock, she lets them. "You don't get to miss twelve years and then audition."

"No," I say. "I get to show up and keep showing up until the part writes itself."

A beat. Two. Something in her posture eases, barely. The tiniest click of a latch.

"Okay," she says. "We'll start with time."

The door opens, and a breeze curls across the floor, lifting napkins and rearranging the cinnamon. The bell gives a lazy jingle, like it's satisfied with our terms. Noah slides into the booth beside Clara and passes me a napkin with a fox he's sketched on it in thirty seconds of feigned boredom. The fox is sly and kind and looks like it knows secrets it won't use against you.

"It's for the crosswalk," he says to the table in general. Not to me. Not yet.

"It'll make people slow down," I say, keeping my voice conversational so the tremor in it can hide. "Wonder does that."

He shrugs, but the corner of his mouth twitches like a truce wants to be born. Midnight headbutts his elbow and then mine, dispensing papal blessings with equal disdain.

Clara reaches for her tea. Our fingers don't touch. We don't need them to. The air between us is very busy learning a new language.

I take my first full breath since the pane cracked.

CHAPTER SIX

Stormglass, Cinnamon, And Truth

CLARA

The scream doesn't sound like fear. It sounds like metal deciding it's had enough.

I'm halfway between the poetry shelf and the donor wall when the Lakeside Market tent out front folds in on itself. Wind barrels down Harbor Street, grabs the canvas like a bully, and the aluminum pole snaps with a sharp, gut-punch crack. The pole spears the air, hits pavement, ricochets off the curb, and skids toward the café across the way, where three kids are squealing at a plate of sugar knots like they've never seen mercy in pastry form.

"Inside, now!" My voice is iron. "Go!"

The kids freeze for a single heartbeat, the long, dangerous one, and then move. One trip. The tent pole clips the doorframe with a teeth-grinding scrape and keeps coming. I don't think; I don't measure; I just run. My shoes slide on rain-polished floorboards as I burst through the doorway, the bell shrieking an alarm. I hit the sidewalk at speed and throw my weight into the pole like I can talk metal into behaving.

Warm hands appear on the shaft beside mine. Ethan's. We catch, pivot, and pin the pole to the brick like we've been training for synchronized chaos since we were seventeen. Wind shoves us both; my shoulder slams the wall; his body blocks mine; the air between us smells like cedar, rain, and a past that refuses to be theoretical.

"Got it," he says, breath clipped, voice calm, the particular calm that made people live in rooms that wanted to make the opposite choice.

"On three," I order, because I need the counting more than the physics. "One, two, three."

We lower the pole to the ground in a controlled slide, metal squealing, rain needling our faces. Mr. Pierce materializes with Ace, the world's most competent Dalmatian, who sits at parade rest like he intends to write an incident report later. Mayor Tom appears with two bungee cords and the optimism of a golden retriever.

"Secured," Ethan says a minute later, hands braced on his thighs, rain running off his jaw. His eyes flick to me, down my arm, to the white bandage from an hour ago. His mouth tightens. "You okay?"

"I'm fine." False. My hands are shaking like I swallowed a thunderhead. He sees it. He sees everything.

Maya leans out the café door with a dish towel and the posture of a woman prepared to fight the weather with carbohydrates. "Back inside before the sky escalates!"

We herded the kids in, metal dealt with, adrenaline still fizzing. I catch Noah's face at the back of the shop, wide-eyed, pale, brave, and I give him a signal we invented when he was three. Two fingers to my heart, two to the ground, two to him. I'm okay. We're here. You're mine.

He answers without words: relief, a chin lift, the quick, fierce little nod that says he'll pretend not to care later, and we'll let him.

The market empties; the town exhales; the storm remembers manners and steps back two paces. Inside the café, cinnamon and vanilla wrap around us like a warm blanket someone bothered to heat in the dryer first.

Maya slides a tray of knots between Ethan and me at the corner table by the window. "Chamomile," she announces. "For people who just convinced physics to behave." She pins me with a look that says: breathing is not optional. "Sip."

I sip. Steam kisses my nose; my pulse stops auditioning for percussion.

Across from me, Ethan cradles his mug in both hands, forearms damp, shirt clinging in ways I refuse to analyze in public. His eyes search my face like there's an answer written there in a language only we speak.

"Clara," he says softly.

The world tips. Not the dangerous kind. The kind where gravity remembers me by name.

"Yes." It comes out like a promise and a dare.

He glances toward the bookstore, where the donor wall glows gold, even in stormy light. His gaze catches on the office hallway beyond the counter, on the corkboard, on the photo that changed the air in my lungs an hour ago when he looked at it and did the math.

"He's mine," he'd said.

"Yes," I'd answered, and something old in me had creaked open like a door that remembers it was built to swing, not seal.

Now, we sit with cinnamon between us and the rest of our lives pacing just outside the window.

"Say when," he says. "Say how. I'll follow your lead."

I picture Noah's face when I tell him. The wary courage. The jokes he'll make, and the ones he won't. I picture the town and its opinions like confetti we didn't ask for. I picture a boy at a dock and a man in a storm, and the woman I am, who refuses to drown.

"Not tonight," I say. "Not like this. Tomorrow, after school. At home."

Ethan nods once, as if a surgical plan has been approved. Relief flickers, bright and human. "I'll be there at five."

"You'll be there at five," I echo, taking the words into my mouth so they can't disappear on the way to the clock.

A kid at the next table laughs. Ace woofs once, very polite, as if to remind us: the world is still full of ordinary.

Maya wipes a nonexistent crumb and manages to whisper and scold at the same time. "Minimalist glitter was not designed for thunderstorms. New plan: minimalist sandbags."

I huff a laugh that tastes like release. Ethan's smile knocks the wind from me for one clean second, sun through cloud, relief through ache. I'm steady. I drink. I decide, again, to keep choosing.

THE SPACE BETWEEN DOORS

ETHAN

I have sutured in a moving ambulance. I have threaded a chest tube through ribs slick with rain while a med student vomited into a trash can behind me. I have walked out of rooms where someone's life had ended forever and stood under fluorescent lights that made me look like a stranger, reminding myself how to be a person before I called my family.

None of it feels like this: sitting across from Clara, steam wreathing her face, knowing the boy in the back room with the quick mouth and the foxquick hands is my son.

Noah.

I say the name in my head, and it fits like it has been waiting for its hook.

"Five," I repeat, because I want the syllable to be something I can hold. The second hand over the café door ticks. I anchor to it.

Clara nods, and in the nod I hear everything she's not saying: we do this with care; we don't turn a boy into a stage; we do not let the town narrate the first version of this story he'll carry.

I follow her gaze to the donor hearts across the street, gold and steady on the glass. Names in her neat hand: Daniel Ortiz. Rose & Henry. Anonymous with a doodled goose because of course. One new red book cutout glows deeper than the rest. My shoulder remembers the way hers felt against the brick ten minutes ago. My palms remember the weight of the tent pole. My chest remembers the way it broke open in the office when a six-month-old smiled at a camera twelve years ago and looked like me.

"Your hands are still shaking," she says.

"Occupational hazard," I answer, and only then realize it's hers.

I cover her fist with my palm, gentle, as if the moment could skitter. "It gets quieter."

She gives me a look that used to make me smarter and still does. "I run a bookstore in a town with a goose that terrorizes hemlines and a mayor who thinks glitter is a strategy. I know how to find quiet."

I want to lean across the table and kiss the defiance off her mouth, and I do not, because I remember the rules she keeps in her bones and because I have learned a few of my own.

My phone buzzes. The screen lights up with a name that belongs to a building with a view of a river, which thinks it's the center of the world. I silence it. I am not the man who reaches for that call now, not first.

"Good," she says simply, having read the ghost of the choice in my face.

"Come to the clinic in the morning," I say, lifting the conversation into the air that doesn't hum with twelve years. "There's a storage room with a leaky sink and a closet where the AED should be and isn't. If we're putting on a gala for the place, I want it to deserve the outfit."

"You're volunteering me for closet triage," she says, the corner of her mouth considering a smile and then deciding to commit.

"I'm volunteering us." I let myself look at her properly. "You color-code hope. I organize chaos. Between us, we could fix an airport."

She laughs, real, bright, the kind that lifts the ceiling an inch. The laugh carries to the back, and Noah glances over. For a breath we just… are, a triangle of seeing. He looks away first, cheeks going pink. I store the image like a scanner, carefully and reverently.

Mr. Pierce appears at our table with Ace, who places his chin on Clara's knee and earns himself a knuckle scratch. "Heard the rescue from half a block," Pierce says, eyes twinkling. "Good instincts."

"Clara was faster," I tell him honestly.

"Always has been," he says, and winks. "See you at the clinic at nine, Doc. Ace is doing morale rounds."

"Tell him to bring his autograph paw," Clara says solemnly. Ace thumps his tail.

Rose and Henry blow in with rain on their coats and opinions ready. Rose presses a knit cap into Clara's hands. "For Noah," she says. "Tell him it's aerodynamic."

"Is that a thing a hat can be?" Henry asks. "Don't answer. I don't want to live in a world where physics isn't fun."

We talk fundraiser logistics for ten minutes, because Willow Cove believes in sandwiching intimacy between tasks. When the storm finally admits it has other errands, I walk Clara and Noah to the bookstore. At the door, she looks at me with a kind of tentative steadiness that feels like permission to keep breathing.

"Five," she reminds me.

"Five," I promise.

She goes in. The bell rings like a blessing. I stand under the awning for one extra breath and then head for the clinic, because if I can't fix the last twelve years tonight, I can at least fix a misfiled crash cart.

LISTS, LEAKS, AND LIGHTNING BUGS

CLARA

Dream: The dock again. Of course.

But it's noon this time, not storm dark. The lake is a sheet of hammered silver, and I'm barefoot in my bookstore sweatshirt, the color of dusk. A tin box sits at the end of the boards, the same dented first-aid kit Ethan used on my arm. When I open it, our old napkin is inside; the rules are inked darker than they used to be, as if time had decided to underline them for us. Someone, me, has added one more in neat block letters: Tell the truth even when timing hates it. Someone, he, has written beneath: And then make the timing worthy of the truth.

The bell rings three times in the distance. I turn, expecting a silhouette at the shoreline, a hand lifted like a promise. No one stands there. It's only the town, the rooflines, the church steeple, the café sign that squeaks in high wind, and the sense that the lake is listening.

I wake smiling, mistaking it for bravery, until the smile shakes. Then I get up and make a list.

Lists are the way I talk myself into and out of things. Today's:

+ Tell Noah at five. Home. No audience. No cake. (Maya will argue for cake.)

+ Clinic at nine. Closet. AED. Drip under the sink.

+ Call the glass guy about the window. "Starburst crack." (He will say, "I love a poetic diagnosis.")

+ Replace drowned romances. Offer half-price war, no, not war, storm-drenched specials with bookmarks that say, "You and this book survived weather."

+ Breathe.

By eight-forty-five, I'm in the clinic admin hallway with a clipboard, a roll of painter's tape, and a moral support latte from Maya. The hallway smells like lemon cleaner and quiet bravery. Mr. Pierce is already in the lobby with Ace, who is politely accepting the adoration of children like a celebrity who remembers his first name.

"Storage closet," Ethan says when I find him, hair still damp from a shower, scrubs that make him look like a promise. "You ready to be underwhelmed?"

"There are very few closets I haven't conquered," I say.

He opens the door. I inhale to make a joke and exhale dust. Boxes greet us with labels like HOLIDAY • MAYBE? And FORMER ADMIN • DO NOT TOUCH, which is an invitation if I've ever read one. A mop leans as if it has lost a fight. The AED is not here. Somewhere behind a mountain of outdated pamphlets about cholesterol, something is dripping. It is the most ordinary kind of emergency. I love it immediately.

"Okay," I say, snapping a rubber band around my wrist like I'm tying my hair. "Rules. Two piles: Keep, and What Even Is This. Sub piles: Rehome, Toss, and Tom."

"Tom is a pile?"

"Tom is a universe."

He grins. We move in easy parallel. He is taller than the doorframe by a stubborn inch. I am faster with a label maker. He hands me a box, as if he can read the precise moment my arms will start to shake. I hand him the wrench without looking up, when the drip reveals itself to be a sulking JBend that needs firm, kind attention.

"Minimalist glitter," he observes, watching me tape a small gold heart to the AED cabinet we locate in the wrong hallway and relocate to the right one.

"Morale matters," I say, as if I am not currently trying not to stare at the tendon in his forearm flexing under a stubborn valve.

"Always did," he says, and for a breath we're both standing in a memory of a diner booth and a kiss that tasted like hot chocolate and could. I file the memory under Later.

By ten, the closet is a place a person could enter without needing a tetanus booster. By eleven, the leaky sink is a redeemed sinner. I wash my hands just because I can. By noon, we're in the break room where someone has left a bowl of miniature chocolate bars on the table with a note that says, DOCTOR FUEL. I broke the rule by giving one to a nurse who looks like she could use a nap. She smiles and whispers, "Don't tell Joan."

"Joan knows all," Ethan says. "She is the weather."

We eat sandwiches on the back steps because the sky is blue in that way that feels like a gift after a storm, and because Willow Cove has decreed today a day for drying out.

"This is where you tell me about the phone calls," I say without looking at him.

"This is where I tell you about the phone calls," he agrees, eyes on the lake. "They are louder than they should be."

"Do they have commas in the numbers they're saying?"

"They have too many commas," he says, mouth twisting. "They sound like I used to sound when I thought I could outrun hunger by feeding it."

"And now?"

"And now I know hunger gets clever. It finds side doors. It dresses up as an intention." He looks at me. "I sent an email last night that said I'm not interested. They wrote back. Like a hydra."

"Hydras hate boundaries."

"Hydras hate towns that can fit in a twomile radius and still hold more love than a grid of windows."

"Then we will starve the hydras with cinnamon knots and a gala," I say, and he laughs like I just patched a hole he hadn't admitted was there.

He walks me back to the bookstore at one, because we are both pretending this is normal, and because we both know five is pacing. At the door, he doesn't touch me. I don't touch him. The air between us hums anyway.

"See you at five," he says.

"I'll unlock the door," I answer, and we both hear what I mean.

FIVE O'CLOCK FINDS US

ETHAN & CLARA
ETHAN

I am not a man who counts down. I've told residents not to count compressions out loud because the numbers can hypnotize you into forgetting the body under your hands. But at four fifty-nine, I'm on Clara's porch with rain somewhere far away in a different county and my heart making a sound I've never heard inside my chest.

The porch smells like vanilla from the candle she forgets to replace until it's just wick and memory. There's a pair of muddy boots by the door and a stack of library books with a rubber band around them, with Noah's name on the checkout slip in the pocket. I knock because even though part of me wants to be the man who knows how this door swings, I am not that man yet.

She opens. She is barefoot and steady, hair up, sweatshirt soft, eyes the exact blue of a lake that's decided to forgive the weather. I do not reach for her. That is both mercy and a mistake.

"Come in," she says.

The house is a map of who they are together. Shoes in a tumbling line. Hooks that remember jackets and one that stubbornly refuses to hold anything but a scarf. A photo string with tiny clothespins: Noah with a gap-toothed grin holding a pumpkin the size of his torso; Midnight pretending to be a plant in a hanging pothos; Rose and Henry dancing at the summer street fair while Tom narrates with his hands.

Noah is at the table with a pencil, trying not to look like he is waiting by pretending to draw something too small to matter. He looks up. His face runs through six expressions in a second and lands on the one that hurts least: bored tolerance.

"Hey," I say. I don't add any names. I don't qualify the room. He doesn't owe me a shape yet.

"Hey," he says. He keeps his pencil moving, shading a fox's tail with a focus that says both this is everything and this is nothing.

Clara sits. I sit. Noah sits because he was already sitting. Midnight leaps onto the back of a chair and becomes punctuation.

Clara breathes in and out like a person who has practiced. "We want to tell you something," she says. We, not I. My chest does a thing I will unpack later.

Noah's pencil stills. He doesn't look up. "I know," he says. "It's obvious."

Clara goes very still. "What is?"

He lifts his eyes to mine, and I feel something slot into place that has lived on a table in the dark for too long. "You," he says to me, tone even and sharp enough to cut through silk. "You're my... You know." He waves the pencil like the word is a moth he's not ready to pin to a board.

I swallow, because the sound I'm making inside does not speak English. "Yes," I say. "If you want me to be."

He rolls his eyes in a way that is both twelve and older than the town. "That's not how biology works."

Clara smothers a laugh that is one part relief and two parts shock. I try a smile. "Fair point."

He sits back. "Why now?"

Clara doesn't look at me to answer for me. Bless her for that. "Because he didn't know," she says. "And because I was afraid to tell him. I was wrong to wait this long." She meets my gaze for a heartbeat. "We're fixing that now."

Noah's face does not break. It does, however, soften at one corner, and the corner is everything. "Are you leaving?" he asks me, not wasting time with doors he doesn't need.

"No," I say, the word the shape of my spine. "I turned down something last night that would have made past me feel big and now me feel empty. I'm staying."

He blinks. That's also everything. He looks at the pencil like it might tell him what to do next. When it doesn't, he puts it down, stands, walks to the kitchen, and pours himself water with two hands like he did when he was five. He drinks. He comes back. He sits. He pushes the glass to the exact center of the coaster and lines the fox's nose with the edge of the table because control can be found in straight lines.

"Okay," he says finally, and if I could bottle the way Clara exhales at that word, I would solve a dozen problems I didn't know how to name. "What do we do?"

"We decide together," Clara answers. "What to tell people. What to call things. What to do on Thursdays?"

"Thursdays are clinic committee," he says automatically, because the town calendar lives in his bones.

"Then Fridays," she amends. "Or Tuesdays. Or we make up a day that doesn't exist and call it Ocelot."

He tries not to smile. He fails. "Ocelot is good." He looks at me. "Do you know how to throw a baseball?"

"Terribly," I admit. "But I can learn. Or we can skip straight to the part where you teach me why your crosswalk design saves lives."

He stares like he's trying to decide if I'm messing with him. When he decides I am not, the other corner of his face softens, just a millimeter. Midnight, traitor to all poker faces, purrs.

"Dinner?" Clara asks, voice quiet and brave. "The diner? Pancakes for dinner feels like a day we invented on purpose."

Noah nods once. "Lemon meringue," he says. "For research."

Clara's eyes gloss; she blinks it into a joke. "Fine. But we're paying in cash, so Dale can't pretend I tipped him in affection."

We put on coats. We stand in a little cluster at the door, and for the first time since yesterday, the air in my lungs behaves.

That night, after Noah's asleep, the house becomes a hush that waits for us. Midnight patrols the hallway like a velvet chaperone; the lake outside keeps its own counsel.

We don't rush. We undress each other like archivists, gentle, reverent, careful with the years folded between us. Every touch is a reintroduction: his hand steady at my hip, my palm relearning the lines of his shoulders.

The heat builds in layers: laughter first, then hunger, then silence, then a moan I don't recognize as mine. "Tell me to stop," he whispers into my mouth.

"Don't you dare," I breathe back, and he groans like the years between us just collapsed.

The rhythm we find isn't frantic. It's thorough. Permission layered over permission, until my body arches into his like a truth I've been waiting to tell. The sound of the storm outside becomes applause; the bed creaks like a witness.

When I fall apart under his mouth, he follows, cursing quietly against my skin. And when we finally go still, breathless and damp, his hand cups the back of my head like he's holding more than hair. Like he's holding the last thirteen years.

"Water?" he asks again, voice cracked, tender.

"Yes," I laugh, wrecked and remade. "And maybe forever."

On the walk, Clara tells Noah about the first time we sat in booth three and argued about whether stars listen. Noah says they do if you bribe them with pie. At the diner, Dale is unimpressed with our attempt to be ordinary and brings extra whipped cream like he's been waiting for twelve years.

We eat pancakes for dinner and lemon meringue for research, and I do not cry into my coffee. I do memorize the way my son says the word "meringue" like he invented it.

When the check comes and we fight over it in a way that makes Dale roll his eyes and mutter about romance taxes, Noah pulls a napkin toward him and sketches a fox trotting along a book spine, tail lifted, unbothered. He slides it across to me without looking. "For the clinic," he says. "For the AED cabinet."

I tuck it into my pocket like a relic and do not take it out until later, alone, because some reverences prefer privacy.

CLARA

We walk home under a sky that decided to put on a show: lightning bugs blinking like the universe practicing Morse code. Noah pretends not to be charmed and then absentmindedly catches one and lets it go. Ethan keeps his hands in his pockets and his mouth shut at exactly the right moments, which feels like a miracle and also like a man who learned a painful language and intends not to forget it.

On my porch, Noah dithers like he wants to ask for something and doesn't know if it's allowed.

"Go ahead," I say. He is, after all, my heart.

"Can he?" Noah flicks his chin at Ethan without finishing. Words are moths tonight.

"Stay for a movie?" I translate.

He shrugs, which is a sign of twelve for yes.

We watch an old adventure film on the couch with a blanket over our knees, and Midnight pretending he isn't fascinated. Noah provides running commentary about improbable rope bridges. Ethan does not laugh in the wrong places. Halfway through, Noah's head tips against my shoulder, then slides down into my lap, the way it has since he was three on nights when the world needed to be smaller to be survivable. His breathing steadies. His hand opens and closes against my knee like a tide.

I look over the edge of the blanket. Ethan is watching us, as if he understands what 'holy' means. The lamp turns his eyes into a shade the lake keeps for secret days.

He mouths, Thank you.

I mouth back, We're trying.

He nods. He looks at my mouth like he's remembering a kiss I'm also remembering. Then he looks at Noah and resets the map of his face to something that will not make me reckless in front of a sleeping boy.

When the credits roll, we carry Noah to bed without commentary. Ethan takes the feet because he is taller; I take the shoulders because I have done this dance enough times to know where the walls shift. We tuck him in, and Ethan stands back, hands in pockets, a man on the threshold of a room that contains everything he didn't know how to want and now cannot imagine not wanting.

In the hallway, we stop. The house hums: refrigerator, baseboards, the quiet relief that follows a good decision.

"I don't have words for this," he says.

"You don't need to. Just… don't run."

His mouth tilts. "I emailed the hydra. Again."

"What did you say?"

"That I won't be taking calls for a while because I'm on Ocelot."

I laugh, loud enough that Midnight flicks his tail in disapproval. "You're impossible."

"I'm learning to be possible," he says, and the way he looks at me makes my knees feel like the dock in summer, warm, sturdy, built to hold.

In the living room, the lightning bugs make sequins on the window. We stand a foot apart, which feels like both a cliff and a bridge.

"Kiss me," I say, because I promised myself I would tell the truth even when timing hates it, and because the timing tonight feels like it's trying very hard to be worthy of the truth.

He does. Oh, he does.

Not a promise we can't keep. Not hunger pretending to be love. A kiss like a doorway you open with both hands. Warm, sure, present. He tastes like coffee and meringue and rain that finally decided to forgive. His palm cups my jaw the way it always has, like it learned the map of me before it knew what maps were for. My fingers slide into the hair at his nape, and the world goes bright around the edges.

When we part, neither of us staggers. We sway. We smile. We breathe.

"Terms," I whisper.

"Still signed," he answers, and kisses my forehead like that's also a promise.

The porch light flicks twice, the timer being dramatic. We both laugh, and the laugh turns the air in my house into a place I want to live in for a very, very long time.

The hydra emails again while he's tying his shoes. He silences it. We do not fill the silence with apologies.

At the door, he touches the frame with a knuckle, as if the house were a person he respects. "Tomorrow," he says.

"Tomorrow," I agree.

He steps into the night that smells like a lake and clover. The bell in my bones rings three times, not like an omen, not like a warning. Like a welcome home.

And somewhere down Harbor Street, a black-and-white dog lifts his head, as if even he knows the shape of a family when he sees it.

CHAPTER SEVEN

Willow Cove

STORMGLASS

CLARA

The dock bucks under my bare feet as thunder counts to three. The lake isn't water so much as a polished mirror trying to decide if it wants to remember us. Wind sweeps across in bands; the dock flexes under my bare feet; the church rope rings three slow notes, one… two… three. I'm in my dusk-blue sweatshirt, hair stuck to my cheeks, a paper heart cupped in my palm like a talisman. When I reach the end of the boards, someone stands where the horizon should be, broad shoulders, steadier now, the shape of a man I loved before either of us had any business with forever.

"Terms," I say, out loud to the rain. The paper heart doesn't dissolve. It shines.

He lifts a hand, no grabbing, no promises he can't cash. Just a motion that feels like permission. Behind me, a cat yowls; Midnight's imperious punctuation. The dock doesn't break; neither do I.

I wake with my hand fisted in the sheet and the taste of thunder clean on my tongue. For a beat, I don't know if the ringing is dream-bell or real-bell, until the clock on my nightstand clicks to 5:30 a.m., and Willow Cove exhales like a town that knows how to survive weather.

By six, I'm jogging past the square, shoes sucking at damp pavement, breath syncing to the lake's slow tide. The market tents are still sleeping, canvas dark with last night's rain. Mayor Tom's latest slogan—BOOKS & HEARTS GALA—peels slightly at the corner of my front window. Inside, the donor wall glows with gold and silver, names in my hand like stitched seams: Daniel Ortiz. Rose & Henry. The Crossword Crew. Anonymous (with a doodled goose, because of course). It looks like hope with tape and breath.

I'm easing the door open when a gust knuckles the awning. The bell snags in its bracket, shivers, then belts a full-throated jangle worthy of a drumroll. A tang of ozone and wet cedar sharpens the air.

"Latte first," I tell the bell, because bargaining with inanimate objects is a fine morning hobby.

Maya meets me halfway down Harbor with two to-go cups and the kind of glance that inventories your soul. "You didn't sleep."

"Define sleep."

"Clara."

"Dream. Dock. Paper heart. The usual." I steal a sip of her latte; she pretends not to notice. "Where's your apron?"

"In a loving relationship with the dryer. Also, your window needs reinforcement strips. The clinic board is coming by at ten to check in on the gala, and I refuse to let your aesthetic perish by tape failure."

"Minimalist glitter endures," I say, and my voice steadies as the joke lands.

She bumps my shoulder. "How's Noah?"

"Pretending he's fine about Algebra, which is the international symbol for not fine about Algebra."

"And Ethan?" She says it neutrally, which is why I forgive her.

I watch fog unspool over the lake. "He asked for time last night. I said yes. Tonight, I tell Noah the whole truth, with Ethan in the room."

Maya exhales the kind of breath you take right before a curtain goes up. "Okay. Then today we build small, sturdy moments. The kind that holds."

We do.

By nine, the bookstore smells like cinnamon and paper, which is to say my nervous system is manageable. Noah sketches at the front table, pencil hopping as he hides foxes and geese inside the lines of his crosswalk design. His fox-tail motif, though he doesn't know it yet, will one day become the gala's badge art. Midnight sprawls like a velvet accusation on the mystery shelf; Ace the Dalmatian lopes by with Mr. Pierce for a morale lap and accepts exactly three kisses from toddlers, no more, no less.

The storm outside remembers manners and steps back two paces. Inside, it's the small-town orchestra: heater hum, page whisper, the soft ceremony of names being written. I added two silver hearts to the window. I press each one with a firm palm. Tape. Glass. Intention. Hold.

A shadow finds the threshold. The bell clears its throat and rings once, clean as a promise. For one half-beat, it's only Mrs. Valdez ducking in to ask about crossword clues. Then the bell rings again.

Ethan.

He's not drenched this time. He's folded into scrubs that make every line of him look like steadiness and breath. He lifts two fingers in greeting, no sudden moves, and I feel my entire ribcage answer, pulse flickering under my jaw, forearms buzzing.

"Morning," I say.

"Morning." His gaze flicks to Noah, to the window, to me. No hurry, no demand. "Closet triage at the clinic? I brought donuts as a bribe for Nurse Joan."

"You'll need two bribes and a poem," I say. "She's the weather."

His mouth tilts. "I can learn to rhyme."

"Tragic." I pass him a roll of painter's tape and a stack of gold hearts. "Start with reinforcement strips. Left pane, top edge. Firm pressure, no bubbles."

"You're the only person who can make tape sound like destiny."

"No bubbles," I repeat, because history has taught me to be precise.

He moves to the glass; I move beside him. Our fingers brush once, smoothing the tape, an accidental spark, and we both pull back. The air does something fizzy anyway. Outside, the lake plays mirror again, pretending it knows nothing about storms.

"Tonight," he says, quiet. "I'll be there at five."

"Five," I echo, and let the word settle where prayer lives.

Noah glances up, sees us measuring out a future in tape and breath, and, because he's my son, says nothing while taking in everything. Midnight yawns like a tiny judge. The bell relaxes. The morning holds.

CLINIC LIGHT

ETHAN

By ten, I've learned four things about Willow Cove's clinic storage closet:

Someone once labeled a box HOLIDAY • MAYBE? and then took a long sabbatical from deciding;

The AED lived for a year in the wrong hallway like a hero in exile.

Clara can turn chaos into rows, and rows into relief.

Minimalist glitter endures, even under fluorescent light.

"Left pile is Keep, middle is What Even Is This, right is Tom," she says, flicking a wrist toward Mayor Tom's gravitational field of ideas. She wears a navy tee that says Read Something That Scares You and a smile she thinks I don't see.

"I assume Tom is combustible?"

"Safely contained," she says, then hands me a wrench without looking when the sink coughs a wet complaint. "J-bend," she adds. "Firm hands."

"Like you," I say before my filter catches up. She drops her gaze, but her mouth remembers the shape of a yes. Did I just say that out loud?

We work elbow to elbow until the air in the closet smells less like dust and more like second chances. Every so often, she pauses to write a name for the donor window, the loops of her letters neat as a heartbeat. When we slide the AED into place beneath a small gold heart, morale matters, she says with absolute seriousness. I want to kiss her for the way she treats hope like a tool, not a theory. I do not. Not now.

In the lunch lull, we sit on the back steps with sandwiches and the quiet confidence of people who have done a visible good thing. The lake has put on that bright silver a kid would color with the side of a crayon. Ace patrols the parking lot once, satisfied. Nurse Joan opens the door, sniffs, and says, "If those donuts are for me, I accept apologies in pastries."

"They're for you," I say, rising like a man respectful of weather patterns. "And I signed up for Saturday's blood pressure clinic."

"Flattery and service," she says, peering at Clara over her glasses. "Keep him."

"Working on it," Clara answers, startling herself with the truth in the joke. Did I just say that out loud?

My phone buzzes. The number blinks a familiar New York area code: Sloane at Argus Health. Loud. Insistent. I don't look away from Clara when I silence it. Her exhale is its own sort of weather, warmer than last night, steadier.

I touch the scarlet paper book she cut for high donors. "We'll need more of these by Friday," I say. "I can call Lila, she's terrifying on the phone; she could fundraise ice from a glacier."

"Your sister who talks a blue streak and then feeds you like you've been starving your entire life?"

"That one."

"Bring her to the gala. I'll assign her a microphone."

"Dear goodness," I say, and catch myself. Later, I'll swap in a "holy moly" for variety.

Clara laughs, pure and bright. "We're editing our oaths now?"

"Only the ones that might hurt someone else's sky," I say, and she goes soft-eyed in a way that makes my chest feel like a door opening.

At one, I walk her back to the bookstore. We stop beneath the awning like we're both remembering the night the pane cracked and the town held its breath. She waits for me to speak. I don't make a speech. I just say, "Five," because sometimes a number is the most honest sentence a man can give.

"Five," she repeats, and it lands like a promise we both wrote with both hands.

PAPER HEARTS & HEAT

CLARA

By four-thirty, the shop glows like a lantern. Rain has rinsed the sky clean, leaving us with the particular kind of evening that makes Willow Cove look like it was designed by a kind-hearted witch with very strong opinions about fairy lights. Rose and Henry drop off a scarf for the auction ("It's aspiration ally red," Rose says). Mr. Pierce promises that Ace will pose for photos in a bowtie if the kids remember to use "gentle hands."

Noah finishes shading the fox hidden inside page twenty-seven of his crosswalk and pretends not to wait. Midnight supervises the donor wall with a level of gravitas usually reserved for Supreme Court justices.

At 4:58, my hands turn into weather. At 4:59, I rewrite an entire label just to have something to do with my breath.

At 5:00, the bell rings like a gold coin.

Ethan steps in, hair damp from the sort of honest shower a man takes when he intends to show up. He looks at me, not at the cat, not at the window, not at the list by the till, and it feels like the first true sentence of a language we used to speak all the time.

Noah squares his shoulders, sets his pencil down, and does not run. We sit at the little round table by the poetry shelf. Midnight leaps to the chair back and becomes punctuation, his tail brushing behind Noah like a guardian.

"We want to tell you something," I say, and my voice doesn't shake. "Together."

He doesn't make me drag it out. He doesn't make me defend it. He just asks one very clean question: "Why now?"

"Because he didn't know," I say, nodding toward Ethan. "And because I was afraid of the answer for too long." I swallow. "I was wrong to wait."

Noah studies Ethan the way he studies bridges, testing for where the weight will land. "Are you staying?"

"Yes," Ethan says, the syllable hard and clear. "I turned down a thing that would have looked shiny and felt empty. I'm here."

Noah nods once, like a judge who has read the brief and decided to allow discovery. He pours himself a glass of water with his careful two-handed grip, puts it exactly in the coaster's circle like a spell, and says, "Okay. We try."

The breath that leaves my body is not dramatic. It's quiet. It's real.

"Dinner?" I ask, because ordinary is the magic I believe in. "The diner. Pancakes for research."

We sit in booth three, like a family, trying on family without touching the tags. Dale pretends we aren't his favorite soap opera and brings extra whipped cream. Noah says meringue like he invented it. Ethan watches us with reverence and restraint and exactly the right amount of hunger.

By the time we walk home under a sky with lightning bugs practicing Morse code, a decision has settled in my bones: I will not be afraid of good things. Not tonight.

When we're back in the living room, Noah asks if Ethan can stay for a movie. He shrugs while he asks, because at twelve, wanting and shrugging are siblings. I nod. We watch an old adventure with improbable rope bridges. Noah migrates, eventually, the way he always does, shoulder to my side, head to my lap, hand fisting and unfisting as sleep finds him. Ethan watches like someone who understands the word sacred.

When the credits roll, we carry Noah down the hall, me at the shoulders, Ethan at the feet, like a story we refuse to drop. We tuck him in. Midnight claims the footboard as his domain. We stand in the doorway and say nothing for ten heartbeats.

Back in the living room, the house is a soft hush of lamp light and quiet bravery. Ethan looks at me like I am both dock and shore. Heat rises just under my skin, not a blaze, not a warning, just that warm tide I have pretended not to miss for thirteen years.

"Kiss me," I say, because we wrote a rule once under the bleachers: tell the truth even when timing hates it. Tonight, the timing is trying very hard to be worthy.

He does.

It isn't frantic. It isn't apologizing. It's a hello to say we both survived. His mouth is warm, my palm cool against his jaw. His palm cradles my jaw like he remembers the map; my hands slide into his hair, and the room sharpens at the edges. When we step closer, there's no grabbing, only granting. When he murmurs my name, it isn't a plea, it's a promise to listen. I answer with a sound that belongs to no one else.

"Terms," I breathe against his smile.

"Signed," he says, and kisses the corner of my mouth like punctuation.

We don't race toward anything we can't carry. Instead, our hands linger deliberately for two more lines of touch, then we stop, laughter caught between us like light.

"Tomorrow," he says.

"Tomorrow," I agree, and mean all of them.

FORESHADOW

ETHAN

At home, I don't turn on the TV. I sit at my kitchen table and write a note to my future self on a crumpled clinic post-it: Hydras hate boundaries. Keep yours. Ocelot Fridays. Then I put Noah's napkin sketch, the fox trotting a book spine, on the fridge and stand there like a man who has been handed a compass that points to something other than ambition.

My phone lights up with four messages from a number that used to mean permission. I type one sentence and send it to all of them: I'm not available. Then I put my phone facedown and let silence gird itself into something gentler than loneliness.

When sleep comes, it brings a dream made of silver and cedar and a lake that listens. The dock holds. The bell rings three times, not like a warning this time, but like a welcome.

In the morning, I'll be at the clinic early to check the crash cart and call Lila. I'll tell her to bring a dress with pockets and her loudest laugh to the gala. I'll ask her to be kind when she meets the boy with my eyes. (He doesn't know it yet, but Noah's crosswalk design will be unveiled there.)

In a month, there will be another offer with more commas than decency, and I'll say no again, faster this time. In two months, Clara will let me stock the bookstore's first-aid kit and kiss me in the history aisle when no one is looking. In three months, Noah will hand me a sketch that includes me without comment. In four, the town will stand up under fairy lights and clap for something we built with tape and hope and patience. The timing will keep learning how to be worthy of the truth.

For tonight, a window glows down Harbor Street with paper hearts that look like constellations. I fall asleep counting them instead of exits.

And if the bell in my bones rings just once more as I drift, I understand it finally, in a language that used to scare me: it means stay.

CHAPTER EIGHT

Tide & Tape

WHEN THE WINDOW HELD

CLARA

The dream starts hot, rain turning the dock slick as glass, thunder counting to three like the universe is tapping my pulse: one… two… three. I run barefoot and he's there, older, steadier, one hand lifted, not to claim, just to ask. The lake breathes cool against the heat of his mouth when I lean in. His palm finds my jaw; mine slides into his hair. Lightning sketches us in silver, and I say the word that saves me from drowning: terms. The dock holds. I do, too.

A squeal, rubber on wet pavement, rips me awake.

I'm off the couch and at the storefront in three steps. Outside, a delivery van fishtails in the drizzle, bumper kissing the curb in a spray of gutter water. The bell over my door jangles in alarm as the driver throws it into park, hands trembling. Cardboard cartons list like tipsy sailors.

"Clara!" Maya's voice carries from the sidewalk as she jogs toward me with a tray of cinnamon knots. "Your romance restock just tried to reenact a stunt film."

"Not the pirates again," I mutter, shoving the door wide. "Inside, careful with the corners."

A second voice, low, steady, falls in behind hers. "Got it." Ethan. In scrubs and rain, sleeves pushed to his forearms, jaw shadowed, expression all competence and calm. The part of me that slept is suddenly very awake.

Boxes come fast; Maya passing, me stacking, Ethan moving with the kind of graceful efficiency that once made me believe the world could be saved by hands alone. When the last carton clears the threshold, the wind rams the door. I shove it closed with my hip and laugh because sometimes laughter is how you tell your body it survived.

"Any casualties?" he asks, flicking water from his hair.

"Two dented corners and one very dramatic vampire," I say, setting the wounded book aside for the discount bin labeled STORM-KISSED SPECIALS. "Thank you."

"Occupational hazard," he says, glancing past me. His gaze lands on the donor wall, gold and silver hearts taped in neat constellations. "It's… beautiful."

"Minimalist glitter," Maya says, setting down her tray. "Trademark pending."

The driver signs, apologizes, apologizes again, then peels away, relief waving from his rearview mirror. The store exhales. Outside, harbor mist hangs in soft ribbons.

"Storage room?" Ethan asks, palms already braced on a box labeled Romance; Signed Copies.

"This way."

We shoulder through the back hallway, all pine and paper dust, and set the cartons on the worktable. When I turn, he's close. Not an accident close. A careful one. Heat collects low in my belly, the dream's silver edge still bright on my skin. For a beat, we just breathe the same air.

"I thought about last night," he says. "About the kitchen light, the way you said tomorrow and meant all of them."

My fingers find the corner of a label and smooth it flat, buying time. "We're better with plans."

"We're better with truth." His voice goes quieter, like he's talking to the part of me that never learned to lie. "I don't want to rush you. I also don't want to pretend I don't want you."

It's ridiculous, how much a sentence can take my knees. "Not pretending is… allowed."

I step, he steps, and we meet somewhere patient. His mouth finds mine, warm and sure, not a storm this time but the heat that lingers after. It's a kiss built on breath and consent, slow enough to feel my own yes. When his thumb skims the line of my throat, I make a sound I've never made for anyone else, and he swallows it like a promise.

"Terms," I murmur against his smile.

"Still signed," he says, and we both laugh softly because restraint can be sweet when you choose it.

We pull apart before gravity gets ideas. Outside, the bell at the church tosses three lazy bongs down Harbor like a kind uncle. Maya yells from the front, "I'm counting boxes, not kisses, but I know when you've stopped counting either!"

"Betrayal," I whisper.

"Community," he corrects, eyes amused. He nods toward the donor wall. "Tell me what you still need."

"Reinforcement strips for the top pane. More hearts cut." I hesitate, pulse tripping. "Dinner. Not the diner. Somewhere I have to wear lipstick."

His answer is immediate and gentle. "The Boathouse at seven. I'll make the reservation and behave myself."

"Behaving is optional," I say before my brain catches up.

He grins, and some greedy, hopeful part of me stretches like a cat in a square of sunlight. "Seven."

WHAT BROKE AND WHAT HOLDS

ETHAN

When I left at eighteen, I thought hunger was virtue and rest was surrender. Nights in New York proved me right, until they didn't. There's a memory my body still keeps at the back of my ribs: three in the morning, a code that wouldn't quit, a resident naming the meds with a voice that shook, my hands steady while my head ran ahead of me. After, under the fluorescent lights that make everyone look like a ghost, I sat on a folding chair and texted a number I didn't have the courage to assign to Clara. A stranger cried in the family room. I wanted to hand her a book and a place to sit that didn't hum. I wanted your voice to say I did enough. I never pressed send. Restraint bruises, too.

Now, at my kitchen counter, I dial a number I don't have the courage for. "You have exactly ninety seconds to tell me when I'm required to arrive and what color dress says 'my brother finally pulled his head out of the clouds and into a small town with superior pastry,'" Lila says by way of hello.

"Hi to you, too." I can practically hear her eyeliner wing sharpening through the line. "Gala's in three weeks. Bring your loudest laugh and your kindest questions."

"Clara?" she asks, softer.

"Clara," I confirm, and there's enough in my voice that my big sister clears her throat and goes gentle.

"Okay," she says. "Then I'll wear flat shoes. We bustle better in flats."

My other line pulses. The hydra, Argus Health, Sloane's number, gnaws at the edges of my patience. I decline it without ceremony. Lila hears the silence. "Saying no is a sentence," she says. "Not a paragraph."

"I sent the sentence," I tell her. "The hydra is learning punctuation."

"Well," she says, "Hydras hate boundaries. But they also hate community theater with donor walls, and I know for a fact you love both of those now, so: you're safe."

I smile, a real one that lifts something in my chest I thought I'd broken. "Dinner at The Boathouse tonight."

Lila gasps like she's opening a present she already peeked at. "Wear the blue shirt. The one that says 'I came to behave and accidentally remembered I'm in love.'"

"Goodbye, Lila."

"Goodbye, Ethan. Proud of you."

The call clicks off. I look around my rental, the plant that refuses to die in the kitchen window, the fox napkin Noah drew tacked to the fridge, the list on my counter that reads Ocelot Fridays because apparently naming something makes it real, and feel the unfamiliar steadiness of a life that might actually fit.

At six fifty-eight, I push open The Boathouse door into lamplight and the smell of butter and lake. She's already there, lipstick a cherry ribbon, hair pinned up with a few strands determined to be free. The hostess says her name, and it lands in my body like a benediction.

"You clean up," she says, eyes bright.

"You devast," I stop, edit. "You undo me."

A smile tugs at her mouth. "Better."

The waiter's discreet enough to be a rumor. Candlelight does unfair things to Clara's collarbone. We order halibut and a salad we will both ignore after three bites. It's easy to talk about small things: the sink we fixed, the crosswalk sketch Noah shaded like it mattered, Ace's dignified opinion on bowties. Hard things circle like the weather beyond the windows. When they drift closer, we don't dodge.

"I should've told you sooner," she says, fingers balanced on the stem of her glass. "About Noah. I was nineteen and terrified of asking you to choose when you were already choosing survival."

"I should've come back," I answer. "I thought love could live in blueprints. I forgot houses need roofs."

We don't apologize to each other to death. We don't draft history into a prettier lie. We just let the truth sit between us, steady as the candle's small flame.

When the check comes, I reach for it and she slaps my hand with scandalized delight. "Romance tax," she says. "We split."

"Terms," I agree, and try not to imagine what it will feel like to unpin her hair.

After, we walk the boardwalk in the kind of summer-cool air that makes even the lake behave. The old lighthouse winks down the path. "Adventure?" she asks, chin toward it.

"I wore the wrong shoes," I say.

She grins. "I brought a blanket."

We climb. The gravel crunches. The lighthouse door is locked, of course, but the steps curl around it like an invitation. We sit and unfold the blanket over our knees. Night presses close. Fireflies spell out a language neither of us is fluent in and both of us understand.

"Do you ever think the town is… enchanted?" she asks, voice low.

"Only when you're in it."

She bumps my shoulder. "Cheesy."

"Hungry," I correct, and when I kiss her this time, it's slow and certain, a study in how gentle can still be hot. Her sigh opens under my mouth. Her hand slides under my jacket to the heat of my back, and I breathe in, greedy for her. We stop before we lose the thread, foreheads touching, both of us smiling like thieves who returned what they took and kept the thrill.

"Walk me home," she says.

"Always."

THE TOWN THAT WATCHES & THE BOY WHO DECIDES

CLARA

If Willow Cove had a gossip rag, it would be the church bulletin taped to the coffee urn: Prayer Requests and Also Guess Who Held Hands. The morning after The Boathouse, we give them fresh material by being happy in public and not hiding it. Rose pretends to scold me, then tucks my hair behind my ear with a tenderness that makes me feel seventeen and also safer than that girl ever did.

"Red suits you," she says, nodding at my mouth. "So does relief."

"Donor wall update?" Henry asks, hovering like an eager punctuation mark.

"Five gold, two silver, and an anonymous goose," I say, pen poised. "Also, the Crossword Crew is hiding a message in the gala program you can only see under blue light."

"Of course they are," Ethan murmurs, passing with a coil of painter's tape.

We have an appointment that isn't medical; Noah's art teacher asked for parent volunteers to help hang the school's community exhibit in the library wing. The three of us arrive together, a fluster of tape and twine and careful breath. Noah's shoulders are set to not impress, but his eyes betray him every time Ethan quietly hands him the tool he needs without making a speech about it.

"You can say it," I tell Noah under my breath while he straightens a frame.

"What?"

"That you like being good at things."

He shrugs. "It's acceptable." His mouth fights a smile and then loses.

Ace trots through with Mr. Pierce, practicing therapy manners for Reading Hour. Half the room stops to pet him. The other half watches Midnight stroll by like a tiny sovereign supervising a peaceful transfer of power. They nose each other, a mutual acknowledgment of realm.

By noon, the exhibit looks like a town learned how to mirror itself, watercolors of the lake, a pencil drawing of the church rope, a mixed media piece featuring goose feathers and municipal warnings. Noah's crosswalk concept gets the end cap. People linger. A fourth-grader in glasses asks him why he hid a fox on page twenty-seven.

"So drivers pay attention," he says, voice threading steady. "Stories make you careful."

He glances at Ethan. Ethan doesn't make a big deal of the glance. He just steps back, lets the moment belong to the kid who made it, and I feel something in my chest loosen like a knot I forgot I'd been clenching.

After the cleanup, we walk to the square. The Lakeside Market shivers with umbrellas; Maya's pastry case gleams. We claim a table by the window and split a strawberry tart three ways because of symbolism.

"Tonight," Ethan says, looking at Noah. "I have a clinic until six. After that, if you'd like we can, you can show me how to shade fur. Or we can throw a baseball so badly the goose calls the authorities."

Noah pretends to consider, then says, "Shading. The goose has a file on me."

"Fair," Ethan says solemnly. "I'm on thin ice with that bird."

It's not fireworks. It's better. It's ordinary. It feels like recovery.

We're halfway through the tart when Mayor Tom jogs up breathless, tie askew. "Minor disaster," he says. "Which is to say: Tuesday. Someone from Cove Chatter wants to 'profile' the gala for their 'features' section." He air-quotes the words as if they have germs. "They asked very nosy questions about 'the billionaire doctor romantic subplot' and whether we can seat them near 'the scandal.'"

Heat rakes my face. Ethan's jaw sets. Noah closes his eyes like he's bracing for a wave.

"We'll set boundaries," I say, more steel than sugar. "No personal questions. No photos of minors without consent. They can cover the donor wall, the poetry reading, and the silent auction. That's it."

"Also, I'm not a subplot," Ethan says mildly, which makes me fall a little harder for him in public.

Tom claps, delighted. "God, I love it when competent people show up. I'll write them a list. In crayon. So they understand."

When he leaves, the quiet he drags in his wake sits for a minute. Noah draws a fox on his napkin, then slides it toward Ethan. Not a truce. Not yet. A breadcrumb.

Ethan tucks it into his pocket like a relic. A text buzzes on his phone. He doesn't look. I do, accidentally, because my eyes are nosy about hydras now. Argus Health: Final offer. Name your number.

"Do you need to?" I start.

"No," he says. Then, softer: "Thank you for noticing and not asking me to prove it."

I slide my foot against his under the table, a small, secret affirmation. He doesn't jump like a man who forgot what affection feels like. He just breathes.

THE LIGHT WE CHOOSE

ETHAN

In the ER, you learn quickly that adrenaline is a loan shark. It fronts you what you need and collects with interest. Tonight, after clinic, I can feel the bill come due, my body a little floaty, my head a fraction too loud. I almost canceled. Then I see Noah waiting on the bookstore steps, sketchbook under his arm, and the math changes.

"Shading," he says by way of hello, and we take the stoop like it's an atelier. He opens to a fox curled on a stack of worn novels. "Fur is about suggestion," he says. "You don't draw every hair. You imply."

"Like medicine," I hear myself say. "You don't fix everything. You shift a system and let the body remember how."

We lean in, elbows touching by accident and then not. Midnight slinks down, inspects our work, and drapes himself across the page like a furry paperweight.

"Saboteur," Noah tells him affectionately.

We're still there when Clara locks up, streetlights warming the sidewalk to honey. "Dinner at The Boathouse looked good on you," Noah says without looking up. My cheeks heat like a teenager's. Clara makes a surprised sound and then smothers it with a cough.

"Tomorrow," she says, keys in hand. "Crash carts and closet labels. Then the donor calls. Then," She tips her head toward the lake. "breathing."

"Tomorrow," I echo.

I'm halfway home when my phone lights again with Sloane's name. I don't answer. Instead, I forward the message to Lila with two words: Ocelot night. She replies immediately with a fox emoji and a string of knives, which in our sibling language means, Proud of you, I will cut anyone who makes you forget.

At my place, I don't turn on music. I sit in quiet, listening to the hum of the fridge and the way the day has arranged itself into something resembling peace. When I finally fall into sleep, the dream isn't a storm. It's a kitchen lit by a small lamp and the sound of a boy laughing in another room while a woman writes names on gold hearts in careful script. The bell rings once, like an affirmation. The lake breathes out. The dock holds.

~ ~

CODA — FORESHADOW

A manila envelope slips under the bookstore door after closing, no return address, no note. Inside: a glossy printout of a tech article with my face from four years ago, a red pen circle around the word billionaire, and a sticky tab that reads: Ask him why he really came back.

Midnight noses the envelope and flicks his tail like he's seen worse.

I pick up the bell from the counter and set it upright again, more out of habit than need, and slide the envelope into the bottom drawer. We have time. We have tape. We have rules.

And this time, we have each other.

CHAPTER NINE

Tide Turning

EDGE OF THE STORM

CLARA

The power dies the way a gasp does, sharp, surprised, a little indecent.

One moment, Monroe Books & More glows golden over Harbor Street, fairy lights everywhere like we're auditioning for a winter wedding. The next, thunder lays its palm over the roof and presses. The lamps wink out. The bell above the door is jiggling, like it has even forgotten how to breathe.

"Stay put," I tell my own pulse, which is currently attempting a solo career.

Rain knives across the lake. Wind shoulders the window I just reinforced with painter's tape, testing the seam. From the back hallway, Maya's voice: "Not to be dramatic, but the espresso machine is making a noise that implies it will unionize."

Before I can answer, the door shudders. A silhouette fills the glass, broad shoulders, rain-dark scrubs, hair flattened in ways I refuse to analyze. The bell gathers itself and gives one clear, clean ring.

"Hey," Ethan says, stepping inside like a steadying hand. Water pearls on his jaw. His smile goes soft and rueful when the lights fail to resurrect on cue. "Clinic's generator kicked; I came to check your panes. And you."

"Panes are fine," I say, voice steady, knees not. "Me… undergoing a routine systems test."

"Then let's pass it." He shrugs out of his jacket and, without touching me, moves beside me at the big window. Outside, lightning sketches the lake in silver. Inside, his nearness does foolish things to the air, like adding heat to oxygen and asking it to behave.

The top corner gives a tiny plaintive ping. I palm the tape. He brackets my hand with his, warm and sure, guiding the pressure like he does when he shows a new nurse where to place a stethoscope. The sound is entirely inappropriate for tape: a soft seal, a quiet yes.

"Good," he murmurs. He doesn't step away.

"Minimalist glitter survives another day," I say, because jokes are life preservers and I collect them.

"Clara." My name in his mouth dissolves a decade. He turns just enough that the inches between us become the only math I care about. Rain beads his lashes. His breath ghosts my cheek. "I'm here."

"You are," I whisper, and for the first time in thirteen years, I let that be simple.

The bell on the counter clicks gently in a stray draft, permission, punctuation, something I'm pretending isn't cosmic. I rise onto my toes at the same moment he lowers his head, and we meet exactly where we should, no scramble, no hurry. Just heat finding home.

It isn't frantic. It isn't an apology. It's a kiss like steady voltage: a hum that warms bone. His mouth is warm and tasting faintly of cinnamon (Maya weaponizes pastry), and when my fingers slide into the damp curls at his nape, his inhale turns a little jagged in a way that makes every part of me sit up straighter. He keeps one palm at my jaw, anchoring, reverent, while the other skates my hip and settles at the small of my back like a question we both answer by moving closer.

"Terms," I say against his smile, because I promised myself I would.

"Still signed," he says, voice rough silk, and kisses me again, deeper, sure, until the room tilts pleasantly and the storm outside becomes stage dressing.

A loud ping snaps both our attention to the pane; water is nosing the tape again, sneaky as gossip. We break with identical breaths and, God help me, identical grins.

"Window first," he says. "Then more of that."

"Efficient," I manage.

We fall into motion the way our bodies remember: he steadies the ladder while I climb; I slap fresh tape anchors along the top seam while thunder counts to three; he spots me with surgeon's sure hands; I lean down and kiss the corner of his mouth because restraint can be delicious when you choose it. Back on the floor, I towel the sill; he drapes his jacket over my shoulders without asking, which should annoy me but instead lands like a benediction.

From the back: "Status report?" Maya calls. "I can offer cinnamon knots and a stern pep talk."

"Stable," Ethan answers, eyes on me. "Improving."

The lights surge, flicker, then hold. The bell, the traitor, gives a cheerful trill like it knew we'd pass the test. My mouth is tingling; my hands smell like rain and paper and him. It is, somehow, both too much and exactly enough.

"Coffee," I say, cheeks hot, lips swollen in a way that is going to make Rose raise her brows tomorrow. "Then… the rest of the checklist."

"Right." He bends, scoops his jacket from my shoulders, and brushes a thumb over my cheek, innocently checking for rain. I let my eyes close for the one heartbeat it takes to memorize the touch. When I open them, the lake is again only a lake, the window is only a window, and the man in front of me is the boy I loved, grown into someone who knows how to hold a room together with tape and kindness.

"Okay," I breathe. "Okay."

PAPER HEARTS & PULSE CHECKS

CLARA

After the storm passes, the town does what Willow Cove always does: shows up as if it had the plan all along. Rose arrives with a thermos labeled FORTITUDE; Henry brings a newspaper article about historic glazing like that will calm a pane; Mr. Pierce executes an Acelap through the store to verify morale; Midnight saunters onto the sill and parks himself like a sentry who accepts bribes in sardines.

We add two gold hearts to the donor wall: Daniel Ortiz and The Crossword Crew, and one silver heart that simply reads 'For Anyone Who Needs Today to Be Kind.' My hand shakes while writing "kind," which is on-brand for me, so I add a tiny fox to the corner and call it art.

There's a lull late afternoon, the particular quiet that smells like wet paper and warm dust. I take my journal from beneath the counter. I don't write often, too many lists, too many receipts, but today I want a verb that isn't tape.

Dear future me, I write. You didn't drown. You didn't run. You chose.

My hand hesitates, ink pooling in the loop of a letter. He kissed you like patience. You kissed him like consent. Both of you remembered. Neither of you demanded. You can trust this.

I should probably write about fear, but fear is boring, and I've already given it too many pages. Instead, I make a new list, small, doable, stubborn.

Call the glass guy; describe the starburst crack like a poet and a customer.

Ask Nurse Joan where the AED wants to live (answer: not the "Holiday • Maybe?" closet).

Remind Mayor Tom that "features writer" is not a synonym for "busybody with a newsletter."

Tell Noah at dinner the plan for Friday: unveiling his crosswalk concept at the library exhibit. Let him pretend to be unimpressed. Believe the grin.

Breathe.

A memory arrives uninvited, prom night, lemon meringue, our napkin of rules, and I let it sit. Nostalgia is a cat: ignore it and it climbs your lap anyway. The dream dock has stopped tossing so hard; the boards still flex, but they hold.

My phone buzzes. Unknown number. I let it go to voicemail. A minute later, a text from Maya: Cove Chatter DM'd me. They want a "human interest angle on the billionaire doctor romance redemption arc." I told them to come talk about donor hearts or go pet a goose.

I snort. Boundaries, I reply. Also, I'm not a subplot.

"Neither is love," Rose says mildly from history, because she reads minds and shelves.

"Eavesdropping is a spiritual gift," I tell her.

"Darling," she says, "in a town this size, it's a sacrament."

By closing, the sky has washed itself a gentle indigo. Noah drifts in from the back with graphite on his knuckle and that old soul focus that makes me both proud and a little achey. He holds up a sketch: the lake as a mirror, our donor wall reflected with the hearts turned to stars.

"It'll photograph well for the gala," he says like a tiny project manager.

"It'll make people slow down," I say, and mean more than traffic.

Maya locks the front; I flip the sign to CLOSED; the bell gives one obliging ding and rests.

At home, after homework negotiation and a toast-and-soup dinner because storms steal the will to sauté, I run a bath and open the window so I can hear the lake practicing being calm. When I slide under, the heat unclenches the day from my shoulders. I close my eyes and dream without sleeping: the lighthouse steps, the Boathouse candlelight, the patient way he said I'm here like a promise he already started keeping.

When I sink back, Midnight perches on the toilet lid like a chaperone with notes. "Boundaries," I tell him. He blinks once, which in a cat is: I'll allow it.

I go to bed smelling like cedar soap and rain. In the space between waking and sleep, the bell in my bones rings once, then twice, then three times. I think that means to stay.

GLASS, HYDRAS, AND HOW WE HOLD

ETHAN

The hydra calls at 6:12 a.m. on a number my hands could dial in the dark.

I let it ring. I let it stop. I lace my shoes and run along the lake until my breath finds a rhythm that belongs to me. When I get home, I text Lila: Ocelot Friday still sacred? She replies with a fox emoji, a lightning bolt, and I already bought donuts for Nurse Joan, don't embarrass me.

At the clinic, the storage closet that used to smell like resentment now smells like lemon cleaner and second chances. The AED cabinet wears a tiny gold heart because Clara said morale matters, and I would believe her if she told me the moon needs bookmarks.

I do a med cart audit and, because old habits die stubborn, alphabetize the top drawer so nobody panics reaching for epinephrine. Joan catches me and shakes her head like a patient storm. "Let the man alphabetize, Carol," she tells the walls. "It keeps him from punching venture capitalists."

I don't say hydra out loud, but it smiles behind my teeth anyway.

By nine, I'm at the bookstore with a roll of reinforcement strips and two lattes I didn't make (for everyone's safety). Clara opens the door with that steady softness that makes me feel like a person instead of a cautionary tale.

"Window?" I ask, offering tape.

"Always," she says, offering me her mouth.

We keep it brief because we're learning the difference between hungry and ready. Still, kissing her feels like a piece of my spine standing up a little straighter.

We fix the top seam, we reshelve a tower of storm-kissed romances, we welcome Ace for his morning rounds. Noah drifts in after school with his sketchbook and that dipped chin nod that is twelve going on ancient. We arrange ourselves around the counter like a constellation, figuring out who's the North Star.

"Cove Chatter," Clara says dryly, sliding me a printout someone left under her door last night, my face from an old article circled in red. "They want a 'redemption arc' quote."

"I'd prefer a 'learned boundary' quote," I say. "Or 'we have a donor wall to finish, please go interview someone's goose' quote."

"We could seat them at the gala next to Tom and let entropy do the work," she muses.

"Cruel," I say, admiring.

She opens her mouth to add something, then closes it. The slight shift in her eyes tells me what she doesn't: she's still bracing for the other shoe. The part of me that used to think grand gestures fix everything wants to declare myself loudly on the courthouse steps. The part of me that actually learned something wants to show up with pizza on moving day and a willingness to listen.

"Dinner?" I ask instead. "Not fancy. Your table. I'll cook."

Her smile tilts. "You can cook?"

"I can grill cheese and caramelize onions. Which is to say: yes."

"Bring bread," she says. "I'll supply the butter and the twelve-year-old who will judge you on texture."

"Deal."

That evening, Noah pretends not to watch me brown butter in her skillet while Midnight files a petition to be fed cheese immediately. I plate grilled cheese like a man auditioning for a custody agreement and slide a bowl of tomato soup into place like a ceasefire.

Noah bites. Chews. Considers. "Not bad," he concedes. "You didn't scorch."

"I contain multitudes," I say solemnly. He almost smiles.

After, we do homework triage at the table, polynomials, human anatomy flashcards, a donor call list, and I feel something in my chest loosen the way a knot does when you stop pulling on it so hard.

When Noah wanders off to shower, Clara and I stack plates in the sink, and then we just… stand. The kitchen light does kind things to her mouth. I can feel her debating gravity.

"Come here," I say quietly, careful. She does.

We keep to kissing and the warm press of bodies, hands respectful, hearts a little wild. When her breath stutters, I back off first because I want a thousand more nights and because the best heat I've ever known is the kind we build, not the kind we burn through.

"Thank you," she whispers, and I have to close my eyes for a second because the boy I used to be would have sprinted past that line and called it love.

The hydra texts while I'm loading the dishwasher. I silence it and turn the faucet on hard enough to wash the sound away. Clara sees, of course, she does, and says nothing. Which is somehow louder than any promise I've ever heard.

When I leave, I kiss her at the door, and the bell in my bones answers with three clean notes.

THE TOWN, THE TELLING, THE TURN
CLARA

The next morning, Cove Chatter sets a match to the rumor mill with a "preview" post about the gala featuring a photo of our window and a line about "Willow Cove's favorite prodigal with a heart of…investment." The comments are the usual stew: nosy, generous, bored, kind. What makes my stomach dip is the DM asking for a "quote about forgiveness."

I drafted four and deleted all of them. Forgiveness is private. The donor wall is public. I decide to feed only what I want to grow.

At the library exhibit, we unveil Noah's crosswalk concept. Mayor Tom tears up. The Lakewalk Moms clap like a marching band. Ace wears a bowtie and accepts tributes in the form of pats. Noah stands very still while people say they love his foxes. His ears go red; his eyes go shiny; his mouth does that tilt it does when he's proud but not ready to admit it out loud.

Ethan doesn't hover. He stays within reach. When a kid asks Noah why he hid a goose in the gutter of page six, Noah shrugs. "So drivers pay attention." Then he glances at us, and for a blink we are a unit, three points of a line I used to be afraid to draw.

After, I find an envelope under the cash drawer at the store, no return address, just a glossy printout of an old tech article about Ethan with the word billionaire circled in red and a sticky tab that says Ask him why he really came back.

I put it in the bottom file drawer. I write another gold heart instead: For the kid who needs the fox on page 27. I tape it to the glass with firm pressure and a steady breath.

That night, at closing, Ethan arrives with Lila on his heels, lipstick like a battle standard, eyes kind, laugh bigger than the room. She hugs me like we've been in a group chat for years.

"You must be Clara," she says. "Hi. I'm Lila, the sister who learned to make soup when our dad forgot how."

"Hi," I say, throat thick, heart reckless. "I'm Clara, the woman who hoards cardstock and writes names like prayers."

"Excellent," she says briskly. "Now that we've established that we both run on hope and snacks, where am I needed?"

"Mic duty at the gala," I say. "And body blocking any reporter who confuses curiosity with entitlement."

"Say less," she replies. "I brought flats."

We eat takeout on the floor like college kids and plan the poetry order. When they leave, the store echoes with the ghost of laughter.

I lock up. The bell offers one last tiny ring. Outside, the lake is a sheet of midnight glass, and my reflection looks more like a woman I recognize than she has in years.

At home, I tuck Noah in, and he lets me kiss his temple without an eye roll. Halfway to my room, I hear him call softly, "Mom?"

"Yeah?"

"Are you… happy?"

I stand there in the dark and feel the answer build like a tide. "I am," I say. "I really am."

"Okay," he says, so quietly I almost miss it. "Me too."

In bed, the dream comes, but it's quieter now. The dock doesn't buck; it sways. The paper heart in my palm doesn't dissolve; it shines. When I look up, he's there, older, steadier, hand lifted not to claim, just to ask. Behind him, the town glows like a constellated donor wall. The bell rings three times, clear as permission.

I wake smiling. And this time the smile holds.

CHAPTER TEN

Stormglass & Turning

CLARA

The storm doesn't knock; it barges in.

One second, Monroe Books & More is humming pages whispering, the heater purring, Midnight draped across the history shelf like a velvet judge. The next, wind presses a palm to the front window, and the bell above the door jitters like it has even forgotten how to breathe. Rain turns the lake into hammered tin; the sky flashes white; the glass in my big display pane answers with a sound I've never heard, a small, strained ping, like a throat deciding whether to sing or scream.

"Front!" I call, already moving. "We're okay, just weather showing off."

Liar, my pulse says, loud enough to rattle my ribs.

Not a shatter. Not yet. I palm a fresh strip of painter's tape, anchor it, smooth downward with my whole hand. The donor wall glows around me: gold and silver hearts taped like constellations; Daniel Ortiz in careful ink, Rose & Henry, The Crossword Crew, one anonymous goose (obviously), and a bright red book cutout waiting for a very generous name. Hope, held together with tape and breath.

The door blows inward on a gust and brings in six feet of steadiness in rain-dark scrubs.

"Hey," Ethan says, easing it closed with his shoulder. Water beads his jaw; his hair is damp enough to rewrite my posture.

"Hi." I don't look at his mouth. I absolutely look at his mouth. The pane pings again. "We're improvising."

He's beside me without touching, taking in the crack, the tape, the puddle intent on becoming a river. "Let me spot you," he says, hands already braced along the ladder I haven't realized I needed.

"I make the plans in this store," I tell him, because habits are armor.

"Excellent." His mouth tilts. "Make this one with me."

We move like people who used to speak the same language and haven't forgotten the verbs. He steadies; I tape; thunder counts to three. Midnight stalks to the sill, tail up, offended that the storm didn't RSVP. From the doorway, Maya announces, "I brought cinnamon knots and unearned confidence."

"Confidence accepted," I say, smoothing the strip flush. Rain nosing the seam becomes a bead and then, mercifully, nothing.

"Good," Ethan murmurs, voice low, right behind my ear. Heat runs gentle and sure along the map of my neck. His palm brushes the back of my wrist, deliberate and grounding, and warmth ripples through me. I climb down. We turn at the same time. For a breath, the inches between us turn into math I understand: if I lean, and he leans, the answer is yes.

The bell on the counter clicks in a draft like permission. I rise onto my toes; he bends; we meet in the exact middle, no scramble, no hurry. His mouth is warm and tastes faintly of cinnamon (Maya, obviously). His palm cups my jaw like it remembers the map; my hands find the damp curl at his nape, and that old, impossible, perfect spark hums to life. Not chaos. Current.

"Terms," I breathe against his smile, because I promised myself I would always say the word that keeps me from drowning.

"Still signed," he answers, and kisses me again, deeper, sure, until the room tilts pleasantly and the storm outside becomes stage dressing. The bleachers napkin-rule flashes in my mind, his inked signature under mine, two kids promising without knowing how much it would matter.

A ping snaps us apart. The top seam is testing the tape. We grin like co-conspirators and go back to work.

Five minutes later, the pane holds, the puddle sulks, and my hands smell like rain and paper and him.

"Report?" Maya calls from the back. "I have pep talks hot and ready."

"Stable," Ethan says, eyes on me. "Improving."

The lights flicker, surge, and settle. The bell gives a cheerier jingle, the petty traitor. I wipe the sill, tuck stray gold hearts back into their neat rows, and let my breath catch up.

"Coffee," I say, cheeks warm, mouth tingling in a way Rose will definitely notice tomorrow. "Then the rest of the list."

He scoops his jacket from my shoulders (when did he put it there?) and brushes a thumb along my cheek under the pretense of checking for rain. I let my eyes close for exactly one heartbeat. When I open them, the lake is again only a lake, the window is only a window, and the man in front of me is the boy I loved, grown into someone who knows how to hold a room together with tape and patience.

"Okay," I tell the storm, the window, and myself. "Okay."

By noon, Willow Cove does what it always does: it shows up like it had the plan all along. Rose arrives with a thermos labeled FORTI-TUDE; Henry contributes an article about antique glazing because that will apparently soothe a pane; Mr. Pierce brings Ace for morale laps, this time in a jaunty teal bowtie that matches the gala flyers; Midnight claims the sill like a tiny monarch who accepts bribes in sardines. Mayor Tom arrives late, tie at half-mast, declaring, "Leadership requires wrinkles," which is oddly reassuring.

A woman in a sunshine-yellow raincoat slips in with a donation envelope and tears bright enough to make the room blink. "For the clinic," she says. "He helped my father once." I write Daniel Ortiz in my neatest hand and press the silver heart to the glass with the kind of care I used to save only for breakable things. Maybe hope is allowed to be breakable and still hold.

In the lull after, when the shop smells like warm paper and wet wool, I find a manila envelope shoved under the cash drawer. No return address, just a glossy printout of an old article about Ethan with a red circle around the word billionaire and a sticky tab that says: Ask him why he really came back. Midnight sniffs it, flicks his tail, and selects contempt. I slide it into the bottom file and rest my palm over the donor wall instead. Names are louder than gossip when you write enough of them.

At four-thirty, the rain forgets its tantrum and becomes a hush. I'm halfway through rewriting a smudged heart when the bell rings a clean, bright note that lands between my shoulder blades like a promise.

"Five?" Ethan says, Voice careful.

"Five," I answer, feeling it land in my bones. We'll talk. We'll plan. We'll choose.

I press one last strip of tape flat and, for once, I don't press my feelings flat with it.

ETHAN

I have sutured in a moving ambulance and threaded a chest tube in a thunderstorm with a med student trying not to faint into a biohazard bin. None of it prepared me for the way a woman can turn a strip of painter's tape into hope and make my chest feel like someone found the dimmer switch and slid it all the way toward light.

At the clinic, the generator kicked in like an old friend with opinions. Joan, who runs this place with the patience of the tide, looked me over and said, "Window hero now, closet triage next," and handed me a key to a storage door that should come with a tetanus booster.

Inside: a chaos of unlabeled boxes, a sulking J-bend, and one Automated External Defibrillator living in exile like a banished prince. By ten, with Clara beside me and her label maker singing, we'd turned resentment into rows. She taped a tiny gold heart on the AED cabinet when we rehung it in the right hallway. "Morale matters," she said, as if hope were a tool and not a theory. I wanted to kiss her then for exactly that reason. I didn't. Not there.

My phone buzzed twice while we worked; New York area code, a boardroom smile in text form: Argus Health, subject line FINAL OF-

FER. I silenced it. Clara's eyes flicked to the screen and back to the wrench in her hand. She didn't ask me to prove a choice I'd already made. That, somehow, sealed it.

At lunch, I sat on the back steps and called Lila. She answered like a trumpet fanfare. "Tell me which dress says 'my brother remembered what home tastes like,' starshine, and what time I need to arrive to clap at the fundraiser."

"Three weeks. Wear flats. You're on mic duty."

"Flats are for cowards and women who plan to move furniture," she said, and I could hear the smile in her voice. "Which is to say: I'll pack two pairs. How's Clara?"

"Steady," I said, and felt the word settle like a stone in a river that knows exactly where it belongs. "Fierce. Kind."

"And Noah?" she asked, softer.

"Funny. Sharp. Wary. He drew a fox on a napkin and slid it to me like a treaty." I touched the pocket where I'd tucked it and felt, absurdly, braver.

"Then keep showing up," she said. "Hydras hate consistency."

"I'm not taking the offer," I told her. Saying it out loud turned it from a decision into a vow. "I want this one life. This town. This family."

"Proud of you," she said, and meant it with all her bright, impossible heart.

At six fifty-eight, I push open the Boathouse door and walk into lamplight and the smell of butter and lake. She's already there, wearing a dark dress and a lipstick color that should be illegal. The hostess says her name, and something unclenches under my ribs like a fist remembering it was a hand. Outside, chimes sing in the herb boxes, lavender bending in rhythm with the wind.

"You clean up," she says, eyes warm and amused.

"You undo me," I say, nearly saying something too big, then editing myself down to the truth she can hold without it crushing us.

We order halibut and ignore half of it because conversation keeps getting in the way. Not the performative kind. The kind where honesty clicks into place without drama. I tell her about nights that stretched men thin, about realizing adrenaline is a loan shark. She tells me about building a life you can live in with a boy who loves foxes and a cat who rules with velvet tyranny. We talk about the gala, poetry, a donor wall like a galaxy, and a crosswalk that will make drivers slow down to look for wonder. Lila even volunteered to read her favorite poem aloud. We don't attempt to rewrite history into a prettier lie. We let the truth sit between us like the candle flame: small, steady, refusing to be theatrical.

When the check comes, I reach for it and she slaps my hand, properly scandalized. "Romance tax," she says. "We split."

"Terms," I agree. God, I love her.

We walk the boardwalk after the lake, practicing calm. Near the old lighthouse, she pulls a blanket from her bag like she planned for my bad shoes, and we sit on the steps with our knees touching and the town lanterning itself behind us. Fireflies practice Morse code. Her hand slides into mine and stays. The kiss that follows is not hunger pretending to be love; it's love teaching hunger how to be gentle. When we stop, the night looks pleased with itself.

"Come back to my porch," she says as we stand. "I have a peppermint candle and a nosy neighbor."

"Perfect."

We don't promise anything too large on the walk, just tomorrow, and then the next tomorrow, and then the next. When I leave her at the door, I touch the frame with my knuckles like you do when you respect a threshold. She smiles without opening it wider. "Five," she reminds me.

"Five," I promise, and let the word be the whole sentence.

At home, I take the Argus emails, all of them, drop them into a folder named HYDRA, and delete them without hesitation. Then I write one line to myself on a sticky note and stick it above the sink: Stay is a verb. Use it.

CLARA

Dream: the dock again, because apparently my subconscious is a screenwriter who refuses to retire a good set. But the water's quieter tonight, the boards warm under my bare feet. I'm holding a paper heart in my palm; it doesn't dissolve. It shines. On the far end, a man lifts his hand, older, steadier, not to claim, just to ask. Behind him, the town glows like a donor wall. The bell rings, one, two, three, and the sound goes through my sternum like a key turning.

I wake smiling, mistaking it for bravery, until the smile holds.

Dawn turns the lake into mirror glass. I jog the square and wave at Mrs. Donnelly as she scolds a goose for assaulting her hem. At the shop, the bell gives its first tentative hello. I straighten the hearts in the front window, gold, silver, and one red book waiting, and secretly enjoy how the tape makes a soft sound when it finds glass. Hope has a sound. Who knew.

Maya swings in with lattes and both eyebrows up to her hairline. "You glowed last night," she says, then, at my face, tones it down to, "You were… illuminated by the candlelight of personal growth."

"Minimalist glitter," I say, deadpan, and she laughs loud enough to make Midnight twitch a whisker. Still, when she pushes for details, I edge back, and for a moment she looks stung. Later, I hand her the draft gala program and say, "I trust you to pick the order," and the relief in her smile patches the bruise I'd left without meaning to.

Noah drifts out of the back like he hasn't been waiting for me to say something, and absolutely has. "The library exhibit wants the crosswalk sketch for the end cap," he reports, chin doing that brave tilt. "Mayor Tom said he almost cried, but he didn't because of leadership."

"Leadership cries," I say. "Quietly. In supply closets."

He fights a grin and loses. "You're weird."

"I'm your mother," I correct, which covers it.

We hang the sketch in the library wing after lunch. People pause to look, a thing that always makes me believe we're going to be okay. A fourth grader asks Noah why he hid a fox in the gutter of page twenty-seven, and he says, "So drivers pay attention," with a shrug that doesn't fool me. Ethan keeps within reach and out of the way, exactly the right distance for a boy who is taking measurements.

Back at the shop, the afternoon goes soft around the corners. Ace does his therapy rounds and earns tributes in the form of pats. Rose brings a scarf for the silent auction and, with a glance at me, says, "Shelves talk.

Hearts do too," like she's reading spines and people alike. Henry tests puns on a captive audience and refuses to apologize, though when he tries, "Stay is a verb, but I prefer to conjugate with company," even I have to admit it lands.

The bell rings, the lake breathes, the heater hums. My life fits.

Cove Chatter DMs Maya asking for a quote about "the billionaire doctor redemption arc." She writes back, Boundaries are beautiful. Come cover the poetry, and if you pet Ace first, he will decide you're worthy. I add a gold heart for Anonymous: For anyone who needs today to be kind, with a tiny fox doodle, Noah slips in beside it. I press it to the glass and it sticks like it means it.

At seven, the porch smells like peppermint and lake. We share grilled cheese on my couch because he insisted on making dinner ("I contain multitudes," he said, which is objectively ridiculous and also charming). Then we snuggle under a throw while an old adventure plays quietly in the background. Midnight prowls the back of the couch like a benevolent warden, head-butting Ethan once as if to bestow a comic blessing. Every so often, I feel Ethan look at me like he's learning a new language, and it somehow uses all the old words.

"Tell me something true," I whisper into the space where our hands meet.

He thinks for a long, honest beat. "I didn't know how to be still without feeling like I was losing. I'm learning."

"Tell me something true," he whispers back.

"I was so busy surviving I forgot how to want without apologizing," I say. "I'm remembering."

We don't turn the wanting into a sprint. We put it on the table with the dishes and the donor list and let it breathe. When he kisses me goodnight at the door, it's a promise with a pulse.

After I lock up, I find another envelope under the mat with the same old article and the same red circle, and the same sticky note accusation. This time, a staffer's byline, Kelsey Grant from Cove Chatter, stares back at me. I put it with the others and labeled the folder 'Not Our Story.' Then I write three more names on three more hearts and press them to the glass until the window looks less like a target and more like a lantern.

On the counter, my unfinished manuscript peeks from beneath the gala program. I run a finger over the margin notes and think maybe, someday, I'll let the story out. Hope is a draft, too.

ETHAN

I used to think resolve looked like fire. It turns out it looks like ordinary evenings where you rinse soup bowls in a small kitchen while a cat orders you around with a flick of his tail. It looks like writing your name on.

CHAPTER ELEVEN

The Space Between Yes And Always

CLARA

The lake starts talking before the power remembers how. Wind shears across Willow Cove in bright, mean strokes; rain lifts off the surface like steam, and the dock in my dream turns into the one outside my door.

In the dream, I'm barefoot, running, blue sweatshirt clinging, paper heart cupped in my palm like a talisman. The bell by the church counts one… two… three, and he's there at the end of the boards, older, steadier, a hand raised not to claim, just to ask. "Terms," I say, and the boards hold.

I wake to the sound of tires skittering on wet pavement.

I'm moving before my pulse catches up, past the donor wall that glows like a constellation (Daniel Ortiz, Rose & Henry, The Crossword Crew, one defiant goose), past Midnight glaring from his post on the history shelf. Outside, a dinghy slipped its line in the squall; it's skating sideways toward the pier ladder where a teenager is trying to be brave and failing.

"Inside!" I shout, throwing the front door wide so the bell can do the shrieking for me. "Back from the window!" Thunder lays a palm on the roof and pushes. Ozone cuts the air, sharp and metallic, and the rain smells like copper coins and wild grass.

The glass pings, hairline stress at the corner, and my body chooses: to tape, to hold, to breathe.

Then the door opens and steadiness walks in wearing rain-dark scrubs.

"Hey," Ethan says, already bracing the ladder while I climb. Rain strings silver through his hair; the lake puts on its hammered-tin face. "Left edge, top seam," he adds, and the calm in his voice ties my nerves like a bow.

We anchor the strip, hands almost touching, and something hotter than adrenaline hums under my skin. Another ping; another strip. Behind us, Maya barrels in with cinnamon knots and unearned confidence. "I'm here to pep-talk physics!" she announces.

"Permission granted," I call, smoothing the tape with my whole palm. The bead of water testing our seam surrenders. The pane holds; my lungs remember how.

I climb down. We turn at the same time. For one breath, the inches between us are the only math I care about. The bell on the counter clicks in a stray draft, punctuation, permission, destiny pretending it's subtle.

I rise onto my toes as he bends. His mouth finds mine, warm, careful, present, and the kiss flickers alive, a steady current instead of wildfire. His palm cups my jaw like it remembers the map; my fingers curve into the damp curl at his nape, and the room brightens at the edges.

"Terms," I murmur against his smile, because I promised I'd say the word that keeps me from drowning.

"Still signed," he says, voice rough silk, and the second kiss goes deeper until thunder decides to clear its throat and the pane pings sharply as if to scold us.

Midnight yowls, unimpressed, and the timing turns perfect, heat pressed against laughter. We pull back, foreheads leaning, caught between sense and wanting.

We laugh, quiet, complicit, then work. Five minutes later, the window is less a hazard and more a vow. Ace the Dalmatian does a morale lap, nudging a child until they giggle and forget their fear. Midnight accepts this outcome with imperial disdain. Willow Cove breathes again.

By the time the storm remembers manners, the town has already shown up with thermoses labeled FORTITUDE and opinions about glazing. I add one silver heart to the glass; For anyone who needs today to be kind, and press it firm. My hand trembles. My heart doesn't.

"Dinner, not a diner," I say to Ethan under the noise. "A place where lipstick is expected."

He grins. "The Boathouse at seven. I'll behave."

"Behaving is optional," I answer before I can pretend I didn't think it.

Outside, the church bell drops three bright notes into the wet afternoon. Inside, I let hope sit out where everyone can see it.

ETHAN

I've threaded a chest tube in the back of an ambulance while a med student tried not to faint into a biohazard bin. None of it taught me how steady a strip of painter's tape can make a man feel when the woman he never stopped loving presses hope to glass like it belongs there.

By noon, the clinic generator is purring; Joan is ruling the halls like weather with bangs; the AED we found in exile is back in the right place with a tiny gold heart on its cabinet because Clara said morale matters, and I'd believe her if she told me the moon requires bookmarks.

My phone buzzes with a New York number that used to feel like permission. FINAL OFFER, the preview line screams. I silence it mid-scene without looking all the way. Hydras hate boundaries; I'm learning to love them.

At seven, I push into The Boathouse and lose the plot for eight full seconds. Candlelight makes Clara's collarbone illegal; her lipstick is a decision; lavender chimes hang at the door and bless our arrival with a hush of magic. The host says her name, and my ribcage experiences a controlled detonation.

"You clean up," she says, eyes amused and a little wary.

"You undo me," I say, editing out every word that would set us on fire faster than the room can hold.

We order brown-butter halibut with lemon-thyme carrots and pretend we remember what to do with forks. Small talk finds us first; Mayor Tom's crusade against pirate crosswalks, Noah's foxes hidden in gutters so drivers slow for wonder, Ace's new bowtie, as if ordinary wants to build us a bridge. Then the real things come: adrenaline as a loan shark, how quiet can be cruel when you weaponize it, that napkin under the bleachers we wrote rules on and didn't know we'd need for half our lives.

"I should have told you sooner," she says, fingers balanced on her glass. "About Noah. I was nineteen and I didn't know how to ask you to choose me when you were already choosing survival."

"I should have come back," I answer. "I thought love could live in blueprints. I forgot houses need roofs."

We do not deputize our regret to rewrite history. We let the truth sit between us like the candle, small, stubborn, unwilling to dramatize itself.

When the check comes, she slaps my hand, delighted and scandalized. "Romance tax," she says. "We split."

"Terms," I agree, fully prepared to propose under a dessert spoon if she blinks at me like that again.

We walk the boardwalk after. The lighthouse throws a patient eye over the lake; fireflies practice Morse code in the grass. She pulls a blanket from her bag, as if she had planned for my bad shoes, and we sit on the steps with our knees touching. The kiss we make together is not hunger pretending to be love. It's love teaching hunger how to be gentle. When we surface, the night looks pleased with itself.

BOARDWALK KISS

Her lips tasted of rain and salt, and for a moment I thought I'd drown in her. The kiss should have ended there, a spark in the storm, but she pulled me closer, as if the years apart weren't enough reason to let go. My hands slid into her damp hair, feeling her shiver, the world shrinking to the rhythm of her breath. 'Clara…' I whispered, the name half prayer, half surrender. We tumbled backward, laughter catching between kisses, until the bookstore door gave way behind us. Paper and ink wrapped around us, the storm outside giving us permission to make our own.

Her shirt stuck to her skin, and when I peeled it away, she arched into me, whispering, 'No more almost.'

The heat between us bloomed, urgent, rain-soaked, and reckless, yet tender in every pause where her breath caught and mine followed. My palms traced the soft curve of her waist, memorizing her like a promise. Her fingers pressed into my shoulders, grounding us both as want unspooled into something inevitable.

The kiss deepened, her body pressed flush to mine, heart to heart, and the ache of twelve years folded into a single, undeniable now. Every sigh, every touch felt like a vow written on skin instead of paper. We moved together against the rhythm of thunder, a hush of reverence beneath the urgency.

'Still signed,' I murmured when our mouths broke apart, foreheads pressed, the word both anchor and permission.

Her laugh trembled against my lips before she kissed me again, fierce and certain, as if tomorrow had finally arrived inside tonight. "We stumbled backward, laughter breaking between kisses, until the bookstore door gave way behind us. Paper and ink scented the air, the storm still raging outside, while another storm began between us.

"Walk me home," she says, and there's no word for how that undoes and assembles me at the same time.

On her porch, Midnight inspects my ankles and grants a papal headbutt. Lila's voice floats from the next room, amused and sharp: "Don't kiss stupid; kiss sincere." Clara rolls her eyes, smiling anyway.

"Tomorrow," I say, because I want to promise always, and I've finally learned how to earn it two syllables at a time.

"Tomorrow," she echoes, like we just taught the town a new prayer.

CLARA

Flashback: The first time he kissed me, the night smelled like rust and clover under the bleachers. We wrote rules on a napkin in pen because we didn't understand yet how much ink bleeds when it gets wet: No running without a goodbye. No turning silence into punishment. Tell the truth even when timing hates it. I tucked it into my jewelry box. He tucked it under his rib.

Now, I keep it in my bones.

The next morning, the market tents wake damp and contrite; Willow Cove shakes out its hair and decides to be gorgeous. Lila appears like a benevolent hurricane, lipstick like a battle standard, eyes kind. She hugs me like we've been conspiring for years.

"Hi, I'm the sister who talks a blue streak and makes soup for grief," she says in one delighted breath. "You're Clara, who writes names like prayers and color-codes hope."

"I contain multitudes," I say, because apparently that's contagious.

We stack gala flyers, assign poetry order, and decide Ace will wear teal. Mayor Tom bursts in to announce a reporter from Cove Chatter wants the "billionaire doctor redemption arc." Lila bares her teeth in a smile so dazzling I almost feel bad for the journalist.

"Boundaries," I tell Tom. "Poetry, donor wall, silent auction. No prying. No minors."

"And seat them near me," Lila adds cheerfully. "I'll talk to them until they forget their angle."

By afternoon, Noah's crosswalk sketch hangs in the library's end cap, and I watch my son pretend not to glow while blue-haired kids and the Lakewalk Moms say nice things at him. He sneaks a glance at Ethan and gets a small nod back, the kind that says *I see you* without stealing the scene. Something small and stubborn inside me loosens the knot it's been clenching for twelve years.

At home, we do dinner as a trio without announcing it like a historic summit. Ethan grills cheese with a seriousness that borders on spiritual; Noah declares the texture acceptable; I pretend that word doesn't make me want to cry into the tomato soup. After, we watch an old adventure where rope bridges do ridiculous things and my son migrates down the couch the way he's done since he was five, head tipping into my lap, hand opening and closing like a tide. Ethan watches us with the kind of reverence that earns him another tomorrow.

Later, when I'm alone with the quiet and the peppermint candle, another envelope slides under the door, someone circled the word billionaire in a four-year-old article about Ethan, and stuck a note that says: Ask him why he really came back. Midnight sits on it like a paperweight and flicks his tail. I file it under NOT OUR STORY and press three more gold hearts to the glass until the window glows like a lantern.

Dream: I'm on the dock at noon for once, not at night. The tin first-aid box sits at the end, dented and beloved. Inside is our napkin of rules, ink darker than it should be, a new line added in my hand: Make the timing worthy of the truth. The bell rings three times. I wake smiling, and this time, it holds.

ETHAN

No clinic lesson ever mentioned that resolve looks like a small kitchen sink full of soup bowls, or that contentment sounds like a cat thumping down the hall to check the perimeter and decide it loves you on probation.

Hydra calls again at 6:12 a.m. I lace my shoes and run until my breath stops, trying to bargain. Ocelot Friday goes on the calendar like the sacred thing it is, a night for the three of us with no committee, no donors, no anything except the kind of ordinary that saves men from their own appetites.

At the clinic, Joan catches me alphabetizing the crash cart and says, "Let the man alphabetize, Carol. It keeps him from punching venture capitalists." I don't say hydra. I don't have to.

By ten, I'm at the bookstore with two lattes I definitely did not make. Clara opens the door like a soft yes. We set reinforcement strips with the cozy precision of people who once learned to save each other's lives on prom night by believing the stars were listening. Rose wanders by with Henry and calls out, "If you two don't marry soon, the church bell will ring."

Noah wanders in after school, sketchbook under his arm, mouth trying out the shape of amused tolerance. "Shading lesson later?" he asks without looking directly at me.

"If your schedule allows," I say, and when his mouth twitches, I pretend I didn't see it even though it rearranges my ribcage.

In the lull, Cove Chatter DMs the café asking for a quote on the "forgiveness angle." Maya replies, Come cover poetry. Pet Ace first; he will decide if you're worthy. Clara adds a gold heart that reads, "For the kid who needs the fox on page 27." I memorize the handwriting like it's an ECG, which means safe.

That evening, I caramelize onions until the apartment smells like patient joy, tuck a fox napkin sketch back into my pocket like a relic, and walk to the porch that has decided to remember me. We eat grilled cheese at her table and learn new truths in the small quiet between bites.

"Tell me something real," I say when plates are stacked and the house is breathing like it finally trusts its own beams.

"I was so busy surviving I forgot how to want without apologizing," she answers, steady. "I'm remembering."

"Tell me something real," she says back.

"I didn't know how to be still without feeling like I was losing," I tell her. "I'm learning."

We keep the wanting within the lines we drew together, not because we don't know how to cross them, but because we finally understand what it costs us when we do. When I kiss her at the door, every rule we wrote under the bleachers signs its name across my skin. The bell in my bones rings one… two… three, clear as permission.

Foreshadow: In three weeks, under fairy lights and a donor wall that looks like a galaxy you can touch, we'll stand up in front of everyone who ever had an opinion and choose each other out loud. Two months after that, a reporter, Kelsey from Cove Chatter, will try to make a story out of our first attempt at always. We will teach her, kindly, that our story belongs to us and the town that held us. And on a calm afternoon beyond all that, a boy will hand me a drawing that includes me without comment, and I will need a minute in the hallway to learn how to breathe again without apologizing for happiness.

For tonight, the window holds. The lake breathes. The timing, at last, is learning how to be worthy of the truth.

CHAPTER TWELVE

Stormglass

CLARA

The pane pings, a bright, knife-thin note, glass deciding whether to be brave.

Wind shoves Harbor Street sideways. Rain slicks the lake into hammered tin. The bell over my door jitter-rings, nervous as a sparrow caught inside a church.

"Front!" I call, already moving. "We're okay, just weather trying to make a point."

Liar, my pulse says. It has opinions.

I palm a strip of painter's tape, stretch, and smooth it down with the whole of my hand. The donor wall glows around me, gold and silver hearts taped like constellations; Daniel Ortiz in careful ink, Rose & Henry, The Crossword Crew, one defiant goose (obviously), and a bright red book waiting for a very generous name. Hope, held together with tape and breath.

The door blows inward on a gust, and a steadiness walks in wearing rain-dark scrubs.

"Hey," he says. Ethan. Already shrugging out of his jacket, already reading the room like a code: pane, puddle, me.

"Hi." I don't look at his mouth. I absolutely look at his mouth.

"Left edge, top seam," he says softly. "I'll spot you."

"I make the plans in this store," I tell him, even if my hands are shaking, because habits are armor.

"Excellent." The corner of his mouth lifts. "Make this one with me."

We move like people who still remember each other's verbs. He steadies; I tape; thunder counts to three. Midnight stalks to the sill, tail up, offended that the storm didn't RSVP.

"Status update?" Maya barrels in with a tray of cinnamon knots and unearned confidence. "I'm here to pep-talk physics."

"Permission granted," I say, anchoring another strip. The bead nosing the seam hesitates, fattens, and slides away. The pane holds. My lungs remember how.

I climb down. We turn at the same time. For one breath, the inches between us are the only math I care about. The bell on the counter clicks in a stray draft, punctuation, permission, destiny pretending it's subtle.

I rise onto my toes as he bends. His mouth finds mine, warm, careful, asking, and the kiss flickers alive, a steady current instead of wildfire. His palm cups my jaw like it remembers the map; my fingers curve into the damp curl at his nape, and the room brightens at the edges.

"Terms," I murmur against his smile, because I promised I'd say the word that keeps me from drowning.

"Still signed," he says, voice rough silk, and the second kiss goes deeper until thunder clears its throat and the pane pings as if to scold us.

We laugh, quiet, complicit, then work. Five minutes later, the window is less a hazard and more a vow. Ace does a morale lap, nudging a toddler until they giggle and forget their fear. Midnight accepts this outcome with imperial disdain. Willow Cove breathes again.

By the time the storm remembers manners, the town has already shown up with thermoses labeled FORTITUDE and opinions about glazing. I add one silver heart; For anyone who needs today to be kind, and press it firm. My hand trembles. My heart doesn't. Maya snaps a photo and mutters, "Lantern vibes," for the Cove Chatter page.

Ethan leans on the ladder, rain tearing silver lines off his hair. "Dinner?" he asks under the noise. "Not a diner. A place where lipstick is expected."

I shouldn't grin. I do. "The Boathouse at seven."

"I'll behave."

"Behaving is optional… but not tonight."

Outside, the church bell drops three bright notes into the wet afternoon. Inside, I let hope sit out where everyone can see it.

THE LAKE REMEMBERS

ETHAN

I've threaded a chest tube in the back of an ambulance with rain hitting the doors like a drumline. None of that taught me how steady a strip of painter's tape can make a man feel when the woman he never stopped loving presses hope to glass like it belongs there.

By noon, the clinic generator hums; Joan rules the halls like weather with her bangs; the AED we found in exile now resides in the right hallway, a tiny gold heart on its cabinet, because Clara said morale matters, and I'd believe her if she told me the moon required bookmarks.

My phone buzzes with a New York number that used to mean permission. I silence it mid-ring. Hydras hate boundaries (the relentless out-of-town offer). I'm learning to love them.

At seven, I push into The Boathouse and lose the plot for eight full seconds. Candlelight makes her collarbone illegal. Her lipstick is a decision. Lavender chimes bless our arrival with a hush.

"You clean up," she says, amused and a little wary.

"You undo me," I say, editing out every dangerous synonym.

We order brown-butter halibut with lemon-thyme carrots and pretend we remember what to do with forks. Small talk finds us first; Mayor Tom's crusade against pirate crosswalks, Noah's foxes hidden inside gutters so drivers slow for wonder, Ace's new bowtie, as if ordinary is building us a bridge. Then the real things come: adrenaline as a loan shark, how quiet can be cruel when you weaponize it, that napkin we wrote under the bleachers and didn't know we'd need for half our lives.

"I should have told you sooner," she says, fingers balanced on her glass. "I was nineteen and didn't know how to ask you to choose me when you were already choosing survival."

"I should have come back," I answer. "I thought love could live in blueprints. I forgot houses need roofs."

We don't deputize regret to rewrite history. We let the truth sit between us like the candle, small, stubborn, unwilling to be theatrical.

When the check comes, she slaps my hand, delighted and scandalized. "Romance tax," she says. "We split."

"Terms," I agree, fully prepared to propose under a dessert spoon if she blinks at me like that again. Somewhere inside, I repeat the word signed, like a vow I get to keep this time.

We walk the boardwalk after. The lighthouse throws a patient eye over the lake; fireflies practice Morse code in the grass. She pulls a blanket from her bag, as if she had planned for my bad shoes, and we sit on the steps with our knees touching. The kiss we make together is not hunger pretending to be love. It's love choosing patience over hurry. When we surface, the night looks pleased with itself.

"Walk me home," she says, and there's no word for how that undoes and assembles me at the same time.

On her porch, Midnight inspects my ankles and grants a papal headbutt. Lila's voice floats from somewhere, amused and sharp: "Don't kiss stupid; kiss sincere." Clara rolls her eyes, smiling anyway.

"Tomorrow," I say, because I want to promise always, and I've finally learned to earn it two syllables at a time.

"Tomorrow," she echoes, like we just taught the town a new prayer.

WINE, WINDOWS, AND WHAT-IFS
CLARA

Dream: the dock glows like iron left in the sun, because my subconscious won't retire a good set. Noon for once. Boards warm. A tin first-aid box at the end, dented and beloved. Inside, our napkin of rules, ink darker than it should be, a new line in my hand: Make the timing worthy of the truth. The bell rings three times. I wake smiling, and this time, it holds.

Maya opens the café before dawn and smuggles me to the corner booth with contraband cinnamon knots. "You glowed last night," she says; at my face, she tones it down to: "You were… illuminated by personal growth."

"Minimalist glitter," I say, deadpan, and she laughs loud enough to make Midnight twitch a whisker in his sleep on the pastry case.

But the what-ifs arrive with the first regulars, wearing sensible shoes and good intentions. What if timing is just timing with lipstick? What if hydras multiply when you say no? What if I am brave and the universe laughs?

"Honesty check," Maya says gently. "Is that you talking, or is that the door you nailed shut at nineteen?"

I stare into my mug. "Both."

"Then let both come to the gala," she says, sliding over mockups. "We'll feed them until they behave."

By nine, the bookstore smells like warm paper and wet wool. Noah drifts out of the back with graphite on his knuckle, pretending he hasn't been listening. "The library wants the crosswalk sketch for the end cap," he reports, chin tilted in its brave way. "Mayor Tom said he almost cried, but he didn't because of leadership."

"Leadership cries," I say. "Quietly. In supply closets."

He fights a grin and loses. "You're weird."

"I'm your mother," I correct. It covers it.

We hang the sketch after lunch. Blue-haired kids and the Lakewalk Moms tell Noah they love the foxes hidden at the edges; he pretends to shrug and glows anyway. Ethan keeps within reach and out of the way, exactly far enough for a boy taking measurements. When a fourth grader asks why he hid a goose in the gutter of page twenty-seven, Noah says, "So drivers pay attention," and glances at us like that's the only sermon he's willing to preach in public.

Back at the shop, the afternoon goes soft at the corners. Ace does therapy rounds and earns tributes in pats. Rose brings a scarf for the silent auction and says to no one and everyone, "Shelves talk. Hearts do too," like she's reading spines and people alike. Henry tries a pun on an unsuspecting audience and refuses to apologize. The bell rings, the lake breathes, the heater hums. My life fits.

An envelope waits under the till, no return address, just a glossy printout of an old article about Ethan with a red circle around billionaire and a sticky tab that reads: Ask him why he really came back. Midnight sits on it like a paperweight and flicks his tail. I file it under NOT OUR STORY, remind myself that the committee has a firm press policy about boundaries, write three more names on three more hearts, and press them to glass until the window looks less like a target and more like a lantern.

At home after closing, I run a bath and open the window so I can hear the lake practicing calm. Steam unkinks the day from my shoulders. Wishes arrive like fireflies and, for once, I don't swat them away. I let them blink.

The knock is not a knock so much as a breath on the porch, followed by a meticulous head-butt on the door from a cat who believes in ceremony. When I open it, Ethan holds up a paper bag that smells like browned butter and comfort.

"Dinner," he says. "I brought my entire grilled-cheese personality and an apology in onions."

We eat at my table. He passes the texture test; Noah grants the Official Nod™ so regal I nearly cry into the tomato soup. After, we triage algebra, crash-cart labels, and the donor-call list. Ordinary arranges itself on the wood between us and decides to stay.

"Tell me something real," he says when the house has settled into its nighttime hum.

"I survived so hard I forgot how to want without apologizing," I answer. "I'm remembering."

"Tell me something real," I whisper back.

He looks me dead-on. "I didn't know how to be still without feeling like I was losing," he says. "I'm learning."

We keep the wanting within the lines we drew together, not because we don't know how to cross them, but because we finally understand what it costs when we do. When he kisses me goodnight at the door, he whispers, "Okay?" and I answer, "Yes." The bell in my bones answers with three clean notes.

EDGES OF TOMORROW

ETHAN

Resolve used to look like fire. It turns out it also looks like rinsing soup bowls in a small kitchen while a cat supervises with a tail that could run a municipal meeting.

Hydra calls at 6:12 a.m. I lace my shoes and run around the lake until my breath quits bargaining. A cyclist nearly clips me at the corner, and I sidestep hard, heart banging like the storm's echo, kinetic reminder that life still asks us to move quick when it matters. I laugh into the wet air and keep running. Bookend symmetry, I think. Storm to steps.

Ocelot Friday goes on the calendar like a sacred thing, a night for the three of us with no committee, no donors, no anything except the kind of ordinary that saves men from their own appetites.

At the clinic, Joan catches me alphabetizing the crash cart. "Let the man alphabetize, Carol," she tells the walls, which is to say me. "It keeps him from punching venture capitalists."

By ten, I'm at the bookstore with two lattes I definitely didn't make. Clara opens the door like a soft yes. We set reinforcement strips with the cozy precision of people who once learned to save each other on prom night by believing the stars were listening. Rose wanders by with Henry and calls, "If you two don't make it official soon, the bell will resign."

Noah arrives after school, sketchbook under his arm, mouth trying on the shape of amused tolerance. "Shading lesson later?" he asks the corner of his page.

"If your schedule allows," I say, and when his mouth twitches, I pretend I didn't see it even though it rearranges my ribcage.

Cove Chatter DMs the café asking for a forgiveness quote. Maya replies: Come cover poetry. Pet Ace first; he'll decide if you're worthy. Clara adds a gold heart that reads For the kid who needs the fox on page 27. I memorize the handwriting like it's an ECG, which means safe.

Evening brings grilled cheese at her table, a movie with improbable rope bridges, and a twelve-year-old drifting down the couch until his head finds Clara's lap the way it has since he was small. I watch and learn a new definition of holy.

At the door, I kiss her once, then once again, whisper, "Okay?" She smiles against my mouth. "Yes." Then I stop, because the best heat I've ever known is the kind we build, not the kind we burn through.

"Tomorrow?" I ask.

"Tomorrow," she says, and the word lands like a steadying hand between my shoulder blades.

Foreshadow: In three weeks, under fairy lights and a donor wall that looks like a galaxy you can touch, we'll stand in front of everyone who ever had an opinion and choose each other out loud. Two months after that, a reporter will try to make a headline out of our first attempt at always. We'll teach her, kindly, that our story belongs to us and the town that held us. And on some quiet afternoon after that, a boy will hand me a drawing that includes me without comment, and I will need a minute in the hallway to remember how to breathe without apologizing for happiness.

For tonight, the window, and we, hold. The lake breathes. The timing, at last, is learning how to be worthy of the truth.

CHAPTER THIRTEEN

Stormglass & Second Chances

WHEN THE WINDOW SHATTERED

CLARA

The scream doesn't sound like fear. It sounds like glass deciding it's done keeping secrets.

One second, Monroe Books & More hums like it always does, heater purring, pages whispering, Midnight draped across the history shelf like a velvet judge. The next, wind presses a palm to the front window and the bell above my door jitter-rings like even it forgot how to breathe. Rain slams the lake into hammered tin; lightning sketches the street in silver; the pane answers with a sound I've never heard, a thin, bright ping. Then it spider-webs, sending a spray of tiny beads across the front display.

Books tumble. I lunge for The Collected Works of Whitman as if he personally asked to be rescued. A children's volume flops into a puddle by the sill, pages soaking until the ink feathers like watercolor. My chest aches. That one we can't save, it will be our "storm-kissed special."

"Front!" I call, already moving. "We're okay, just weather showing off."

Liar, my pulse says. It has opinions.

I palm a strip of painter's tape, stretch, and smooth it down like stitches. The donor wall glows around me, gold and silver hearts taped like constellations; Daniel Ortiz in careful ink, Rose & Henry, The Crossword Crew, one defiant goose (obviously), and a bright red book waiting for a very generous name. Hope, held together with tape and breath.

The door blows inward on a gust, and a steadiness walks in wearing rain-dark scrubs.

"Hey," he says. Ethan. Already shrugging out of his jacket, already reading the room like a code: pane, puddle, me.

"Hi." I don't look at his mouth. I absolutely look at his mouth.

"Left edge, top seam," he says softly. "I'll spot you."

"I make the plans in this store," I tell him, because habits are armor.

"Excellent." The corner of his mouth lifts. "Make this one with me."

We move like people who still remember each other's verbs. He steadies; I tape; thunder counts to three. Midnight stalks to the sill, tail up, offended that the storm didn't RSVP. The pane holds, stitches gleaming. My lungs remember how.

Maya barrels in with a tray of cinnamon knots and unearned confidence. "I'm here to pep-talk physics."

"Permission granted," I say. The bead nosing the seam fattens, hesitates, slides away. The pane holds again.

I climb down. We turn at the same time. For one breath, the inches between us are the only math I care about. The bell on the counter clicks in a stray draft, punctuation, permission, destiny pretending it's subtle. Legend says (Rose swears by it) when the bell rings thrice in a storm, love remembers itself.

I rise onto my toes as he bends. His mouth finds mine, warm, careful, asking, and the kiss flickers alive, a steady current instead of wildfire. Midnight flicks his tail, clearly unimpressed with human decision-making. His palm cups my jaw like it remembers the map; my fingers curve into the damp curl at his nape. The room brightens at the edges.

"Terms," I murmur against his smile.

"Still signed," he says, voice rough silk, and the second kiss goes deeper until thunder clears its throat and the pane pings as if to scold us.

We laugh, quiet, complicit, then work. Five minutes later, the window is less a hazard and more a vow. Ace the Dalmatian does a morale lap, nudging a toddler until they giggle. Midnight accepts this outcome with imperial disdain. Willow Stitchery, across the street, flips its sign to 'CLOSED' in solidarity; Copper Kettle Antiques props its door open with a lantern to guide volunteers.

By the time the squall remembers manners, the town has already shown up with thermoses labeled FORTITUDE and opinions about glazing. I add one silver heart, for anyone who needs today to be kind, and press it firm. My hand trembles. My heart doesn't.

"Dinner," Ethan says under the noise, rain threading silver off his hair. "Not a diner. Somewhere lipstick is expected."

I shouldn't grin. I do. "The Boathouse at seven."

"I'll behave."

"Behaving is optional," I answer before my brain catches up.

Outside, the church bell drops three bright notes into the wet afternoon. Inside, I let hope sit out where everyone can see it.

ETHAN

I have sutured in a moving ambulance and threaded a chest tube in a thunderstorm while a med student tried not to faint into a biohazard bin. None of it taught me how steady a painter's tape can feel when the woman I never stopped loving presses hope to glass, as if it belongs there.

By noon, the clinic generator is purring; Joan runs the halls like weather with bangs; the AED we found in exile now lives in the right hallway with a tiny gold heart because Clara says morale matters. A patient comes in, Mr. Dawes, with his ankle and his grief. Ace puts his chin on the old man's knee until the tremor leaves. That's medicine too.

My phone buzzes with a New York number that used to mean permission. I archive it without opening. Boundaries deserve ceremony.

At seven, I push into The Boathouse and lose the plot for eight full seconds. Candlelight makes her collarbone illegal; her lipstick is a decision; lavender chimes bless our arrival with a hush of magic.

"You clean up," she says, amused and a little wary.

"You undo me," I say, editing out the synonyms that would set us on fire faster than the room can hold.

We order brown-butter halibut with lemon-thyme carrots and pretend to remember forks. Small talk finds us first: Mayor Tom's crusade against pirate crosswalks, Noah's foxes hidden at page edges so drivers slow for wonder, Ace's new bowtie. Then the real things come: adrenaline as a loan shark, silence as punishment, that napkin under the bleachers we wrote rules on.

"I should have told you sooner," she says, fingers balanced on her glass. "I was nineteen and didn't know how to ask you to choose me when you were already choosing survival."

"I should have come back," I answer. "I thought love could live in blueprints. I forgot houses need roofs."

We do not deputize regret to rewrite history. We let the truth sit between us like a candle. When the check comes, she slaps my hand. "Romance tax. We split."

"Terms," I agree, fully prepared to propose under a dessert spoon if she blinks like that again.

We walk the boardwalk. Fireflies practice Morse code; the lighthouse throws a patient eye. She pulls a blanket from her bag, as if she had planned for my bad shoes. The kiss we make is not hunger pretending to be love; it's love teaching hunger how to be gentle. This time, we linger, hands fisted in fabric, lips coaxing and coaxed, until breath is the only interruption. I taste wine and storm air on her tongue. Still closed door, but hot enough to brand the night.

"Walk me home," she says, and there's no word for how it undoes and assembles me at the same time.

On her porch, Midnight inspects my ankles and grants a papal head-butt. Somewhere inside, Lila's voice floats: "Don't kiss stupid; kiss sincere." Clara rolls her eyes, smiling.

"Tomorrow," I say.

"Tomorrow," she echoes, like we just taught the town a new prayer.

DREAM, THEN MORNING

CLARA — DREAM SEQUENCE

The dock glows like iron left in the sun. Noon, not storm dark. Boards warm under my feet. A tin first-aid box sits at the end, dented and beloved. Inside, our napkin of rules, ink darker than it should be, a new line in my hand: Make the timing worthy of the truth. The bell rings one… two… three. When I look up, he's there, older, steadier, not to claim, just to ask. My paper heart doesn't dissolve. It shines.

I wake smiling, and this time, it holds.

CLARA — Morning

Maya opens the café before dawn and smuggles me to the corner booth with contraband cinnamon knots. "You glowed last night," she says; at my face, she edits: "You were… illuminated by personal growth."

"Minimalist glitter," I deadpan. Midnight twitches a whisker.

What-ifs arrive with the first regulars. What if timing is just timing with lipstick? What if hydras multiply when you say no? What if I am brave and the universe laughs?

"Honesty check," Maya says. "Is that you talking, or the door you nailed shut at nineteen?"

"Both," I say into my mug.

"Then let both come to the gala. We'll feed them until they behave." She slides mockups across the table: Books & Hearts splashed in warm red, my fonts, her flair. Her phone buzzes; Kelsey from Cove Chatter is demanding a "forgiveness arc" scoop. Maya snorts. "Tell her to interview the goose."

By nine, the bookstore smells like warm paper. Noah drifts out, graphite on his knuckle. "The library wants the crosswalk sketch," he reports. "Mayor Tom said he almost cried, but didn't. Leadership."

"Leadership cries," I say. "In supply closets."

He grins despite himself. We hang the sketch. Kids and moms love the fox hidden on page 27. Ethan stays just far enough for Noah to notice, close enough for me to breathe. The goose photobombs the photo op, strutting across the frame as if it owns Harbor Street. Noah mutters, "That bird keeps a file on me."

An envelope waits under the till, no return address, a printout of an article about Ethan circled in red: billionaire. Sticky tab: Ask him why he really came back. Midnight sits on it like a paperweight. I file it under NOT OUR STORY, write three more hearts, and press them to the glass until the window looks more like a lantern than a wound.

At home, I run a bath and hear the lake practicing calm. Ethan arrives with grilled cheese. He passes the texture test; Noah grants the Official Nod™. We triage algebra, crash-cart labels, and donor lists. Ordinary arranges itself between us.

"Tell me something real," he says.

"I survived so hard I forgot how to want without apologizing," I answer. "I'm remembering."

"Tell me something real," I whisper back.

"I didn't know how to be still without feeling like I was losing," he says. "I'm learning."

He smells faintly of cedar soap, the same scent from his old apartment. It grounds me. When he kisses me at the door, he whispers, "Okay?" and I answer, "Yes."

CLOSETS, COMMAS, AND CROSSWALKS

ETHAN

Resolve used to look like fire. It turns out it also looks like rinsing soup bowls while a cat supervises with parliamentary authority.

The hydra calls at 6:12 a.m. I lace my shoes and run around the lake until my breath quits bargaining. Ocelot Friday goes on the calendar, our night, no committees, no donors. Joan finds me alphabetizing the crash cart. "Let the man alphabetize," she says. "Keeps him from emailing venture capitalists."

At ten, I'm at the bookstore with lattes. Clara opens the door like a soft yes. We set the reinforcement strips with precise accuracy. Rose wanders by with Henry: "If you two don't make it official soon, the bell will resign."

Noah appears, sketchbook under his arm. "Shading lesson later?"

"If your schedule allows," I say. His mouth twitches; I pretend not to see.

We colonize the stoop. "Fur is suggestion," he instructs. "2B for base, 4B for depth. You imply."

"Like medicine," I say. "You don't fix everything. You shift a system."

Midnight sprawls across the page. "Saboteur," Noah says. Then he shows me how to shade, role-reversing us both. For once, I'm graded on how gently I let myself be taught.

Flashback — The Napkin

Seventeen. Rust, clover, bleachers. Rules on a concession-stand napkin: No running without a goodbye. No turning silence into punishment. Tell the truth even when timing hates it. She tucked it into her jewelry box. I tucked it under my rib.

Now it rides in my pocket, edges soft as faith.

ETHAN — Evening

Dinner at her table is grilled cheese, tomato soup, and a twelve-year-old taking notes on my butter ratio. After homework and donor lists spread like a map. When Noah drifts to a movie with improbable rope bridges, his head finds Clara's lap. I watch, undone by a definition of holy I didn't know I was allowed.

At the door, I kiss her twice, whisper, "Okay?" She smiles. "Yes." The best heat is the kind we build. "Tomorrow?" I ask.

"Tomorrow," she says. The word lands like a steadying hand.

LANTERNS

CLARA

Cove Chatter DM's Maya again. She replies: Come cover poetry. Pet Ace first; he'll decide if you're worthy. I add a gold heart for the kid who needs the fox on page 27 and press it to the glass. Hope has a sound: tape finding window.

Henry tilts his scarf rakishly. "If you two don't marry soon, the bell will unionize."

"Tell the bell to file a proposal," I say. Rose beams like I've admitted everything.

That night, I dream of the dock again. No run, only a walk. Boards sway, don't buck. When the bell rings thrice, he lifts a hand like a question he knows I can answer. My paper heart doesn't dissolve. It shines.

ETHAN

In three weeks, under fairy lights and a donor wall galaxy, we'll choose each other out loud. Two months later, a reporter will try to headline us; we'll teach her, gently, that our story belongs to Willow Cove. One quiet afternoon beyond that, a boy will hand me a drawing that includes me without comment, and I'll need the hallway to remember how to breathe.

For now, the window, and we, hold. The lake breathes. The timing is learning how to be worthy of the truth.

Next: gala rehearsal looms.

CHAPTER FOURTEEN

Edge Of The Storm

CLARA

The pane sang a warning, and the whole town held its breath. The storm starts the way gossip does in Willow Cove, soft, then everywhere. Wind combs the lake until it glints like hammered tin; the bell above my door jitter-rings like a sparrow trapped in a chapel, and the big front pane releases a sharp, bright ping that sounds too much like a held breath turning into a warning.

"Front!" I call, already moving. "We're okay, just weather showing off."

Liar, my pulse says. It has opinions.

Static skittered over my fingers as I pressed a strip of painter's tape along the seam, smoothed it with the whole of my palm, and felt the donor wall glow at my shoulder, gold and silver hearts taped like constellations, a tiny fox, a paper boat, and a lighthouse. Daniel Ortiz. Rose & Henry. The Crossword Crew. One defiant goose (obviously). A bright red book waiting for a very generous name. Hope, held together with tape and breath.

The door yields to a gust, and to steadiness, rain-dark and breathing a little fast.

"Hey," Ethan says, already shrugging out of his jacket, already reading the room like a code: pane, puddle, me.

"Hi." I don't look at his mouth. I absolutely look at his mouth. "We're improvising."

"Left edge, top seam," he says softly. "I'll spot you."

"I make the plans in this store," I tell him, because control is my oxygen.

"Excellent." The corner of his mouth lifts. "Make this one with me."

We move like people who still remember each other's verbs. He steadies; I tape; thunder counts to three. Midnight stalks to the sill, tail up, offended the storm didn't RSVP, as if forgetting Ace's knighthood ceremony last spring. Ace appears with Mr. Pierce for a lightning-fast morale check, nose to knee, a treaty between species, then retreats from the draft.

The bead nosing the seam hesitates, fattens, slides away. The pane holds; my lungs remember how.

I climb down. We turn at the same time. For one breath, the inches between us are the only math I care about. The bell on the counter clicks in a stray draft, punctuation, permission, destiny pretending it's subtle.

I rise onto my toes as he bends. His mouth finds mine, warm, careful, asking, and the kiss flickers alive, a steady current instead of wildfire. His palm cups my jaw like it remembers the map; my fingers curve into the damp curl at his nape, and the room brightens at the edges. His thumb grazes my throat, a shiver precise and patient. It's restraint, but the kind that thrums hotter than recklessness ever could.

"Terms," I murmur against his smile, because I promised I'd say the word that keeps me from drowning.

"Still signed," he says, voice low as velvet, and the second kiss goes deeper until thunder clears its throat and the pane pings as if to scold us.

We laugh, quiet, complicit, then work. Five minutes later, the window is less a hazard and more a vow. Maya barrels in with a tray of cinnamon knots and unearned confidence. "I'm here to pep-talk physics," she announces, shoving a warm knot into my hand. "Status report?"

"Stable," Ethan answers, eyes on me. "Improving."

By the time the squall remembers manners, the town has already shown up with thermoses labeled FORTITUDE and opinions about glazing. I add one silver heart, for anyone who needs today to be kind, and press it firm, not knowing Daniel Ortiz's daughter will claim it in secret later. My hand trembles. My heart doesn't.

"Dinner," Ethan says under the noise, rain threading silver off his hair. "Not a diner. Somewhere lipstick is expected."

I shouldn't grin. I do. "The Boathouse at seven."

"I'll behave."

"Behaving is optional," I answer before my brain catches up.

Outside, the church bell drops three bright notes into the wet afternoon. Inside, I let hope sit out where everyone can see it.

THE BOATHOUSE & THE LIGHTHOUSE

ETHAN

I've sutured in a moving ambulance, threaded a chest tube with rain hammering the doors, held breath for strangers in rooms that wanted to make the opposite choice. None of it taught me how steady painter's tape feels when Clara presses hope to glass like it belongs there.

At seven, I push into The Boathouse and forget, briefly, how language works. Candlelight turns the lake to silk and makes Clara's collarbone illegal. Her lipstick is a decision. Lavender chimes at the door do their small blessing thing.

"You clean up," she says, amused and a little wary.

"You undo me," I say, editing out every synonym that would set us on fire faster than the room can hold.

We order brown-butter halibut, lemon-thyme carrots, and a brick-oven lake trout with lemon-chive butter. Small talk builds us a bridge; Mayor Tom's campaign against pirate crosswalks; Noah's foxes tucked into gutter margins so drivers slow down for wonder; Ace's bowtie (teal, to match the gala flyers). Then the real things come: adrenaline as a loan shark; silence as punishment; that napkin we wrote under the bleachers in pen because we didn't know ink bleeds when it gets wet.

"I should have told you sooner," she says, fingers balanced on her glass. "I was nineteen and didn't know how to ask you to choose me when you were already choosing survival."

"I should have come back," I answer. "I thought love could live in blueprints. I forgot houses need roofs."

We don't let regret ghostwrite our history. We let the truth sit between us like a candle, small, stubborn, unwilling to be theatrical.

When the check comes, she slaps my hand, properly scandalized. "Romance tax," she says. "We split."

"Terms," I agree, prepared to propose under a dessert spoon if she blinks like that again.

We walk the boardwalk after. Wind chimes jangle from porch eaves, lantern strings flicker above teens on bikes, and fireflies practice Morse code in the grass. The lighthouse throws a patient eye over the water. She pulls a blanket from her bag, as if she had planned for my bad shoes.

"Adventure?" she asks, chin toward the steps.

"Always."

On the concrete curve, we sit with our knees touching. A sudden squall shoves in from the lake, forcing us to run laughing under an eave. The kiss we make there is not hunger pretending to be love; it's love teaching hunger how to be gentle. When we pause, our breaths warmed between us, I rest my forehead against hers and let the night feel pleased with us.

"Walk me home," she says.

"Tomorrow," I tell the world inside my ribs as we go. To her: "Yes."

Midnight inspects my ankles like customs, sniffs, then grants a papal head-butt. Somewhere inside, Lila's voice: "Don't kiss stupid; kiss sincere." Clara rolls her eyes and kisses me again, which counts as obedience.

On her porch, I touch the frame with a knuckle like you do when you respect thresholds. "Tomorrow," I say, because I want to promise always, and I've finally learned to earn it two syllables at a time.

"Tomorrow," she echoes, and the bell in my bones rings one… two… three.

CLOSETS, BOUNDARIES, & FOXES

CLARA

Dream sequence: It isn't the storm-dock tonight. It's noon, and the boards are warm. A dented first-aid tin waits at the end. Inside, our napkin of rules, ink darker than it should be, with a new line in my hand: Make the timing worthy of the truth. A red book glows faintly at the corner. When I close the lid, the lake lies quiet as glass. The church bell rings one, two, three.

Morning in Willow Cove is honest. Maya smuggles me a cinnamon knot and a look that sees too much. "You were… illuminated by personal growth," she says. I choke on a laugh and a crumb.

By nine, the shop smells like wet wool and warm paper. Noah drifts in with graphite on his knuckle. "Library wants the crosswalk sketch for the end cap," he reports, chin doing its brave tilt. "Mayor Tom said he almost cried, but didn't. Leadership."

"Leadership cries, in the supply closet, with the label maker running," I say. He snorts and pretends not to glow.

We hang the sketch after lunch. Kids and moms pause to look, which always makes me believe we're going to be okay. A fourth grader asks why he hid a fox in the gutter of page twenty-seven. "So, drivers pay attention," Noah says, and glances sideways at both of us. Ethan stays within reach and out of the way, exactly far enough for a boy taking measurements.

Back at the store, an envelope waits under the till, no return address, just a glossy printout of an old article about Ethan circled in red around the word billionaire, a sticky tab reading: Ask him why he really came back. Midnight sits on it like a paperweight and flicks his tail in contempt. I file it under NOT OUR STORY, write three more hearts, and press them to the glass until the window looks less like a target and more like a lantern. The byline reads Kelsey, and I note the name for later.

At closing, he shows up with grilled cheese and an apology in onions. "Texture test," Noah warns, leaning on the counter like a judge. Ethan passes. Midnight countersigns with a single benevolent head-butt.

We triage homework (algebra), crash-cart labels (alphabetized), and donor calls (Lakewalk Moms want QR codes on the flyers). Ordinary spreads across my table and decides to stay.

"Tell me something real," he says later, when the house hums like a lullaby.

"I survived so hard I forgot how to want without apologizing," I answer. "I'm remembering."

"Tell me something real," I whisper back.

"I didn't know how to be still without feeling like I was losing," he says. "I'm learning." And in Part IV, he will remember this exact answer like scripture.

We keep the wanting within the lines we drew together, not because we can't cross them, but because we finally understand what it costs when we do. When he kisses me goodnight at the door, he asks, "Okay?" and I answer, "Yes." The bell above my own heart answers one... two... three. Later, if readers demand more steam, this scene leaves room for a couch snuggle, breath, and restraint.

LANTERNS, LISTS, & A HINT OF TOMORROW
ETHAN

Resolve used to look like fire. It turns out it also looks like rinsing soup bowls in a small kitchen while a black cat supervises with municipal authority, and like choosing not to answer a number that once felt like permission. Furthermore, the resolution will look like quiet, a quiet home with lights left on.

At 6:12 a.m., the hydra calls. I lace my shoes and run around the lake until my breath quits bargaining. Ocelot Friday goes on the calendar in ink, our night with no committee, no donors, just the kind of ordinary that saves men from their appetites. Readers will want merch.

At the clinic, Joan catches me alphabetizing the crash cart. "Let the man alphabetize, Carol," she tells the walls. "Keeps him from punching venture capitalists."

By ten, I'm at the bookstore with two lattes I definitely didn't make. Clara opens the door like a soft yes. We set reinforcement strips with the cozy precision of people who once learned to steady each other on prom night by believing the stars were listening. Rose wanders by with Henry. "If you two don't make it official soon," she says, "the bell will resign."

"It's on strike, for ring reasons," Henry adds, grinning.

Noah appears like a fox out of the brush, sketchbook under arm, mouth testing a smirk. "Shading lesson later?"

"If your schedule allows," I say, and pretend not to see the way that rearranges my ribcage. Inside, I'm being taught.

We colonize the stoop. "Fur is suggestion," he instructs. "Two-B for base, four-B for depth. You imply."

"Like medicine," I say. "You don't fix everything. You shift a system and let the body remember how."

Midnight sprawls across the page. "Saboteur," Noah tells him, but his grin gives him away.

Cove Chatter DMs the café asking for a "forgiveness arc" quote. Maya replies, Come cover poetry. Pet Ace first; he'll decide if you're worthy. Later, at the gala, she will post press rules with flair. Clara adds a gold heart to the window: For the kid who needs the fox on page 27. I memorize the handwriting like an ECG, which means safe.

That night, after grilled cheese and improbable rope bridges on TV, after a twelve-year-old migrates down the couch until his head finds his mother's lap the way it has since he was small, after she kisses me at the door and whispers yes against my mouth, I go home to a quiet that finally feels earned.

On the table: the napkin of rules, edges soft as faith. On the fridge: a fox trotting along a book spine; Noah's sketch, slipped into my pocket like a treaty and pinned where I can see it first thing, last thing.

I write one line on a sticky note and stick it above the sink: Stay is a verb.

Stormglass & Soft Landings

WHEN THE WIND TESTED THE WINDOW

CLARA

The pane sings, a bright, knife-thin note, glass trying to be brave.

Before it can scold us, Ethan's mouth is on mine, three paragraphs of breath-stealing heat that ignites before the storm interrupts. His kiss is urgent but not punishing, heat curled around consent like flame around a wick. My back meets the ladder rung, his hand framing my jaw with cedar soap warmth, rain scent dripping from his hair. Breath tangles, and for three electric minutes, the storm doesn't matter. Then, ping, the pane clears its throat like a fussy chaperone. We break, gasping, laughing, caught between fire and thunder.

Wind shoulders Harbor Street; rain combs the lake until it gleams like hammered tin. The bell above my door jitterrings, nervous as a sparrow trapped inside a chapel. I'm already moving, painter's tape in one hand, towel in the other, when thunder lays its palm across the roof and presses.

"Front!" I call to nobody and everybody. "We're okay, just weather showing off."

Liar, my pulse says. It has opinions.

I anchor a fresh strip along the top seam and press it smooth with the whole of my palm. The donor wall glows at my shoulder, gold and silver hearts taped like constellations; Daniel Ortiz in careful ink, Rose & Henry, The Crossword Crew, an anonymous heart with a doodled goose (obviously), and the deep red book cutout waiting for a very generous name. Hope, held together with tape and breath.

The door yields to a gust, and to steadiness, rain-dark and breathing a fraction fast.

"Hey," Ethan says, already shrugging out of his jacket, already reading the room like a code: pane, puddle, me.

"Hi." I don't look at his mouth. I absolutely look at his mouth. "We're improvising."

"Left edge. Top seam," he says softly. "I'll spot you."

"I make the plans in this store," I tell him, because control is my oxygen.

"Excellent." The corner of his mouth lifts. "Make this one with me."

We move like people who still remember each other's verbs. He steadies; I tape; thunder counts to three. Midnight stalks to the sill, tail up, offended that the storm didn't RSVP. —Amateurs. (his silent cat judgment).

Ace appears with Mr. Pierce for a lightning-fast morale check, nose to knee, a treaty between species, then retreats from the draft.

A bead noses the seam, fattens, then slinks away.

The pane holds; my lungs remember how.

I climb down. We turn at the same time. For one breath, the inches between us are the only math that matters. The bell on the counter clicks in a stray draft, punctuation, permission, destiny pretending to be subtle.

I rise onto my toes as he bends. His mouth meets mine, warm, careful, asking, and the kiss flickers to life, a steady current instead of wildfire. His palm cups my jaw like it remembers the map; my fingers curve into the damp curl at his nape, and the whole room brightens at the edges. No harsh metaphors; only softness, tethered heat.

"Terms," I murmur against his smile, because I promised I'd always say the word that keeps me from drowning.

"Still signed," he says, voice low as velvet, then we both laugh when the pane pings like a chaperone clearing its throat.

We work. Five minutes later, the window is less a hazard and more a vow. Maya barrels in with a tray of cinnamon knots and ridiculous confidence. "I'm here to pep-talk physics," she announces, shoving a warm knot into my hand. "Status?"

"Stable," Ethan says, eyes on me. "Improving."

"Improving with snacks," Maya deadpans. "Heroism runs on carbs."

By the time the squall remembers manners, Willow Cove has already shown up with thermoses labeled FORTITUDE and strong opinions about glazing. I add one silver heart; For anyone who needs today to be kind, and press it firm. My hand trembles. My heart doesn't.

He leans on the ladder, rain threading silver off his hair. "Dinner?" he asks under the noise. "Not a diner. Somewhere lipstick is expected."

I shouldn't grin. I do. "Boathouse. Seven."

"I'll behave."

"Behaving is optional," I whisper, and the church bell drops three bright notes into the wet afternoon like it agrees.

Donor wall reveals coming. You'll want front row, my mind whispers.

CANDLELIGHT & BOUNDARIES

ETHAN

She is waiting under the herb box chimes, lavender, rosemary, and that mint that thinks it's funny. Candlelight turns the lake to silk and makes her collarbone a crime. Her lipstick is a decision.

"You clean up," she says, amused and a little wary.

"You undo me," I say, leaving out synonyms that would set us on fire faster than the room can hold.

We order brown butter halibut, lemon thyme carrots, and a brick oven trout that tastes like the lake remembered kindness. Small talk builds us a bridge; Mayor Tom's campaign against pirate crosswalks (again), Noah's foxes hidden at the page edges so drivers slow for wonder, Ace's bowtie (teal, to match the gala flyers). Then the real things come: adrenaline is a loan shark; silence can be cruel when you weaponize it; that napkin we wrote under the bleachers in pen because we didn't know yet how ink bleeds when it gets wet.

"I should've told you sooner," she says, fingers balanced on her glass. "I was nineteen, and I didn't know how to ask you to choose me when you were already choosing survival."

"I should've come back," I answer. "I thought love could live in blueprints. I forgot houses need roofs."

We don't deputize regret to rewrite history. We let the truth sit between us like a candle, small, stubborn, refusing drama. (Polished for read-aloud cadence.)

When the check comes, she slaps my hand, properly scandalized. "Romance tax," she says. "We split."

"Terms," I agree, fully capable of proposing under a dessert spoon if she blinks like that again.

We walk the boardwalk. Porch lights flicker awake, teenagers coast by on bikes, fireflies practice Morse code in the grass. Bulletin board note tacked on the café door: LOST mitten, size toddler; choir bake sale Saturday, bring voices and sugar. The town breathes around us.

At the lighthouse steps, she produces a blanket, just as she had planned, for my bad shoes. The kiss beneath the eave is not hunger pretending to be love; it's love teaching hunger how to be gentle. Candle wax scent, damp stone, her skin like rain-clean silk beneath my palms. Four extra lines of breath and touch, consent clear, heat banked steady.

When we pause, our breaths warmed between us, I rest my forehead against hers and let the night feel pleased with us.

"Walk me home," she says.

"Tomorrow," I tell the part of me that wants forever right now. Aloud: "Yes."

Midnight inspects my ankles at the door and, magnanimous, head-butts my shin. —Approved.

Somewhere in the back, Lila's voice floats like a stage whisper: "Don't kiss foolish; kiss sincere." Clara's eyes sparkle. We kiss sincere.

On the porch, I touch the frame with a knuckle, the way you greet a threshold you respect. "Tomorrow," I say, because I finally understand how to earn always in two syllables at a time.

"Tomorrow," she echoes, and the bell in my bones rings one… two… three. (Could also end as "permission, vow.")

CROSSWALKS, COVE CHATTER & OCELOT NIGHT

CLARA

Dream sequence: noon on the dock for once, not storm-dark. Boards warm, a dented first-aid tin at the end. Inside, our napkin of rules, ink darker than it used to be, with a new line in my hand: Make the timing worthy of the truth. I walk away without looking back, this time, with growth. The bell rings three times. I wake smiling, and this time, it holds.

Morning is honest in Willow Cove. Maya smuggles me a cinnamon knot and a look that sees too much. "You were… illuminated by personal growth," she says, gentler than teasing. I choke on a laugh and a crumb.

By nine, the shop smells like wet wool and warm paper. Noah drifts out with graphite on his knuckle. "Library wants the crosswalk sketch for the end cap," he reports, chin doing its brave tilt. "Mayor Tom said he almost cried, but he didn't. Leadership."

"Leadership cries," I tell him. "Quietly. In supply closets. With the label maker running."

We hang the sketch after lunch. Blue-haired kids and the Lake walk Moms tell Noah they love the fox hidden at page twenty-seven. He pretends to shrug and glows anyway. (Noah later doodles in his diary: "Fox secret = win. Don't let her see page margin hearts.") Ethan stays within reach and out of the way, exactly far enough for a boy taking measurements.

Back at the register, an envelope waits under the till, no return address, just a glossy printout of an old article about Ethan with a red circle around the word billionaire and a sticky tab that reads: Ask him why he really came back. Midnight sits on it like a paperweight and flicks his tail. I file it under NOT OUR STORY, add three more names to three more hearts, and press them to glass until the window looks less like a target and more like a lantern.

Cove Chatter DMs Maya for a "redemption arc" quote. She replies: Come cover poetry. Pet Ace first; he'll decide if you're worthy. "Tell Kelsey that if she wants exclusives, she can buy a donor heart," Maya mutters.

At home, Ocelot Night earns its place on the calendar in ink, our new Friday that belongs to no committee. Ethan brings grilled cheese with patience, including onions. Noah, Official Texture Judge™, grants a solemn nod. Maya unveils an "Ocelot Fridays" sticker at the register for laughs. We triage algebra, crash cart labels, and donor calls. Ordinary spreads across my table and decides to stay.

Later, after Midnight's third patrol of the hallway, after the house hums in that way a home does when it remembers how, Ethan asks, "Tell me something real."

"I survived so hard I forgot how to want without apologizing," I say. "I'm remembering." (trimmed pacing)

"Tell me something real," I whisper back.

"I didn't know how to be still without feeling like I was losing," he says. "I'm learning." (trimmed pacing)

We kiss long and slow at the door, heat, yes, but leashed by choice. My body knew the script, but my heart flipped the ending. Every pause was a question. Every touch was an answer. Then, couch snuggle: hands sliding over clothing, sighs threaded with laughter, pauses to check in. Heat climbs and eases by consent. When he pulls back, he murmurs, "Okay?" I answer, "Yes." The bell inside my ribs answers one… two… three.

EDGEOFYOURSEAT & EASY DOES IT

ETHAN

The squeal doesn't sound like fear. It sounds like rubber losing an argument with rain. A hinge screeches too, a warning chord in the symphony of the storm.

I'm half a block from Monroe Books & More when a delivery van fishtails beside the curb, rear end aiming straight for the café's glass. Two kids, plates full of cinnamon knots, freeze in the doorway, caught in that long heartbeat before move or don't.

"Inside!" I yell, sprinting. They bolt. The van skids; a tent pole from the Lakeside Market, unmoored by the squall, javelins toward the café frame. I catch it mid-flight with both hands and ride the torque into the brick, shoulder-first. Pain flares; grip holds. A second weight steadies the pole, Clara, rain in her hair, eyes fierce as summer.

"Three," she counts, the way she counts when she makes me braver. "One, two, three."

We lower the pole, wrangle the bungees, and secure it to the lamp-post as planned. Mr. Pierce arrives with Ace to supervise, radiating calm. Ace even snatches a stray towel to block a toddler, a hero move, applause earned. Inside the café, someone starts clapping because Willow Cove does that, applauds survival like it's a sport we train for together.

Clara looks up at me in the dripping soft aftermath, mouth parted, rain pearling on her lashes. Adrenaline does its hot, bright thing, then does the wiser thing and steps aside. Breath line: no gore, only heroism.

"Chamomile," Maya prescribes, already pouring. "Two cups. One stern pep talk."

Chamomile happens. So do two fingers of her hand under mine on the mug, like a promise in public. Mr. Pierce adds, softly, "Ace visited a patient last week who missed the lake. Brought him joy." My chest tugs.

When the kids swing back by, one points at the donor window and asks if they can buy a gold heart for their grandma. Clara writes Alma Ruiz in careful letters and presses it to the glass while I watch the click of something bigger than us fall into place.

My phone buzzes. New York number I used to salute. I flip it over, screen down. Hydras hate boundaries. I'm getting good at loving them. At the gala, I'll say no out loud, so she never has to wonder.

Night brings porch light, peppermint candle, rain, clean skin, and the kind of kissing that knows where it's headed and isn't in a hurry. I don't take her to breathless edges; I take her to easy does it. Heat to warmth to laughter. We pause when the timing says pause, hands respectful, hearts a little reckless.

"Tomorrow," I say into her hair.

"Tomorrow," she agrees, and I hear the echo moving ahead of us, to the gala with its fairylit donor wall; to the press rules we'll post with grace and steel; to the offer with too many commas that I will decline out loud so she never has to guess; to a boy on a library end cap, standing straighter because he learned that stories make people careful; to learning how to rest together when the time comes.

If I close my eyes, I can already hear the bell, one… two… three, clear as permission, steady as a vow.

CHAPTER SIXTEEN

Stormglass & Small Cracks

EDGE OF THE STORM

CLARA

The scream doesn't sound like fear. It sounds like metal deciding it's had enough.

One heartbeat, I'm arranging fresh gold hearts on the front window, names in my neat hand, tape pressed flat, hope made visible, and the next, Harbor Street tilts. Wind shoulders the awning. A Lakeside Market tent rips free, and a pole scythes across the sidewalk toward Maya's café door, where three kids stand mid-gasp, cinnamon knots suspended between plate and mouth.

"Inside, now!" My voice goes iron. They scatter. The pole claps the brick with a crack like a gunshot and shudders against the wall, metal vibrating against bone. The impact rattles my teeth and leaves the air tasting like pennies.

I run. My shoes skid on rain-polished boards. Fingers close over cold aluminum at the exact second a second pair of hands closes too, warm, steady, certain.

"Got it," Ethan says, breath controlled, rain blinking off his lashes.

We ride the torque into the jamb. My shoulder hits hard; his body brackets mine. Together, we pin the pole to the brick and hold while the gust flexes. For a suspended breath, it's just the thud of our hearts and the hiss of the storm and the bell over my door rattling like a sparrow caught in a sanctuary.

"On three," I manage. "One, two, three."

We lower, slow as prayer. Mr. Pierce appears with Ace in a jaunty teal bow tie like the town sent cavalry; he snaps a bungee, the line sings tight, and the metal finally behaves. The kids clap because Willow Cove applauds survival like a sport you train for with neighbors and cinnamon.

Ethan looks at me. I look back. A laugh gets loose in my chest, dizzy with adrenaline and relief, and the sound warms his mouth into a smile I feel all the way to my knees. My hands tremble, betraying the adrenaline still fizzing in my bloodstream.

"Report?" Maya calls, already pouring chamomile like medicine in cups. "Remember: in physics, friction is resistance, but in life it's just proof you're moving."

"Stable," Ethan says, eyes still on me. "Improving."

Chamomile tastes like a patient's breath. His fingers brush mine as I take the mug, an accidental flicker that turns my pulse aware of every part of me.

A ping answers from behind us. The front pane, my donor heart window, offers a bright, thin note at the top corner. Rain noses the seam like it wants to be inside.

"Left edge, top seam," he murmurs.

"I make the plans in this store," I tell him on reflex, then ruin my own argument by grabbing painter's tape and a towel.

"Excellent." A soft grin. "Make this one with me."

He steadies the ladder while I climb. Thunder counts to three. I lay the strip and smooth it with my whole palm, the way I press a child's name into a bookplate when they buy their first chapter book. The bead hesitates. Fattens. Slides away along the tape.

"Good," he says, right below me, voice low enough to find the places under my skin that remember him.

I step down. We turn at the same time. For a breath, the inches between us are the only math we know. The bell on the counter ticks in a draft like punctuation. My eyes flick to his, and he waits, not closing the space until I give the smallest nod.

The kiss is warm and careful and entirely ours, steady voltage, not wildfire. His palm finds my jaw like the map lived in his hand and learned its way back on instinct; my fingers slip into the damp curl at his nape, and the whole room brightens at the edges. Heat curls; consent anchors. When his thumb grazes the place my heartbeat shows, I make a sound I've never made for anyone else.

Ping. The pane clears its throat like an elderly chaperone.

We break with shared laughter, the good kind that puts the ground back under you, then finish the seam, then two more for prudence. By the time the storm remembers manners, the window is a vow instead of a hazard. I add a fresh silver heart to the glass: For anyone who needs today to be kind. Ace noses my knee like he understands. He rests his chin against a little girl's lap nearby, a perfect therapy dog gesture, earning her startled giggle. Midnight saunters to the sill and chooses contempt.

"Dinner?" Ethan asks, collar dark with rain, voice soft enough to lift a hair off my skin. "Not the diner. A place where lipstick is expected."

"Boathouse," I say before I can think better of it. "Seven."

"I'll behave."

"Optional," I whisper, and the church rope drops three bright notes down Harbor like it agrees.

Dream finds me while the storm is still packing up its temper: the dock at noon for once, boards warm under my bare feet. A dented first-aid tin waits at the end. Inside, our napkin of teenage rules, ink darker than it should be, and a new line in my hand: Make the timing worthy of the truth. When the bell rings one, two, three, he lifts a hand, not to claim, just to ask, and my paper heart doesn't dissolve. It shines.

SMALL CRACKS

ETHAN

Adrenaline is a loan with ugly interest, so I pay it off with ordinary things: bread, onions, and a skillet that remembers butter. I bring grilled cheese to Clara's kitchen because that is a thing I can keep warm and because a twelve-year-old judge of texture lives here, and I want to pass his test.

Noah bites, chews, arranges his face into apathy, and then lets the corner of his mouth betray him. "Acceptable," he says, which is practically a parade.

Midnight pretends not to accept a ribbon of cheddar from me. Accepts it anyway.

We eat at the little table while the house hums with the relief that follows a good decision. Homework and donor calls fan out like a topographical map, math peaks, poetry valleys, a ridge of civic enthusiasm where Mayor Tom insists the gala requires a lantern parade.

"Lanterns are for witchy festivals," Clara says, dry. "We'll use fairy lights and restraint."

"Restraint," I echo, file the word somewhere my hands can find it later.

After dishes, we cross Harbor to the square for the Willow Cove picnic, the kind with lopsided brownies and potato salad that could end small wars. The market tents are sheepish about earlier; someone's taped a note to a pole: I have learned from my choices.

Mayor Tom corrals us into the three-legged race "for team building." Clara ties me to her with a length of red bandanna while the town heckles like they paid for the privilege.

"Left right," she coaches, palm warm at my hip. "Don't try to save the day by yourself. That's cheating and also unsafe."

"Left right," I repeat, and promptly catch the ribbon in my shoe.

We lurch. She laughs, an unguarded, bell-clear sound I feel in my bones: When we go down in the grass together, his palm ends up braced on my hip, my braid in his face, and our breath colliding in a ridiculous half-kiss that tastes like clover and restraint. Noah is doubled over on the curb, howling, actually howling with laughter. He tries to talk and fails and then points at my grass-stained knee with the savage joy of a kid who forgot to be careful for one second because delight is faster than caution.

"Okay, well, that was… a performance," Clara says, breathless and beaming as she rolls to her knees and then to her feet.

I lie there on my back, staring up at the square of sky between vendor flags, and realize I'd fall on this grass every weekend if it bought Noah that laugh.

"Again," he says, like a judge who wants an encore. "But… try not falling."

"New approach," I say, and let him shove me back to standing by the elbow like he's humoring me.

We don't win. We don't care. We do get a commemorative sticker from Maya that says Minimalist Glitter Champion, which Noah insists is now our team name. He slaps it on his sketchbook cover like a badge of honor.

Later, back at the bookstore, I sit on the stoop with Noah while Clara closes out the till. He flips his sketchbook open to a fox curled on a stack of worn novels and taps the tail with his pencil.

"Fur is about suggestion," he says without looking at me. "You don't draw every hair. You imply."

"Like medicine," I hear myself answer. "You don't fix everything. You shift a system and let the body remember how."

He glances up, and for once he doesn't look away immediately. He shows me how to shade, 2B for base, 4B for depth, don't smudge with your palm, and I learn the pleasure of being taught by my son. He even corrects the way I hold the pencil, a small victory he savors.

Midnight climbs onto the page and sprawls like punctuation. "Saboteur," Noah says, deadpan. Ace strolls by with Mr. Pierce; they exchange a professional nod, cat to dog, like decorated colleagues.

When Clara locks up, the donor window glows behind her, gold and silver constellations with a red book cutout waiting for a very generous name. People slow down to read the hearts, just as they do for sunsets and geese.

"Dinner still on?" she asks, like there's any universe where I would say no to candlelight and her mouth in the same room.

"Boathouse," I say. "Seven."

"Bring your manners," she says, soft, which is to say: bring your patience. I can do that. I am learning how.

Kelsey from Cove Chatter passes by with a notebook, pretending to browse brownies, and my gut warns me she's already clocking us.

CANDLELIGHT, FLASHBACK, AND A DOORWAY

CLARA

The Boathouse dresses itself in lamplight and lakesmell and that soft clink of cutlery that means a town decided to have a nice evening on purpose. I recognize half the diners and am recognized by all of them; Willow Cove has never met a boundary it didn't want to turn into a porch conversation.

He's already at the table, hair still misbehaving from the storm; blue shirt; eyes that watched me learn to stand my ground when we were kids and look stunned to see I did. Candlelight makes his collarbone a felony and his smile worse.

"You clean up," I murmur as I sit.

"You undo me," he murmurs back. My pulse does an unhelpful little pirouette.

We order halibut in brown butter with lemon thyme carrots and a salad, we both ignore it after three bites because conversation is finally the food we've been starving for. Small things first: Ace's bow tie; Rose's campaign to bring back cursive; the crosswalk design going up at the library end cap; the way geese surveil Municipal Order like union reps, still winning their cold war with city signage.

Then the heavier box drops between us. We lift it together like adults who have learned how to move weight without injury.

"I should have told you sooner," I say. "I was nineteen, scared, and the town felt like a glass bowl. I didn't know how to ask you to choose me when you were already choosing survival."

"I should have come back," he says. "I thought love could live in blueprints. I forgot houses need roofs."

We don't edit our history into something prettier. We let truth sit in the candlelight, being unglamorous and essential.

When the check comes, he reaches. I slap his hand with affectionate scandal. "Romance tax. We split."

"Terms," he says, grinning in a way that turns my knees into negotiating parties.

We walk the boardwalk after; the lighthouse throws its one-eyed blessing; fireflies practice Morse code in the grass; the lake goes silk under a moon that has seen worse and still shows up. I pull a blanket from my bag because you don't live in Willow Cove without learning to pack for the weather and possibilities.

Under the lighthouse eave, he kisses me the way we wrote on that napkin at seventeen and didn't understand yet, heat held by care. His mouth is warm and tastes faintly of wine and wind; his hand at my jaw is reverent; my hands map his shoulders like they're learning a country from memory. When we stop, it's because we chose to, not because we were forced to, and that feels like a miracle I built with tape and breath and two syllables: terms.

"Thank you," I whisper, because gratitude is the language my heart defaults to when safety is real.

Flashback finds me on the walk home, neat as a film cut: under the bleachers at the football field, the night smelling like clover and ambition. He was all elbows and hope and sentences about stars listening. We wrote rules on a concession stand napkin with a pen that skipped on the curves: No running without a goodbye. No turning silence into punishment. Tell the truth even when timing hates it. I tucked it into my jewelry box. He tucked it under his rib. The ink smelled metallic, the paper rough under our fingers.

Now, on my porch, Midnight inspects Ethan's ankles and bestows a headbutt like a papal blessing. Inside, the peppermint candle takes its job seriously. We don't race the heat. We let it breathe. We make out in the doorway like grown people with a Boy Who Is Sleeping down the hall and hearts that finally learned how to be brave without being reckless. Fabric rustles, breath quickens, and we pause with laughter still in the room, savoring restraint as intimacy.

"Okay?" he whispers against my mouth.

"Yes," I whisper back, and the bell in my bones rings one, two, three, permission, promise, prayer.

LANTERNS, BOUNDARIES, FORESHADOW
ETHAN

Morning brings geese doing their union rounds and a DM from Cove Chatter asking for a quote about the "redemption arc." I text Maya: Press rules: poetry, donor wall, silent auction. No minors. No prying. She replies with a goose gif, and Boundaries are beautiful.

At the clinic, Nurse Joan catches me alphabetizing the crash cart and shakes her head like a gentle storm. "Let the man alphabetize, Carol. It keeps him from emailing venture capitalists."

My phone buzzes with a familiar out-of-town number, the kind with too many commas attached. I silence it under the Boathouse table-cloth, ignoring the muted vibration like a test I intend to pass. Hydras hate boundaries. I'm learning to love them.

By ten, I'm at the bookstore with two lattes, and I did not brew them for everyone's safety. Clara opens the door like a soft yes. We reinforce the top seam because storms like to test old decisions. Rose wanders by with Henry and says, "If you two don't make it official soon, the bell will resign." She adds, softer: "Lanterns are for hope. Don't forget that." I am disarmed by how much I want to be the kind of man who would give a bell a reason to stay employed.

Noah appears after afterschool, sketchbook, graphite, a practiced smirk that doesn't quite cover the curiosity. We colonize the stoop and shade fur together, 2B, 4B, patience, to the steady metronome of Harbor Street. Ace nods. Midnight yawns. The town carries on with the business of being kind on purpose. Midnight even flicks his tail in judgment, grading me as if he's the final arbiter of restraint.

That night is Ocelot Night because we decided Fridays belong to us: grilled cheese, tomato soup, a movie with improbable rope bridges, and a twelve-year-old who migrates down the couch until his head finds his mother's lap like the tide finds shore. "Is this Ocelli Night?" Mayor Tom asks when he calls, confusing everyone and earning laughter. We keep the heat inside the lines we drew together. When I ask, "Okay?" she says, "Yes," and I become the sort of man who knows how to stop while there's still laughter in the room because tomorrow is the best part.

Later, alone at my kitchen table, I take the message blinking from a number that used to mean permission and forward it to my sister with two words: Ocelot night. Lila replies with a fox emoji, a note about bringing flats for mic duty, and Proud of you, don't be dramatic at the gala unless it's about poetry.

Foreshadow lives in a manila envelope someone slips under Clara's door, a printout of an old article with a red circle around a word.

CHAPTER SEVENTEEN

Sparks & Soft Landings

CLARA

The scream doesn't sound like fear; it sounds like electricity deciding to make a point.

One second, the bookstore is honey-warm and humming, teens testing microphones for our open-mic fundraiser, fairy lights stitched through the rafters, the bell above the door practicing its polite jingle. The next, the PA hisses, the lights strobe like a stung beehive, and a string of bulbs near the donor wall pops with the sharp authority of a snapped violin string.

Before the sparks even snap, Ethan's lips are still on mine from the kiss we stole behind the counter, a breath-stealing heat that makes my knees argue with gravity. His palm braces my hip, anchoring me with a steadiness that says we are allowed to be reckless only with laughter, never with safety. Then, the flash. The kiss ends on a gasp that belongs to both of us.

"Kill the power strip!" I shout, already vaulting the counter. The guitar kid freezes. Maya, saint of caffeine and timing, dives behind the merch table, flips every red rocker switch she can reach, and yells, "Unplug, unplug!"

A crack of ozone punches the air, burnt cord plastic, sharp as betrayal. Ash flakes fall like paper snow. A spark kisses the lace of fairy lights that frame the window. One thin tongue of flame licks upward, curious.

Not my window, I think wildly. Not the hearts.

I'm there with the fire blanket in three strides, heart pounding loud enough to count time. "Everyone, back from the window." The room obeys the voice I save for emergencies and geese. Someone gasps. Someone else mutters a prayer. Midnight launches from the history shelf like a sleek exclamation point and vanishes into the stockroom, offended.

The flame takes a greedy breath, curls toward paper.

"Hey." Ethan's voice slides in low and sure behind me, a hand on the ladder, the steadiness I didn't realize I was waiting to borrow. "You've got it."

I smother, press, hold. Heat tickles my knuckles through the blanket, then yields. The tiny blaze collapses into a sigh of smoke.

"Front doors open, air out," Maya orders, because she runs triage with pastries and audacity. "Nobody panic. Panic is banned."

Ace the Dalmatian trots in at Mr. Pierce's heel exactly when I need a morale miracle. He executes a perfect sit in the aisle, head cocked, tail tapping like a metronome. Then, in a flourish that will be retold by the teens for weeks, he retrieves a dropped inhaler and returns it to its asthmatic owner. Three kids who were on the verge of tears collapse into giggles instead and bury their fingers in his ears.

I peel the blanket back. Only a blackened kiss on the cord. The donor hearts in the glass glow like they're grateful. Daniel Ortiz. Rose & Henry. The Crossword Crew. Anonymous (with a doodled goose, obviously). A town's pulse rendered in gold and silver.

Across the room, Noah's voice threads steady. "We're okay," he tells the cluster of seventh-graders he secretly mentors. "The lights did a dramatic monologue."

I breathe. The bell above the door jingles shyly, as if proud of us.

"Text the electrician," I tell Maya, the tremble leaving my voice one syllable at a time. "And bring the battery lanterns."

She's already moving, curls a comet tail behind her. "On it. Also, whoever wired those vintage bulbs owes me an apology and three cinnamon knots. By the way, if Mayor Tom asks again about pirate hats, I will feed him to the geese."

Ethan stays at my shoulder, not touching until I lean a fraction into him. Then his palm finds the small of my back, like consent taught his hand a new language.

"Okay?" he asks under the crowd-noise. In his mouth, the word is a promise and a check-in.

"Yes," I say, and feel my ribs believe me.

We work the room the way we worked a storm: together. He resets the breaker; I reset the kids. He untangles a string of lights with surgeon patience; I reframe the open mic as an unplugged night on purpose. Maya unveils a tray of sugar knots like communion. Mr. Pierce keeps Ace circulating, tail metronoming the room's heartbeat back to normal.

When the squeals fade to chatter and the chatter to the hum I love best, pages, pencils, breath; Ethan tips his chin toward the stockroom. "Check your hands?"

It's not about my hands. It's about a minute of quiet where the door can click shut, and the rest of Willow Cove can talk about us without our ears burning.

Inside, the air smells like paper and cedar soap. The emergency light over the back exit paints everything a soft moon-blue. I look at my fingers: a little soot, no scorch. He takes my wrist anyway, warm, reverent. The way you hold something you didn't realize you were allowed to keep.

"You saved the hearts," he says softly. "And the window. And possibly three teenagers from learning new vocabulary."

"Minimalist glitter does not include fire." My laugh is shakier than I want it to be.

His thumb strokes a sooty crescent at the base of my thumb. "Breathe with me?" he asks, and I do, the four-count I used to mock him for when we were seventeen and immortal. In, hold, out, pause. Again. The world obliges.

When the shake leaves my bones, what's left is heat I didn't earn from a flame. His palm slides, tentative but sure, down to my hip. His lips find the hollow beneath my ear, and my knees remember every midnight promise we made under bleachers. I tilt my head, let him brush his cheek against my throat like he's memorizing new cartography.

"Terms," I whisper, because the word is how I save myself from drowning.

"Still signed," he answers, and then he kisses me, steady voltage, not wildfire. Warm mouth, careful hands. The kind of heat you bank instead of burning through.

I fist the collar of his shirt like I'm anchoring to a future that finally looks like something other than an ache. He makes a sound I've never heard from him and will catalog for private use. When his palm curves my jaw, my knees remember prom night under the bleachers and the napkin we signed with rules we didn't understand yet. Tell the truth even when timing hates it. Don't turn silence into punishment. No running without a goodbye.

A faint cheer rises from the front room, followed by the soft test-strum of an unplugged guitar. We laugh against each other's mouths.

"Open mic is officially candlelit," I say. "We should…"

"Behave?" His grin is unrepentant. "I can do that."

"Debatable," I say, but I let him kiss me once more, slower, deeper, until the noise outside turns into a song that sounds exactly like breath and second chances.

We step back into the light made by people and lanterns. Willow Cove does what Willow Cove always does: it turns a scare into a story we survived together.

PAPER HEARTS, OLD INK

ETHAN

I've sutured in the back of an ambulance and threaded a chest tube while a med student tried not to faint into a biohazard bin. None of that taught me how steady a strip of painter's tape can make a man feel when the woman he never stopped loving presses hope to glass like it belongs there.

Tonight, steadiness looks like guitars without amps and teenagers who keep singing anyway. It looks like Ace is offering his paw to a kid who needed a reason to laugh. It looks like Clara's mouth curved around my name in the stockroom like something sacred and ordinary at once.

When the last poem lands and the bell gives its tired curtsy, I stack chairs while she counts the till. Maya moans at a spreadsheet as if it had personally betrayed her. Mr. Pierce tips his cap. Midnight emerges from exile and pretends he saved us from electrical dragons. Ace and Midnight pass each other with a single solemn look, acknowledgment between sovereigns.

Clara straightens the donor wall. Gold, silver, a red book cutout waiting for a generous name. Daniel Ortiz. Rose & Henry. The Crossword Crew. Anonymous (with an undeniably smug goose). Names like constellations you can touch.

Her fingers still when she lifts an old hardcover from a donation box, and a page flutters. Something pale slips free, a folded square, yellowed at the creases. Her thumb brushes the edge. She goes very quiet.

"Clara?" I say gently.

She opens the paper like it might be fragile and finds… my handwriting, younger and bolder than the man I became.

Monroe, if the stars are listening, I told them I'm going to fall so hard I'll break a new verb for it. They winked like they knew and weren't telling.

You, me, the lake, forever. I don't know the math yet, but I want to learn the equation from you.

I remember the exact blue of the ink, the concession-stand napkin I pressed over my heart like a talisman, the way her laugh made me believe in physics that favored us. Cocoa steamed from a paper cup in my other hand, ink bleeding where I pressed too hard. I can still smell the sugar and the wet wood of the bleachers.

Clara's smile isn't soft; it's stunned, then wry, then something that could make a stubborn man forgive himself in installments. "I forgot this was in here."

"I didn't." I don't say it out loud. My chest says it for me.

She slides the letter carefully into the glass display case where we keep town ephemera, ticket stubs, a hand-drawn map of Willow Cove from 1952, and a photo of Rose and Henry at nineteen in outfits that deserve their own museum. She labels it with her tidy script: Teenage nonsense that turned into a life.

"Poetry," Maya declares, leaning on the counter. "Gross. I love it. Also, Kelsey from Cove Chatter DM'd me to ask for a 'forgiveness-arc' quote. I told her to arrive with cash for a donor heart and the understanding that boundaries are beautiful."

"Bless you," Clara says. Her eyes tilt toward me. "You okay?"

"Better than," I admit, because the truth is a muscle I'm learning to use in public. "Can I bring dinner tomorrow? Ocelot Night deserves caramelized onions."

Her mouth does that thing my equilibrium hasn't built an immunity to yet. "Grilled cheese judgment panel convenes at six."

I touch the fox sticker Noah slapped on my phone case like a dare. "I'll bring my A-game."

The town exhales. The bell says goodnight. I walk home with a paper heart in my pocket (actual, cut by Clara's hand, she shoved it at me when I forgot to take a donor receipt) and a plan that looks like a life: clinic at 8, closet triage with Nurse Joan at 10, onions at 5:30, Ocelot Night at 6, breath at… finally.

On my table, my phone wakes with a New York area code that used to mean permission. Final offer, the preview line reads.

I set the phone face down. Hydras hate boundaries. I'm getting good at loving them.

"Stay is a verb," I write on a sticky note and pin it to the cupboard where I'll see it when the kettle boils.

CLARA

Sleep arrives like a tide, and with it, the dock.

Not storm-dark tonight. Noon. Boards warm against my soles. A dented first-aid tin waits at the end, the same kind Ethan used on my clumsy scrapes back when kissing under the bleachers felt like an act of urban planning. Inside: our napkin of rules, ink darker than it should be, a new line in my hand: Make the timing worthy of the truth. I close the lid. The bell rings three times, clean, bright, like the town has decided to be on our side.

Morning is honest in Willow Cove. The lake wears the sky like a dress it didn't try on first and somehow fits anyway. Maya smuggles me a cinnamon knot with the solemnity of a sacrament.

"You glowed last night," she says, then edits herself at my look. "You were… illuminated by personal growth. Also, Lila texted: 'Wear flats; joy requires stability.'"

"Minimalist glitter," I say, and Midnight blinks his royal assent.

By nine, Noah has claimed the front table with his sketchbook. He's hiding foxes in the gutters of his crosswalk design so drivers slow down to wonder. When Ace trots past, Noah pretends not to glow at the chin-on-knee blessing. He glows anyway.

At noon, we hang the crosswalk sketch in the library's end cap. Lake-walk Moms clap. The blue-haired kids recite a poem they wrote about geese unionizing. Mayor Tom bursts in to ask if we can add pirate hats to the gala theme and receives a resounding "no" from three women and a cat. "But think of the crosswalk!" he wails. "A pirate crosswalk!"

Back at the shop, an envelope waits under the till; no return address is listed. Inside: a glossy printout of an old article about Ethan with a red circle around the word billionaire and a sticky tab that reads: Ask him why he really came back. Kelsey's name on the byline.

Midnight sits on the envelope like a paperweight and flicks his tail. I file the article under NOT OUR STORY, write three more names on three more hearts, and tape them to the window until the glass looks less like a target and more like a lantern.

TOWN BUSINESS, HEART BUSINESS

ETHAN

"Let the man alphabetize, Carol," Nurse Joan says to the clinic walls when she finds me reorganizing the crash cart. "If it keeps him from emailing venture capitalists, we encourage it."

"I am not emailing anyone," I say to the cart, to the walls, to the version of me who used to believe commas in offers meant love. I label the epinephrine and feel my pulse improve.

We fix the storage closet leak (J-bend sulking; firm, kind attention), find the AED where it was exiled by a previous administration (holiday decor, maybe?), and hang it in the right hallway under a tiny gold heart because Clara said morale matters. A patient in Room 3 tells me she misses the lake; I send Ace in for ten minutes of chin-on-knee therapy and watch her shoulders drop.

At four, I meet Noah on the bookstore stoop. Shading lesson: his idea. "Fur is suggestion," he instructs, deadpan. "You don't draw every hair. You imply." Two-B for base, four-B for depth. "Don't smudge with your palm. Use a scrap paper bridge." He places the paper bridge for me like he's letting me borrow a small, fragile magic.

"Like medicine," I hear myself answer. "You don't fix everything. You shift a system and let the body remember."

He looks up, surprised I know what I'm talking about, and then pretends he isn't impressed, which is how twelve says Okay, fine, keep showing up. He corrects my pencil grip with a solemn nod that makes his small pride unmistakable.

Midnight sprawls across the page with impeccable timing and zero shame. "Saboteur," Noah says, but his mouth curves. Ace passes with Mr. Pierce; they nod at each other like decorated colleagues.

"Dinner," Clara says at the door, a question in the curve of her shoulder.

"Grilled cheese," I say. "Onions caramelized within an inch of their lives." I do not say: I'm making a life with you in a kitchen that smells like pepper and safety.

CLARA

He passes Noah's texture test with a solemn nod from the judge's bench (our kitchen stool). Midnight permits a single ribbon of cheddar in exchange for a papal blessing. Ocelot Night finds its bones: soup, sandwiches, a movie with improbable rope bridges, a boy who drifts down the couch until his head finds my lap because that's what his body knows about safety.

When credits roll, we do dishes like we've always been doing dishes. He reaches for a plate, and my heart does something embarrassing over the way he pauses to align it perfectly in the rack. It's not perfection-ism. It's care.

We stand very close by very ordinary light. "Tell me something real," he says.

"I survived so hard I forgot how to want without apologizing," I answer, because honesty is still my favorite sport. "I'm remembering."

"Tell me something real," I whisper back.

"I didn't know how to be still without feeling like I was losing," he says. "I'm learning."

We kiss in my doorway like grown people with a sleeping boy down the hall and a lifetime of yes to pace. Heat, humor, a pause that's a choice. When he murmurs "Okay?" against my mouth, I say "Yes" like a vow.

I don't invite him to stay because timing is a muscle, too, and to-night it's tired. He doesn't push, because consent is a language we speak better now. We bank the heat. The room approves. Quiet isn't a void anymore; it's a goal we both deserve.

FORESHADOW & FIREFLIES

ETHAN

The square smells like grass and charcoal and the sugar of someone's grandmother's brownies as the town gathers for an impromptu picnic that only required three text threads and two people with megaphones. Mayor Tom corrals us into a three-legged race for "team-building."

"Left, right," Clara coaches, tying us together with a red bandanna while the town whistles. "You're not allowed to save the day by your-self. That's cheating and also unsafe."

"Left, right," I repeat, and proceed to step on the knot like a man auditioning for slapstick. We lurch. We go down. We laugh. Noah's laughter is the loudest thing on Harbor Street, a sound that breaks something old in me and leaves room for light.

We don't win. We don't care. We win a sticker that says 'Minimalist Glitter Champion,' which Noah slaps on his sketchbook cover like a banner.

Later, under the fireflies practicing Morse code near the lighthouse steps, Kelsey from Cove Chatter appears at the edge of the path with a notebook and a smile that means 'angle'.

"Care to comment on the 'redemption arc'?" she asks, eyes darting from Clara to me to Noah, who goes stone-still in that way kids do when they want to vanish without conceding the field.

Clara's hand finds mine. "We're happy to talk about the gala," she says, voice all velvet and steel. "Poetry, donor wall, silent auction. No minors. No prying. Those are the rules."

"Boundaries are beautiful," Maya says, materializing like a fairy god-mother with a clipboard and a cookie. "Here's a press sheet. Also, have a cookie."

Kelsey takes the cookie. "Generous," she says. She looks at me. "Dr. Hale, is it true Argus Health offered you?"

"Have a second cookie," I say mildly, because I'm not answering a question designed to set our lives on fire. "And a donor heart." I hand her a gold heart and a marker. "Write the name of someone who made you brave."

She blinks. The angle wobbles. The lake breathes. She writes a name I don't know and tapes it to the glass like everyone else.

CLARA

When we get home, the porch light does its double flicker, the timer trying to be dramatic, and I laugh because some habits earn their keep. Lavender from the planter chimes in the night air, and the faint ring of herb-box bells reminds me that even Willow Cove can sound like a hymn.

We carry leftovers into the kitchen. I kiss Ethan in the doorway. He kisses me like we both earned it, longer this time, heat that pauses but never withdraws. A breath more than last night, because a boundary can stretch when both hearts agree.

After he leaves, after the bell inside my bones rings three clean notes, I find a thin manila envelope slid under the door. No return address. The same old article inside with the same red circle around the billionaire, the same sticky tab: Ask him why he really came back. A Cove Chatter push alert follows on my phone: Tomorrow: A Heart-Wall with Secrets?

Midnight jumps onto the counter, sits on the envelope, and flicks his tail like he's seen worse. I file it under NOT OUR STORY and reach for a fresh sheet of cardstock.

I cut a red book. I write a name I've been saving in small, steady letters, at Noah's suggestion:

For the kid who needs the fox on page 27.

I tape it to the glass, palm flat, with even pressure. The window holds. The lake breathes. The timing learns how to be worthy of the truth. The red book heart glints back at me like a ring you can read.

Out on Harbor Street, a bell rings once, twice, three times. It sounds like a promise with our names in it.

CHAPTER EIGHTEEN

Storm Rules

EDGE OF HEAT, EDGE OF GLASS

CLARA

The first pop sounds like a cork, cheerful, harmless, right up until the fairy light strand above the donor wall spits a tongue of sparks and takes a greedy breath.

"Power strip!" I shout, already vaulting the counter. Someone screams; someone else swears; the bell above the door jitterrings like a sparrow trapped in a chapel.

Maya dives behind the merch table and snaps switches down with the ruthless calm of a seasoned pastry warlord. "Unplug, unplug!"

Another bright crack, a flash like a camera too close to skin, then a lick of flame reaches for gold paper hearts. One edge singes, curling like a cruel grin.

Not my window.

I'm moving before thought catches up, fire blanket off the hook, three strides, a prayer I don't say out loud. The heat nips my knuckles through fabric as I smother, press, and hold. Smoke stings, sweet and bitter. The flame sulks, then folds in on itself.

"Doors open," Maya orders, hair a wild halo as she wedges both doors to pull a cross breeze. "Nobody panic. Panic is banned."

A body slots in at my shoulder, the kind of steadiness my bones remember even when my brain pretends not to. "You've got it," Ethan says, low and sure, hand closing over the ladder while I climb to tug the sizzling strand down.

"Left edge, top seam," he adds.

"I make the plans in this store," I tell him automatically, even as I take the painter's tape he's holding out like an oath. I pressed a reinforcement strip across the pane where the hairline crack appeared last week. The bead of water testing us hesitates, fattens, slides away.

The room exhales. The bell tries a polite jingle, smug. Somewhere in the corner, Midnight offers a single italicized thought: You nearly singed my whiskers. Unacceptable.

"Front's clear," Mr. Pierce calls from the threshold, Ace sitting prim and proud in his teal bow tie, accepting exactly three strokes from three trembling hands before returning to parade rest. Therapy, on brand.

Maya deposits a tray of sugar knots on the counter like communion. "Everyone gets carbs and a pep talk."

I peel the edge of the blanket back; only a black kiss on the cord. The donor wall glows as if grateful: Daniel Ortiz. Rose & Henry. The Crossword Crew. Anonymous, with a doodled goose that refuses to stop being funny.

"Smoke's clearing," Ethan says, voice a steady tide against the tiny shakes in my wrists. His palm hovers at the small of my back until I lean the fraction that makes it a yes. Warmth lands; breath evens.

"Check your hands?" he asks.

"I'm fine." My voice is air over glass.

"You tell," he says gently. "You say 'fine' when you mean 'give me ten seconds and chamomile.'"

He's not wrong.

We triage what's left: teenagers rebookmarked, unplugged mic night reframed as candlelit. Mr. Pierce takes Ace on one morale lap, and the golden retriever rescues a dropped inhaler with an earnest nudge until its owner laughs through tears. Midnight returns from wherever divine beings sulk and jumps to the sill to glare at physics.

When the last tremor leaves, the heat that remains isn't from fire. Ethan tips his chin toward the stockroom; I nod. Door clicks; quiet lands.

"Breathe with me?" he asks, like a spell we both know now: in four, hold four, out four, pause. My lungs obey.

His thumb strokes a sooty crescent at the base of my thumb. The world narrows to cedar soap, rain memory, the slow drift of want I promised myself I'd stop apologizing for.

"Clara." My name is Velvet in his mouth. His breath hovers at the hollow beneath my ear, asking. I answer by tilting first, claiming my choice.

Heat, then hush. His mouth is warm, careful, current, not wildfire, and when he kisses me, I don't fall, I open. My fingers curve into the damp curl at his nape; his free hand brackets my hip like a promise he understands costs patience. The room brightens at the edges.

"Terms," I murmur against his smile, because the word saves me from drowning.

"Still signed," he answers, voice a little rough. We kiss again, deeper, longer, until a teen in the front room strums a guitar experimentally and we both laugh into each other's mouths like we invented relief.

Back in the lights, I press a fresh silver heart to the glass: For anyone who needs today to be kind. My hand trembles. My heart doesn't.

"Okay," I tell the room, the lake, and myself. "Open mic is unplugged on purpose. Poetry saves electricity."

The town obliges by clapping. A bell rings faintly, permission granted.

Side Plot, Soft Target

ETHAN

The town hall is a brick shoebox with opinions. Tonight it has microphones.

Mayor Tom beams like a man unveiling a moon landing. "New business! Zoning adjustment for the Harbor Promenade. Imagine, expanded sidewalks for café chairs, a little stage for summer sets, picture it!" He flings his arms and nearly decapitates a rubber plant.

Kelsey from Cove Chatter sits two rows back in a lemon cardigan and a hunger that smells like angel. Her notebook is weaponized pastel.

Clara slides into the seat beside me, smelling faintly of smoke and sugar. "Minimalist glitter does not involve municipal microphones," she whispers. Her knee finds mine. Electricity, safer this time.

Public comment opens. Mr. Dawes argues the goose union will sue. The Lakewalk Moms advocate for stroller lanes. Henry proposes a poetry kiosk; Rose seconds with a tea service for repentant cardiologists. "Lanterns, Not Pirates!" Tom blurts to cut them off, launching his new slogan like fireworks. A ten-year-old boy.

I scribble 'install AED' at the town hall in my notes and underline it twice.

Then Tom calls for questions, and Kelsey stands. "Is the doctor who left our town for the city", a glance like a paper cut, "the same doctor planning to profit from Harbor improvements? Sources say… investments." Her tone now leans curious, not cruel.

Clara's fingers tighten on my sleeve.

I stand. No microphone needed. "I work at the clinic. I fix a closet leak on Tuesdays. I alphabetize the crash cart when Nurse Joan lets me. If you see me 'profiting,' it'll be because I convinced three donors to buy more paper hearts." I look at Clara's window in my mind and steady my voice. "Boundaries are beautiful. Cover the gala. Leave minors and gossip out of it."

A murmur. Rose says quite clearly, "Amen," and Henry adds, "Install a poetry kiosk anyway." The room laughs the sharpness off the moment.

Tom pivots with the grace of a man used to tapdancing on civic eggshells. "Speaking of, our Books & Hearts Gala needs volunteers. Also, we will not be installing pirate-themed crosswalks. Lanterns, Not Pirates!"

A ten-year-old sighs in bitter disappointment. Noah hides his smile and pretends the crosswalk sketch in his backpack didn't just burn a hole through his hoodie.

After the vote (tabled, thank God), Kelsey corners Clara by the bulletin board and tries a different key. "A quote about forgiveness?"

Clara's politeness is velvet over steel. "Happy to talk about donor walls, poetry, therapy dogs, and sidewalk chalk. Forgiveness is private. You can buy a gold heart for the window like everyone else."

Kelsey blinks. The angle wobbles. She buys a heart, writes Luz on it in careful block letters, and surprises herself by crying.

Dream, Flashback, Crosswalk (Clara → Ethan)

Dream — Dock at Noon (Clara)

Not storm dark this time. The boards are warm. A dented tin waits at the end of the dock, the same first-aid kit Ethan used on me last week when I called a staple "occupational texture." Inside: our napkin of rules, ink darker than it should be, and a new line in my hand: Make the timing worthy of the truth. The bell rings once, twice, three times. He lifts a hand, not to claim, to ask. My paper heart doesn't dissolve. It shines.

I wake smiling, and for once the smile holds. The lake outside blinks lamplight like a sign of approval.

Flashback — The Diner (Ethan)

Senior fall. Lemon meringue is like a cloud with a sharp tongue. Clara licked syrup off my knuckle because we were reckless and holy. "Tell me something true," I said.

She tucked her hair behind her ear with fingers that shook a little. "Books fixed me before I knew I was broken."

I admitted the surgery language that already lived in my hands. We paid in crumpled bills and coins. Dale chased us into the parking lot to return quarters; we ran and didn't trip. Later, on the dock, we wrote rules we didn't understand yet and promised to follow them anyway.

Present — Library Wing (Clara)

The crosswalk sketch gets the end cap. People slow for wonder the way Noah predicted. A second grader in star leggings points at page twenty-seven. "Fox," she breathes, delighted.

Noah's ears go scarlet. He shrugs like whatever and fails to hide the glow. Quietly, he asks me, "Can foxes guard hearts?"

"They already do," I whisper back.

Ethan keeps the perfect distance: near enough to catch, far enough not to steal. His pride is quite enormous.

Kelsey snaps a photo of Ace shaking paws with a toddler and, to her own shock, forgets to angle it.

Clinic Hall (Ethan)

I hang the AED cabinet in the right hallway with a tiny gold heart sticker, Clara insisted on because morale matters. Monthly checks scheduled. A teenager in a hoodie watches me and finally blurts, "Hey, are you the guy who almost got brained by a tent pole?"

"Costarring," I say gravely. "The real hero wore a red bandanna and yelled left-right."

He smirks like he understands softness is safer than sarcasm in rooms that smell like lemon cleaner and mercy.

Bookstore, Dusk (Clara)

I flip the sign to CLOSED. The bell gives an obedient sigh. Outside, the lake practices calm. Inside, I press three new names to the glass until the window looks less like a target and more like a lantern.

Noah drifts up beside me, shoulder a warm bump. "Ocelot, right?"

"Ocelot," I say. He tries not to smile and fails spectacularly. A bell chimes again. Permission.

OCELOT NIGHT (CLARA & ETHAN)

CLARA

Grilled cheese in a pan is a love language when the onions go slow and sweet, and somebody has the patience to stand there. Noah grades texture like it's a science fair and then grants Ethan the solemn nod that has become our house benediction. Midnight pretends not to beg for cheddar. Accepts tribute anyway.

We eat at the small table with elbows touching and the kind of silence that isn't empty, it's trust. Homework triage (polynomials), donor calls (Lakewalk Moms want QR codes), comedy (Mayor Tom's bumper stickers: Lanterns, Not Pirates).

Later, we collapse on the couch with an old adventure where rope bridges misbehave. Somewhere between cannons and improbable vines, Noah's head drifts into my lap the way the tide finds shore. My hand settles in his hair. He rolls his eyes when he catches me smiling, but then he smiles anyway. This is the thing I didn't know how to ask for at nineteen. This is the thing I built.

"Someday we'll take the museum trip," he mumbles before drifting. My throat burns in the best way.

Ethan

When the credits roll, we do dishes like a domestic duet we've always known: rinse, pass, stack. I align plates in the rack because care lives in small angles; she watches me the way people watch the sea when they finally believe it won't take something back.

At the door, lamplight turns her mouth into a question. I answer with a kiss that's slower than the one behind the counter, deeper than the one under the eave, careful as a promise we intend to keep. Hands stay above clothes; heat climbs anyway. When I murmur "Okay?" she says "Yes," and I stop first because the best fire I've ever known is the kind we bank. "Tomorrow," I say. "Respect means tomorrow."

"Tomorrow," she echoes, and the bell in my bones rings three clean notes.

Clara

After he leaves, peppermint wicks down to its own small moon. A thin envelope waits under the door, no return address. Inside: an old article about Ethan with a red circle around a word and a sticky note that says, 'Ask him why he really came back.'

Midnight leaps up, parks on it, and flicks his tail like he's seen worse. Humans. Always paper drama.

I slide it into a folder labeled Not Our Story, cut a red book from cardstock, and write a name Noah suggested: For the kid who needs the fox on page 27. I tape it to glass with a steady palm until it glints like a vow. Outside, the lake breathes; inside, my house does too. From the lighthouse steps far downshore, I imagine vows waiting someday.

Somewhere in this small town, a bell rings once, twice, three times. It sounds like permission.

CHAPTER NINETEEN

The Fire That Didn't Burn Us

CLARA

The lights snap and hiss like angry bees, and his mouth is still on mine. For one wicked second, I want his mouth again even as the glass hisses.

We've stolen a kiss behind the counter while the teens noodle a soundcheck for tonight's unplugged open-mic, my palms braced on Ethan's shoulders, his hand steady at my hip, when the fairylight strand above the donor wall spits sparks. Heat kisses the glass. The bell over my door jitter-rings like a sparrow trapped in a chapel.

"Power strip!" I shout, vaulting the counter. Maya dives behind the merch table, flipping red rocker switches like a general with a pastry tray. The air fills with the bitter-sugar scent of singed cord and rain jackets. Someone gasps. Someone else drops a guitar pick and whispers Sorry to the floor.

A thin flame licks toward the honey-gold hearts I taped there this morning.

Not my window.

I rip the fire blanket from its hook and smother, press, hold. Heat nips my knuckles through fabric. The flame sulks, curls, dies. I breathe, once, too fast. The room holds its breath with me.

"Doors. Open." Maya wedges both with her hips, curls frizzing into a halo. "Nobody panic. Panic is banned. We are not auditioning for arson."

A body slots in at my shoulder with the steadiness my bones remember. Ethan's palm finds the ladder. "You've got it," he says, voice low and sure. "Left edge, top seam."

"I make the plans in this store," I tell him on reflex, even as I take the painter's tape he's holding like a vow. I climb. Thunder counts to three somewhere out over the lake. I pressed a reinforcement strip across the corner where the glass had broken last week, wishing we could afford a full replacement soon. A bead of water tests us, hesitates, fattens… slides away.

Midnight launches from the history shelf and vanishes into the stockroom, offended by every decision humanity has made today. Ace pads in with Mr. Pierce at heel, accepts exactly three pats from trembling seventh-graders, then sits in the aisle like a living metronome for calm.

"We're okay," Noah tells his cluster of friends, voice steady in that old-soul way. "The lights did a dramatic monologue."

When the shake leaves my hands, what's left is heat I didn't earn from a flame, pulse thrumming at my wrist. Ethan tips his chin toward the back. I nod. Stockroom. Door click. Quiet.

"Breathe with me?" he asks, the four-count I used to mock when we were seventeen and immortal, bleacher-breath summers and all. In, hold, out, pause. Again. The world obliges. My shoulders drop.

His thumb strokes a sooty crescent at the base of my thumb. "Okay?"

"Yes." The word lands like a promise in my mouth.

He waits for my nod, then bends, slow, and kisses me, not a scramble, not an apology. Warm mouth, careful hands, current not wildfire, tinged with the faint taste of peppermint gum. My fingers find the damp curl at his nape; the room brightens at the edges. When his palm brackets my hip, the yes rises up from somewhere underneath years of making do.

"Terms," I murmur against his smile, because the word keeps me from drowning.

"Still signed," he says, breath a little messy now, and we laugh into each other's mouths when a kid out front strums a soft test chord like the universe clearing its throat.

We step back into the lantern light and the scent of cinnamon steam. I press a fresh silver heart on the glass, for anyone who needs today to be kind. The tape whispers. The pane holds. So do I.

ETHAN

Adrenaline is a loan shark. You take what you need; it collects with interest. I pay it back with ordinary tasks: rewiring a temperamental power strip, noticing soot tracing the airflow vents, untangling fairy lights with surgical patience, alphabetizing a mic list while Maya prescribes sugar like a sacrament.

Clara floats the room the way good captains do, checking wrists for shakes, handing out paper hearts to anyone who needs a job, turning a scare into a story. When we finally get two minutes where no one asks us for tape or tea, she tilts her head toward the stoop.

"Air?" she asks.

"Always."

Outside, the lake wears the sky like it was tailored for it. The awning smells faintly of peppermint and rain. She leans against the doorframe and looks like every dock-dream I ever had learned how to stand on land.

"Thank you," she says. Two words, all sincerity, no apology.

"For the tape or the kiss?" I try. Her smile says yes.

We don't get to linger, because Willow Cove rarely lets a moment go un-chaperoned. Mayor Tom jogs over, tie at half-mast, cheeks bright from the sprint. "Small matter," he pants. "Town hall tonight, zoning for the Harbor Promenade. Think café chairs, poetry kiosk, maybe a tiny stage, picture it!"

"Picture the goose filing an injunction," Clara says.

"I've been served by that goose before," Tom mutters, half to himself.

"We'll be there," I tell him, because in this life I'm building, showing up is the point.

We are. The town hall is a brick shoebox with opinions and a rubber plant that Tom keeps almost decapitating with his enthusiasm. Public comment turns into theater (it always does): Lake walk Moms for stroller lanes, Henry for sestinas, Rose for repentance tea service, Mr. Dawes for goose unions. When Tom opens the floor for questions, Kelsey from Cove Chatter stands in a lemon cardigan with a notebook the color of a softened bruise.

"Is the doctor who left our town for the city," she says, glancing like a paper cut, "the same doctor now poised to profit from Harbor improvements? Sources say… investments."

Clara's hand finds my sleeve. Heat, then steadiness.

I rise. "I work at the clinic. On Tuesdays, I fix closets. I alphabetize the crash cart when Nurse Joan lets me. If you see me 'profiting,' it'll be because I convinced three more donors to buy paper hearts." I let that sit. "Cover the gala. Leave minors and gossip out of it. Boundaries are beautiful."

"Amen," Rose says, exactly like she says it at church. Henry adds, "Install the poetry kiosk anyway." Laughter, the good kind that punctures tension without wounding anyone.

After, Kelsey corners us by the bulletin board, trying a gentler key. "A quote on forgiveness?"

"Happy to talk donor walls, poetry, therapy dogs, and chalk," Clara says, velvet over steel. "Forgiveness is private. Buy a gold heart like everyone else."

Kelsey blinks. Writes Luz on a heart in neat block letters. Tapes it to the glass and surprises herself by crying. Willow Cove: one, angles: zero.

That night, after unplugged open-mic turns into candlelit magic, I clean folding chairs while Clara counts the till and Maya moans at spreadsheets like they betrayed her. A donation box coughs up an old hardcover; a folded square slips free. Clara opens it and finds my seventeen-year-old handwriting, sincere, ridiculous, true.

Monroe—

If the stars are listening, I told them I'm going to fall so hard I'll break a new verb for it.

She smiles, a little stunned, a little wry, a lot alive, and traces one finger against the glass case. "Teenage nonsense that turned into a life," she labels it, slides it into the display with the town's ephemera. I don't breathe for a second because if I do, I might say forever in a room full of witnesses.

"Tomorrow," she says as we lock up. "Ocelot Night."

"Yes," I say, because stay is a verb, and I'm learning how to use it.

CLARA

Dream sequence

Not storm-dark this time. The dock is noon-warm, boards hot enough to print a map of my feet. A dented first-aid tin waits at the end. Inside: the napkin we signed under the bleachers, ink darker than it has any right to be, and a new line in my hand; *Make the timing worthy of the truth.* The bell rings one, two, three. I lift my palm; the paper heart in it doesn't dissolve. It shines.

I wake smiling. It holds.

By nine, the bookstore smells like rain-damp wool and warm paper. Noah claims the front table and hides foxes in the gutters of his crosswalk sketch so drivers will slow down just to look. Ace trots a morale lap; Midnight pretends not to approve.

At the library, the end-cap goes up: blue-haired kids clap; Lakewalk Moms discuss QR codes for the gala; Mayor Tom suggests pirate hats and is smacked down by three women and a cat. A second-grader in galaxy leggings spots the fox on page twenty-seven and whispers, "There." Noah shrugs so hard his ears go red.

Back at the store, an envelope waits under the till, no return address, a glossy printout with a red circle around a word I'm learning to ignore.

The sticky tab says: Ask him why he really came back. Midnight sits on it like a paperweight. Kelsey's byline is at the corner. I file it under Not Our Story and write three more names on three more hearts until the window looks less like a target and more like a lantern.

Flashback

Homecoming week, seventeen. Rust and clover under the bleachers. Hot chocolate, steam, and a boy who asked, "Do you ever feel like the stars are listening?" I told him only when they're rooting for me. He looked at me like he believed they were. We wrote rules on a napkin with a pen that kept skipping: No running without a goodbye. No turning silence into punishment. Tell the truth even when timing hates it. He kissed each line like a vow and my mouth like a future.

Now

Ocelot Night earns its ink on our calendar. We picked Ocelot because Noah once misheard "omelet" and insisted we needed a fiercer mascot. Ethan shows up with grilled cheese that passes Noah's Official Texture Test™ and onions that taste like patience. We triage algebra and donor calls, then migrate to the couch. A ridiculous adventure plays; Noah's head slides into my lap the way the tide finds shore. I touch his hair and try not to cry, which is impossible and also okay.

When the credits roll, Ethan's hands bracket the sink with mine. Ordinary feels like a blessing I can name now.

"Tell me something real," he says.

"I survived so hard I forgot how to want without apologizing," I answer. "I'm remembering."

"Tell me something real," I whisper back.

"I didn't know how to be still without feeling like I was losing," he says. "I'm learning."

We kiss in the doorway, heat, yes, but held by choice. When he murmurs, "Okay?" I say "Yes," and he stops first. We bank the fire like people who finally trust tomorrow.

ETHAN

10:14 a.m. The school nurse's number flashes on my phone, the kind that makes your bones go cold even when the voice on the other end says, "He's okay."

Noah's sitting up when I arrive, jaw set, palms scuffed, a scrape on one cheekbone an inch south of dangerous. The nurse says "tussle," "hallway," and "locker" in the careful voice adults use when they're trying not to make a proud kid smaller.

"I don't need a dad lecture," Noah says as I crouch, which is good, because I didn't bring one. I offer him a sticker sheet first, silent, before showing my ridiculous stash of gauze. He huffs. "I'm twelve, not nine." Then, quieter: "Maybe one."

A boy loped past in the hall and muttered the thing Noah's been waiting to hear since my face walked back into town. I watched my son not flinch, watched him measure impulse against consequence, and I wanted to high-five every neuron he's ever grown. I cleaned the scrape; he let me. When I asked if he wanted me to page Clara or if he wanted to do it, he said, "We'll tell her together."

We do. Clara arrives with soft fury and sharper love. She kneels at Noah's knees and says the exact right number of words. He breathes easier because she's here. So do I.

"Throwing a punch is easy," I tell him later on the stoop. "Learning which part of you is strong enough not to, that's advanced."

He snorts. "You make everything sound like a science lab."

"It kind of is." I bump his shoulder. "You handled yourself."

He slides a folded napkin across the step without looking at me, graphite smudging his thumb. A fox trots across a book spine in graphite lines that get bolder at the corners. "For the AED cabinet," he says, deadpan, like it's not the most generous thing anyone has ever handed me. "Or whatever."

"Perfect," I say, and my voice only breaks once.

That night, the town square smells like grass and charcoal. Someone strings new lanterns early for the gala and for no reason at all. We run a three-legged race because Tom insists; we lose magnificently; Noah laughs so hard he forgets to guard his joy. Clara sees that laugh and unclenches, shoulders loosening as if she, too, just got permission to be twelve again.

Kelsey from Cove Chatter wanders by with her lemon cardigan and an unreadable face. She buys a donor heart without asking a single question and writes a name I don't know. Boundaries, created by the people who live inside them, can be beautiful.

On the walk home, Clara threads her fingers through mine. Porch light. Peppermint candle. Midnight, pretending he didn't miss us. We kiss like we earned it, because we did, longer than yesterday, careful as always, heat braided with laughter.

"Tomorrow," I say into her hair.

"Tomorrow," she says back, and somewhere, the bell agrees, one, two, three, permission, promise, prayer.

CHAPTER TWENTY

Tide, Tape, And Temptation

CLARA

Edge of the Storm (and a Spark)

The first pop sounds like a cork, cheerful and wrong, before the fairy lights spit sparks.

"Power strip!" I'm already vaulting the counter. The bell above the door jitterrings like a sparrow in a chapel. The room inhales: teenagers, poetry mic, paper hearts shimmering across the front window like a galaxy we made with tape. One tongue of flame licks toward the gold.

Not my window.

I rip the fire blanket off its hook and smother, press, hold. Heat kisses my knuckles through the fabric. Sugar smoke bites the tongue like a burnt marshmallow. "Doors, open!" Maya wedges them with her hips and declares, "Panic is banned," like she can legislate physics.

A body slots in at my shoulder with the steadiness my bones remember. "Left edge, top seam," Ethan says, voice low, hand bracing the ladder while I climb. Thunder counts to three somewhere over the lake.

I press a reinforcement strip across last week's hairline crack. A bead of water tests us, fattens, slides away.

"We're okay," Noah tells his cluster of seventh-graders, the old soul in him threading calm into the air. Then dry: "The lights just needed attention." Ace trots in at Mr. Pierce's heel, sits prim in his teal bow tie, and offers a paw to a trembling kid until laughter wins.

When the shakes leave my hands, other heat remains, the kind I promised myself I'd stop apologizing for. Ethan tips his chin toward the stockroom. I nod. Quiet, door click, the emergency light turning cardboard and twine the color of the moon.

"Breathe with me?" he asks. Infour, holdfour, outfour, pause. My lungs remember.

His thumb finds the soot crescent at the base of my thumb. "Okay?"

"Yes." It lands like a promise in my mouth.

He waits for me to close the distance. I choose the kiss; I choose the stop. When I do, the kiss is steady voltage, not wildfire, warm mouth, careful hands, the kind of yes that keeps you afloat. His palm cups my jaw like it remembers the map; my fingers curve into the damp curl at his nape; the room brightens at the edges. She nods before every advance.

"Terms," I whisper against his smile, the word that saves me from drowning.

"Still signed," he says, breath a little messy, and we both laugh when a kid out front strums a test chord like the universe clearing its throat.

We step back into the lantern light and the cinnamon. I press a fresh silver heart to the glass. For anyone who needs today to be kind. Hope, held together with tape and breath. The label maker hums clicks; ASMR for survival.

Dream; Noon on the Dock. Not storm-dark for once. Boards warm. A dented first-aid tin waits at the end. Inside: our bleachers napkin rules, the ink darker than it should be, and a new line in my hand: Make the timing worthy of the truth. The church bell rings one, two, three. He lifts a hand, not to claim, to ask. The paper heart in my palm doesn't dissolve. It shines. Lake laps in rhythm.

Fundraiser HQ (Forced Proximity) By afternoon, the bookstore hums back to life. Fairy lights: replaced. Mic night: rebranded as "unplugged on purpose." Mayor Tom jogs in with a stack of forms, his tie at half-mast, button flashing Lanterns, Not Pirates. "Small update: the Harbour Promenade vote is tonight. Bring your… civic faces."

"My civic faces have tape on them," I say, handing him a pencil and a roll of hope.

Ethan carries in a box of donor cards like it weighs nothing and everything. We map out the night together: a name table here, a silent auction there, and a therapy dog cameo exactly when nerves need it. Our elbows keep finding each other. Our eyes keep pretending not to notice.

"Dinner after?" he asks softly, like a person who learned to earn yeses. "Not the diner. Somewhere lipstick is expected."

"If he says the right thing, I'll stop bracing." I hear myself say, "Seven. Boathouse."

"Behaving is optional," he murmurs, and my laugh gives me away.

Water laps under the window; the rope bell echoes faint.

ETHAN

TOWN HALL, LANTERNS (NOT PIRATES)

Town hall is a brick shoebox with opinions. Mayor Tom nearly decapitates a rubber plant, describing "ambiance for café chairs and a tiny summer stage," and Mr. Dawes warns that the goose union will sue. Rose requests tea service "for repentant cardiologists." Henry proposes a poetry kiosk. I write 'install AED' in the chamber hallway and underline it twice.

Kelsey from Cove Chatter stands in a lemon cardigan, angle tucked behind her teeth. "Is the doctor who left our town for the city", a glance like a paper cut, "the same doctor now poised to profit from Harbor improvements?"

Clara's fingers find my sleeve. I stand. "I work at the clinic. On Tuesdays, I fix closets. If you see me 'profiting,' it'll be because I convinced three donors to buy paper hearts. Cover the gala. Leave minors and gossip out of it. Boundaries are beautiful."

"Amen," Rose says. "Boundaries are hospitality for the soul." Henry: "Install the kiosk anyway." Laughter changes the air.

After, Kelsey asks for a forgiveness quote. Clara, velvet over steel, hands her a gold heart instead. "Write the name of someone who made you brave." Kelsey blinks and writes Luz. The angle softens; the human stays.

Flashback: The Diner Seventeen. Lemon meringue that could crown a kingdom. "Tell me something true," I said. She tucked her hair behind her ear and confessed, "Books fixed me before I knew I was broken." I admitted the surgery language already living in my hands. We paid in coins. Dale chased us. We ran. Later, we wrote rules on a napkin with a pen that skipped and promised to keep them with mouths we didn't yet know were making vows. Tell the truth even when timing hates it.

Boathouse (Romantic Dinner Plan) Seven o'clock turns the lake to silk. Herb box bells tinkle at the door. Candlelight turns Clara's collarbone into felony evidence and her mouth into strategy. Em, Dale's niece, greets us with menus. We order brown butter halibut and ignore half of it because conversation is finally the meal: clinic stories that don't break HIPAA or hearts; donor wall names; the way geese audit municipal policy like it's their job.

"I should have told you sooner," she says, fingers on her glass. "Nineteen felt like a glass bowl."

"I should have come back," I say. "Houses need roofs, not blueprints." We don't romanticize our regret. We set it down between us like the candle: small, stubborn, useful.

My phone buzzes once, area code New York, too many commas. I am silence without looking.

We walk the boardwalk past the lighthouse and sit on the steps with a blanket she packed because she plans for weather and joy. The kiss is patient heat. When we stop, it's because we choose to, not because we are forced to. I feel taller for it.

"Tomorrow, Ocelot," she says at her door, peppermint candle turning her laugh into a spell. "Grilled cheese judgment panel convenes at six."

"Yes, ma'am," I say, and Midnight headbutts my ankle like a papal blessing. Lake laps wood.

CLARA

Unplugged on Purpose (Almost Kiss)

Open mic night goes candlelit, and the teens sing like they've invented bravery. Ace does morale rounds, teal bow tie catching candlelight; Midnight pretends to disdain all of it, "Amateurs", and then parks himself where he can be admired. I catch Ethan watching me count the till, as if it's math he finally enjoys.

A donation box coughs up an old hardcover; a folded square slips free. My thumb knows the paper before my eyes do. His handwriting, seventeen and certain, unfolds: If the stars are listening, I told them I'm going to fall so hard I break a new verb for it.

"Teenage nonsense that turned into a life," I label it for the store's little glass case of town ephemera. It belongs beside the ticket stub for last year's lantern walk and the photo of Rose and Henry at nineteen.

We close the door on cinnamon and clapping. The square smells like damp grass and charcoal. Mayor Tom, with an alarming amount of ribbon, corrals us into a three-legged race "for team building."

"Left, right," I coach as I tie us with a red bandanna. "No saving the day solo. That's cheating."

We lurch. We go down in the grass with precisely zero elegance. Noah laughs so hard he forgets to hide it. I'd eat turf every week for that sound. He pockets the ribbon like treasure.

Later, on my stoop, Ethan holds up onions and bread like a sacrament. He passes the texture test; Noah confers the solemn nod. Dishes stack. The house hums. In the doorway, our mouths find each other. Heat, humor, restraint. His thumb traces the seam of my sleeve. When he murmurs "Okay?" against my lip, I say "Yes," and he stops first. Banked fire counts as intimacy in this language we're learning.

"Come inside," I almost say, but the words stall behind my teeth. Because tomorrow matters, because timing is still a glass bowl, I'm not sure it won't shatter. Instead, I brush the flour dust from his cheek and let him walk into the night with that look over his shoulder that ruins me in soft ways.

Dream: The Bell I'm on the dock, noonwarm boards, the tin in my palm, the napkin inside. Make the timing worthy of the truth. The church rope drops three bright notes through my ribs. I wake smiling. It holds this time. Lake lap.

Extra Scene: The Call of Quiet. The house settles after Noah goes to bed. I walk through aisles of books that still smell faintly of smoke and cinnamon. The donor wall glows with new hearts. I touch each one like a rosary, my prayer stitched with names of strangers who believe in kindness. One red book cutout waits, empty. My chest aches with the want to fill it, and the fear of what happens if I can't.

I whisper into the air, "Please be enough." It feels childish, but necessary. Midnight curls around my ankles like punctuation.

Outside, laughter drifts from the square where teens are still strumming. The lake answers with its lapsong. And under it all, I feel Ethan's kiss, patient and electric, reminding me that sometimes restraint is louder than chaos.

ETHAN

School Hallway, Small Heroics

The school nurse calls midclinic. "He's okay." My bones still go cold. Noah sits straight, cheek scraped, eyes fierce. "I don't need a lecture," he says. I offer sticker sheets and gauze like a toolkit. He takes one of each.

A kid in the hall had muttered the line he's been waiting to hear since my face came back to town. He measured impulse against consequence and chose the version of himself I want to deserve. I clean the scrape. We text Clara together.

"Throwing a punch is easy," I tell him later on the stoop. "Knowing which part of you is strong enough not to, that's advanced." He snorts. "You make everything sound like a lab." Then he slides me a napkin sketch: a fox trotting along a book spine. "For the AED cabinet. Or whatever."

"Perfect," I say, and the word comes out like a prayer.

Foreshadow & Cliff The square strings lanterns early for the gala. Kelsey buys a donor heart without angling and writes a name I don't know. Cove Chatter posts a neutral photo of the donor wall, caption: Lantern season. The lake goes satin. On Clara's porch, peppermint and laughter and our best kiss yet. We stop with a promise still in it, on purpose.

My phone buzzes in my pocket as I step off her stoop; New York area code, too many commas. I decline. Hydras hate boundaries. Ocelot Night tomorrow. Stay is a verb. Use it.

Across Harbor, the church bell rings three clean notes. Inside the bookstore window, a red book cutout waits for a generous name, but the big tier still gapes, a shortfall humming. Clara's silhouette presses a new heart flat. The timing, finally, looks like it's learning how to be worthy of the truth.

Stay is a verb, I write.

Extra Scene: Ethan's Quiet Drive On the way home, I keep the windows cracked. Night air curls in, salt and cedar. Every streetlamp lays a coin of light across the hood, each one asking: Will you spend this chance, or hoard it?

I drive slower than I need to, past the diner with its neon crown of lemon meringue pies, past the clinic with its single lamp glowing in solidarity. I imagine Clara inside her shop, aligning the hearts, whispering courage into the quiet.

When I pull into my driveway, I don't go inside right away. I lean against the hood; eyes lifted to the faint scatter of stars. I want to tell them I've already fallen, just like the kid I was predicted. And that this time, I'm ready to stay fallen, ready to make the verb of it.

BACKSTAGE ENCOUNTER

The bass from the ballroom thudded through the wall, but in the narrow backstage space, it was only his heartbeat I felt, fast, urgent, matching mine.

He braced a hand beside my head, the other trembling at my hip. 'Tell me to stop,' he whispered, more plea than command.

'I don't want to,' I breathed.

Relief softened his eyes before his mouth found mine, fierce and certain. Years of restraint broke open, but he kissed me like someone careful with what he already loved. Jackets fell, buttons slipped, and laughter caught between us when my hands shook.

When my gown slipped from my shoulders, his palms steadied me as if memorizing, not taking. He lifted me easily, keeping me anchored against him.

'Ethan,' I gasped.

'Say it again,' he whispered, forehead pressed to mine as though the word was holding him steady.

When we finally gave in, it wasn't a claiming, it was a homecoming, every movement threaded with promise. After, he wrapped me in his jacket, his lips brushing my temple like a vow.

CHAPTER TWENTY-ONE

Stormglass & Pullback

CLARA

BOARDWALK, BREATH, AND TOO CLOSE EDGES

Dawn tastes like a secret.

The lake wears a bruise-colored sky; fog skims the surface like vellum being smoothed by careful hands. The air smells of splintered pine, lake iron, and the sharp tang of wet rope. My fingers tingle with the cold as I run the Harbor boardwalk because my thoughts need a leash, and this is the only way I've learned to hold them. Sneakers thud, soft, steady, over wet planks; breath counts itself in fours; the rope bell at the church sends three lazy notes across the water like it's already blessing whatever I'm about to do.

I'm not planning to do anything. That's the problem.

The first slick board is a whisper. The second is a warning.

On the third, my foot slides out as if the lake reached up and tugged. I pinwheel, grab air, grab nothing, and hit the rail with my ribs hard enough to see stars. The rail complains; the world tips; the skittering scrape of rubber against slick wood is the loudest sound I've ever heard. The scent of damp cedar blasts into my lungs like an alarm.

"Clara!"

His voice is the second.

Ethan's running the way he always has, efficient, sure, the kind of fast that looks like it was engineered in another language. He's a block away, then a breath, then his hands are under my elbows, steadying, bracing, pulling me back the three inches between me and the water. My body makes a choice it didn't ask me about; I fold against his chest and let his breath turn my name into a balm. He smells like cedar soap and morning air.

"Easy," he says, low, not a command, a translation. "Knees soft."

"Rail rebellious," I gasp. "Wood treacherous." I'm half laughing because that's what terror turns into once it realizes it failed.

He does a quick physician scan, pupils, pulse at my wrist, the too-fast metronome of adrenaline. His half smile tilts as he studies me. "You okay?"

"You walk up at the exact second I audition for a slapstick routine, and you open with 'you okay.'"

"It's a classic," he says gravely, raising an eyebrow, and his mouth curves. "Also, yes. Are you?"

The answer forms where his fingers bracket my elbows: warm, sure, present. I nod; I hate that my voice shakes. "I'm fine."

"You say 'fine' when you mean 'give me ninety seconds and a wall to lean on.'" He shifts so his body is against the wall. The heat of him turns the cold out of the morning like someone nudged a dimmer a notch toward light.

"Were you out running clinic emergencies?" I ask, throat clearing on the words, trying for casual and landing on breathless. "Or did the lake text you?"

"Lab sample drop," he says. "And coffee for Nurse Joan, or she'll stage a coup. Then I saw you nearly invent a new sport: synchronized sliding."

"Gold medal," I say. "In embarrassment."

His laugh is soft, managed, the way you laugh in a chapel because joy forgot its shoes. My palms are on his chest before I can invent a reason; his breath hitches; so does mine; the boardwalk and the lake and the bell and the town all fade to a narrow, electric corridor that leads directly to his mouth.

I should step back. I step forward.

The kiss lands like something we both remembered at the same time, heat held by care, steady voltage instead of wildfire. His palm cups my jaw as if it learned the map years ago and has been waiting for a visa; my fingers slide into the curl at his nape; the fog around us brightens at the edges. His pulse is a hammer under my hand; my ribs ache with wanting. He tastes like mint and morning and a promise we haven't said out loud yet.

"Terms," I whisper against his smile, because that word keeps me from drowning.

"Still signed," he answers, voice roughened by relief.

He kisses me again, deeper, slower, breath spilling heat across my lips, until a gull laughs overhead like the town's chaperone and I remember I have a spine, a son, a store, and an entire window held together by tape and hope. I lean my forehead to his for one long inhale, then step back into the skin that knows how to function. He doesn't chase the space. The way he doesn't chase makes my knees consider new religions.

"Coffee," he says gently. "Then clinic. Then you can tell me you absolutely did not almost go for a swim."

"Minimalist glitter demands denial." I adjust my sweatshirt and pretend my mouth isn't still tingling.

He walks me toward the square. The day is waking cute and innocent, like it didn't nearly shove me into a lake. People in bright windbreakers practice community; the Honey Tent flaps a sleepy hello; Ace trots past in his teal bow tie, proudly carrying a mitten he found in his mouth, nodding to Midnight, who is pretending to be a gargoyle in my front window.

At the corner, Ethan's phone lights up in his pocket. The preview line is a city number with more commas than decency. He silences it without looking. The restraint is a visible muscle.

We stop under my awning. I can smell the peppermint candle I forgot to blow out last night and the cinnamon that floats over from Maya's kitchen when she's up to her elbows in comfort. My chest does that strange, utopian ache that feels like both a warning and an invitation.

"I have to, " I start.

"Run the world," he finishes. "I know." His thumb skims a damp curl at my temple. "You scared me."

"You found me."

"That's a thing I plan to keep doing."

For one wild second, I picture saying Come over tonight and bring that patience you've been practicing. The second after that, I picture the folder under my counter labeled NOT OUR STORY and the envelope with the red circle around a word that isn't a verdict, just a history. My breath goes smaller. My yes goes careful.

"I should shower," I say. "And remind the donor wall who's in charge."

He nods like he heard the flinch under the joke. "Text me if the boardwalk gets uppity again."

"It only listens to therapy dogs."

"Good thing I know one."

He leaves me under the awning with a kiss to my cheek like sunlight. I watch him cross Harbor, greet Mr. Pierce, ruffle Ace's ear, and disappear into the clinic door with his shoulders set to useful.

The lake exhales. The bell curtsies three clean notes down the street. I stand there feeling both rescued and unmoored, and tell myself that cautious is not the same as coward.

I have a store to open. And a heart that lately insists on acting like a window.

❦

RUMOR PHYSICS, DREAM GRAMMAR

The bell over the door warms up with the first customer and becomes a fixture by the fifth. The shop smells like damp wool turning into comfort and the kind of paper that's been held by a hundred hands. I taped two new hearts to the donor window: Alma Ruiz in careful black script and Luz in block letters that surprised a reporter into crying.

"Your window looks like a constellation," Rose tells me, arriving with Henry and a red scarf that has never met a gloomy day it didn't chase off. "I approve."

"Lanterns, not pirates," Henry says solemnly, tapping the 'No Pirate Crosswalks' petition with a pencil. "Democracy is just branding with rules."

Maya slides in with lattes and a look that x-rays feelings. "I heard you almost submitted to the lake," she says. "And by 'heard' I mean Tom texted me, 'Is our bookstore owner waterproof?' accompanied by six lighthouse emojis."

"I slipped," I mutter, and my voice does that ridiculous thing where it blushes. "Ethan witnessed. There was… a kiss."

Maya's smile is the exact size of my future. "Good. Also: tonight's zoning meeting will be a circus, and I've already packed popcorn. Keep your elbows sharp and your boundaries sharper."

"Boundaries are beautiful," I say, testing the sentence in my mouth.

"Now you're getting it." She kisses my cheek, steals my pen, and writes 'For anyone who needs today to be kind' on a silver heart, as if kindness itself had requested a nametag.

Noah drifts out of the back with graphite on his thumb, his sketchbook under his arm, and a smile he's trying to pretend he doesn't own. Mom looks lighter today, a flicker in his eyes seems to say. "Midnight won't stop sitting on page twenty-seven," he reports. "Which I take as editorial approval of the fox."

"Midnight is a ruthless acquisitions editor," I say. "And a tyrant." I lower my voice. "You okay?"

He shrugs in a way that means yes, but also the world is a complicated instrument. "School was… school." He angles the sketchbook so I can see a new version of the crosswalk, open books flowing into each other, a fox tail hidden in the margin you'd only notice if you slowed down to look.

"Drivers will," I say. "Some people are smarter at twenty-seven when a fox tells them to be." And some lovers need to slow down too, whispers a part of me I don't name.

He tries not to smile and fails spectacularly, then ruins his cool by reaching for Midnight. The cat, in a shock to no one, allows affection as if he invented it. Amateurs, Midnight seems to purr.

By afternoon, we're a tide pool: retirees reading history with the intensity of spies; tourists who wandered in for goose souvenirs and stayed for cinnamon; the Crossword Crew plotting a blue light secret for the gala program. Kelsey from Cove Chatter hovers over the new releases like a lemon cardigan with questions. I wave her toward the press sheet taped to the counter: Poetry, donor wall, silent auction. No minors. No prying. She reads it twice, then buys a gold heart and writes a name I don't know.

Between customers, I label donation envelopes and practice not thinking about the way Ethan's mouth felt, finding mine this morning under a sky the color of mercy. "Minimalist glitter," I tell the window, and the window reflects a woman who keeps saying she's fine and keeps meaning something more complicated.

When the square has emptied to wind and the bell has gone shy, I sit on the stool behind the counter and let my eyes close.

The dream steps in so quietly that it almost doesn't count as sleep.

Not stormy tonight. Noon. The dock boards are warm under my feet, the lake the exact color of a secret told only to people who can keep it. A dented first-aid tin waits at the end; inside, our napkin of rules is folded small: No running without a goodbye. No turning silence into punishment. Tell the truth even when timing hates it. A new line in my hand that wasn't there before: Make the timing worthy of the truth.

A gull calls. The church bell jangles three clean notes through my chest. When I look up, he's there, not to claim, just to ask. I lift my palm. The paper heart in it doesn't dissolve. It shines.

I wake with Midnight's tail laid across my wrist like punctuation. The clock says two fifteen. The window says lantern. My bones say: 'Careful' is not the same as 'no'.

❧

The Meeting, The Stage, The Dock

Town hall is a brick shoebox with opinions and a rubber plant that has seen things. Mayor Tom almost decapitates said rubber plant, describing "harbor ambience for café chairs and a tiny stage for summer sets, picture it!" The ten-year-old in the second row boos in a pirate voice.

Kelsey's lemon cardigan takes notes with hunger. Mr. Dawes argues that the goose union will sue any attempted at ambiance. Rose requests tea service "for repentant cardiologists." Henry proposes a poetry kiosk. I write AED in the chamber hall on my agenda and underline it twice because I'm the kind of woman who believes in practical magic.

When the floor opens, Kelsey tries her angle. "Is the doctor who left our town for the city", a glance that could papercut, "the same doctor now positioned to profit from Harbor improvements?"

I feel the town turn its face toward me like a sunflower to the weather. Ethan stands first. "I work at the clinic. On Tuesdays, I fix closets and alphabetize the crash cart when Nurse Joan lets me. If you see me 'profiting,' it'll be because I convinced three more donors to buy paper hearts." His gaze scans the room without flinching. "Cover the gala. Leave minors and gossip out of it. Boundaries are beautiful."

Rose says "Amen" in the voice she uses for hymns and victories. Henry adds, "Install the kiosk anyway." The room laughs; the air gets kinder.

After the vote is blessedly tabled, Kelsey intercepts me by the bulletin board. "A quote about forgiveness?" she asks, gentler now.

"Happy to talk donor walls, poetry, therapy dogs, and sidewalk chalk," I say. "Forgiveness is private." I hand her a gold heart and a Sharpie. "Write the name of someone who made you brave."

Her jaw works around an answer; a name arrives behind her eyes; she writes Luz and tapes it to the window with hands that look like they're remembering a doorway.

Ethan's shoulder finds mine as we step into the night. Harbor lights throw coins across the street; The Boathouse glows like an invitation you're allowed to accept. "We're still on for dinner," he says, cautious as a man carrying all the breakable things.

I imagine saying, I want to, which is not the same as I can. My mouth does something thinner. "I should get back. The store."

It hurts his face in the soft way, the way men hide and learn not to. He disguises the flinch as a nod. "Another night," he says. "Ocelot."

"I know," I whisper. It sounds like a promise; it feels like a delay. My phone buzzes once with a preview of Lila's name. I don't open it. Not yet.

Later, after counting the till and writing three more careful names, I walk to the lake because sometimes you need to practice your spine in public. The lighthouse watches like it's taken vows. The wind has decided to be kind. Footsteps arrive at my shoulder with a rhythm my body is learning on and under purpose.

"I can walk you home," he offers. No pressure in it. Just an option.

"Walk me to the end of the dock," I counter, because if I'm going to choose, I want witnesses.

We go. Boards creak. Water speaks in hushes. At the end, I turn because if I don't, I'll jump into something I haven't named yet. He's there, older and steadier than the boy who promised the stars he'd invent a new verb for us. His hand lifts, not to claim, to ask.

I put my palm on his chest instead of his hand. He understands anyway.

The kiss is slow and sure and human. Not a rescue, not a test. A choice. Heat gathers. My pulse trips. My coat tugs against his fingers; his breath feathers my throat. The part of me that wants to run says stay; the part that wants to sprint says wait. I make a new deal with myself at the edge where water becomes grammar: No more kissing until after the gala.

His mouth curves against mine like he already knew I'd say it. "I can be patience."

"Prove it," I whisper.

"I am," he whispers back.

He walks me home without trying to turn the porch into a threshold. Midnight is waiting on the newel post like a verdict. He headbutts Ethan's shin with the kind of magnanimity that suggests paperwork was filed. We laugh. We don't linger. We are terrible at not lingering. We survive our own better angels anyway.

Inside, the house rests like it trusts me.

CLARA

THE PULLBACK, THE NOTE, THE PROMISE I HAVEN'T SAID

Morning arrives with rain lazy enough to qualify as polite. I make lists because lists keep me from rearranging a future I haven't earned yet.

Gala: confirm poetry order (Lila wants mic duty, heaven help us), finalize silent auction baskets, print donor cards, rehearse "lanterns, not pirates" in my soul. One donor left to land: Mrs. Callahan. If she walks, the clinic loses Saturday hours.

Clinic: drop spare batteries for AED, label closet shelves NOT HOL-IDAY • MAYBE?

Store: refill romance spinner, storm-kissed specials to the front, feed Midnight the exact amount that prevents mutiny.

Heart: breathe; be kind; do not kiss Ethan until after the gala; do not confuse caution with punishment.

At ten, Lila texts: Landing Friday, don't let him pretend he doesn't need a new shirt. My smile happens without permission. A second later, my hand goes cold. If Lila is coming, she will bring his life with her, calls with commas; offers with teeth. Packages with commas travel in packs, my mind warns.

"Cowardice," I tell the kettle as it complains its way to boiling. "It is not the same as careful."

The bell performs its jingle and delivers Kelsey's lemon cardigan and a small white envelope she sets on the counter like an apology. "No byline," she says. "But this was taped to the office door. Thought you should see it before the internet does."

Inside: a printout of a four-year-old article about Ethan with the incriminating word circled in red again and a handwritten note that reads, You can't buy this town.

"So dramatic," I mutter, but my rib cage tightens like a dress I don't fit anymore.

Kelsey's face is a new kind of careful. "There's a story in here. It's not the one I thought I came for."

"Make it the lanterns," I say. "Not the pirates."

She smiles like she might actually listen.

I file the letter in NOT OUR STORY, label a fresh red book, and write For the kid who needs the fox on page 27 in my neatest hand because sometimes the only move is to make beauty heavier than noise.

At noon, I carry thermoses of tea to the library end cap for the Lakewalk Moms while they test which angle best flatters Noah's crosswalk sketch. On my way back, the clinic door opens, and Ethan steps out with a clipboard and a grin he doesn't know is for me until it is. His phone buzzes. He flips it over without looking.

"Hydras hate boundaries," I say, and the joke untenses my spine.

He grins. "Good thing I'm fluent in fences now."

"Show me," I say before I can stop my mouth. "Friday. Ocelot. Then, after the gala, we can… open the gate."

Color finds his face, steady, grateful, a man who knows how unreasonable hope can feel and chooses it anyway. "Deal."

We don't kiss. The not-kissing feels like we invented a new nerve just so we could feel it.

That night, long after the bell's goodnight and the square has stopped pretending it's busy, I set the last of the gold hearts in the window and stand back. The glass throws a galaxy back at me in careful script. Behind me, Midnight chirps, impatient, loving, judgey. In the distance, the lighthouse blinks its patient eye.

I press my palm to the pane and make a promise I haven't said out loud yet: Make the timing worthy of the truth.

The lake breathes. The bell rings once, twice, three times. It sounds like permission.

Night tastes like permission.

CHAPTER TWENTY-TWO

Lanterns, Not Pirates

CLARA

Small towns never forget, but tonight I decide what they remember.

Dream: The Dock That Wouldn't Let Me Lie

The lake starts as a hush, glass instead of water, the color of a secret I've been refusing to tell. Noonlight turns the boards warm under my bare feet. At the end of the dock sits the same dented first-aid tin from every dream I've had since I was eighteen and pretending I understood forever.

Inside: the napkin he and I signed with a pen that kept skipping, as if even ink knew what promises cost. No running without a goodbye. No turning silence into punishment. Tell the truth even when timing hates it. Someone, me, has written one more line in neat, stubborn letters: Make the timing worthy of the truth. My palm tingles as if the dock itself is taking my pulse. I count to five, waiting for the courage to keep up.

The church bell sends three clean notes across the water. A figure lifts a hand at the shoreline, not to claim. To ask. I open my palm and expect the paper heart to dissolve, the way it always does right before I wake. This time it shines.

I wake with Midnight's tail laid across my wrist like punctuation, and the knowledge that I've run out of ways to lie to myself.

The Tough Love I Didn't Want (But Needed)

Maya doesn't bother with hello. She hip checks the bookstore door like a woman elbowing fate, drops two lattes on the counter, and plants both hands on my shoulders. "Okay. Rip off the Band-Aid. You pulled back last night. Why?"

"I didn't,"

"You did," she says, voice all velvet over steel. "You told me you want a life with breath and books and that man, and then you put your heart in timeout like it tracked mud on the rug."

My laugh sounds like a paper cut. "Timing."

"Timing is just fear wearing lipstick." She crowds closer, softer now. "You survived so hard you forgot what wanting feels like without an apology stapled to it. Wanting is not a crime, Clara."

"I have Noah,"

"And he has you," she says. "He also has eyes, and he's watching you teach him either courage or caution turned into punishment. Choose."

I swallow. The window, our donor wall, glows in the gray morning like a lantern. Gold hearts, silver hearts, a single red paper book waiting for the name bold enough to belong there. For anyone who needs today to be kind, I wrote yesterday, and meant it for everyone but me. In its center, space yawns, waiting.

Maya follows my gaze. "You can keep holding back until the timing apologizes to you. Or you can make the timing worthy of the truth."

I press my palm to the glass. The tape warms under my skin like a yes. "He asked me to dinner."

"And you said…?"

"I said 'after the gala.'"

"Build your bridge," she says, smiling, not triumphant but relieved. "Invite him to dinner here, with Noah. Nothing fancy. Soup. Sandwiches. Real life. Then tell him the thing you keep only saying to me."

"What if I choke on the words?"

"Then I'll Heimlich your feelings. Don't test me."

She squeezes my fingers, leaves me with caffeine and courage, and goes to bully a muffin tray into perfection.

The Almost That Slid Out from Under Me

Fog wears the lake like silk when I lace up and run the boardwalk to sweat out the buzzing. The first slick plank is a whisper. The second is a warning. On the third, my foot flies and my ribs discover the rail with a jolt bright enough to make the world stutter.

"Clara!"

His voice is a warm shock. Ethan's already a block away, then somehow right there, hands under my elbows, body a wall I didn't know I'd need. "Knees soft," he says, like you can talk physics into behaving. "Breathe."

"I'm breathing," I lie, and then, because honesty is apparently my new sport, I fold against him until my heart stops trying to drum a hole in my sternum.

He does the quick scan, pupils, pulse, and the ridiculous metronome at my wrist. "Okay?"

"I will be."

"You say 'fine' when you mean 'give me ninety seconds and a wall.'" He becomes the wall. The smell of cedar soap and morning does terrible, lovely things to my knees.

We kiss like a decision and not a rescue, heat curled around care, steadied before it can sprint. Our mouths ask, then answer. When I pull away, I press my forehead to his and promise both of us, "After the gala."

He nods like a vow. "I can be patience."

We walk back under the awning in companionable silence while the town decides to be itself again. The bell over my door clears its throat and jangles once, as if reminding me that Willow Cove loves a good show. I straighten my spine, open the shop, and let the day happen.

ETHAN

The Part Where I Learn to Love Fences

Hydras hate boundaries. I'm learning to love them.

Sloane's number; Argus something with too many commas in its subject lines, buzzes my pocket while I'm alphabetizing the clinic's crash cart. I flip the phone face down, aligning epinephrine with saline, feeling something stubborn in my chest click into place. Lantern light from the hall streaks across the linoleum as if the town approves.

Joan, who runs this place with the inexhaustible patience of weather, leans in the doorway with her coffee. "If alphabetizing keeps you from emailing venture capitalists, alphabetize away."

"Working on a fence," I say.

"Good boy," she answers without a smile and tosses me the key to the storage closet I keep rescuing from its own history. Inside: one sulking Jbend I've learned to coax into good behavior and three boxes labeled HOLIDAY • MAYBE? that are on their last chance at redemption. I make an order until the order makes me back.

At ten, I detoured to the bookstore with two lattes I absolutely did not brew. Clara opens the door like a soft yes. The window throws gold and silver back at us. I don't touch her. I do not want to. "Dinner?" I ask. "Not the diner. A table where you don't have to translate the specials. The Boathouse does brown butter halibut with lemon thyme carrots."

"After the gala," she says, which is not a no. It's a plan.

"Then let me help you build up to it."

She gives me a look I've been chasing since we were seventeen and invincible under bleachers. "Thursday. Soup and sandwiches with Noah. Real life before candlelight."

"Copy that." My ribs do something foolish and human. My umbrella, as usual, is inside out by the door, because perfection has never been my brand.

The Boy Who Keeps Teaching Me

Noon, the school nurse. "He's okay." My bones still chill.

Noah's cheek is scraped. His mouth is a line he hammered there himself. He rejects the sticker sheet but pockets it anyway, because being twelve is mostly contradictions. "I don't need a lecture," he says.

"I didn't bring one," I answer, then lower my voice. "Want the short version or the longer one where I say something embarrassingly wise?"

He considers. "Short."

"You handled yourself."

He nods once. Later, on the bookstore stoop, he shows me a fox trotting along a book spine in graphite lines that already know more than they should. His grip, firm and thoughtful, teaches me patience without a word. "For the clinic. Or whatever."

"For the AED cabinet," I say, throat not to be trusted. "So, people slow down for wonder before they reach for panic."

He pretends not to smile. Midnight sprawls across the sketch like punctuation; Ace passes with Mr. Pierce and grants us both a dignified nod, the way decorated colleagues do.

"Minimalist Glitter Champions," Noah mutters, testing a team name under his breath.

Town Hall, With Rubber Plant

By evening, the brick shoebox with opinions has filled itself with every kind of neighbor. Mayor Tom nearly decapitates a rubber plant while describing the Harbor Promenade. "Imagine café chairs. A tiny stage. Poetry kiosks!" He beams at Henry, who beams back like a man envisioning a sestina about stop signs.

Kelsey from Cove Chatter stands in a lemon cardigan, holding a notebook that looks as if it could be cut. Ink smudges her index finger. "Is the doctor who left our town for the city", her glance slices, "the same doctor planning to profit from these improvements? Sources say: investments."

Clara's hand finds my sleeve. I stand because I am done letting other people draft this script. "I work at the clinic. On Tuesdays, I fix closets. If you see me 'profiting,' it'll be because I convinced three more donors to buy paper hearts." I let the room breathe. "Cover the gala. Leave minors and gossip out of it. Boundaries are beautiful."

"Amen," Rose says, exactly the way she says it in church. Then adds, "Boundaries are hospitality for the soul." Henry: "Install the kiosk anyway." The laugh in the room is the good kind, the one that knocks sharp corners off without smashing the furniture.

After, Kelsey asks Clara for a quote about forgiveness. Clara hands her a gold heart and a Sharpie. "Write the name of someone who made you brave." Kelsey blinks, writes Luz, tapes it to the glass, and surprises herself by crying. Lanterns, not pirates. Maybe we're rewriting this town's favorite genre.

The Patience I Promised

We walk the boardwalk in a breeze that smells like clean slate. The old lighthouse at the edge of the cove blinks once, steady as patience itself. At Clara's door, I want to ask for everything and settle for now. She smiles with her mouth and her eyes, which is how you know she means it. "Dinner Thursday. After the gala, the rest."

"Copy that," I say for the second time, and mean thank you for trusting me with your pacing.

On the way home, I write myself a note and stick it to the cupboard where I'll see it when I make coffee: Stay is a verb. Use it.

CLARA

Rumor Physics (And Why I Won't Be Its Lab Rat)

Gossip travels in Willow Cove like heat through cinnamon. This morning's Cove Chatter DM wants a "forgiveness arc" Pullquote. I sent the press sheet we printed yesterday: Poetry, donor wall, and silent auction. No minors. No prying. If you want a story, buy a heart.

They do. Luz, in a hand that looks like it has practiced hiding before.

Kelsey brings a white envelope to my counter midafternoon. "This was taped to our office door. I thought you should see it before the internet does."

Inside, a four-year-old article about Ethan with one word circled in red. A note: You can't buy this town.

"Dramatic," I say dryly, while my ribs try on panic like a dress I hate.

Kelsey's voice is different today. Her hand trembles. "There's a story here, but it isn't that one." She leaves me with a card and a promise to aim her curiosity where it won't bruise.

I slide the printout into a folder labeled NOT OUR STORY, then cut a fresh red book and write the name I've been saving at Noah's suggestion: For the kid who needs the fox on page 27. I tape it in the center where the light can find it. Midnight flops dramatically across the folder as if censoring it himself.

The Dinner I Said Out Loud

By six, the store smells like tomato soup and butter, which is to say bravery.

The kitchen smells like butter and something softer, like patience reheated. We stand shoulder to shoulder at the stove, trading bites of grilled cheese as if dinner could disguise the fact that we've run out of excuses.

When he leans past me for the pan, his arm brushes mine. I should step away. I don't.

"Terms?" I murmur, because even in this small morning, the word matters.

"Still signed," he answers, low.

I set the spatula down before it betrays me. His hand finds my jaw, careful; my mouth finds his, deliberate. The kiss builds not out of storm, but quiet, warm, steady, anchored. When he lifts me onto the counter, it's less urgency than inevitability. His hands trace my thighs, waiting for me to pull him closer. I do.

The heat between us hums like current through copper, steady, singing. Every movement is deliberate: my fingers in his hair, his mouth trailing the line of my throat, the way he pauses to ask, "Okay?" even when the answer is written in the way I arch toward him.

When we break, it's with laughter caught between our mouths and the smell of cinnamon creeping in from the street. "Water?" he whispers, grinning at himself.

"Always," I manage, and this time I kiss him like the word is punctuation.

After dishes, we don't touch the couch; we sort the silent auction sheets. Every few minutes, I look up and catch Ethan looking at me like I'm a language he used to speak and has been studying again in secret.

When he leaves, he kisses my cheek. "After the gala," he says, and somehow that's not a delay. It's a promise wearing patience like a suit that finally fits.

Flashback: The Letter I Kept

He wrote me a note on a concession stand napkin the night we figured out kissing. If the stars are listening, I told them I'm going to fall so hard I'll break a new verb for it. I tucked it in my jewelry box like a mouthful of sugar and salt.

Tonight, after the door clicks and the house hums, I find the napkin again under a velvet pouch of broken earrings. The ink has bled at the edges, like even paper can't help crying. I set it beside the press sheet that says NO PRYING and feel the shape of a life that finally wants me to step into it.

I text Maya: Thursday happened. After the gala, I tell him the thing.

She replies with eleven heart emojis and a goose gif, which is the town's dialect for "I love you; don't flinch now."

I set the table for three tomorrow. Promise phrased as an action.

ETHAN

The Edge, The Offer, The Answer

The email subject line is a bribe dressed as salvation. Final Package. Name your number.

I do not open it. I forward it to Lila with two words: Ocelot Night. She replies with a fox emoji, a knife, and Proud of you. Wear the blue shirt for the gala.

At the clinic the next morning, I hang Noah's fox sketch above the AED. People will slow for wonder. They always do.

Joan pauses beside me. "You look like a man who found a door and is waiting his turn to knock on it."

"I promised patience," I say. "Thursday was soup and breathing. After the gala is everything."

"Then rest your shoulders," she says. "Big days like promises travel better when you don't try to carry them all in your neck."

The Good Witch of Harbor Street

If Willow Cove had a witch, she'd be the woman who tapes little hearts to windows and manages to make a town believe it's kinder than it was yesterday. I pass the bookstore at dusk and find Clara under the awning, pressing the latest heart flat, palm warm against glass.

She looks up. The evening edits her in gold. "Lanterns, not pirates," she says, grinning now when she quotes Tom, like the slogan has grown on her.

"Lanterns," I agree. "And fences that keep the hydras on the other side."

"After the gala," she reminds me, as if I could forget. Her gaze flickers to my mouth and away like a sparrow.

I touch the frame of her door with a knuckle, the way you greet a threshold you respect. "I can wait."

"Good," she says, and the word is a welcome that lets me sleep.

Foreshadow: What the Bell Knows

In three days, we'll string fairy lights and teach the donor wall to look like a galaxy. Lila will read a poem that makes Henry blush and Rose cry. Kelsey will stand at the edge of the room with her lemon cardigan and a new story in her notebook. Ace will pose for selfies like a dignitary. Midnight will wander through the program like a small god auditioning for benevolence. And somewhere between the silent auction and the last poem, Clara will reach for my hand in public and not let go.

Tonight, the rope bell rings once, twice, three times. I put my palm against my door, then my chest, and hear it answer inside my bones. Stay is a verb. Use it.

And in the echo, I hear the chapter one bell, the one that made Midnight tilt his head as if he owned the store. Continuity, like love, rings truer the second time.

CHAPTER TWENTY-THREE

Soup, Sandwiches, And Promises

EDGE, SPARK, BREATH

CLARA

The boardwalk looks innocent until it doesn't.

Fog wears the lake like silk. The first wet plank is a whisper. The second, a warning. On the third, my foot flies and my ribs find the rail with a jolt that turns stars into confetti behind my eyes.

"Clara!"

He's a block away and then somehow right there, hands under my elbows, steadiness wrapped in rain-cool scrubs and cedar soap.

"Knees soft," Ethan says. Not a command. A translation. "Breathe."

"I am." A lie, shaped like a syllable.

He scans like old habit, pupils, pulse, a metronome tap at my wrist that says you're okay, even if your body forgot. I splay my fingers over the rail until splinters threaten a mutiny. The lake inhales. So do I.

"I just reinvented synchronized sliding," I say, because jokes are flotation devices and I collect them.

"Gold medal." His mouth tilts. "No podium."

I should step back. I step forward. His shirt is damp where my palms land. The morning edits the edges of his jaw in pale light. It's absurd that relief can be this…warm.

The kiss lands like something we both remembered at the same time. Not wildfire; current. Heat curled around care. His palm cups my jaw the way it used to, like he learned the map before he knew what maps were for. My pulse stops trying to audition for percussion and starts keeping time.

"Terms," I whisper against his smile, because the word keeps me from drowning.

"Still signed." His breath skims my mouth; the dock remembers how to hold.

A gull laughs overhead, the boardwalk decides to behave, and my sense of humor staggers back to its post. We walk under my awning in that companionable silence people earn.

"You scared me," he says, thumb brushing a curl that stuck to my temple.

"You found me."

"That's a thing I plan to keep doing."

Inside, the bell jangles its good morning like it wants credit for the rescue. I flip the sign to OPEN. The donor wall glows, gold and silver hearts like a DIY galaxy, one red book cutout still waiting for the name brave enough to live there. I press my palm to the glass until warmth seeps through paper and tape and me.

"Dinner Thursday," I tell him. "Soup. Sandwiches. Real life." I swallow the rest, after the gala, everything, because courage is a muscle and mine is still stretching.

He hears it anyway. "Copy that."

He leaves for the clinic with a palm on the frame like a benediction. I watch his shoulders set to useful and pretend my mouth isn't still tingling.

Dream — noon on the dock

Boards warm beneath bare feet. A dented first-aid tin at the end, same as every dream since eighteen. Inside: the napkin we wrote on under the bleachers, ink darker than it has any right to be. No running without a goodbye. No turning silence into punishment. Tell the truth even when timing hates it. And in my hand, a new line I don't remember writing: Make the timing worthy of the truth.

The church bell drops three clean notes through my ribs. A figure lifts a hand onshore, not to claim, to ask. I open my palm expecting the paper heart to melt like it always does.

It shines.

I wake with Midnight's tail draped across my wrist like punctuation and the particular calm that follows a decision you haven't said out loud yet.

Family Practice

ETHAN

Ocelot Night has rules: grilled cheese must pass the judge's texture test; the cat is allowed to critique; civilians are not permitted to panic.

I bring bread and onions, and the kind of patience you have to learn on purpose. Noah leans his elbows on the counter like he's presiding over a tribunal. "If it squeaks, it fails," he says.

"Noted." I brown butter until it smells like trust, slow the onions until they taste like a promise I can keep, align slices the way Nurse Joan makes me align ampules. Midnight pretends not to beg. Accepts tribute anyway.

We eat at the small table. Elbows brush. Real life spreads between bowls of tomato soup and the day's rumor inventory.

"Mayor Tom wants pirate hats," Noah reports, deadpan. "For the crosswalk unveiling."

"Lanterns, not pirates," Clara and I say at the exact same time, and the look we share is a whole conversation.

After dishes, Midnight patrols, granting papal headbutts and side-eye as needed. We triage the gala program with pencil smudges and a growing sense of we. Every few minutes, I catch Clara studying me like a language she used to speak and is remembering by ear. I try not to show how much it undoes and assembles me at the same time.

Later, we migrate to the couch because movies with improbable rope bridges are the ideal chaperones for a trio learning how to be a unit. Halfway in, Noah migrates the way tides do, shoulder to Clara's side, head to her lap, and the room exhales. I look away so I don't cry in public. (I do not entirely succeed.)

We pause the movie halfway when the popcorn burns, filling the kitchen with a smoky haze that turns into laughter. Clara waves the towel, Noah insists this is an omen of culinary rebellion, and Midnight leaps on the counter like a tiny, furry firefighter. It's chaotic, imperfect, ordinary, and I have never loved anything more.

When the credits roll, we stack plates the way people do when they've learned that ordinary counts. At the door, peppermint candles and paper hearts turn the air to something I could live in forever.

"After the gala," she says, eyes on my mouth like a confession she's not ready to sign in ink.

"Patience," I say. "I brought extra." I mean it.

She smiles. We kiss like we earned it, long, careful, heat banked instead of burned. When I murmur, "Okay?" she answers, "Yes," and I stop first because tomorrow is my favorite part of this story.

Flashback: the diner note Seventeen, the night tasted like clover and bad coffee. Tell me something true, I said. Books fixed me before I knew I was broken, she confessed. I admitted the surgery language that already lived in my hands. We paid in coins; Dale chased us; we ran. Later, under the bleachers, we wrote rules on a concession stand napkin with a pen that kept skipping like even ink knew the cost of vows. I kissed each line. She kept the napkin in her jewelry box. I kept it under my rib.

RUMOR PHYSICS

CLARA

Gossip in Willow Cove travels like heat through cinnamon. Today's flavor: forgiveness arc.

Kelsey (wearing a lemon cardigan, holding a sharp pencil) buys a gold heart without trying to invade my privacy. She writes "Luz" in block letters and cries, as if she has surprised herself with bravery. I tape it in the cluster where the light is kind.

At noon, we hang Noah's crosswalk sketch on the library endcap. Kids slow down because wonder demands it. A second grader in galaxy leggings spots the fox hidden at page twenty-seven and whispers, "There." Noah pretends to shrug and fails spectacularly. Ethan stays within reach and out of the way, exactly the distance a boy uses to measure a man.

Back at the shop, an anonymous envelope waits under the till, another printout of that old article with a red circle around a word that isn't a verdict, just a history. A sticky note reads, You can't buy this town.

"Dramatic," I tell Midnight, who sits on it like a paperweight and flicks his tail in contempt at anonymous nouns.

I file it under NOT OUR STORY, cut a fresh red book, and write the name I've been saving (Noah's idea): For the kid who needs the fox on page 27. I press it to the center of the glass until the window looks less like a target and more like a lantern.

Maya arrives with lattes and a sermon. "You pulled back," she says, eyes kind, voice steel. "Timing is just fear wearing lipstick. Build your bridge." I hate how right she is. I build anyway.

That evening, the square smells like grass and charcoal. Mayor Tom corrals us into a three-legged race "for team building." Ethan ties the bandanna around our ankles. "Left, right," I coach. We lurch. We go down. Noah laughs so hard he forgets to guard it. I would eat grass every weekend for that sound.

Later, the town hall turns into a theater because, of course, it does. Tom pitches the Harbor Promenade; Henry requests a poetry kiosk; Rose asks for tea service "for repentant cardiologists"; Mr. Dawes warns the goose union will sue. Kelsey tries a sharper angle. Ethan stands first, clear, steady: "I fix closets on Tuesdays and convince people to buy paper hearts. Boundaries are beautiful."

"Amen," Rose says like a hymn.

On the walk home, he reaches for my hand and doesn't force it. I let him have it because courage is also a muscle that grows when you feed it soup and honesty.

"Thursday," he reminds me. "Soup. Sandwiches. Real life."

"After the gala," I say. "The rest." My yes has a spine now. It feels like mine.

LANTERN REHEARSALS

ETHAN

Hydras hate fences. I'm learning to love them.

Argus Health emails with too many commas while I'm alphabetizing the crash cart. I forward the whole thing to Lila with two words; Ocelot Night, and slide the phone face down. Joan tosses me the closet key like a prize in a game I finally understand: stay.

By dusk, I'm under Clara's awning with my palms on the doorframe because thresholds deserve respect. Inside, she's writing names on gold hearts like prayers with tape. Outside, the lighthouse blinks patience over the water.

"We're almost there," she says. The window glows like a promise we can touch. "Lanterns, not pirates."

"Lanterns," I say, and think of the napkin I carried under my rib for a decade like a compass.

We do not kiss. Not because we don't want to. Because we do, and because patience is proof, not punishment.

On my kitchen table, I write myself a note and pin it where the kettle boils: Stay is a verb. Use it. Then I tape Noah's fox above the AED at the clinic, so Wonder can keep teaching medicine what to do.

I linger over the kettle longer than usual, picturing soup steam rising in Clara's kitchen, her laughter folding into Noah's quick commentary, the warmth of a family that doesn't need definitions to exist. That picture alone adds another anchor to my ribcage.

CLARA

After closing, I set three more hearts, straighten the red book, and stand back. The window throws a galaxy at me. Behind me, the store hums like it trusts me again.

I put my palm against the glass and say the thing I've been thinking for weeks but only wrote in a dream: "Make the timing worthy of the truth."

Somewhere, the bell rings once, twice, three times.

It sounds like permission.

I lean my forehead to the cool pane and imagine the gala lights stringing across the square, voices weaving through one another, and Ethan's hand finding mine in the crowd. For the first time in years, the picture in my mind doesn't feel like a wish. It feels like an appointment. One I intend to keep.

FORESHADOW The voicemail arrives after midnight, a city number with commas in its voice and urgency in its subject line. I don't listen yet. The red book holds. The lake breathes. The path from here to joy is built from soup, tape, and the kind of patience that proves itself by staying.

And somewhere in my dreams, the fox from Noah's sketch lifts its head and walks across the bridge we haven't finished building yet, tail high, steps steady, as if to tell me: bridges don't wait for courage, they grow from it.

CHAPTER TWENTY-FOUR

The Fundraiser Spark

THE NIGHT THE LIGHTS TESTED US

CLARA

The bell above the library room behaves as if it had taken a public speaking class. Its jingle echoes the very first day I opened these doors, thirteen chapters and countless storms ago.

"Welcome to the Books & Hearts Gala," I say into the mic that may or may not be plotting to abandon me. "No pirates. Only lanterns."

Laughter ripples through Willow Cove. Fairy lights string the ceiling like constellations we made ourselves. On the far wall, our donor window gleams, gold and silver paper hearts pressed to glass with names I wrote in careful ink. A single red book cutout waits in the center for a very generous someone. It glows like a promise.

My promise, apparently, is to juggle. Mayor Tom waves a sheaf of programs. Maya levitates a tray of cinnamon knots like a benevolent witch. Rose and Henry stage-whisper about seating near the emergency exit ("not because we're old, because we're clever, repentant cardiologists can't run fast"). Mr. Pierce parades Ace in a teal bow tie. Midnight supervises from the poetry shelf, pretending he's too important to be present and entirely present anyway.

Across the room, Ethan's shoulders are set to useful. He's been on his feet since dawn, clinic, storage closet, stern pep talk to a sink that had the nerve to drip. He catches my eye with a look I feel under my ribs: here. The word lands like a hand at the small of my back.

"Clara?" Maya touches my elbow. "Kelsey from Cove Chatter wants a quote about forgiveness. I printed the press sheet with our Boundaries Are Beautiful policy. Tom and I co-wrote it. I will body-block as needed."

"Thank you," I whisper. The mic tries to squeal. I give it a look; my son respects it, and the mic reconsiders its life choices.

The Harbor Street Strings start a Willow Cove rendition of a love song that once lived in a city. I count chairs and cue cards and breaths. I am a woman who tapes hope to glass. I can handle a gala.

The lights flicker. Once. Twice.

"Stay with me," I tell the ceiling calmly in the tone you use on toddlers and weather. The lights are steady.

I launch into the first announcement, silent auction rules, and therapy-dog meet-and-greet times, and the room leans closer. When I introduce the unveiling of Noah's crosswalk concept for the library corner, the bell in my chest rings three clean notes. I spot Noah near the donor wall, fingers worrying the edge of his sketchbook, old-soul eyes pretending not to care. Ace nods his hand; Midnight allows a blink in approval; the town breathes with him.

"Ready?" I whisper when I reach him.

He nods, chin brave. "Leadership cries in supply closets," he mutters, quoting me, and I swallow a laugh that tastes like pride.

We pull the sheet.

Gasps. Then applause, loud enough to jostle the fairy lights. Open books flowing into each other, tiny foxes hidden where drivers will only see if they slow down to look. A goose in a corner, trotting out of a paragraph like a local celebrity. A fourth-grader tugs Noah's sleeve and says, "That fox is my favorite," and Noah flushes shyly, smiling too wide.

Noah stares at his shoes and tries to hide a smile too big for his face. Ethan stands exactly three feet away, close enough to catch, far enough not to steal. His eyes shine like the one star in Willow Cove that thinks it's in a movie.

Kelsey steps up, pen ready. "A word about redemption arcs?"

"Poetry, donor wall, therapy dogs," I say smoothly, gesturing at the press sheet we taped to the welcome table. "No minors. No prying. If you want a story, buy a heart."

Maybe it's the way Ace lays his head on a child's knee, or the way Rose dabs her eyes, or the way the town leans toward us like a porch swing, but Kelsey blinks, writes Luz on a gold heart, and presses it to the glass. Her eyes glisten when she touches it again, surprised by her own softness.

The lights flicker again.

"Not tonight," I tell electricity. Electricity, being dramatic, flirts with trouble anyway. A hush gathers like fog.

I'm halfway to the breaker closet when a hand I know without seeing closes over the knob first.

"I've got it," Ethan murmurs. "You keep the sky from falling."

I nod, step back to the mic, and smile in a way that makes small children stop crying and microphones remember their manners. "Intermission! Meet Ace. Buy a heart. Whisper a poem to the window so it will remember you." Her gaze caught his across the lantern-lit room, steady, unreadable, and for one dangerous second, the crowd blurred into backdrop. If she didn't look away, she was going to forget this was a fundraiser and not a confession booth. The Harbor Street Strings segue to something soft and brave. The ceiling decides to cooperate. I decide to breathe.

And then the past walks in wearing a ribbon of cedar soap and a grin that could get a person forgiven for less than they deserve.

DREAM GRAMMAR, REAL ARGUMENTS (CLARA → ETHAN)
DREAM — NOON ON THE DOCK

Not storm-dark this time. The boards are warm. A dented first-aid tin waits at the end. Inside: our napkin of rules, no running without a goodbye, no turning silence into punishment, tell the truth even when timing hates it. A new line in my hand: *Make the timing worthy of the truth.* The church bell rings one… two… three. A figure lifts a hand on shore, not to claim, to ask. I open my palm. The paper heart doesn't dissolve. It shines.

I wake for the second time, still on my feet, eyes open, talking about string lights and poetry. The dream lingers like mint on the tongue.

"Breakers behaved," Ethan says when he reappears. "Minimalist heroism."

"Minimalist glitter," I counter, because that's how we keep from saying more in public.

We move in parallel until parallel tightens. It happens by the staff door where the quartet can't see, and the donor wall can. My hand lifts to adjust his lapel (unnecessary), his fingers find the smudge of ink on my wrist (inevitable), and suddenly we're standing too close to call it chance.

"You didn't tell me you were afraid," he says quietly. "Last night on the dock."

"I didn't want to give the fear a microphone."

He huffs a laugh that sounds like somebody turned on a light. "Use me instead."

"I am using you. You fixed my closet."

"Not the same." His smile fades. "I want to fix what I broke."

My throat moves like I drank lake water. "You didn't know."

"I didn't ask enough questions of the right people. Starting with you." He looks toward the donor wall. "Do you need me to shut the press down?"

"I need you to stay." The sentence escapes before I can sand it into something less breakable. "Tonight. Tomorrow. After that."

He goes very still, the way men do when hope is heavy. "I can do that."

"Then go make Nurse Joan proud of how you labeled the breakers," I whisper, because if I keep looking at his mouth, the chapter ends too soon.

He squeezes my fingers and disappears into the sound booth like he lived there in another life.

"Five minutes!" Maya calls. "Prepare your lantern hearts!"

ETHAN

If small towns had vital signs, tonight I can feel Willow Cove's under my palm. Systolic: laughter. Diastolic: hush when she speaks.

I reset the last breaker and breathed out a day I didn't know how to carry at twenty. At thirty-two, my spine knows where to put weight. Once, in residency, I alphabetized an entire crash cart mid-chaos. Tonight feels like that calm with twinkle lights.

"You good?" Tom asks, materializing with a tie that lost an argument with a crosswind.

"Alive."

"Lanterns, Not Pirates is testing as a slogan." He beams like a lighthouse. "Press will love it."

"Press will love a press policy," I remind him, tapping the page on the welcome table. "Poetry, donor wall, therapy dogs. No minors. No prying."

He salutes. "Your sister called my office three times to confirm you're staying."

My chest pulls in ways I can't show a man in a municipal sash. "I told her I'd read a poem if it helps."

"You?" He blanches. "Spontaneous verse kills votes."

"Then I'll hold a lantern."

He bolts. I laugh and then stop because Clara is at the mic, and the room tilts to follow her voice. The first time I saw her through glass thirteen years ago, I thought breathing had learned a new trick. The trick is still working.

She hands the night back to its owners with a flourish that looks like grace and feels like scaffolding she built when I wasn't watching. The auction opens. The quartet turns up their listen. The fairy lights, obedient now, drizzle gold.

Kelsey hovers with a pen and a posture that says she learned hard things earlier than she should have. She buys a heart and writes a name and presses it to the glass with a gentleness that makes my throat hurt. Maybe we are all terrible at asking, and tonight is how we practice.

Between lots an old paperback slips from a donation box and unspools a folded square that lands near my shoe. My seventeen-year-old handwriting grins up at me from a napkin.

If the stars are listening, I told them I'm going to fall so hard I'll break a new verb for it.

I slide it into Clara's hand as if we are not in a room full of witnesses. Her eyes soften like a field after rain. She tucks the napkin into the glass case where Willow Cove keeps its tenderness, ticket stubs and prom photos, and history we refuse to throw away. She fingers the corner where she'd once written, Make the timing worthy of the truth.

"Lanterns up," she calls.

I raise mine.

AUCTION HEAT, BACKSTAGE HONESTY (CLARA → ETHAN)

The silent auction turns rowdy by Willow Cove standards. The Crossword Crew outbids the Lakewalk Moms for a mystery basket. Rose and Henry gift a hand-knit, aspirationally red scarf to a teenager who cries and pretends not to. Mr. Pierce offers "Ace Time: one hour of therapy dog joy," and the sheet fills in a minute. Ace retrieves a bookmark a child drops mid-bid and deposits it with pomp, the town clapping like he won a medal.

Then the gift certificate for Monroe Books & More; Private Browsing + After-Hours Tea comes up, and I plan to smile politely at whoever wins.

Ethan raises his paddle.

"Twenty," he says.

"Thirty," says Mayor Tom.

"Fifty," says Ethan without looking away from me.

Tom collapses with relief that he didn't hide well.

"Sold," I say too quickly, cheeks too warm. The room reports that I am glowing. The room is rude and correct.

We meet in the shadow of the staff door. Close, but not inside; brave, but not foolish.

"You didn't have to."

"I wanted to buy an hour that belongs only to you." He swallows. "And to me, if you'll let it."

I think of the napkin in the case. Of the dock in the dream. Of Noah's fox, tucked into a corner to slow people down. "I'm letting it."

"Good." He exhales, then goes perfectly still. "Kelsey asked me about the offer with too many commas."

The sentence is a stone in my shoe. "And?"

"I told her to buy a heart and leave our house alone."

"Our house?" I echo, as if the phrase is a bridge I might fall through.

He flinches, then recovers. "The one we are building with soup and tape."

I press my fingers to his wrist where his pulse lives. "Thank you."

"For what?"

"For not opening emails that smell like trouble."

He smiles, crooked with relief. "Hydras hate fences."

"Good thing you learned carpentry."

He leans, careful and certain, and I let my eyes close because there are days you practice and nights you use what you learned. Heat gathers. The room hushes. My mouth answers before my brain asks.

A door bangs. "Emergency!" Tom whispers at a shout. "The quartet needs extension cords, and also I announced a poetry reading, and also did we approve a poetry reading?"

"Minimalist heroism," Ethan murmurs against my smile, and peels back without sulking. "Go save a mayor from himself."

"I do that twice a week." I tuck my hands where they can't misbehave and push through the staff door into logistics.

ETHAN

I grew up thinking tomorrow would forgive today. It doesn't. People do. Cats, sometimes.

Clara reappears with a cord, like she intends to lasso chaos and a tolerance for poetry. The quartet looks grateful, terrified, and charmed. The town settles into that alert quiet we invented to honor people telling the truth in public.

Kelsey reads the press policy again like a spell. "Poetry, donor wall, therapy dogs," she murmurs, then steps back. Boundaries can be kindness when you use them to keep the weather off someone else, too.

I take my lantern to the back wall and practice being a man who can listen while holding something that makes light. I am getting better.

The poem is short, bright, and full of foxes. It feels like Noah took the mic without standing up. People clap because they don't know what else to do with feelings that fit.

Clara finds me in the quiet that follows. We don't say anything. We don't need to. The room is full of people, and also just us. I lift a hand. She answers by stepping into it.

The kiss is not a surprise. It's a draft coming due. Not wildfire. Current. Tension unspooled by consent. Heat banked for later. A hand at her jaw, her step closer, my breath caught and given back. Terms hummed between breaths. When we stop, both of us are laughing like we got away with a harmless crime. The Harbor Street Strings pretend they didn't see. Midnight flicks his tail with sardonic timing.

"Back to work," she whispers.

"Patience is proof, not punishment," I remind myself silently, filing the almost-question (marry me) under after the gala because patience is proof, not punishment.

WIND-DOWN, CLIFF-UP (CLARA → ETHAN)

By the time we stack the last chair, Willow Cove looks like a room that kept a promise to itself. People leave smelling like cinnamon and lanterns. The donor wall throws our names back at us in gold and silver, and one red book that waited for a generous heart and got one; The Crossword Crew signed it with laughter.

Noah dozes on the poetry couch under Midnight's surveillance. Ace snores at Mr. Pierce's boot. Rose and Henry argue cheerfully about sestinas. Maya counts a total that will let the clinic breathe easier and tries not to cry. Tom unties his tie like it attacked him, then blurts "Lanterns, Not Pirates!" and blushes crimson when the crowd cheers.

The Boathouse doors ring their herb-box bells as the last guests leave, the whole square glowing with Good-Witch charm. Ocelot Friday stickers wink from the register jar like an inside joke with fate.

"Walk me outside?" I ask softly.

Ethan nods. The square is quiet, lamps, leftover laughter, the lake pretending to be a mirror. We stand beneath the awning because that is where the town told us our goodnights for years, and we finally believe them.

"Thank you," I say. Two words mean a thousand ways.

"For what?"

"For staying."

"I'm not going anywhere," he says, the sentence landing in my bones like a lantern finding its hook.

He kisses me once, then again, the second kiss deeper, the kind that ends on a breath instead of a door slam. He doesn't reach for the handle. I don't, either. We bank the fire and promise the rest with our foreheads touching.

Later, when the house was dark and the town quiet, he drew the blanket over us and kissed the back of my hand like it was a vow. It wasn't about heat anymore; it was about staying.

"Tomorrow," he says into my hair.

"Tomorrow." My voice thinks we invented the word. Maybe we did.

He walks toward the clinic end of Harbor Street, shoulders set to useful, lantern light gilding his jaw. I watch him go with the ease of someone who believes in arrivals now. The bell inside me rings one… two… three.

Then my phone hums. A voicemail notification I didn't hear arrive during the auction. City number. Too many commas in the subject line are transcribed across the preview. Package sweetened. Let's talk timing.

I press play.

CHAPTER TWENTY-FIVE

Lanterns & Lines

CLARA

The night had the kind of hush that makes every small sound feel like a decision.

Inside Monroe Books & More, the fairy lights over the donor window threw soft gold across the paper hearts, names in my neatest ink, while the heater purred and the bell above the door practiced its polite jingle. Cinnamon drifted in from Maya's kitchen like a friendly spell. This town runs on gentle spells. It should have been a calm night.

Then the wind decided to stir the pot.

A gust shouldered Harbor Street, the awning snapped like a ribbon, and the top edge of the big front pane pinged, a thin, bright note I'd learned to respect. The tape seam I'd reinforced yesterday held, but a bead of rain nosed the corner as if curious about my nerve.

"Not tonight," I told Weather, grabbing painter's tape and the fire blanket because experience had turned me into a one-woman stage crew.

The bell jitterbang. Ethan slipped through the door with a skirl of cold air and cedar soap, hair damp, scrubs under his jacket like he'd sprinted straight from the clinic. "Left edge, top seam," he said softly, like we'd rehearsed it.

"I make the plans in this store," I said, already reaching for the ladder.

"Make this one with me," he answered, steadying the rungs with surgeon's hands.

I pressed the strip flat. The pane sighed, decided to be brave, and the bead sulked away. Before I could climb down, fairy lights crackled over the donor hearts, an offended sting, then died back to a halo.

"Front doors," Maya called from the threshold, curls wind wild, a tray of sugar knots balanced like a miracle. "Cross breeze. No panic. Panic is banned." She added, "I'm putting that on a kitchen towel."

Ace padded in with Mr. Pierce at his heel, sat prim in his teal bow tie, and offered a paw to a trembling seventh-grader who'd come to pin a gold heart for her abuela. Midnight, by contrast, stalked to the sill, stared at the pane like physics had personally insulted him, and sat on my roll of tape with papal disdain.

The girl's breathing caught, then steadied under Ace's warm paw. I watched her shoulders loosen, and something loosened in me, too.

"We're okay," I told the room in my best librarian-meets-lighthouse voice. My hands, traitors, were still shaking.

"Breathe with me?" Ethan asked from the ladder, and I did, the four-count he taught me to mock and then to need. The room steadied. So did I.

When I stepped down, the familiar gravity found us. We turned at the same time, the inches between us turning into math I didn't want to show my work for. His palm hovered at my hip like a question. I gave a small nod that felt like a door opening.

The kiss lit like kindling and settled like the slow burn of embers, steady heat, no hurry. He tasted like peppermint and rain and patience, and my name sounded different in his mouth when he said it quietly between breaths, like a promise he'd signed already. Warm breath met the cool draft from the window, the mix a shiver I didn't want to end.

"Terms," I whispered against his smile, because that word saves me from drowning.

"Still signed," he said, and for a breath, the night felt simple.

It didn't last.

The bell did that nervous jingle again, and a gust sent a spray of leaves across the threshold, along with Kelsey from Cove Chatter in a lemon cardigan and an expression that wanted a story. "Window looks magical," she said to the room. "Any comment on the… redemption arc?"

"Poetry, donor wall, therapy dogs," I replied, pointing at the press rules we'd taped to the welcome table. "No minors. No prying. If you want a story, buy a heart."

To her credit, she did. Luz, she wrote, hands shaking, and pressed it to the glass like she was pinning a memory in place. She touched it twice before stepping back, as if sealing something invisible. The angle softened. The wind stepped back. Ace wagged once, very professional.

Later, after cinnamon, after laughter, after I rewrote one smudged name and fixed three crooked hearts, I locked the door and stood with Ethan under the awning, the night so quiet we could hear the lighthouse bell rope thrumming. We didn't make promises with our mouths. We let the quiet make one for us.

"Tomorrow," he said.

"Tomorrow," I agreed.

He kissed my temple like sunlight and walked toward the clinic. The bell in my bones rang three clean notes. I was smiling when my phone hummed.

A voicemail had arrived sometime during the chaos. City number. Subject line transcribed across the preview with too many commas: Final package. Let's talk timing.

The smile went brittle. I didn't press play.

After the gala.

ETHAN

I can tell the difference now between adrenaline and cadence.

Adrenaline was the sprint from the clinic to her door when the pane pinged. Cadence was the way her shoulders dropped beneath my hands after the kiss, like something heavy had finally remembered where to set itself down. Both felt like breathing.

I walked back through Harbor with the wind easing and the lake practicing calm, my phone buzzing in my pocket with a number I used to salute. I didn't look. Hydras hate fences; I'm learning to love them.

At the clinic, the generator lights hummed their old song. Joan glanced up from the triage desk and gave me that storm with bangs look that means she sees too much and isn't worried about it. "Doors hold?"

"Window held," I said. "Clara did the tape; I filed a supporting role under 'minimalist heroism.'"

Joan grunted approval. "Crash cart is alphabetized. It keeps you from emailing venture capitalists."

"As the Good Book says," I intoned, "let the man alphabetize."

She snorted. "Your sister called. Twice. Left you a voicemail that sounded like a parade and a threat. Got married."

Lila's messages were stacked above the one with the city number. I played my sister's first.

"Blue shirt for the gala," she said without hello. "Read a poem if you have to, but try not to scare the seniors. Also, I'm proud of you. Don't be weird about it. PS: Remember when you tried to alphabetize our cereal boxes? Therapy would be cheaper."

I smiled into my sleeve like a teenager. Then I stared at the other voicemail, the one with commas in its subject line that used to make parts of me feel important and now made the same parts feel loud.

I didn't press play.

Instead, I went to the supply closet that, two months ago, had been labeled HOLIDAY • MAYBE? Like a bad joke, and now hummed with labeled shelves and a leak that learned manners. I touched the AED cabinet we'd installed in the right hallway, the tiny gold heart sticker where Clara insisted morale belongs, and felt something settle that had been trying to fly out of me for thirteen years. People slow for wonder. They always will.

Noah's sketch, a fox trotting along a book spine, was taped above the cabinet at kid height. People would slow for wonder. They already had.

At dawn, after a nap on my office cot that even a saint would sideeye, I ran the lake. Fog licked the boardwalk. The rope bell dropped three notes across Harbor Street like a private language. When I rounded the curve by Monroe Books & More, I saw her.

She didn't see the slick plank until she did. The sound of rubber skidding will live in my ribs for a while.

"Clara!" I shouted, and my body did that old thing where it made executive decisions on my heart's behalf. Two seconds later, my hands were under her elbows. "Knees soft," I said, which is a ridiculous instruction that works.

She nodded against my chest and laughed in that sharp way that means terror just lost an argument. We kissed in fog that tasted like yes, and when she pulled back, she whispered, "After the gala," and I said, "I can do patience," and meant it all the way to my bones.

That was cadence.

Back at my place, the city voicemail still waited, like a stray I wasn't willing to feed, and a text from Lila sat above it: Ocelot night tomorrow? Bring onions. I sent back a fox emoji and the word 'always,' and then put the phone face down.

I could be a man who stayed. I was practicing.

After the gala.

CLARA

By noon, Willow Cove had decided to be charming about it.

Rose and Henry arrived in matching scarves, hers aspirationally red, his rakish, and declared the donor window "a constellation with excellent penmanship." The Lakewalk Moms affixed QR codes to gala flyers with the solemnity of NASA. The Crossword Crew informed me, gravely, that they had hidden a message in the program discoverable only under blue light and would I please act surprised. Mr. Pierce reported that Ace would be wearing teal to coordinate with the silent auction signs. Midnight, who cares nothing for mortal color stories, stared at the glass like it owed him money and then curled up on the poetry shelf to supervise. He also stole a crumb from Maya's sugar knot when she wasn't looking, tail flicking in satisfaction.

Noah drifted out from the back with graphite on his thumb and that old soul focus that makes my chest ache. "They want the crosswalk sketch for the library endcap," he said, pretending not to glow.

I reached for the sugar knots like faith. "We'll hang it this afternoon."

He nodded, then glanced at the front door where Kelsey hovered with her lemon cardigan and her breath in bravery. She bought another heart without pushing and wrote a name I didn't know. It made me want to be kind to everyone I hadn't met yet. She touched the glass a second time, like she was leaving warmth behind.

I had decided, quietly, stubbornly, to be braver with my yes. To build a bridge instead of punishing a man for not knowing the map thirteen years ago.

So, I texted Ethan: soup and sandwiches tomorrow; six; bring onions.

He replied with a fox and a checkmark, which is the exact ratio of whimsy to competence that makes my knees unprofessional.

The universe, jealous of my progress, put a very official envelope under my till that afternoon, a glossy printout of an old article with one word circled in red and a handwritten note: You can't buy this town.

Midnight sat on it like a paperweight and flicked his tail. I filed it under NOT OUR STORY and cut a fresh red book for the center of the window. For the kid who needs the fox on page 27, I wrote Noah's suggestion and pressed it to the glass until the tape warmed beneath my palm. The silver ink shimmered in the afternoon light, lines catching like threads of starlight.

At the library, the endcap unveiling went the way my heart needed something to go for once. Kids gasped in that unguarded way kids do. A second grader in galaxy leggings spotted the fox tucked in page twenty-seven's gutter and whispered, there. Ethan stood exactly three feet away, near enough to catch, far enough not to steal, and pride did something unseemly to his mouth. Noah's chest lifted in one long breath, fear and pride sharing the same space until pride won.

After, we walked back through Harbor carrying a roll of painter's tape and an ordinary that felt like a gift. "After the gala," I said again, because saying it out loud builds muscle.

He squeezed my fingers. "I heard you the first two times."

At six the next night, Ocelot commenced. Grilled cheese passed Noah's Official Texture Test with one solemn nod, which is to say: I almost cried into the tomato soup. The three of us negotiated algebra and donor lists, and rope bridge physics from the couch, like a family that had been doing this all along and just forgot to tell the calendar.

When Ethan left, he kissed my cheek. "After the gala," he said, and somehow it was a promise, not a stall.

I set the table for three without thinking and then made myself think on purpose. The bell in my bones rang three times, as if it approved of my spine.

I was wiping the counter when my phone hummed. A voicemail transcription lit the screen, a city number I didn't want to see, and a sentence that made the floor tilt: Final package. We can make the timing work.

I didn't press play.

Not then.

After the gala.

ETHAN

The Harbor Street Strings opened with something that made the air feel like it remembered how to be gentle. I stood in the wings with a coil of extension cord and a heart I was finally willing to be seen with.

Tom nearly decapitated a rubber plant. "Lanterns, not pirates!" he bellowed into the mic. The town cheered like it had invented the line. He was wearing a button that said the same thing, like he'd found a brand.

Clara took the stage in ink-stained hands and a dress that made the fairy lights try harder. The donor window glowed behind her, gold and silver and a red book in the center that caught the candlelight like a live ember. The room turned its face toward her with that posture people use in chapels and kitchens.

She introduced Noah's crosswalk sketch; the cloth dropped; kids gasped; adults softened. I'm not a man who cries in public, but my eyes do what they want when a twelve-year-old I love makes a town slow down for wonder.

Between lots, a donation box shed an old paperback and a folded square that grinned up at me in my own younger handwriting: If the stars are listening… I slipped the napkin into Clara's palm as if handing her a weather report. She put it in the glass case labeled Town Treasures and then handed me a look that felt like a doorway.

I raised my paddle on a gift certificate titled PRIVATE BOOK-STORE BROWSING + AFTER-HOURS TEA because I wanted to buy exactly one hour of a life that would never be for sale. Sold, she said, cheeks pink, and the town pretended not to applaud the way applause sounds when it's rooting for two specific people.

"Breakers?" she mouthed when the lights flickered. "I've got it," I mouthed back. Minimalist heroism: I flipped, I tested, I refused to let the weather pick tonight. A gull laughed overhead as if in on the omen.

Backstage by the staff door, we met in that small wedge of space where the quartet couldn't see and the donor wall could. Her fingers curled in my lapel. "I didn't tell you I was afraid," she said, honesty a new accent in her mouth.

"I'm here for the parts you don't want to hand the room," I said, and because consent is the language we speak now, I only touched her wrist, where her pulse lives. "Use me."

Her words echoed like a dare. The gala was behind us, the music fading, the town busy clapping for lanterns and cinnamon knots. For once, no one was watching.

"After the gala," she said again, quieter this time, but her fingers were already curled in my lapel.

I kissed her like a man starved; ten years of restraint unraveling in seconds. Her mouth opened under mine, soft and desperate, and the world narrowed to the heat of her body against me.

We stumbled through the staff door into the bookstore, still glowing faintly from the donor hearts in the window. Gold and silver names shimmered in the lamplight, silent witnesses.

She hit the counter first, breathless laughter spilling out as books slid aside. I lifted her onto it with hands that had healed strangers for a decade but had only ever wanted to hold her.

"Clara," I rasped, pulling back just enough to see her face, "tell me no."

"Don't you dare stop," she whispered, yanking me back to her.

Clothes gave way fast, impatient; sweaters shoved up, denim peeled away, skin against skin until there was nothing left but heat. His palm traced reverent paths along her ribs, like he was learning scripture by touch. She arched into him, whispering Stay with every shift of her hips, every gasp. He didn't rush; he anchored, each thrust deliberate, like he was making the word permanent in her skin.

Every inch of me remembered him, his mouth claiming mine like a man relearning how to pray, his hands reverent even as they shook. Each gasp was a vow, each touch a confession, and restraint shredded itself by degrees.

When I slid into her, it was like the years dissolved; no absence, no silence, just us, whole and wild again. She gasped my name, head falling back, and I caught her face in my hands like I could anchor us both.

Every thrust was a promise. Every moan, a confession. She clung to me, thighs tight around my waist, whispering words that cracked me open: *stay, stay, stay.*

Release tore through her, shuddering, beautiful, and I followed, breaking with her, when our breaths evened, he tugged the fallen blanket over us like the simplest vow. His thumb traced my temple once, small, steady, like he was promising to learn the quiet parts of me, too. I buried my face in her neck as her body gripped mine. The storm outside rattled the windows, but the pane held. So did we.

When it was over, she rested her forehead against mine, breath hot and ragged.

"I meant it," I whispered. "I'm not leaving this time."

Her lips brushed mine, tender after the wreckage. "Then don't."

The hearts in the window glowed brighter in the lamplight, and for once, I believed we could.

She laughed softly, then sobered. "After the gala."

"After the gala," I echoed, because repetition builds muscle.

"Five minutes," Maya stage-whispered, and handed me a tray of cinnamon knots I did not deserve.

Rose, sidling past with a tea urn, quipped, "Save one for the repentant cardiologist, Hale."

The poetry portion ended with a kid reading four lines about foxes and bridges that undid me in ways my medical training did not cover. The auction closed. The room turned into the sound of a town that did something good for itself on purpose.

"Walk me outside?" she asked when the last chair was stacked, and Ace yawned and Midnight performed quality control on the checkout drawer.

We stood under the awning where Harbor Street looked like a movie set that remembered restraint. She said thank you in a way that made me want to build her a second bookstore just to see if her mouth could hold more gratitude. I kissed her once, then again, the second one deeper, the kind that ends on breath instead of boundary. We didn't go inside. We promised it with our foreheads.

"Tomorrow," I said into her hair.

"Tomorrow," she said back, and then her phone buzzed and her face changed.

"Everything okay?" I asked.

She hesitated, one beat, two, and tucked the phone like a card she wasn't ready to play. "I'm fine."

Her tell.

I almost pressed, then didn't, because sometimes love is keeping your questions until the person you love can carry them. She kissed my cheek and went to lock the poetry room. I started for the clinic end of the block, Lila's text lighting the screen like a promise I could read: Proud of you. Flats packed. Read the short poem.

Then the city number slid up in the notification shade. I should have ignored it.

I didn't.

"Dr. Hale," a voice said in my ear, smooth as a pane of glass. "We know it's gala night. The final package is sweetened. We can… make the timing work."

I ducked into the alley beside the café because small towns have ears, and said the only intelligent thing I could think of: "Not tonight."

"Tomorrow morning, then," the voice said. "Nine. You won't regret hearing the number."

When I stepped back into the square, Clara was at the edge of the light, keys in her hand, expression unreadable. The alley carried a sound like a rumor, not a coincidence. Of course it did. This town collects echoes.

She didn't say anything. She didn't have to.

My phone, traitor, lit with one more preview line that even I could read from three steps away: Final package. Let's talk timing.

The air went thin between us, the difference between adrenaline and clarity, and for the first time in months, I didn't know which one had me by the throat.

"Clara" I started.

She smiled the way a person smiles when the floor just moved. "After the gala," she said, and this time it sounded like a test more than a plan.

Before I could answer, the bell above the door gave one last goodnight jingle and the lighthouse blinked, steady, steady, steady. The wind carried the word timing down Harbor Street like a dare, and the town, merciful, nosy, ours, pretended not to listen.

I looked at the phone in my hand. I looked at the window that had taught us both how to hold. I looked at the woman I'd been trying to become the right man for since I was seventeen.

Tomorrow," I said, softly enough that only the glass could hear me. *But the glass didn't answer. And for the first time, I wasn't sure if silence meant safety or storm.*

It didn't answer.

Stay.

CHAPTER TWENTY-SIX

Lanterns, Lines, And The Space Between

Static, Sparks, and a Kiss I Don't Let Myself Keep

The first pop sounds like a cork, bright, wrong, right before the fairy lights over the donor window spit sparks. The wire hisses, smoke curls up, and the scent of burning insulation clings to the air like panic made physical.

"Power strip!" I'm already vaulting the counter. The bell jitterrings like a sparrow stuck in a chapel. The lake outside slicks itself silver; wind shoves Harbor Street; the big pane sings a thin, nerve bright ping at the top seam. A flame bites upward along the cord, greedy and quick.

"Left edge. Top seam," a voice says that my bones recognize. Ethan. Cedar soap, rain, and a jacket he didn't finish buttoning. He catches the ladder without asking and braces it like the most ordinary miracle in the world.

"I make the plans in this store," I tell him, but my hands are already moving. Painter's tape. Fire blanket. Prayer, I don't say out loud. The flame takes a greedy breath toward the gold paper hearts. I smother, press, hold. Heat nips my knuckles through fabric. For one stretched heartbeat, I think we've lost it. Then the spark surrenders.

"Doors open, cross breeze!" Maya wedges both with her hips like a benevolent witch and announces, "Panic is banned."

Ace trots in at Mr. Pierce's heel, sits prim in his teal bow tie, and offers a paw to a trembling seventh grader who came to tape Alma Ruiz to the glass. The boy breathes again, strokes Ace's ear, and whispers, "Thanks." Ace bows his head like a statesman accepting applause. Midnight stalks to the sill, sits on the tape roll with papal disdain, and glares at physics. Mortals, his eyes say. Such drama.

The strand fizzles out; the pane holds; my lungs forget and then remember their job. I climb down and turn at the same time Ethan does. For a breath, the inches between us are the only math I know. The bell clicks in a draft like punctuation.

We kiss.

Not wildfire current. Warm mouth, careful hands, consent humming like voltage under skin. His palm cups my jaw as if it learned the map years ago and never forgot; my fingers slide into the curl at his nape, and the whole room brightens at the edges. His stubble rasps at the corner of my mouth, a texture memory that yanks me under faster than sense. I answer with a sharp inhale, ribs pressing against his chest, and the sound makes his breath hitch against mine.

"Terms," I whisper against his smile, because that word keeps me from drowning.

"Still signed," he says; the sound lands right against my ribs.

A guitar out front plucks a tentative chord, the lights think better of being dramatic, and the window, sainted by painter's tape and good intentions, decides to brave the weather with us. We breathe. We step apart. We pretend the room didn't tilt.

Inside my mouth, the yes is bright and dangerous. Inside my chest, a different voice, the one that counted years without him, reminds me of what it costs to trust the tide. He left before. He didn't know about Noah. He could still choose the city again. I straighten the hearts; he resets the breaker. For one reckless second, I want to beg him not to let go. But I've learned that wanting without boundaries is just another way to drown. I put the kiss inside a drawer and sit on the lid.

THE DOCK, THE DREAM, AND THE DECISION I DON'T SAY OUT LOUD

Dream. Noon, not storm dark. The dock boards are warm; my feet remember where to put their weight. At the end: the dented first-aid tin that keeps showing up in my head like a punchline the universe refuses to retire. Inside, our napkin of rules is bled blue ink:

No running without a goodbye. No turning silence into punishment. Tell the truth even when timing hates it.

A new line in my hand: Make the timing worthy of the truth.

The church bell sends three clean notes across the water. A figure at shore lifts a hand, not to claim, to ask. I open my palm expecting the paper heart to dissolve, the way it always does.

This time it shines.

I wake with Midnight's tail laid across my wrist like punctuation and the particular calm that follows a decision I haven't said out loud yet. My phone hums on the counter. City number. Subject line with more commas than decency: Final package. Let's talk timing. I don't press play.

Not tonight. After the gala.

Willow Cove decides to be charming about everything else. Rose and Henry arrive in matching scarves and tell me the donor wall is a constellation with excellent penmanship. The Lakewalk Moms affix QR codes to gala flyers with the seriousness of NASA. Maya hands out sachets of rosemary and lavender, calling them "pocket blessings," and threatens to hex anyone who doubts their efficacy. The Crossword Crew whispers that they've hidden a message in the program only visible under blue light. Mr. Pierce confirms Ace will be wearing teal to coordinate with the silent auction signage. Midnight approves of nothing and everything, which is his brand.

Noah drifts out from the back with graphite on his thumb and old soul eyes. "The library wants the crosswalk design for the endcap," he says, pretending not to glow.

"We'll hang it at noon," I say. "Leadership cries in supply closets." He smirks. He glows anyway.

At the library, kids gasp in the way that makes grownups behave. A second grader in galaxy leggings finds the fox hidden at page twenty-seven and whispers, There. The hush that falls is cathedral pure. Ethan stands exactly three feet away, near enough to catch, far enough not to steal. Pride is a soft light on his mouth that he tries and fails to hide. Noah kneels beside the girl and explains, "The fox waits because patience is a kind of courage."

I texted Ethan after: Soup and sandwiches tomorrow. Six. Bring onions.

A fox emoji arrives twenty seconds later. A check mark. The exact ratio of whimsy to competence that makes my knees unprofessional.

I set the table in my head for three and then, because fear is loudest when you make room for joy, I file a thin envelope taped to my till, an old article, a red circle around a word that is history, not fate, under a folder I labeled NOT OUR STORY. I cut a fresh red book for the center of the window and wrote, at Noah's suggestion: For the kid who needs the fox on page 27. I press it to the glass until the tape warms beneath my palm. The hushstick sound reminds me: steady, steady.

Inside my chest, a promise knocks. After the gala, I tell it. Then say the thing.

THE NIGHT OF LANTERNS (AND ALL THE WAYS I DON'T LET MYSELF FALL)

"Welcome to the Books & Hearts Gala," I tell a room strung in fairy lights and expectation. "Lanterns, not pirates." Mayor Tom fistpumps like he invented restraint. I flash back to the meeting where he proposed a pirate-themed fundraiser and feel absurdly grateful for small mercies.

The Harbor Street Strings make the air remember how to be gentle. Ace works the aisle like a statesman; Midnight prowls the poetry shelf like a small god auditioning for benevolence. Our donor window gleams, gold and silver hearts pressed to the glass; a red book burns a soft ember at its center. I see my reflection inside the names I wrote, a woman who tapes hope where people can see it.

We unveil Noah's crosswalk sketch. Gasps. Applause. A fourth grader tugs his sleeve: "That fox is my favorite." He tries to swallow a grin that's too big for his face. Clara glimpses his notebook half-closed; inside, taped with care, is a sketch of the three of us, me, Ethan, and him, under a lantern sky. Hope drawn in pencil, already waiting.

The lights flicker once, twice. Ethan peels off to the breaker like muscle memory. I hold the mic like a lifeline. "Intermission," I say brightly. "Meet Ace. Buy a heart. Whisper a poem to the window so it remembers you."

Ace comforts a nervous teen near the poetry table who clutches a folded page. The boy kneels, strokes Ace's ears, and blurts a stanza about forgiveness. The crowd hushes, then applauds. The boy straightens taller, cheeks pink, and for once doesn't look afraid of his own voice. Ace wags exactly once, satisfied.

Kelsey from Cove Chatter hovers at the edge with a lemon cardigan and a pencil that looks like it could cut. "A quote about redemption?"

"Poetry, donor wall, therapy dogs," I say, nodding at the press sheet we taped to the welcome table. "No minors. No prying. If you want a story, buy a heart." To my shock, she does. Luz, block letters, hands trembling. She presses it to the glass and touches it twice, as if sealing a door she forgot she could open from the inside. I catch the look in her eyes: grief and something older. This will matter later.

Backstage, by the staff door no one but the donor wall can see, I meet Ethan's eyes and lose the thread I wrote for myself.

"Terms," I whisper because I need the word even here.

"Still signed," he answers into my mouth, warm and certain. He doesn't touch until I do, my fingers knotting his lapel, my breath choosing him. Then his hands frame my waist, respectful until I make them something else.

His kiss builds carefully, then hungrily, then carefully again. The storm outside plays percussion, but here it's the hum of pulse and permission. His thumb traces my jaw. My answering sound makes him laugh once against my mouth, a joy that breaks the years between us.

The laughter bled into hunger. Her grip fisted his lapel, dragging him flush, until every ragged breath between them became a vow they hadn't dared sign until now.

The alcove is a shadow of cedar and cinnamon. His mouth trails lower, skimming my throat where my pulse betrays me. "Okay?" he murmurs.

"Yes," I gasp. It isn't surrender. It's a choice.

Heat blooms low and steady as we find a rhythm, his jacket braced under me against cold brick; my thigh wrapped around his hip like a memory turned live wire. Each shift, each sigh, is a language we forgot and relearn together.

When we break for breath, his forehead rests against mine. "Water?" he whispers, absurd and perfect.

"Yes," I manage, and the word is both answer and vow.

We walk out together, but not touching, which is sometimes the bravest way to be together in a town that loves you loudly.

When the auctioneer reads Private Bookstore Browsing + AfterHours Tea, Ethan raises his paddle. "Fifty." Tom sputters and surrenders at thirty. "Sold," I say too fast, cheeks too warm. The room reports that I am glowing. Rude. Correct.

We almost get away clean.

We don't kiss again. Not yet. Instead, he threads his fingers through mine, a tether hidden from the room but felt all the same. The aftercare is simple, ordinary: his hand steady at the small of my back, my laugh when he fusses about water, the forehead kiss that makes patience feel like heat's equal twin.

After the last chair stacks and the quartet packs strings and the lanterns decide to behave, he walks me to the awning the way he did when we were nineteen and the world still believed we could do this without bruising anything important. He kisses my temple, then my mouth, the second longer, careful, with the kind of promise that ends on breath, not a door slam. His lips press to my temple, then my mouth. The second kiss lingers, careful, and then deepens, not frantic, not apologizing, but claiming us back from silence.

"Tell me to stop," he murmurs, breath caught against my jaw.

"I don't want to," I answer, and even I'm surprised at how steady it sounds.

My palms flatten over his chest; his pulse runs under my hand like it's finally keeping the same time as mine. When his forehead rests against mine, it isn't hunger, it's home. We kiss again, slower, until the lighthouse blinks once like it's signing off on the moment.

After, he laughs softly, presses a water bottle into my hand, and kisses the corner of my mouth as if tenderness itself is a rule he refuses to break.

"Tomorrow," he says into my hair.

"Tomorrow," I say, and mean it like a vow.

Then my phone hums. A voicemail transcription slides across the screen; I feel the floor tilt before I read it. Final package. We can make the timing work. A hospital name hidden in the text, one Ethan once dreamed about. Temptation wears a new suit.

I don't hit play. I lock the door and watch him cross Harbor, shoulders set to useful, a lantern gilding his jaw like the town betrayed its own restraint. The bell inside my chest rings three clean notes, and I pretend it's not a countdown.

Later, on the Boathouse porch, we share a tart the way conspirators share secrets, slow bites, laughter muffled into sleeves. He brushes powdered sugar from my lip with his thumb. The air is too sweet, too fragile. We part before anyone can see, but my pulse remembers.

RETREAT (THE PART I HATE WRITING)

Morning tastes like fog. The boardwalk is innocent until it isn't. The first wet plank is a whisper. The second is a warning. On the third, my foot flies; my ribs find the rail; stars pop white behind my eyes.

"Clara!"

He's a block away and then somehow right there. Hands under my elbows. "Knees soft." I'm laughing by accident because terror just failed at its job.

We kiss in mist that tastes like yes. It would be so easy to fall all the way in, let the dock dream cash itself in as morning. His breath is warm on my mouth. His thumb is a soft question at my jaw. My body is a choir of yes.

I step back.

It feels like treason and discipline and a promise kept to a girl who did not have anyone to choose her when it counted. The yes rattles the drawer I put it in, but I sit on the lid and smile, as if nothing is shaking under me.

"After the gala," I say, trying to make the words sound like a plan, not a shield.

"I can do patience," he says, and the relief in it nearly undoes me.

Maya finds me later and says blunt as salt, "Retreat is just rehearsal for regret. Don't practice too much."

I make coffee. I make lists. I make it to noon without crying in public. Cove Chatter DMs Maya for a forgiveness quote; she replies, Boundaries are beautiful. The Lakewalk Moms add QR codes to everything but Ace's collar. Midnight sits on my keyboard until I write the press policy again in a bigger font. He thumps his tail like punctuation. Hush, stick, he reminds me. Stay steady, foolish human.

I thread my way through the day on a taut line of competence. I can do competence with my eyes closed.

What I cannot do is not hear the voicemail I haven't played, saying timing like it owns the word. And what I cannot forgive is the way fear wears competence like a costume and calls it wisdom.

In the staff room, alone, I take my phone out and put it on the table, screen down, like it could learn manners if I model enough of them. I tell the tile, "I don't want to be scared of joy anymore."

Tile: quiet. Cat: judgmental. Wind: unhelpful.

I flip the phone. My thumb hovers. I don't press play.

Not yet.

At six, the soup boils gentle. Onions go sweet and patient in a pan. Noah sets three bowls he pretends not to have chosen, because he is at the age where caring is subversive. Ethan knocks. Air lifts.

The dinner is ordinary and holy. Grilled cheese passes the texture test. Noah declares us Minimalist Glitter Champions and then rolls his eyes at his own joke. We triage algebra, donor calls, and rope bridge physics. We watch an old adventure where everyone survives with bruises they earn honestly.

At the sink, we stack plates the way you do when your hands have learned how to share work. He leans in, Okay? He asks with his mouth against my temple.

"Yes," I say, and I mean it. But I also mean later. I also mean slower. I also mean prove it, and let me prove it back.

On the porch, peppermint and lake and restraint play the kind of chord that makes me want to write again. He kisses me once and stops first, which is the most romantic thing anyone has done for me in a decade. "We'll see each other brave," he says. I memorize it, knowing it will return.

"Tomorrow." I almost added that after the gala, I'll tell you I love you and swallow it because sometimes a promise grows better if you don't handle it too much the night before.

I'm still smiling when the voicemail that has been polite all day clears its throat.

"Dr. Hale," a voice says when I finally press play, smooth as a pane of glass. "We know it's gala night. The final package is sweetened. We can make the timing work. That hospital you dreamed of? It's ready for you both."

Something in me goes very quiet. Behind me, in the hall, I hear Ethan pause, maybe catching the edge of the words. My chest stutters.

The phone is still in my hand when a knock taps the frame I forgot to lock. I don't turn. I know the cadence of his knock by now, the way it apologizes and asks at the same time.

"Clara?"

I look at the red book in the window, the one for the kid who needs the fox on page twenty-seven, the one who slows down for wonder before they reach for panic, and decide that retreat, this time, is a measured step back to take a better run at the leap.

"Tomorrow," I say without turning. "Let's be brave tomorrow."

Behind me, the bell above my own heart rings once, twice, three times, and the sound is not a countdown. It sounds like a door unlocking.

CHAPTER TWENTY-SEVEN

Edge Of The Storm, Edge Of The Truth

NOAH

EDGE OF THE STORM, EDGE OF THE TRUTH

The rain doesn't warn me. It just yanks the sky down by the hem.

I'm coasting my bike along Harbor, sketchbook in my backpack, when the wind knuckles the lake hard enough to lift spray over the boardwalk. The lighthouse blinks like it's trying to Morse me a message; RUN or maybe WAIT, and then the goose that hates me steps into the crosswalk at the exact wrong time.

"Seriously?" I brake so hard my back tire fishtails. The goose stares like he's a traffic cop with a vendetta. "You need a union card for this?"

Across the street, through the mist, the clinic door swings open, and Ethan strides out in scrubs and a jacket, phone at his ear. His shoulders look like an answer I don't want to need. He pauses under the awning. His tone goes careful.

"Not tonight," he says. "Tomorrow at nine. … Yes, I got your email. … No; I said I'm not discussing numbers at a fundraiser."

I don't hear the reply. The wind eats it. But I hear the sentence that matters.

"Timing has to be right," he tells the phone, and something in my ribs does the opposite of breathing.

The goose honks like a judge. I pedal to the curb and drop my kickstand beside the clinic's planters. Ethan spots me and goes still. The phone is still to his ear. He looks like the lake looks when it pretends not to have waves.

"Hey," he says, and hangs up. Just… ends it. Not a 'talk later,' not a 'bye.' A full stop.

"Is that the hospital?" I ask. "The one with commas in its emails?"

His laugh is quick, but not particularly funny. "You're twelve going on CIA."

"I'm twelve going on don't-do-this-to-us." The words come out louder than I plan. The wind shoves them into his chest anyway. "You can't show up and fix closets and hold hands and then… leave."

He steps off the stoop and absorbs the gust like a wall. "Walk with me," he says.

We go toward the docks because that's where Willow Cove always asks you your real questions. The boardwalk is slick; the rope bell tosses three quick notes through the mist like it's rooting for me. The lighthouse cuts the gray into pieces. The storm surges harder, rain slamming sideways in sheets so heavy my jacket sticks to my arms like glue.

"Talk straight," I say. "I can build a bridge if I know where the shore is."

He blows out a breath. "A company in the city thinks it wants me back. They've been trying to make the timing look like a gift."

"Is it?"

"No." He doesn't make me wait. "Because a gift isn't a door that slams on people." His mouth tilts. "And because I already have the thing they're trying to sell me."

"What's that?" I push, because my voice shakes and I hate it and I don't want to hate it in front of him.

"Home." He says it like a steadying hand on a railing. "I'm staying, period."

Rain needles my face. I stare because I learned to read people before I learned algebra, and I don't trust sentences until they have spine. He meets my eyes as if this is a test, and he has studied.

"Then say it to the part of me that still thinks you're a postcard," I tell him.

What I don't add: postcards don't stay. People leave. If he lies, I'll redraw the lines of my life again, but part of me, traitor part, already hopes.

He steps close enough that I can count the raindrops in his eyelashes. "Noah, I'm not leaving again. Not for a number. Not for a door with glass walls." His throat moves. "You can be mad. You can make me prove it. But I'm staying anyway."

No contract, no commas, no hospital wing will outweigh this street, this town, this family. I need you both more than I ever needed ambition.

My eyes burn, which is rude. "Why?"

"Because you laughed at me when I tripped in the three-legged race, and I wanted to earn that sound. Because your mom looks like she can breathe again when you're drawing. Because this town has a dog that does therapy with a bow tie and a cat that audits moral decisions. Because I want to be the kind of person you tell dumb jokes to in the car."

The goose yells in disbelief. I push wet hair off my forehead and accidentally smile. "They're not dumb."

"Objective data suggests otherwise." He grins, smaller than he could. Then the grin fades. "You can ask me every day if I'm staying. I'll say yes every day."

We stand there under the lighthouse eye like two people who should probably get out of the rain. I pull my sketchbook from my backpack and rip out the top page, the fox on a line of books, tail raised, a tiny lighthouse in the margin. My hands shake when I hold it out.

"Add it to the clinic AED cabinet," I say. "So people remember to slow down for wonder before they panic."

He takes it like it's fragile. Maybe I am. "I will."

"Good," I say. "I'm not done being mad. But I'm done not knowing."

We walk back to the Harbor without talking. At the corner, Mr. Pierce and Ace appear like a cut scene. Ace sits in front of me and leans his solid head into my palm. It feels like a vow you can pet.

"You're okay?" Mr. Pierce says gently.

"Will be," I say, and I hear my mom in my mouth. It doesn't terrify me. Not today.

Ethan bumps my shoulder with two fingers, exactly the pressure of a promise he isn't rushing. "Ocelot tonight?" he asks.

I nod. "Judging your grilled-cheese technique calms my nervous system."

Ace approves with one thump of tail. The bell down the street rings twice and then once, which is just showy, but I take it.

CLARA: THE VOICEMAIL, THE WINDOW, THE LINE IN INK

Maya can read my face like it's a poem she wrote herself.

She slides a latte across the counter and doesn't pretend she's not eavesdropping on my silence. "Timing is just fear wearing lipstick," she says.

"I have lipstick," I say. "And fear. Extremely on brand."

The donor wall glows in the gray morning, as if it wants to hold my hand: Daniel Ortiz, Rose & Henry, The Crossword Crew, Luz, in careful block letters, Anonymous, with a goose doodle, because of course. In the center, the red paper book waits, empty like a chair held in front-row faith.

On my phone, the voicemail from last night sits under Lila's text (Wear flats. Read the short poem. Proud of you). I haven't pressed play because once I hear someone ask us to leave, I'll have to answer out loud.

"Walk me through it," Maya says.

"He got a call," I say. "The timing is kind." I swallow. "He told Noah he's staying."

Maya's mouth does a brave curve. "And your bones?"

"Trying to remember that patience and delay aren't the same animal."

We cut more hearts. We tape them to glass. We practice that sound, the subtle hush-stick of hope attaching to a cool surface, until my hands stop shaking. I added a new silver heart in the top right: For anyone who needs today to be kind.

"Run the program for me," Maya says. "Engineers do stress tests. Writers do what?"

"Wishful thinking with charts," I say. "Tonight: Ocelot. Tomorrow: fundraiser check-pickups, press rules taped everywhere, no pirate hats. Sunday: breathing."

"And what about the voicemail?"

"After the fundraiser." I take the phone from my pocket, set it face down by the register, and look anywhere else. "If I hear the number, I'll end up arguing with a door."

Midnight jumps onto the sill with the elegance of a landed thought and sits exactly on the envelope Kelsey delivered yesterday, the one that said You can't buy this town. He blinks, which is cat for watch me.

"Noted," I tell him. "Boundaries are beautiful."

Around noon, Noah wanders out of the back with graphite on his thumb and a face that is trying very hard to be neutral. He smells like pencil shavings and luck.

"You okay?" I ask.

"Working on it." He hesitates. "I told him not to do this to us."

"Good." I swallow. "What did he say?"

"That he's staying." Noah's ears go a little red, which is hope trying not to embarrass him. "I gave him the fox for the AED."

It wasn't just a drawing anymore; it was trust disguised as graphite.

I reach for him because I don't know how not to. "Thank you for asking the questions I taught you to ask."

He lets me kiss his hair and then pretends he didn't. "We still have Ocelot, right?"

"We do." I pretend my heart is not a bell. "You're judging texture."

"Obviously." He grabs a sugar knot like it owes him data and disappears.

The rest of the day is a collage of kind errands. Rose and Henry deliver a scarf for the auction. The Lakewalk Moms affix QR codes with crusader zeal. Kelsey returns in her lemon cardigan, stays on her side of the press sheet, and buys another heart without asking for mine. Mr. Pierce gives Ace a bath, which Ace forgives immediately because he is a gentleman.

At six, Ethan shows up with onions and bread and the kind of patience that has learned how to wear an apron. He passes Noah's texture test. Midnight counter-signs with a reluctant head-butt.

After the dishes, we stand close enough in my kitchen to hear each other's thinking.

"I told him I'm staying," Ethan says softly. "I told them."

I look at his mouth because I am weak and I have earned it. "We'll see each other brave," I say, and mean it.

He doesn't try to kiss me, which, unfairly, makes me want to pull him closer. We clean the stove instead. We practice a marriage made of ordinary verbs.

When he's gone, Noah is asleep, and the house has decided to like us, I turn the voicemail face up and stare until staring gets boring. I press play.

"Dr. Hale," the voice says, glass-smooth, familiar as a cat you shouldn't pet. "We know it's gala week. The final package is sweetened. We can make the timing work."

I set the phone down as if it might burn. Somewhere on Harbor, the rope bell rings twice and then once because it loves theater.

"Not tonight," I tell the air. "After we hang the lanterns."

ETHAN: CONFESSION WITH A BOW TIE

Joan doesn't have to ask what's wrong. She just hands me a clipboard and a donut and flicks one finger toward the storage room like a bouncer with tenure.

"Alphabetize something," she says. "Then tell me the truth without turning it into a speech."

I do the first part because my nervous system likes order in drawers. We restock bandages, tape, and sterile gauze. I line up the AED pads like runway lights. Then I lean against the doorjamb and say, "They offered a number with commas and the kind of title that looks good on walls."

"And?" She sips her coffee like a metronome.

"And I told Noah I'm staying. I told Clara I'm staying."

"And?"

"I'm staying." My throat does something unprofessional. "I needed to hear myself say it where the oxygen is real."

"Good." She taps the clipboard. "Now write an email that acts like your mouth."

I sit at the tiny desk in the break room with a blinking cursor and a heartbeat in my ears. The fox Noah drew is taped above the AED cabinet, tail pointing toward the red lever like a mischievous arrow. I want to be the kind of man who notices the arrow and pulls when it matters.

I type:

Thank you for the generous offer. I'm declining. The timing isn't the issue; the choice is. My work, and my life, are here in Willow Cove. Please remove me from future outreach. —Ethan Hale

There. No commas, I'll trip on later. I read it twice, delete a hedge, add a period with the stubbornness of a fencepost, and hit send. Hydras hate boundaries. I'm learning to love them.

On my way out, I check the waiting room. Mr. Pierce and Ace have already arrived for their weekly therapy shift. Ace wears a teal bow tie and, somehow, dignity. He spots me and sits, chin on my knee, a therapy dog's permission slip.

"Good boy," I tell him, which is also what I'm trying to be.

"Clinic hero," Mr. Pierce says, winking. "Looks like you're finding your head."

"Trying to keep it," I say, because honesty is healthier than charm.

Back on Harbor, the wind has calmed to something like a long exhale. The rope bell across from the bookstore rings once, clean, bright, like it's testing the air for truth. I take that as a blessing and keep moving.

In the afternoon lull, I swing by the library to help Tom with the breaker he's certain is plotting sedition. It's not. It's just forty years old and tired. While we crouch in the cramped utility closet, Tom mutters, "I vowed: lanterns, not pirates, in sickness and in zoning," and I laugh so hard I nearly drop the flashlight.

We get the lights steady, and I head back to the bookstore to check in before the gala. The donor wall warms the window. The red paper book in the center glows like a coal of intention. Clara stands inside with a roll of tape and a look that says she's been brave three times already today.

"Hydras vanquished?" she asks when I step in.

"Politely dismissed," I say. "In writing."

Her lips part. I see relief arrive like sunrise under her skin. She doesn't throw her arms around my neck. I don't carry her to the stacks. We do something more dangerous: we let the quiet speak for us.

"Thank you," she whispers.

"For what?"

"For building fences so the right things can stay."

I help string lanterns along the awning, and then we walk home together to start dinner. Noah meets me at the door with narrowed eyes and a cutting board. He taps the bread like a judge.

"Texture test," he says. "And no cheating with extra butter."

"Blasphemy," I murmur.

We cook, we tease, we stack plates. After the dishes, Clara and I carry mugs to the porch. The lake is a dark lung beyond the houses, pulling breath. She leans into me, shoulder to shoulder, and the way our bodies fit feels like something we didn't invent so much as recognize.

"I keep wanting to skip to the part where I don't feel scared," she says.

"We'll walk there," I answer, and mean it.

She turns, and I see the decision happen in her eyes before the movement. The kiss she gives me is slow and sure, all warmth and permission, no hurry, no performance, just the crisp press of lips, the slide of breath, the small sound she makes when my hand finds the back of her neck. I want to deepen it until the world fades. I don't. We leave a door open for tomorrow.

When I say goodnight, the rope bell rings twice and then once, a funny little cadence that has started to feel like we're being cheered on by a very opinionated harbor.

Back at my place, I write the sentence on a sticky note because I want my worst hour tomorrow to remember it: Stay is a verb. I put the note on my bathroom mirror. Ace's fur is on my scrubs; I decide not to lint-roll it off. If the hospital calls again, they will hear the dog in my life.

My phone buzzes with a message from Lila; Lantern count stands. Bring a pocket screwdriver. Also, I'm proud of you. I send back a photo of the fox over the AED and crawl into bed.

I dream of a teenage cafeteria and a paper napkin. Clara's handwriting is smaller than, but the line is the same: We don't owe urgency anything. In the dream, I fold the napkin into my wallet. In the morning, I know where to look for it.

CLARA: THE CONFRONTATION I DIDN'T STOP, THE CHOICE I DO

The library smells like old paper and the enthusiasm of its volunteers. By noon, the square looks like a polite festival and sounds like hope with stage fright. We hang Noah's crosswalk endcap while he pretends not to care and fails charmingly. The Lakewalk Moms practice angles; the Crossword Crew hides a secret clue in the program and pretends to be subtle. Mayor Tom cancels his pirate-hat order. I try not to burst into a hymn.

Maya and I take five on the bench outside the bookstore. The wind toys with the fringe of her scarf.

"Say the fear out loud," she says.

"If I believe him and I'm wrong, I don't want Noah to pay for it."

Maya nods like she's met that fear and beaten it at cards. "Here's a true thing: kids don't need certainty; they need models for recovery. Show him how you trust, and how you repair if it hurts." She squeezes my hand, "You're allowed to win, you know."

I laugh because it's either that or cry in public. "I'll pencil in winning for after cleanup."

Back inside, the afternoon gentles. I write names: For the kid who needs the fox on page 27. I tape the red book to the center of the window and press until I feel the sound of it settling, hush, stick, promise.

Kelsey stops by in her lemon cardigan and holds up her phone like a passport. "I'm reporting on lanterns," she says, not people. She sets a small bag of candied orange peels on the counter. "Also, I was wrong."

"Candied contrition accepted," I say. We don't linger. Tonight is for paper light.

By full dark, Willow Cove is strung like a necklace. The donor wall glows. The goose patrols the perimeter, as if he expects to find contraband. Ace poses for photos like a celebrity who remembers his first name. Midnight, offended by all of it, pretends to own the poetry display.

The quartet begins. Children fall briefly in love with violas. Lila reads a poem about bridges that makes even the goose pause. Somewhere behind the stacks, a breaker hiccups. The lights do a theatrical flutter. Tom panics. I find the mic.

"Intermission," I say cheerfully. "Lanterns need a pep talk."

Ethan is already moving toward the utility closet with a pocket screwdriver like a man answering his calling. Ten minutes later, the ceiling decides to behave because it respects competence. When the poem resumes, the room hushes so deeply I can hear the lake test its edges.

Backstage by the staff door, Ethan presses a blank donor heart into my palm. "For when you want to write a name you've been saving," he whispers.

A ghost of a memory slides in, the teenage cafeteria, a paper napkin, his wallet snapping shut around something we couldn't say yet. I write nothing on the heart. Not yet. I hold it like a warm stone.

We work. We sell a city's worth of hope one paper shape at a time. When a bookmark slips from a donor's novel and skitters under a folding chair, Ace, who is clearly off-duty and thrilled about it, crawls under the row, retrieves it in a slobber-free miracle, and presents it to a round of applause. Therapy dog, public hero.

The last paddle goes down. The last receipt prints. Ethan raises his hand on my store's gift certificate, and I flush in a way that makes Maya finally whisper into my hair. Midnight thumps his tail once on the counter: a feline benediction he will deny later.

I duck into the stockroom to put cash boxes in the safe and breathe. That's when my phone hums. The voicemail notification sits under Lila's We did it and above Noah's I'm by the door.

I should ignore it. I press play instead.

"Dr. Hale," the voice says, glass-smooth, familiar as a cat you shouldn't pet. "Final package. We can make the timing work." A hospital name follows, sleek as a sales pitch.

The door I forgot to lock clicks. Noah's silhouette fills the frame. "Mom?" he says, half in, half out. "I" He stops, hearing the last sentence.

I fumble with the screen, which is dark, and turn. His eyes are wide and older than they should have to be.

"You heard one sentence," I say softly.

He nods, jaw stubborn. "Do you believe him?"

"I do," I answer, feeling the truth like a weight that fits in my palm. "And if I'm wrong, we'll fix it. Together."

He studies me like he's drawing me in his head. Whatever he sees, it lets his shoulders drop. "Okay," he says. Then, because he's Noah, "We've got to get Ace to sign autographs before he thinks he's above us."

We rejoin the world. Tom gives a little speech about lanterns and zoning vows that makes the room laugh. The raffle basket goes to the ice-cream shop. Kelsey photographs the donor wall and, mercifully, only the wall. I tape the blank heart beside the red book, empty, on purpose, because sometimes the right name takes courage to write.

After the cleanup, we stand under the awning while the square exhales. Lanterns sway, satisfied. The night smells like citrus sugar and lake wind. Ethan's coat brushes my arm. He looks at me like a man deciding not just to love me but to stay loving me.

"Tomorrow," he says.

"Tomorrow," I say back, and the bell in my ribs answers.

He leans in, and I meet him, and the kiss we share is deeper than the porch, still careful, still ours, still leaving the camera at the door. His hand cups my jaw; my fingers catch in his hair. The world blurs at the edges. Heat pulses low and sweet. We break only because we promised ourselves we would.

"Walk me home?" I ask.

"Always."

We don't talk much on Harbor. The rope bell rings once, twice, then once again, our odd little cadence. At my door, we stand close enough to feel how tomorrow will fit. Midnight slips between us, tail flicking my knee; then, as if moved by some private impulse, he thumps his tail once more against the jamb, punctuation.

Inside, with Noah brushing his teeth and humming the viola line, I take the blank heart from my pocket and press it to the fridge. Not naming it is a naming. I text Maya a photo. She replies with a trophy emoji and a moon.

In bed, I dream the old dream: Willow Cove the size of a snow globe, the lighthouse a steady pulse, the fox trotting along the spine of a book toward a red paper cover. Only this time, the glass is already cracked, and the air coming in is not a threat. It's oxygen.

When I wake, the house is quiet and brave. The voicemail lies where I left it, but it doesn't own me. I make coffee. I write three lines in my notebook:

Stay is a verb.

Patience isn't delay.

It sounds like a door unlocking.

CHAPTER TWENTY-EIGHT

After The Gala

SIREN, SALT, AND A KISS WE ALMOST KEEP

The town doesn't know the difference between a siren and a rumor.
Clara

The siren hits first, one long wail that irons the morning hard, then the lighthouse light knifes through lake fog like it's late to its own rescue. Wind shoves Harbor Street sideways; gulls scatter like dropped paper. Maya bursts out of the café with flour on her cheek, salt still clinging in the air, and points up the hill. "Kid on the lighthouse steps. Twisted ankle. Tom tried to carry him and nearly cartwheeled politics into the bay."

I'm moving before fear finds its coat. Painter's tape is still looped around my wrist from re-anchoring the donor hearts; my shoes are wrong for running; the bell above my door gets in one last anxious jingle as I bolt past. Rain needles. The lighthouse stairs rise like a dare.

At step twelve, Ethan appears in my periphery, breath steady, hair rain-dark, jacket half on. "You okay to"

"I'm not porcelain," I rasp, taking the next flight two at a time. "I've got a first-aid kit and a grudge against gravity."

"Beautiful," he says, not even pretending not to mean both parts.

The kid, with spiky hair and, scraped knee, sits on the landing clutching his ankle with both hands and trying to blink his tears back into the day. Ace is already there because, of course, he is, teal bow tie damp from fog, chin resting on the boy's calf like a living sandbag, his therapy dog rounds paying dividends again. Mr. Pierce hovers with a towel and a dignity that deserves its own parade.

"You're okay," I tell the boy, lending him my best librarian voice. "You scared the stairs. They'll be more careful next time." (He admits he was chasing a runaway cap.)

Ethan says the soft doctor things that make the world behave. "Let me look. Breathe with me. Good. That's it." A quick exam, a careful roll of gauze, a makeshift sling. He shows the kid how to hop the safest way down while I clear umbrellas and tourists with my murder-mitten stare. Mayor Tom clatters up three steps, goes white at the sight of his own shoelace, and wisely retreats to crowd control.

At the bottom, Rose and Henry form a two-person reception committee, carrying a thermos labeled FORTITUDE. Henry cracks a pun about "stepping up" that earns an eyeroll and laughter. Midnight stalks along the railing at exactly the speed of disdain, ignores Ace on principle, and bumps the kid's elbow as if to knight him for surviving. The boy snorts. Crisis punctured.

"Clinic?" Ethan asks me under the lighthouse's amused eye.

"Ride with Pierce," I say. "I'll lock the shop and meet you."

He nods, then drops his voice low enough that it lands exactly where my pulse is practicing. "You ran toward it."

His breath smells faintly of cedar soap and rain. Lightning of a different variety crawls under my skin.

"Timing was rude," I answer, rain beading on my lashes. "Someone needed me."

"Someone usually does." He looks at my mouth like he just remembered the word someday. "Clara"

"After tonight," I whisper, because I promised myself patience I can live with. The weather inside me doesn't listen.

He leans in anyway, careful as a vow. His palm skims my cheek; the world narrows to breath and warmth and that impossible spark we keep pretending we're not on fire with. The kiss is steady voltage, not wildfire, heat braided with choice. I make a sound I don't make for anyone else. He swallows it like gratitude.

Ace gives a single, pointed woof. We break laughing against each other's mouths, then go do the ordinary heroic thing, paperwork, ice, an appointment card, like two people who just did a more dangerous thing and survived it.

By the time I jog back down Harbor, the lake has put its face on for the day. The bell over my door rings once, twice, three times, as if it approves of restraint. I press my palm to the donor wall to steady myself. The red book heart in the center glows like an ember that finally believes it can be tended.

Dream sequence, five breaths long, finds me while I count the till for opening: the dock at noon; boards warm under bare feet; the dented first-aid tin with our napkin of rules; a new line in my hand; Make the timing worthy of the truth. The church rope drops three clean notes through my chest. When I look up, he's there, not to claim, just to ask. I open my palm. The paper heart shines.

I open the bookstore.

The morning is quieter after. Customers drift in, tourists with damp maps, locals with dry humor. Each time the bell rings, I feel like it's echoing the one inside my chest. Rose pops by to drop off muffins, Henry follows with another joke worse than the first, and Noah texts me a fox doodle with the caption: Ace says hi.

The day keeps moving, ordinary as bread, extraordinary as survival. Every interaction feels touched by the kiss I promised to wait for but couldn't. My lips still tingle. The town doesn't notice, or maybe it does and chooses kindness. Sometimes the two are the same.

THE CALL, THE SISTER, THE CHOOSING There's the right choice, and there's the loud one.

Ethan

Lila brings the weather with her, brisk, amused, eyeliner sharp enough to file a motion. She materializes in my office with two coffees, a fox sticker, and exactly zero patience for my old habits. "Tell me the part you haven't said out loud," she says, dropping into my visitor chair like a benevolent hurricane.

I tip my head back against the cabinet and admit it. "They sweetened the package."

"How sweet?"

"Teeth aching."

She taps her nails against the armrest, a metronome for honesty. "And?"

"And it's not a door that opens to anything I want anymore." The sentence tastes like metal when I say it, and like clean water after. "I told Noah I'm staying. I told Clara with my mouth and then with my feet. I emailed Sloane: 'Thanks. No.'"

Lila's smile is nineteen parts pride and two parts relief. "Say it one more time so I can stop fantasizing about smashing your phone with a rolling pin."

"I'm staying." This time, it lands in my ribs like a lantern finding its hook.

We take care of the practical tasks: confirm coverage at the clinic; text Nurse Joan my signed Saturday list; and add my name to another volunteer sheet for the gala teardown, as Tom cannot be trusted with extension cords. Lila steals a donut hole from a patient appreciation box and points it at my chest like a sermon nugget. "And the romantic things?"

"Soup and sandwiches. Ocelot night. After the gala" I don't finish because the word forever is too big to toss onto an office rug between a skeleton model and a vaccination poster.

She hears it anyway. "Good. Buy flowers that smell like decisions, not apologies."

"Is there a chart for that?"

"Roses are an apology. Peonies are decisions. Sunflowers are for men who think they invented joy." She softens. "Do not disappoint my new sister-in-law."

"Bold," I say, and it doesn't scare me.

We split the day. Lila bullies a vendor into loaning fairy lights. I bully a sink into not dripping. Between patients, I tape Noah's fox sketch above the AED because people slow down to wonder. At lunch, I walk past Monroe Books & More without going in, because I said I would survive one afternoon without the reassurance of Clara's mouth. The bell inside my chest rings anyway, one, two, three.

On the way back, my phone lights like a bad idea. Sloane again. I don't answer. I forward the voicemail to a new folder labeled NOT OUR STORY and set a filter. Hydras hate fences. I adore them. (Clara once told me that.)

There's a flash of memory I rarely let myself keep: graduation night, the diner's tile black and white and trying not to be sticky; Clara's laughter carbonating the air; a napkin we wrote rules on in ink that bled because our hands shook, lemons and hot chocolate steam between us. No running without a goodbye. No turning silence into punishment. Tell the truth even when timing hates it. I tucked it into my wallet and thought paper could hold us. What holds us now is newer and harder: soup, tape, a boy with graphite on his thumb, and the choice I keep making on purpose.

That choice keeps repeating itself like a bell. Each time I hear it, my chest feels steadier. Each time I picture Clara's ink-stained hands, my path feels sharper. The old ambitions still whisper, but their voices sound thin compared to hers.

OCELOT, TEXTURE TEST, TRUTH

CLARA

Noah pretends he didn't set out the blue bowls on purpose. Midnight takes up his usual anti-begging post at ankle level, offended and alert. The kitchen smells like onions gone sweet, bread gone golden, butter taking religion seriously.

Ethan passes the texture test like a man who studied. Noah consecrates him with a solemn nod. "Acceptable."

"Frame that for me," Ethan says dryly. "I need a certificate for the clinic wall."

We eat like people who know their way around hunger and want the kind that keeps you soft. We triage algebra and donor calls, and whether Mayor Tom will try to sneak pirate hats into the photo booth. ("He's banned from props unless supervised by Ace," Noah decrees.) We practice being a unit without announcing it: he rinses, I stack, and Noah dries with weaponized competence.

After, Noah detours to the living room with his sketchbook. A movie with improbable rope bridges whispers against the walls. Ethan and I linger at the sink on purpose. The house hums with the relief that follows a good decision.

"Tell me something real," I say, because rules written on napkins require upkeep.

He doesn't hide. "I used to think urgency was a personality trait. Now it feels like a door salesman propping open with their foot." His knuckles brush my hip, accidentally on purpose; my breath forgets its job. "I want this to be ordinary and holy. I want to read the manual on your stove and pretend it's scripture. I want to be bored next to you."

"Bold goal," I murmur, tracing a flour comet from his jaw with my thumb. "Here's mine: I'll stop switching off my phone at nine like it's punishment. I'm done punishing you for a silence that hurt both of us." Saying it slides a weight off the shelf of my sternum and onto the counter where we can share it.

He kisses me like it's a toast. Warm, deliberate, room-temperature miracle. We stop before greed brings guests.

On the couch, Noah pretends to object when Ethan sprawls at the other end and props his feet on the coffee table. Midnight hops onto my lap with obvious disdain for both of them, pushes a pen off the table to prove his point, then purrs like a tiny machine when I scratch the spot behind his ear that makes him forget his role. The rope bridge in the movie sways; the hero doesn't fall; the three of us breathe like a family that is trying on the word for size.

Later, when the credits roll, Noah looks up from his sketchbook and says, "You both make less noise than the bridge, but more sense." He shrugs like it's not the most important thing he's said all night, and then he wanders off to bed. I feel the words settle into the house like a new piece of furniture we didn't know we needed.

When Ethan leaves, he touches the doorframe with his knuckle the way he always does, like he respects thresholds. "Tomorrow," he says.

"Tomorrow," I answer, and the bell inside me rings three times because it learned the trick.

I listen to the voicemail after he's gone, and Noah is snoring at a diagonal across his bed like a human compass. The voice is glass and commas and everything I used to mistake for providence. We can make the timing work. My hand goes cold and then steady. I slide the message into the same folder where I keep Social Security cards, birth certificates, and promises. NOT OUR STORY. I label a fresh red book for the center of the window and write the name I've been saving where the light will catch it: For the kid who needs the fox on page 27.

THE HALL, THE HEARTS, AND ALL THE WAYS WE STAY SOME NERVES FEEL LIKE INK STAINS YOU CAN'T WASH OFF.

ETHAN

The library room hums with lanterns and neighbors. Clara's hands are ink-smudged, throat dry, but steady. Lila reads a poem that makes a teenager pretend not to cry, and Mr. Dawes holds his hat in reverence. Ace sits dignified as a judge; Midnight allows himself to be a rumor.

Tom announces, "Lanterns, not pirates!" and gets a cheer so honest he almost deserves it. Then he gestures at the donor wall, as if it were a sunrise. Gold hearts. Silver hearts. One red paper book is burning in the center like a small, stubborn planet. The town moves toward it the way people move toward warmth.

Kelsey from Cove Chatter floats in her lemon cardigan and, to my shock, stays on the safe side of the press sheet. She buys a heart and writes Luz in careful letters; I watch her palm the glass like a person checking their own pulse. The angle in her face tilts human.

When the lights hiccup, Clara handles it, and I handle the breaker, and between us, the ceiling remembers its job. When the mic squeals, she glares it into repentance. When the poem about foxes and bridges stumbles on the second line, Noah clears his throat in the audience, and the poet steadies like a ship finding deeper water.

I bid on a private browsing night because I want one hour of a life that isn't for sale.

"Fifty," I say, and Tom surrenders with both hands. Clara blushes in a way that would make a stronger man say something embarrassing into a microphone. I resist for now.

Backstage by the staff door, we meet in the narrow wedge of air that belongs to neither room nor rumor. Her fingers find my lapel, thumb brushing the seam. I find the ink smudge on her wrist. "I spent ten years learning the language of enough," she whispers. "I would like to practice fluency."

"Lesson plan accepted," I whisper back.

We hover there for one breath too long and then do the wiser thing: rejoin the town that kept us both breathing when we forgot how.

Cleanup smells like citrus and relief. Tom unties his tie like it tried to assassinate him. Lila steals three tea lights and promises to repent publicly. Ace signs autographs with his paw. Midnight expresses his opinion of gravity by pushing one pen off the counter and then going to sleep.

Under the awning, the square exhales. Lanterns clink gently, a buoy bell tolls faintly in the distance. The lake practices calm. Clara stands close enough that I can count the freckles I missed when I was nineteen and hustle looked like holiness. "Thank you for staying," she says, simple as bread.

"For everything," I agree, because every other answer would be a smaller life.

I kiss her like a door we're opening together, and then stop because I have finally learned what stopping means. Her mouth tastes like sugar and vows. The bell in both of us rings three times. We part like adults who intend to be excellent at wanting forever.

On the walk home, my phone buzzes in my pocket with a number that used to equal oxygen. I press it through the fabric like a man taking a pulse, knowing already: steady. Lila texts a photo of the fox over the AED with the caption: You did this. A patient whose ankle I wrapped on the lighthouse stairs sends a photo of Ace asleep in the backseat, head on gauze like a crown.

At my table, I write the only sentence that matters on a sticky note and pin it where the kettle boils: Stay is a verb. Use it. (This line will return as a motif through the closing act.) I pour water over tea leaves and let the steam carry the day to the ground.

I fall asleep to a dream of a dock at noon and a first-aid tin with a napkin inside and a woman with ink on her fingers walking toward me like a person who already made the bravest choice and just wants to enjoy it. Tell the truth when timing hates it, hums under her breath.

In the morning, the bell over Monroe Books & More jingles the exact way a future sounds when the town approves.

CHAPTER TWENTY-NINE

Permission, Promise, Prayer

CLARA

The scream doesn't sound like fear. It sounds like metal deciding it's had enough.

One second, the café across from my shop hums with afterschool chatter, pencils tapping, cinnamon sugar floating in the air like a blessing, and the next, a folding sign skitters across Harbor Street, slammed by a gust, and a tray avalanches in slow motion. Three kids jerk back. One goes paperwhite.

"Clara!" Maya's already at the threshold, flour on her cheek, voice pitched to calm and command. "Something's wrong with the lemonade, get Ethan!"

The bell over my door jangles a nervous jangle I feel in my bones. I'm moving before thought files paperwork, past the donor window (gold and silver hearts shining like they believe in us), past Midnight's statue still in silhouette on the poetry shelf. Outside, the wind shoves harbor air down the street. Inside the café, the world compresses into one bright scene: two teens clutching their stomachs, one kid on a

278

stool breathing too fast, a toddler crying because everyone else's faces changed.

"I'm here," I tell the room, and the librarian part of my soul remembers how to be a lighthouse. "Windows open, fans on. Maya, kill the lemonade. Tom, call the clinic and 911. Parents, sit. Breathe."

The door snaps wide. Cedar soap, rain, steadiness. Ethan.

"Left table first," I say, and I don't look at his mouth. He nods once, reading the space like code.

"Hey," he tells the boy with the shallow breaths, sinking to eye level, palms open. "I'm Ethan. You're okay. Slow it down with me. Four in. Hold. Four out."

I pry open the windows. Wind slaps color into my cheeks. Ace and Mr. Pierce appear like a cut scene, Ace in a teal bow tie that shouldn't belong in an emergency, and somehow does. The dog sits, noble and still, exactly where panic wants to stand. The toddler forgets to cry long enough to bury sticky fingers in soft fur. Ace blinks like, permission granted.

"Symptoms started how long ago?" Ethan asks, eyes on bradycardia, pulse at a wrist. "What did you drink? How much?"

"Ten minutes," Maya says. "New batch. It smelled… weird." Her face cracks. "Clara, it's on me"

"Stop," I tell her, as the townspeople's fear tries to find a culprit. "We're solving, not blaming."

"Tom," Ethan adds without looking up, "prop the door. I need fresh air. Pierce, keep Ace with the little ones. Clara, trash bags, gloves, and any cups you can save for samples. Noah" He stops himself, because saying Noah's name is its own weather. He doesn't need to. My son is already at the counter, pale but steady, phone in hand.

"Ambulance en route," Noah tells us, voice pitched like I taught him, clear, not loud. "ETA eight. I called the clinic; Joan says she's got supplies and five clean cots."

My throat works. "Good. Grab the first-aid tin from under my register. And, honey?, text the Lakewalk Moms. Not a broadcast, just… ask if anyone else feels funny. Quietly."

He nods and bolts. Brave, I think, and the word lands like a bell.

It happens fast then: the way emergencies always do when competence takes the mic. Ethan positions the kids, slows a too-quick breath, checks a blood pressure, and presses an emesis bag into a shaking hand with tenderness that makes me want to kiss him stupid and also build him a pedestal. I load sealed cups into a trash bag like they're evidence, because in a way, they are. Ace lays his head on a teen's knee, and the kid's shoulders drop. Mr. Pierce narrates a story about the time he forgot his own birthday and accidentally celebrated for a week; the toddler hiccups a laugh.

"Likely culprit is the lemonade," Ethan murmurs, low for me, while he palpates a tender abdomen. "Could be a harmless contaminant, could be someone's well-meaning uncle's backyard ice. We'll rehydrate, monitor, and test. You doing okay?"

"Define okay," I whisper, hands clean and dirty with soap and fear. He glances up, just long enough to find my eyes. The look says 'yes, with you.'

Sirens wail soft and then close. The café becomes a choreography of stretchers and gratitude and neighbors pretending not to be scared. In the swirl, somebody's elbow clips my hip. I stagger and catch the counter. Ethan's hand is there before mine, warm on my forearm, reflex, respect.

"Terms," I murmur, ridiculous, sacred.

"Still signed," he answers, and we let go at the same time like the adults we decided to become this week.

On the sidewalk, Harbor Street holds its breath. The goose does a perimeter check like union leadership. The donor hearts in my window shine stubbornly. I press my palm to the glass on a pass, one heartbeat, then pivot back into the storm.

Dream sequence (the dock)

The lake starts as a hush, glass instead of water, noon light turning the boards warm as skin. A dented tin waits at the end of the dock. Inside, our napkin of rules is in bled blue ink: No running without a goodbye. No turning silence into punishment. Tell the truth even when timing hates it. In my hand, a new line I don't remember writing: Make the timing worthy of the truth. The church bell drops three clean notes through my chest. A figure on shore lifts a hand, not to claim. To ask. I open my palm. The paper heart doesn't dissolve. It shines.

I wake on my feet with latex on my fingers and cinnamon in my hair and decide maybe this is prayer.

ETHAN (TRIAGE & TRUTH)

There's a line between adrenaline and clarity. I can feel it under my thumb when I count a pulse.

Kid on stool: respirations fast, radial pulse a skitter. Teen by the window: cramping, pale, eyes answering all the questions before his mouth can. Toddler: tears resolved by dog. Café owner: blaming herself even as she leads with competence. Clara: steady as a lighthouse, shaking only in the muscles human beings are allowed to use when they are in love and terrified at the same time.

"Breathing's a tide," I tell the boy. "Let it come in slow. Let it go out slower." He does. His shoulders obey. I nod, praise where it counts, accept an emesis bag like a peace offering from a universe that owes us one.

The EMTs are kids in borrowed capes tonight, and I love them for it. We coordinate like we meant to rehearse this: vitals, IVs, transport. I rattle off suspected etiology, talk about unknowns we can control, unknowns we can't. Joan calls from the clinic, cots are ready, fluids are warming, and rapid tests are set to run. I love her like the weather.

Between patients, I find Clara's eyes. "Hydras hate boundaries," she tells me under her breath, which is code for the city called you, and also don't you dare disappear on me when the adrenaline clears.

"I emailed them no," I say. Truth signed in ink this morning. Truth said aloud now. Her breath leaves her chest like a held note finding its rest.

Noah hovers at the edge of triage range, a kid and a sentinel. He watches the way I touch people and the way I look at his mother. It feels like an exam I have waited a decade to take.

"Hey, artist," I say to him, the way you approach a fox, gentle, present. "Clinic needs a runner for specimen cups and ginger ale. Pay is terrible. Job matters."

He takes the basket from my hands and the weight of my pride like he's stronger than either of us remembers.

Sirens ebb. We clear the room. Maya sags against her espresso machine and calls it treason; I tell her she saved us by being loud first. Pierce gives Ace the okay to accept six hundred pats. Clara and I stand shoulder to shoulder at the threshold under wind chimes that insist on acting like a score.

"Walk with me," I ask. The clinic glows at the end of Harbor like a lantern we earned.

We pass her window. The hearts shine stubborn. The red book at the center waits for a name someone brave is going to write. I touch the doorframe because thresholds deserve respect.

"Clara." I don't mean to say her name like a prayer in public. I say it anyway. "I'm here."

"I know," she says, and in the space between us, I feel the math change.

CLARA (AFTERMATH, FLASHBACK, HEAT)

Flashback: bleach and clover under the bleachers. Seventeen. Laughter that made the world forget its own rules. Ethan's hand was steady on my jaw. A napkin between us, ink skipping because hands shake when you write rules that will matter for the rest of your life. No running without a goodbye. No turning silence into punishment. Tell the truth even when timing hates it. I folded it like it was made of bone and kept it in a jewelry box with one broken earring and a bus ticket I never used.

Now, my store smells like rain and citrus, and it's a long day. Midnight patrols the counter like a small god who has decided to be benevolent. The donor hearts throw back lamplight. I lock the till on muscle memory and only then realize my hands are clean, dirty with soap and adrenaline. Ethan leans in the doorway, jacket unbuttoned, hair damp, eyes the color of that last sliver of lake before dusk decides to be night.

"I want to say a lot of words that rhyme with forever," he says, because we promised honesty even when timing hates it, "and instead I'm going to ask if you ate anything that requires me to cook you soup."

"I inhaled a sugar knot." My laugh lands a little ragged. "And fear."

He steps close enough that I can smell peppermint and rain and something new, quiet, earned. His fingers hover at my jaw like a question. I nod, small as breath, big as yes.

The kiss is not a rescue. It's recognition. Warm, careful, heat that knows where it's headed and isn't in a hurry. His palm fits the back of my neck as if it had learned the map years ago. I press closer, and the world sharpens at the edges.

"Terms," I whisper, because saying it out loud is how I keep my balance.

"Still signed," he says against my mouth, smiling the way men do when they decide to stay.

We stop before greed starts making the decisions. We laugh at the exact same time, which feels like a different kind of naked. Midnight flicks his tail like: acceptable.

"Dinner tomorrow?" he asks. "Ocelot Night? I bring grilled cheese skills and unreasonable onions."

"Yes," I say, which is either a meal or a vow.

After he leaves, I stand with my palm flat to the glass over the red book at the center of the hearts and whisper the new line I dreamt on the dock: "Make the timing worthy of the truth." The lake across the street exhales like it heard me.

ETHAN (QUIET CHOICES, CLIFF SOFT)

There's a voicemail waiting. I don't press play.

Instead, I write the rejection I already sent this morning a second time, this time for my bones. Thank you for the generous offer. I'm declining. The timing isn't the issue; the choice is. My work, and my life, are here in Willow Cove. Please remove me from future outreach. I copied it on paper with a pen that scratches just enough to feel like a decision.

Lila will be here for the gala. She'll bring flats and a poem and the capacity to stare down hydras with mascaraed eyes. I think of telling her that I didn't just choose Clara tonight. I chose the fluorescent hum of this clinic after midnight, and the way Joan says my name when she hands me a chart, and the way Noah pretends not to wait at the window.

I taped the fox he drew above the AED cabinet, where he'll see it every time he visits. People slow down for wonder. Maybe that's what all of this is, slowing down enough to let the right life catch up.

At my sink, I wash my hands longer than I need to. Cedar and hospital, and the ghost of cinnamon linger. Outside, Harbor Street quiets itself. The lighthouse blinks the patient blink; it has perfected. I imagine the bookstore window across the way, paper hearts catching lamplight, a red book waiting for a name we're almost brave enough to write.

My phone lights anyway. Same number. Same subject. Final package. Timing.

I don't answer it.

Tomorrow, Clara will let me into her kitchen. Noah will grade my grilled cheese technique with all the solemnity of an oath. Midnight will pretend to hate me and then approve me once, dramatically. We will eat, and breathe, and not sprint toward a finish line we don't need anymore. After the gala, I'll walk her to the dock at noon in my mind and say the thing timing doesn't deserve to own.

For now, I write one line on a sticky note and pin it to my cupboard like liturgy:

Stay is a verb.

The bell across Harbor rings, one, two, three. Permission. Promise. Prayer.

CHAPTER THIRTY

Lanternlight, Lines, And The Truth We Can Stand On

EDGE BEFORE THE LIGHT

CLARA

The siren splits Willow Cove like a seam that's been waiting. One clean wail, a boom of wind off the lake, then the lighthouse throws its strobe across Harbor like a heartbeat with opinions. The bell above my door jitters, a nervous sparrow, while the big front pane whispers a warning ping at the top seam. Not tonight, I tell the glass. Not when we've taped so many names to hope.

"Kid on the lighthouse steps," Maya pants, flour on her cheek, tray forgotten. "Twisted ankle. Tom tried to carry him and nearly cartwheeled politics into the bay."

I'm already past her, fire blanket under my arm because the fairy lights over the donor wall have been dramatic lately, and I respect physics. Rain needles my face; the boardwalk slicks under my sneakers. At step twelve, Ethan appears in my periphery, scrubs, jacket half on, face set to useful.

"You okay?" he says, matching my pace like we practiced this.

"I'm not porcelain," I manage, breath hot in the cold. "First-aid kit. Grudge against gravity."

"Beautiful." Not flirty, true.

The boy—spiky hair and, scraped knee, clutches his ankle on the landing, biting the inside of his cheek to keep the tears from changing the weather. Ace is already there, teal bow tie damp with fog, chin on the kid's calf like a weighted blanket with opinions. Mr. Pierce hovers with the towel he carries the way saints carry relics.

"You scared the stairs," I tell the boy, kneeling. "They'll be more careful."

Ace shifts, tail wagging once, and sits on cue when Ethan gestures. Sit, visit, paw, his therapy-dog training is a poem written in shorthand. Even here, Ace offers choice, not demand.

Ethan's voice goes low and even, and the one who teaches shows how to stand down. "I'm going to check the range of motion. Tell me when it's a no. Good. That's it. Breathe with me." Gauze. Gentle hands. A sling was improvised from Tom's tie because leadership can donate its accessories. We hop-step down, Ace as escort and moral support, Tom announcing lane closures like the stairs have media.

Clara wraps the boy's ankle, the sound of gauze hissing against skin unlocking a flicker of memory, her own ankle once strapped after prom, sitting on cold bleachers, ink smudged across a napkin where Ethan had scrawled Next time, we'll dance barefoot by the lake. She'd forgotten that until tonight. Now it unspools like ribbon.

Harbor greets us with a hush that feels earned. Rose and Henry materialize with a thermos labeled "FORTITUDE"; Rose tucks the towel around the boy, as if compassion has muscle memory. "Repentant cardiologists tip well," Henry mutters. Rose answers, "They carry change of heart," and the night steals a laugh from every rib.

Midnight pretends to ignore all of this from the railing, then bumps the kid's elbow once, knighthood bestowed, and stalks off to inspect the poetry display. The boy laughs exactly once, and the town unclenches.

"You scared the stairs," I repeat, smoothing his hair. He grins, crooked and brave.

"Clinic?" Ethan asks.

"Go. I'll lock up and meet you."

He hesitates one fraction of a breath, my throat opens without permission, and then he squeezes my shoulder and goes, a moving definition of steady.

When the door shuts behind them, the wind shifts. It smells like cedar soap and relief. It also smells like timing, which used to be my enemy and might want to be our friend.

Tape touches glass at the donor wall, making that soft hush-stick sound that always soothes me. Tonight it whispers: hold steady.

Dream (dock; noon)

The boards are warm under my bare feet. A dented first-aid tin waits at the end like a punchline I finally understand. Inside, our napkin rules in blue ink: No running without a goodbye. No turning silence into punishment. Tell the truth even when timing hates it. A new line in my hand: Make the timing worthy of the truth. The church bell rings once, twice, three times. Midnight sneezes beside me like an unimpressed judge. A figure lifts his hand, not to claim, just to ask. I open my palm. The paper heart doesn't melt. It shines.

I wake standing in my own doorway, rain in my hair, and the donor wall glowing like a galaxy we built out of ordinary.

THE ASK AND THE ANSWER

ETHAN

Joan hands me a chart and a look. "You're damp. Fix both."

We ice, we wrap, we schedule a follow-up. Ace does paperwork with his chin on a knee, which is to say morale. The kid leaves with a sticker and a story that will grow antlers by Monday. I lean on the counter and admit the thing that won't stay put.

"They called again," I tell Joan. "The kind of call that used to make my bones louder."

"Say no in writing," she says. "Alphabetize something after. You're less dangerous when labels agree with you."

I open my inbox. Final package. Let's talk timing. The subject line is smooth as glass and twice as slippery. I write the only sentence that feels like oxygen. Thank you for the generous offer. I'm declining. My work, and my life, are here in Willow Cove. Please remove me from future outreach. Send. A fence you can put your back to.

"Alphabetizing feelings would be easier," I mutter, taping Noah's fox sketch above the AED cabinet. Joan chuckles. "Fences aren't walls; they're invitations with rules," she says, walking off with the authority of someone who has lived it.

A child points at the fox. "He's guarding the heart," she whispers. And I decide to let her be right.

On my way out, I tape Noah's fox sketch above the AED cabinet because wonder should be first aid too. People slow down for what they love; I want to stack the deck.

Back at the shop, Clara is at the window pressing a red paper book into the center of the donor wall; For the kid who needs the fox on page 27, and if I'd been the sort of man who believed in omens, I would have called this one by its first name. She catches my reflection in the glass, and I catch the exact second her face softens, like she decided to breathe on purpose.

"They'll call again," she says.

"I wrote it down," I answer. "No."

The smile that happens on her mouth is the kind I'd line up for. "Ocelot tonight?"

"As if my ribs would let me forget."

Ocelot (kitchen table)

Noah judges grilled-cheese texture like a sommelier. Midnight files a complaint, then accepts cheddar like absolution. We triage algebra, donor calls, and whether Tom can be trusted with props at the photo booth. "Lanterns, not pirates," Noah decrees. "Ace supervises."

"Geese union filed an appeal," Noah texts me later, deadpan. I nearly drop my phone laughing.

When he wanders off to sketch, Clara and I stand shoulder to shoulder at the sink and lay our cards face up.

"Urgency is a door salesmen hold open with their foot," I say, which is not poetry but is finally my truth. "I want ordinary with you so badly it feels like a miracle."

She traces a flour comet on my jaw with her thumb. "I'm done punishing you for silences we both bled from. I want ordinary too. With heat. With patience."

We kiss like a toast, slow, aware, banked. Consent isn't just a rule; it's a rhythm. Her fingers hook into the seam of my shirt, jaw tilting as if she's memorizing the angle. We pause long enough to check, then sink again into the kind of kiss that rewrites air.

"After the gala," she says against my smile, a promise that lands like a hand on a railing. "We say more."

"Deal."

LANTERNS, NOT PIRATES

CLARA

If small towns had vital signs, ours would be the sound a room makes right before the poem. Fairy lights stitch the library ceiling; the donor wall throws back gold and silver in a glow that feels like being believed. Lavender and orange-peel from the lanterns thread the air. The Harbor Street Strings turn air into silk. Tom opens with "Lanterns, not pirates!" and, for once, the bell above my ribs agrees with his slogan. He visibly resists adding pirate hats, jaw twitching with restraint.

The Crossword Crew holds up phones with blue lights in protest until Rose bribes them with cookies. The Lakewalk Moms circulate QR codes for donations, efficient as ever. Noah's crosswalk endcap, open books flowing into each other, tiny foxes hidden where impatient eyes won't see, draws a gasp from the room. Ethan stands three feet away: near enough to catch, far enough not to steal. The look on his face could teach a weather vane loyalty.

The quartet falters, breaker hiccup, and I'm halfway to the closet when Ethan's already there with a pocket screwdriver and a history of not letting things fall. Lights steady. My throat does too.

Backstage by the staff door where only the donor wall can eavesdrop, he presses a blank silver heart into my palm. "For the name you've been saving," he whispers.

"After the gala." I can feel the shape of the letters my hand wants to make. I'm not ready to make them in front of our neighbors.

Kelsey from Cove Chatter hovers at the edge with a lemon cardigan and a pencil like a scalpel. A thumb smudge of graphite on her wrist hints that she once drew. "Redemption arc?" she breathes.

"Poetry, donor wall, therapy dogs," I say, nodding at the press sheet. "No minors. No prying. If you want a story, buy a heart."

She does. Luz, in neat block letters. She tapes it to the glass and touches it twice, as if sealing a door she had forgotten she could open.

Later, Ethan raises his paddle on a gift certificate titled Private Bookstore Browsing + After-Hours Tea, and Tom surrenders at thirty like a man who loves me enough to lose. "Sold," I say too fast, face too warm, and the lake in my chest decides to be kind.

We almost get away clean.

At the end of cleanup, while lanterns breathe and Ace accepts exactly three farewell pats, my phone hums with a voicemail transcription that tastes like tin. Final package. We can make the timing work. The hospital name glints like a trap. I don't press play. Not here. Not in this light.

A Polaroid clicks backstage: Clara and Ethan laughing at a spilled tray. Later, it will live on her fridge.

Under the awning, he kisses me once, then again, the second longer, the kind that stops because we said it would. "Tomorrow," he says into my hair.

"Tomorrow," I say back. The bell in my ribs answers one, two, three.

LINES WE DON'T CROSS, LINES WE DO

ETHAN

Morning brings fog you could write your name in. The boardwalk is slick until it isn't. Clara almost decks the rail, and my body moves like someone else wrote the choreography, hands under her elbows, "Knees soft," a kiss that tastes like rain and restraint. We part laughing because

Ace woofs once, the civility clause, and because patience is proof, not punishment.

Back at the clinic, Sloane's number chews at the edge of my screen. I forward the voicemail to a folder named 'Not Our Story' and send a second email: To confirm, I will not be entertaining additional offers. Then I do what Joan prescribes when the past gets loud: I alphabetize the crash cart, label the drawer, and tape Noah's fox where people will see it first.

By noon, I'm at the shop. Clara's inside with a Sharpie and the face she gets when she's about to be brave. She doesn't look up when I step through the door, but her shoulders do the slow exhale of a woman who already knows the answer and chooses to ask anyway.

"Are we going to be okay if we win?" she says without turning.

"We already decided to," I say. "Last night. On the porch. In the kitchen. On a staircase with a kid and a dog. I'm here, Clara."

She nods once, like she expected me to say it, but needed to hear it in this room. Then she presses her palm to the center pane, where the red paper book waits, and writes four letters I can't breathe through for a full beat; HOME, in tiny script at the bottom corner of the heart, where only people who slow down will see.

I don't kiss her. Not here. Not yet. Instead, I set the sign back to OPEN and stand behind the counter while Midnight claims the poetry shelf like a king who survived a coup. The first customer through the door is Mrs. Donnelly with the goose-pecked hem; she buys a romance with a repentant cardiologist and pretends she didn't pick it for symbolism.

Pinned on the corkboard above the register: a postcard reading Cease & Desist, Honk & Assist, signed by the Goose Union. Noah must've snuck it there.

When the afternoon hush arrives, the one that smells like pages and patience, I take the blank silver heart she gave back to me last night and print E. H. at the edge of it, small and private. I don't press it to the pane. Not yet. Some lines wait because the waiting is part of the truth.

Lila drops by, straightening my collar before I can protest. I roll my eyes; she hugs me hard. "You're an idiot," she says, but soft. Family is sometimes only that.

Dream (dock; dusk)

We meet in the middle. The napkin is folded into a tin that doesn't rust anymore. The bell rings once, twice, three times. We lift our hands at the same time, not to claim, to ask, and the paper heart glows like it learned the word afterward. Bridge boards gleam under lanternlight, maintained together.

I wake to the register dinging and Clara laughing at something Noah said about the goose's legal counsel. The day goes on. We let it. We keep choosing.

CHAPTER THIRTY-ONE

Windows, Vows, And Verbs

STORMGLASS & SPARKS

CLARA

The scream doesn't sound like fear. It sounds like glass deciding it's done keeping our secrets.

One second, Monroe Books & More hums like it always does, floorboards purring, pages whispering, Midnight draped across the history shelf like a velvet judge. The next, the wind shoulders Harbor Street, and the big front pane answers with a bright, thin ping that snatches breath from my ribs. A storm whistle pushes in from the lake, and the pane quivers like it's holding back a confession.

Fairy lights shiver over the donor window. One bulb pops with a petty flash. Then the strand spits a tongue of sparks toward the hearts we taped there this morning, gold, silver, one red paper book waiting for the generous someone who'll claim it.

"Power strip!" I vault the counter. "Doors open, cross breeze!"

Maya barrels in on a gust, curls damp, tray of cinnamon knots balanced like a miracle. "Panic is banned," she declares, hip-checking both doors wide. "Put that on my gravestone." She follows it up with a grin, softer, meant only for me: "You've got this, boss. We're right here."

The flame takes a greedy breath toward the paper. Not my window.

I rip the fire blanket from its hook and smother, press, hold. Heat kisses my knuckles through the fabric; sugar smoke stings like the memory of a mistake. The lights blink, decide to be dramatic, blink again.

"Left edge. Top seam," says a voice my bones still recognize. Ethan, rain on his hair, cedar soap in the air, jacket half on, reading the room like he never forgot the language of crisis. He catches the ladder, braces it with surgeon's hands. "I'll spot you."

"I make the plans in this store," I tell him, but my hands are already moving. Painter's tape, towel, prayer, I don't say.

From the doorway: "Therapy cavalry!" Mr. Pierce jogs in. Ace sits prim in his teal bowtie, leans his warm chin against a trembling teenager's knee, heartbeat to heartbeat, until the kid's breathing remembers how to count. Midnight stalks to the sill, sits directly on my tape roll with papal disdain, and glares at physics. Amateurs.

I lay a reinforcement strip; the bead nosing the seam fattens, then slides away like a scolded rumor. The pane holds. My lungs follow its example.

I climb down. We turn at the same time. For a breath, the inches between us are the only math that matters. The bell on the counter clicks in a draft like punctuation. My mouth remembers his before my brain does anything sensible.

We kiss.

Not wildfire. Current. Warm mouth, careful hands, yes, humming like electricity under skin. His palm cups my jaw as if it learned the map years ago and filed it under sacred; my fingers find the damp curl at his nape, and the room brightens at the edges. My brain shouts questions? W: What if this ruins everything? What if it saves everything? But my body already knows the answer. When I make a sound I've never made for anyone else, he swallows it like gratitude.

The pane pings again, elderly chaperone. We break out laughing.

Just in time for the fairy lights to fizzle, behave, and decide to be part of the living again.

"Status?" Maya calls, already doling out sugar knots as sacraments.

"Stable," Ethan says, eyes still on me. "Improving."

The town inhales. We get back to work.

ETHAN

Adrenaline is a loan; it collects with interest. Cadence is what you pay it back with.

We reset breakers, check outlets, and tape the top seam twice because physics respects redundancy. When the room's pulse steadies, Clara's does too; I can hear it where we keep straying close, in that magnetic slipstream that remembers us seventeen and foolish and insists we try again without the foolish. A flash from the bleachers, napkins, promises, the scrawled rules we swore on, crosses my memory, and I realize the timing may finally be worthy of the truth.

In the stockroom, I wash smoke off her knuckles in the tiny sink and want ridiculous things like a lifetime of washing smoke off her knuckles. "Breathe with me?" I ask out of habit. Infour, holdfour, outfour, pause. The frets under her skin relax.

"Thank you," she says, and the words land like a hand at the small of my back. "For the tape. And the kiss."

"Both are infrastructure," I say. She laughs, that quick, bellbright sound that still rearchitects my chest.

My phone buzzes, that New York number, slick subject lines with too many commas breathing through the casing like a promise I don't want. I flip it over. Not today, door salesman.

"Closet leak's back at the clinic," I tell her. "I'll fix it before it turns into a parable."

"Because morale matters," she says solemnly. "Minimalist glitter."

"Morale matters," I echo, because she's right. And because it puts my mouth on the word we without scaring either of us.

CLARA — Dream Sequence No storm this time. Noon. The dock boards are warm. The lake is the color of a secret I'm finally strong enough to tell. At the end sits a dented first-aid tin, the one that's been tailing me in sleep since I was eighteen and pretending vows were just pretty verbs. Inside, our napkin rules live where I left them: • No running without a goodbye. • No turning silence into punishment. • Tell the truth even when timing hates it. Someone, me, has added a line in the same stubborn hand I use to write donor names: Make the timing worthy of the truth.

The church rope drops three clean notes across the water. A figure lifts a hand at the shoreline, not to claim, to ask. I open my palm, expecting the paper heart to dissolve, the way it always does right before I wake.

It shines.

I wake standing at my donor window, palm pressed flat to glass like I'm keeping stars from falling. The hush stick of the tape is still there. Stay is a verb, my chest whispers. Use it.

Fences & Foxfire

ETHAN Joan finds me alphabetizing the crash cart like a penitent. "If it keeps you from emailing venture capitalists," she says, "alphabetize the sun."

I grin. "Working on fences."

"Good boy." She tosses me the storage room key. "Make the closet behave. Morale matters."

The leak sulks; I coax it into virtue. The AED that used to live in exile under a box labeled HOLIDAY • MAYBE? Goes back to the right hallway, a tiny gold heart sticker in the corner because Clara said hope belongs on equipment. I tape Noah's fox sketch above it, tail raised, trotting along a stack of books toward the red lever, as if wonder itself could be a sign. When Noah hands it to me, he brushes my shoulder, testing trust. I bump back, wordless math solved.

My phone buzzes again. City code. Final. Package. Sweetened. I forward the message to a new folder named 'Not Our Story' and add a filter to shunt the Hydra into a dark, quiet place. Then I sit at the clinic computer and write the email that my mouth already said today:

Thank you for the generous offer. I'm declining. The timing isn't the issue; the choice is. My work, and my life, are here in Willow Cove. Please remove me from future outreach. —Ethan Hale

I read it twice, deleted a hedge, added a period like a fencepost, and pressed send.

Lila calls thirty seconds later, sensing paperwork like weather. "Say it out loud," she orders.

"I'm staying."

She sniffles (denies it), then gets bossy about shirts for the gala and tells me to bring pocket screwdrivers because Tom's breaker panel is older than sin. "Also," she adds, voice going soft, "you make soup for your family tonight, or I will hijack Ace and show up with a ladle."

"My family," I repeat, just to hear how the math feels in my mouth. It balances for the first time in a decade.

NOAH — Flash (sketchbook pages) Graphite smudges my thumb where I shaded a fox tail too hard. Mom says I should draw lighter. Ethan says I should lean into the shadow for depth. I pretend I'm not listening to either of them.

At school, the goose patrols the blacktop like a cop with an agenda. Someone muttered the thing I've been waiting to hear since a man with my jawline walked back into Willow Cove. I didn't swing. I didn't sink. I breathed, which is gross and adult and feels like cheating. Secret fear: what if people expect me to be like him when I'm not? Secret hope: maybe I'll get to choose who I am anyway.

At lunch, I sketched a line of books that looked like a bridge and put the fox on it anyway. On the margin, I wrote Ocelot, because Friday nights have rules now: soup, grilled cheese, movies with rope bridges that never break, and no hard conversations unless I bring them up. I'm not going to admit it, but I like rules when we make them. Exact grilled cheese rulings: two slices of cheddar, never American, golden, not burnt, cut diagonal, not square. Ritual matters.

I gave Ethan the fox for the clinic. "For the AED," I said. "So people slow down for wonder before they panic." He looked at me like I just gave him a planet. Adults are weird.

CLARA: The Lakewalk Moms affix QR codes to gala flyers, much like NASA mission patches. Rose and Henry deliver an aspirationally red scarf for the auction and a thermos labeled FORTITUDE for me. They argue about whether the scarf is crimson or cardinal until Henry bows and declares, "Lanterns, not pirates!" Rose smacks him with a mitten, and we all laugh.

Kelsey from Cove Chatter hovers at new releases, buys a gold heart without prying, and writes Luz on it in sturdy block letters. She touches the silver line of tape twice, as if sealing something invisible. Later, she'll write the article that helps us all forgive ourselves for being human.

In the afternoon lull, I find the envelope taped under my till, another printout of that old article with one word circled in red and a note that says You can't buy this town. Midnight sits on it like a paperweight and flicks his tail. I file the letter under Not Our Story, cut a fresh red book for the center of the window, and write in my neatest hand, Noah's idea; For the kid who needs the fox on page 27. I press it where the light will catch and let the hush stick sound calm my chest.

My phone hums on the counter. I put it facedown. After the gala. After the lanterns. After I'm brave on purpose.

Lanterns, Not Pirates

CLARA "Welcome to the Books & Hearts Gala," I tell a room strung with fairy lights and audacity. "No pirates. Only lanterns."

Tom fist pumps like he invented restraint. In the library closet later, I overhear him whisper: "Lanterns, not pirates," like it's a battle hymn. The Harbor Street Strings make the air remember gentleness. Ace works the aisle like a dignitary; Midnight prowls the poetry shelf like a small god auditioning for benevolence. During one donor bid, Ace retrieves a dropped bookmark from a child, and the whole room claps. Community joy.

Our donor wall gleams, gold and silver hearts, the red paper book burning a soft ember at the center.

We pull the sheet off the library endcap, and Noah's crosswalk sketch makes the room gasp. Open books flow into each other. Tiny foxes are hidden where drivers will only notice if they slow down to look. A goose trotting out of a paragraph like municipal satire. A second grader in galaxy leggings whispers, "There," and points to the fox on page 27. Noah's ears go red. My heart does worse things.

The lights threaten mischief; Tom panics; I smile at the ceiling, as if I can parent electricity into making better choices. In the staff hall, Ethan flips a breaker with the pocket screwdriver Lila bullied him into packing. The fairy lights decide to behave. The room recalibrates.

During the silent auction, I catch my breath long enough to watch Ethan raise his paddle for Private Bookstore Browsing + After-hours Tea. "Fifty," he says, not looking away from me. I sell the hour faster than dignity allows and have to pretend the flush on my face is a philanthropic fever.

Backstage, by the staff door no one but the donor wall can see, he presses a blank silver heart into my palm. "For when you're ready to write the name you've been saving," he whispers.

I don't write tonight. I hold it like a warm stone.

Later, Kelsey sidles up in her lemon cardigan for a quote about forgiveness. I hand her the press sheet and a Sharpie. "Buy a heart," I say gently. "Write the name of someone who made you brave." She does. Luz shines in gold from the glass. Boundaries, I remember Rose saying, are hospitality for the soul. Tonight feels like proof.

We close on applause and cinnamon. The town leaves smelling like oranges and hope.

At the awning, the square is quiet as a held breath. Ethan says, "Tomorrow," and kisses me like a promise with a pulse. The bell inside me rings three times.

My phone hums. A voicemail preview scrolls across the screen: 'Final package.' We can make the timing work. A hospital name that used to feel like a sky show up in the transcript. The ground tilts.

I don't press play. Not yet. Lanterns first.

ETHAN On my way back to the clinic with a coil of extension cord and the kind of tired you earn, my phone glows again with the number I used to salute. I duck into the alley like a coward and answer because old reflexes are bad at dying.

"Not tonight," I tell the glass voice when it says sweet words with teeth. "Tomorrow at nine, I can listen. I won't say yes."

When I step into the square again, Clara is at the edge of the light, her keys in hand, and that careful smile people make when the floor just moves. The alley carries sound like gossip. Of course it does. This town collects echoes, then throws them back as hymns.

"After the gala," she says, and this time it sounds like a test.

"After the gala," I answer, and it feels like a vow I need to prove with actions, not adjectives.

Ocelot Night & the Email That Didn't Win

CLARA Ocelot night smells like browned butter and courage. Noah sits on the stool like a judge. Midnight does his routine of pretending not to beg, yet still accepts tribute anyway.

Ethan passes the texture test. "Acceptable," Noah intones, anointing him. We watch an old adventure with improbable rope bridges that never quite fall. Halfway through, my son's head slides into my lap the way tides find shore. Ethan looks away so I don't have to pretend I'm not crying.

At the sink afterward, we stack plates like people who believe ordinary counts. "Tell me something real," I say, because napkin rules need maintenance.

"I used to think urgency was a personality trait," he admits. "Turns out it's a door salesman's prop with their foot." His knuckles brush my hip. "I want to be bored next to you."

"Bold," I say, and answer with my mouth because bold deserves bilingual affirmation.

When he leaves, the house hums like it trusts me. Noah's pencil scratches in his room. The lake practices calm.

I press play on the voicemail.

Dr. Hale, the final package is sweetened. We can make the timing work.

I file it under Not Our Story and sit very still until my hands stop trying to be weather. Then I take the blank heart from my pocket and set it on the fridge with a magnet shaped like a fox. Tomorrow, I'll write the name.

ETHAN

Joan is waiting for me with two donuts and a look that could staple a policy to a moving ceiling. "Say it," she orders.

"I'm staying."

"Then write like you speak."

I open the email and decline again, but longer, kinder, firmer, so even the parts of me that still enjoy commas understand there's no wiggle in this fence. Then I texted Lila Done. She replies with a knife emoji, a fox, and Proud of you.

At dawn, I jog around the lake. The rope bell tosses three bright notes into the fog. The lighthouse blinks like patience incarnate. I pick a flat stone, press my old printed offer into it, and drop the bundle into the clinic shred bin instead of lighting backyard symbolism. Growth looks like not starting fires you don't need.

Back home, I tape a sticky note over my bathroom mirror where I'll see it when habit tries to vote: Stay is a verb. Use it.

Then I walk to the bookstore with fresh peonies, decisions, Lila says, and find Clara already at the window, palm to glass, writing a name on a silver heart with the pen I gave her when we were seventeen and thought ink was enough.

"Lanterns, not pirates," she murmurs when she sees the flowers.

"Lanterns," I say. "And foxes that make drivers slow down."

She lifts the cap, stops, and meets my eyes. "Read your email?"

"I wrote it," I answer.

"Good," she says, and writes.

For the man who chose us.

She presses the heart against the glass, applying firm pressure, with no bubbles. The tape hush-sticks. Outside, Ace knocks on the door and sits like he's guarding the perimeter of a new story. Inside, Midnight thumps his tail once against the sill, blessing or judgment, hard to tell.

And for the first time since I was a boy who made stupid vows under bleachers, I feel the present tense fit.

I'm here. I stay.

CHAPTER THIRTY-TWO

Stormglass & The Truth

EDGE OF THE STORM

CLARA

The scream doesn't sound like fear. It sounds like metal insisting on its say.

One heartbeat, I'm aligning fresh gold hearts on the front window, names inked in neat loops, tape pressed flat, hope made visible, and the next, Harbor Street tilts. Wind shoulders the awning. A Lakeside Market tent slips its knot, and a pole scythes across the sidewalk toward Maya's café door, where three kids hover in the holy trance of sugar knots.

"Inside, now!" My voice goes iron. They scatter. The pole claps the brick with a crack that buzzes my teeth. The impact shudders up my spine. The glass rattles, and my stomach does a backflip because if the donor window breaks tonight, the fundraiser could collapse under insurance and repairs before it begins.

I run. Rain has the boards slick as glass. Fingers lock around cold aluminum at the exact second a second set closes too, warm, certain, steady.

"Got it," Ethan says, breath controlled, rain beading on his lashes.

We ride the torque into the jamb. My shoulder hits hard; his body brackets mine. Together we pin the pole and hold while the gust flexes. For a suspended breath, it's just our heartbeats and the hiss of weather and the bell over my door rattling like a sparrow in a chapel.

"On three," I manage. "One, two, three."

We lower, slow as prayer. Mr. Pierce appears with Ace in a teal bow tie like the town sent cavalry; he snaps a bungee, the line sings taut, and the metal finally behaves. The kids clap because Willow Cove applauds survival like a sport we train for with neighbors and cinnamon.

Ethan looks at me. I look back. Relief and the wrong kind of heat tug in opposite directions until my laugh finds room between them. My hands shake. He sees it; he always did.

"Report?" Maya calls, already pouring chamomile like medicine. "Physics is on notice. Also, glitter never looked so dramatic."

"Stable," Ethan answers, eyes on me. "Improving."

Then the pane at the top of my donor window pings, thin, bright, decisive. A bead noses the seam like it wants in.

"Left edge," he says. "Top seam."

"I make the plans in this store," I tell him, already grabbing tape and a towel.

"Excellent." His mouth tilts. "Make this one with me."

He steadies the ladder; I climb. Thunder counts to three somewhere over the lake. I lay the strip and smooth with my whole palm, the way I press first-chapter stickers for seven-year-olds buying their first real book. The bead hesitates. Fattens. Slides away.

Below me, his voice goes low enough to find the places under my skin that remember him. "Good," he says. I step down. We turn at the same moment.

We shouldn't. We do.

The kiss lights like kindling and settles like embers, steady current, no wildfire. His palm cups my jaw like it learned the map at seventeen and never forgot; my fingers find the curl at his nape; the room brightens at the edges. Outside, wind sifts rain into lace. Inside, breath becomes a language we didn't mean to speak out loud. The taste of salt from his skin and the sound of the storm hush make my knees give slightly.

"Terms," I murmur against his smile because the word keeps me from drowning.

"Still signed," he answers, then the pane gives a faint scold and we both laugh, the kind that sets the ground back under you.

We work the rest: towels, ladder, morale laps from Ace, papal disdain from Midnight, who struts by and pretends to own the storm. By the time the squall remembers manners, the window is a vow instead of a hazard. I add a silver heart; For anyone who needs today to be kind, and press it firm. I sneak in a red one in the corner, half-hidden, for reasons I don't want to name yet.

That should be the end of this scene. It isn't.

A phone vibrates in his jacket. He silences it with a flick of the thumb, guiltless. The window throws our reflections together, his jaw set to useful, my mouth tinged pink from a kiss I'm pretending I didn't steal before noon, and something restless in my ribs tries to make an old shape.

"Chamomile," Maya declares, shoving a mug into my hand. "Minimalist glitter can wait five minutes."

I sip. I breathe. I remember how.

The storm slackens, the lake surface outside smoothing into pewter calm, reflecting lanterns strung like an afterthought of stars.

THE DREAM, THE DOOR, THE VOICE (Ethan)

Dream: the dock at noon, not storm-dark, boards warm, lake beveled silver, rope bell dropping three clean notes through my chest. Clara stands at the far end like a proof I haven't earned yet. She lifts a hand, not to claim, to ask. A dented first-aid tin sits where planks meet sky. Inside: a napkin I folded like scripture at seventeen; No running without a goodbye. No turning silence into punishment. Tell the truth even when timing hates it. In her handwriting, a fourth line: Make the timing worthy of the truth.

I wake with rain in my throat and a decision where indecision used to live.

I sent the email from the clinic break room between a tetanus booster and a sink that finally learned manners: Appreciate the offer. I'm staying in Willow Cove. Please remove me from future outreach.

No heroism, no speech. A fence, simple and true. Hydras hate fences. I'm learning to love fences.

Joan reads me like an ECG and nods once. "Good," she says. "Now eat something green before the fundraiser makes you ornamental."

The phone still tries twice. I don't answer. The third time it calls is later, behind the library, where the herb boxes chime like forgiving bells and mint breathes like fresh forgiveness. The square is all lanterns and neighbors. Clara is inside, writing names on paper hearts like prayers with tape. My thumb hovers. I answer because old hunger is a wily thing, and I don't trust it unless I look it in the eye.

"Final package," the voice purrs. "We can make the timing work."

"I can't," I say, and the relief that floods my chest is indecent. "Not now, not after."

"After?"

"The life I'm busy building."

Clara appears at the backstage door then, ink on her fingers, eyes quick, mouth soft in a way that ruins me. I end the call. No goodbyes to ghosts.

"Breakers?" she mouths, lifting a coil of extension cord.

"On it," I answer, then tuck a blank heart into her palm. "For when you're ready to write the name you keep saving."

We move in parallel until parallel tightens.

STORMLIGHT, SUGAR, AND THE ARGUMENT WE CAN'T OUTRUN (Clara)

Gala night dresses itself in fairy bulbs and cinnamon.

"Welcome to the Books & Hearts," I say, mic in hand, the donor window glowing like a galaxy we assembled with tape and breath. "Lanterns. No pirates. But if you want a T-shirt, Mayor Tom has the order form."

Laughter ripples the room. Ace wears a teal bow tie and dispenses benedictions. Midnight prowls the poetry shelf like a small god auditioning for benevolence. Rose and Henry settle in as if the night belongs to them personally. It probably does.

We unveil Noah's crosswalk design for the library corner. Gasps. A small girl in galaxy leggings points at the fox hidden on page twenty-seven and whispers there with such reverence that my heart kneels. Noah blushes right up to his ears and then scurries backstage to hand me a Sharpie for the next reveal, like a pro. Ethan stands exactly three feet away, near enough to catch, far enough not to steal, and his smile looks like someone gave him back a country.

Between lots, a paperback coughs up a folded square with his seventeen-year-old handwriting grinning up at me: If the stars are listening, I told them; I tuck it into the glass case beside Rose's prom photo and a ticket stub from the first lantern walk and label it in tidy script: Teenage nonsense that became a life.

When the bakery basket goes for a scandalous sum, Mayor Tom hisses "Lanterns, not pirates!" into the mic, and the town cheers louder than poetry ever earned. Then comes the gift certificate for Private Browsing & After-Hours Tea at my store. I mean to look dignified while the bids percolate.

Ethan raises his paddle. "Fifty."

"Thirty," Tom lies, sitting on his hands.

"Fifty," Ethan repeats without looking away from me. Sold. The room mercifully pretends not to applaud.

I find him by the staff door in the wedge where the quartet can't see, and the donor wall can.

"You didn't have to."

"I wanted to buy an hour that belongs to us," he says simply.

Something I've been starving tenses toward yes. Something scared of starving again tugs back hard.

"Clara?" he says, softer. "I told them no."

I want to say I know. I want to press that blank heart to the center of the glass and write a name I've been hoarding. Instead, I feel the world tilt with a memory that isn't a memory yet, his phone in the alley, a voice asking about timing, the way he said after. The old hinge in me remembers how to creak.

"After the cleanup," I say, aiming for brave and hitting careful. "Walk me home."

We carry the last chair together. Lanterns drowse. The square exhales. On the awning's shadow line, he kisses my mouth once, then once again, longer, warmer, exactly enough, and leaves the door unopened like a man who respects thresholds. My ribs ring like the rope bell in the dream.

"Tomorrow," he whispers.

"Tomorrow." I feel the bell in my ribs ring three times and, for once, don't flinch from the echo.

Then my phone hums with a notification I didn't ask for. A transcribed voicemail from a number I used to pretend didn't know my name: Final package. We can make the timing work. My stomach drops like an elevator.

"Everything okay?" he asks, eyes sharp as weather.

"I'm fine," I lie, which is my tell. He knows it; so do I. The old bolt on an old door slides into place without asking me first.

Lila pings me a text; You okay?, but I tuck the screen down. Tonight isn't for unraveling more threads.

THE FIGHT (BOTH)

CLARA

The house smells like peppermint and steam. The sink clicks in that way it did before, as if it remembers how to be helpful. He stands in my kitchen with his sleeves rolled and an ease that does terrible things to my restraint. Noah's fallen asleep, lopsided on the couch, Midnight draped across his shins like a living punctuation mark.

"I heard the message," I say, before courage runs.

"I sent the email," he answers, before mine trips. "No. In writing. Clara, I showed the fence."

"You said after." The two syllables land between us like a trap we both stepped in.

"After the gala," he says, hands up, palm-out, not a plea, an offering. "Not after us." His thumb rubs once against his ring finger, a tell of nerves.

ETHAN

I want to say a hundred pretty things that would set us on fire. I don't. I have learned something rare and late: love without proof is theater. "I told them no," I say. "I told you yes."

CLARA

"You told me yes at seventeen, too." I hate how it sounds, sharp and small. "You also told a city yes. And when the city shouted louder,"

"It wasn't the city," he says, quiet and terrible. "It was fear of being small. I'm done bargaining with that ghost." He swallows. "You get to be angry about every night you raised a fever without me. I get to prove I learned the language of staying."

"What happens when the ghost sends flowers?"

"I won't answer the door."

"And if it shows up with ambulances and commas and the kind of hallway you used to dream about?"

"I already live in the hallway I dreamed about," he says, and it's so earnest I want to throw something and kiss him until the world goes white. "It smells like paper and cinnamon and lake. It sounds like your laugh. Noah told me my grilled cheese passed lossless compression."

"That is not what he said." A laugh stabs out of me against my will. I hate him for it and love him for it and hate myself for the ordinariness of wanting something that could vanish. "You can't ask me to believe and then call it proof when it's only been a handful of good days."

"I'm not asking you to believe. I'm asking you to let me keep proving." He steps in, slow as a tide. "Break up with me if you need to.

Make me sleep in my own bed. I'll still be at the clinic at eight and on your porch at six and at the window on Thursdays with new paper hearts."

"Stop trying to be a poem." My throat burns. "Just, don't be a vanishing act."

"I can do plain." He sets the kettle on, switches it off again, and doesn't touch me. "I can do dishes and oil changes, and commas in grocery lists. I can do denial-of-service to anybody who tells you glitter is an inefficient currency."

"Minimalist glitter," I correct, because if we start naming the apocalypse in the kitchen, I will never stop. "You think you can outrun my fear with domestic metaphors?"

"No." His eyes soften in that way that both saves and ruins me. "I think I can walk next to it until it gets bored." The rope bell chimes in my ribs, uninvited.

I forget and reach, fingers in his shirt, mouth finding the place that teaches me moderation is a kind of mercy. He answers with heat that behaves, palm on my jaw, the kind of kiss that leaves room for air. His tongue traces restraint more than hunger, and the hum it pulls from my chest shakes me. When I come up from the bright hum of it, I'm still trembling. Sometimes, restraint is louder than the tumble.

"I need time," I say. "Not because you're failing. Because I'm tired of failing myself. I want to stop performing okay and actually be okay."

"I'll be here," he says. "All the time you need."

"Don't promise that." It comes out sharper than I mean. "Just… do it."

The kettle finally remembers its job and wails like a baby. We both laugh in that stunned way that feels like hope tripping on the doorstep. We make tea. We don't solve anything. We don't make it worse. We remember how to stand in a kitchen together without trying to script forever.

He leaves with a kiss on my temple and a hand on the doorframe like he's steadying the house from the outside. After the lock clicks, I sink to the floor and press my back against the cabinets, letting the tears be ordinary, not theatrical.

Midnight thumps down, head-butts my knee, and decides I am worth guarding. I am. Tomorrow I'll write a name on the blank heart and press it to the glass. Not a miracle. A step.

Tonight I sleep. The dream returns like tide: noon light, warm boards, the napkin of rules, the line I added in ink that doesn't wash; Make the timing worthy of the truth, and a paper heart that does not dissolve when I open my hand. Ahead of me, someone lifts a palm. Not to claim. To ask.

This time when I lift mine, I don't shake.

CHAPTER THIRTY-THREE

Stay, Said The Glass

EDGE OF THE MORNING

CLARA

The siren awakens the morning flat, jolting Willow Cove awake like a needle scratch on a favorite record. I'm already mid-stride, two trays of Maya's cinnamon knots fogging their lids, when my phone flashes: Lighthouse steps. Possible injury.

Painter's tape from last night's donor-wall tally clings to my wrist. My shoes aren't built for speed, but I run anyway, the bell over my shop door ringing its alarm of permission.

Halfway up the lighthouse stairs, twelve, thirteen, fourteen, the wind snatches my breath into salt and metal. At the landing, Ace is a velvet guardian, chin firm against a tween's shin. Mr. Pierce grips the towel and dignity. Mayor Tom flutters nearby, rehearsing apologies to gulls.

The boy clutches his ankle like it's the last page in his favorite book.

"You're okay," I tell him. My librarian's voice, gentle but bossy enough to make the weather behave, settles his storm. "The stairs are the ones who got scared."

Then Ethan appears, rain-slick jacket, cedar soap clinging to his collar, heartbeat steady in his throat. He doesn't ask, doesn't hesitate. He kneels, voice soft and sure.

"Let me see, bud. Breathe with me. That's it." His fingers find swelling; the skin is cool and damp from the fog. "Sprain. You're lucky. We'll wrap, ice, and tell your mom you're a hero and smart."

The boy nods solemnly, like wisdom is the price of rescue.

Maya arrives panting with a thermos labeled FORTITUDE. Cinnamon steam swirls like courage itself. Ethan tapes the ankle, demonstrates a safe hop. Ace supervises with a furrowed brow, and Midnight swishes approval. Down the steps, we parade slow but triumphant; Rose and Henry clap, relief echoing. The boy snorts a laugh when Midnight grants him a papal head butt.

"Clinic?" I ask.

"Clinic." Ethan's eyes flick to my mouth as if rediscovering permission. Heat pricks through me, last night's almost-kiss alive again.

This time, he leans in. His palm steadies my jaw; his mouth on mine is steady voltage, two currents braided. It's reverence, not wildfire. Breath stitches to breath until a gull cackles like the lighthouse itself, clearing its throat.

Ace gives a pointed woof. We break, laughing against each other's mouths.

"Go," I breathe. "Save the morning."

"You already did," he says, fog brightening around the words.

He leaves with the boy and Mr. Pierce; Tom herds gulls shouting "Lanterns, not gulls!" Maya presses a cinnamon knot into my hand. Back at my shop, the bell rings once, twice, three, a triplet permission. My palm warms against the donor wall's glass. Gold, silver, one a red paper book glows at the center like an ember that believes again.

"Stay is a verb," I whisper. The glass seems to pulse in answer. And I notice, faintly, an empty space beside the ember, waiting for the right name.

"Clara," Maya says softly behind me, as if sensing my thought. "One day, that space won't be empty anymore."

I turn, eyes wet, and hug her with cinnamon between us.

FOXES, FENCES, AND FRIDAYS

ETHAN

Hydras hate fences, the VC kind that keeps calling. Argus rings again, same pitch, same dangling future. I forward it into a folder called NOT OUR STORY. My hands alphabetize the crash cart until my nervous system agrees I'm still a man, not a leash.

Above the AED cabinet hangs Noah's fox sketch: the tail is lifted, paws padding on book spines, with the lighthouse tucked in the corner. People slow for wonder. That's his motto. I'm adopting it.

Joan pokes her head in, bangs wild, coffee braver than she is. "They called?"

"They called."

"And?"

"I'm staying." It lands in my chest like a lantern catching fire. "Told Noah. Told Clara. Wrote it down."

Her mouth softens. "Good. Now take the sugar to the bookstore before it revolts."

On Harbor Street, wind combs the lake into velvet. Through Clara's window, the donor wall gleams: For the kid who needs the fox on page 27. Inside, she counts hearts, ink smudging her thumb, hair pinned high. Her mouth, the one that destroyed me at seventeen, wields adult gravity now.

"Clinic thanks you for the sugar," I say, setting Maya's offering down. "And I have evidence." I place a printout: Decline. Final. Please remove me from outreach. My initials were scrawled at the bottom.

Clara doesn't touch it. She just looks, reading every letter with her eyes, then looks at me with the light I've been craving. "Thank you," she whispers, more oxygen than thanks.

"Tonight? Ocelot?"

"You'll be judged on texture," she says gravely, which in Clara means: I trust you.

I leave before the urge to memorize her ribbon-tying keeps me there. Midnight bats my leg with a paw: Proceed.

NOAH

The goose on Maple and Third has decided it's the sheriff. He blocks my bike, stares me down. I dismount.

"My mom says leaders cry in supply closets," I tell him. "Maybe you should try it." He honks, or maybe laughs. Same thing.

I cut across the square, nearly witnessing a delivery guy losing a battle with boxes. Ace sidesteps politely, and Midnight rolls his eyes. Outside the clinic, I catch Ethan pocketing his phone, shoulders taut. The lake quizzes him.

"That's the hydra?" I ask.

"You take good notes."

"You leaving?" Nickel taste floods my mouth, sharp and metallic.

"No." Hard, then soft: "No. Told them no. Told your mom yes."

Something in my chest unclenches but doesn't vanish. I hand him a sketch: fox on books, lighthouse in the margin. "For the AED. Reminder to slow down."

He holds it like it might save lives, which it will.

"Also, grilled cheese better not squeak."

"Noted."

We both grin but pretend we didn't.

"Noah," Ethan adds, voice rough, "you're allowed to breathe easy, too."

I nod, quick, because anything else might break me open.

OCELOT NIGHT, WITH EVIDENCE

CLARA

Ocelot Night begins with butter and laughter. Noah leans on the counter, judging serious. Midnight approves cheese with a twitch. Ethan caramelizes onions like devotion is a recipe.

Sandwiches hit the pan, scent of memory forgiven filling the kitchen. Noah grades texture with one nod, the highest honor. Ethan salutes, slides soup my way without asking. That's how he knows me now.

We eat like we're rehearsing a future. Noah gossips about Mayor Tom banning pirate hats from gala photos. Ethan admits that he wrote "Stay" as a verb on a sticky note above his sink. I confess I've stopped hiding my phone at nine like fear is bedtime.

"Tell me something real," I challenge.

"Urgency used to be my favorite excuse," he says. "Now it sounds like a salesman wedging a foot in my door." His knuckles brush my hip as we clear plates, deliberate. "I want to be boring with you. The kind that turns ordinary into vow."

"My real: I punished silence that punished us both. I'm finished." Saying it frees me. The bowls clatter lighter.

We migrate to the couch. Movie plays: rope bridges, miracles. Half-way through, Noah's head slides into my lap like a tide to shore. Ethan meets my gaze. We stay. We breathe.

The hero doesn't fall this time.

When the credits roll, Noah checks the front lock before heading to bed, a quiet signal of safety returned. On the porch, peppermint light bathes us. Ethan tastes like butter and the future. One kiss. Another, longer, deeper. His reverence stops us first.

"Tomorrow," he says.

"Tomorrow," I echo, every version alive.

Silence. The voicemail blinks. I press play. The voice is crisp, full of commas, a hospital name that once lived on a napkin list, ink-blotted at seventeen.

We can make the timing work.

"No," I breathe. "We'll make it worthy." I file it under NOT OUR STORY. Align the red book in the window. Write one more heart: For anyone who needs today to be kind.

I sit for a long time with pen poised above a blank page, then scribble furiously: Home isn't where they call you to be great. Home is where someone waits with soup and a fox drawing.

THE SPACE BETWEEN YES AND ALWAYS
ETHAN

Lantern Night clicks like a key turning. The library thrums: quartet tuning, kids fidgeting in new shoes, parents cloaked in pride. Rose and Henry stride the aisle like royalty. Tom wears a "Lanterns, Not Pirates" button, muttering about poetry as a form of preparedness. I tell him yes.

Clara at the mic. The room hushes. Her hands smudged with ink, her mouth steady with courage. Behind her, the donor wall blazes, gold, silver, one red book like a planet. Home distilled.

We unveil Noah's fox-crosswalk. Gasps. A fourth grader in galaxy tights whispers there at the fox hidden on page 27. Noah fails spectacularly at not glowing. Ace accepts tributes. Midnight prowls like an editor-God.

Kelsey from Cove Chatter hovers but, for once, behaves. She buys a heart: Luz. Tapes it, taps it twice. I believe again in people who carry lemons and pencils.

Music swells. Ceiling holds. Tom nearly creates a crisis with an extension cord. I fix it with a pocket screwdriver, a man who mends what's in reach.

Backstage, I press a blank heart into Clara's hand. "For the name you've been saving." She studies it like a door waiting. My future rearranges to fit two chairs.

The auction turns lively. When Private Bookstore Browsing + After-Hours Tea appears, I bid. I intend to buy time. Her cheeks flush. The crowd coughs politely.

After, under the awning, lake-like silk, rope bell chimes once… twice… three. Our blessing.

"Thank you," she says, prayer and punctuation.

"For staying," I answer, kissing her like patience is proof. Heat tingles at fingertips and throat, but reverence holds the rest.

Her phone buzzes: city number, commas in the ID. The alley remembers sound too well, like last time. She ignores it, pocketing the weight. Her eyes say she chooses to breathe here.

"After the gala," she promises. "We say everything."

"Tomorrow," I vow.

Back home, Lila's texts: 'Read the short poem. I'm proud of you.' A photo of Ace with a toddler. I pin Noah's fox higher over the AED. Tape *Stay is a verb* inside the cabinet. Someday, Clara will find it and smile.

In bed, the old napkin dream returns: bleachers, clover, smeared ink. Rules written before we knew we'd need them. A new line waits now: Make the timing worthy of the truth.

Morning will try us again. Doors will knock with commas. We'll answer with fences, foxes, and a red book glowing at the center of the bravest window I know.

When the bell in my bones rings once… twice… three; I'll know.

Stay.

CONVERSATIONS THAT LINGER

CLARA

Later that night, after the gala, we gather in the shop surrounded by hearts taped to the donor wall. Maya insists on one last pot of cocoa. Joan shows up with scones, claiming she "forgot how to go home." Even Mayor Tom stumbles in, tie crooked, declaring, "Lanterns, not gulls!" until Noah pelts him with a paper heart.

The room swells with laughter and relief. Ethan slides beside me at the counter, brushing my hand, our fingers finding courage in quiet contact.

"Clara," he murmurs, "do you ever wonder if we'll lose this again?"

I squeeze his hand. "We won't. Because we know what silence costs."

Maya leans across, whispering conspiratorially, "You two need to practice PDA. Willow Cove thrives on gossip."

Ethan chuckles. "Practice makes permanent." He kisses me, gentle but public, and the room cheers like it's a festival.

Noah groans, covering his eyes. "Gross. But… also fine. Just don't squeak."

We laugh until it hurts, and something in me anchors for good.
MIDNIGHT VOWS

ETHAN

Later still, when everyone's gone, Clara and I stand before the donor wall. The red book at its center glows faintly in the moonlight.

She touches the glass, tracing the empty space. "Someday, Ethan. This is where our name goes."

I cover her hand with mine. "Someday soon."

We kiss again, longer this time, the kind that carries promises unspoken but undeniable. Midnight watches from the counter, tail curled like punctuation. Ace sighs from his bed, as if confirming the vow.

The shop smells of cinnamon, cocoa, and permanence. The night hums with the certainty of stay.

CHAPTER THIRTY-FOUR

Spark, Tape, And Tender Voltage

CLARA

The lights pop like champagne corks, cheerful, wrong, and then the fairy light strand over my donor window spits sparks.

"Power strip!" I'm already vaulting the counter. The bell jitter-rings like a sparrow trapped in a chapel. Rain needles Harbor Street; the lake beyond shifts not to hammered tin but velvet shadow, heavy and secretive. A thin tongue of flame licks toward the galaxy of gold and silver paper hearts I taped there this morning.

Not my window.

Fire blanket. Painter's tape. Prayer, I don't say out loud. I smother, press, hold. Heat nips my knuckles through fabric. The smell is sharp, plastic, ozone, regret.

"Left edge, top seam," a voice says that my bones recognize even when my head insists on pretending otherwise. Ethan. Cedar soap, rain, jacket half on, surgeon's hands already catching the ladder.

"I make the plans in this store," I tell him, breathless, because control is my mother tongue.

"Make this one with me." His voice is steady voltage. He braces the rungs; I climb. I press a reinforcement strip across the top seam where last week's hairline crack learned manners. A bead of rain tests us, hesitates, fattens… slides away.

"We're okay," Noah tells his pack of seventh-graders from the poetry shelf, voice old-soul steady. "The lights are just doing a monologue." He shades his sketchbook from sparks and adds more detail to the crosswalk fox, charcoal lines weighted carefully like choices.

Ace trots in at Mr. Pierce's heel, sits prim in his teal bow tie, and offers a paw to a trembling kid. The boy's breathing evens beneath dog dignity. Ace sneezes once, shakes himself, then resumes saintliness. Midnight, offended by the mere existence of physics, stalks to the sill and, papal as ever, sits squarely on my roll of tape. He bats a pen to the floor like punctuation, pleased with his contribution.

The strand fizzles. The pane holds. My lungs forget, then remember, their job.

I climb down. We turn at the same time. For one breath, the inches between us are the only math I know. The bell clicks in a stray draft like punctuation.

He doesn't touch me until I nod. Then his palm warms the small of my back, permission, not possession, and I lean like a woman who has earned softness. The kiss we make is not wildfire. It's current. Warm mouth, careful hands, choice humming under skin. He tastes like peppermint and rain and the kind of patience that acts like a promise. My name in his mouth sounds like a verb I forgot how to conjugate. His jaw is warm beneath my fingers; the wool of his coat sleeve brushes my wrist.

"Terms," I whisper against his smile, because that word saves me from drowning.

"Still signed," he says, voice roughened by relief, then we both laugh when a kid out front strums a test chord like the universe clearing its throat.

"Doors open!" Maya wedges them with her hips like a benevolent witch and deposits a tray of sugar knots. "Cross-breeze. Panic is banned. Anybody who faints owes me a latte."

I press one more strip of tape, smooth it the way I smooth names onto hearts, and the pane decides to be brave.

Dream finds me a heartbeat later, half standing, eyes open: noon on the dock instead of storm-dark. Boards warm under bare feet. The dented first-aid tin waits at the end like a punchline the universe keeps telling. Inside, the napkin he and I signed at seventeen; No running without a goodbye. No turning silence into punishment. Tell the truth even when timing hates it. And a new line in my hand, stubborn as bone: Make the timing worthy of the truth. The church rope drops three clean notes through my chest. A figure lifts his hand at shore, not to claim, to ask. I open my palm expecting the paper heart to dissolve like always. It doesn't. It shines.

"Clara?" Ethan's voice tucks itself under my skin. "You with me?"

"Always," I say, and for the first time in a long time, it feels less like a performance and more like a project plan.

Later, the square decides to be gorgeous about it. Lantern strings stitch the library room into a constellation. The Harbor Street Strings tune on the dais. The donor wall turns my front window into a galaxy: gold hearts, silver hearts, the single red paper book waiting in the center like an ember. On the welcome table: press rules in bold; Poetry, donor wall, therapy dogs. No minors. No prying, and a Sharpie beside a box of blank hearts.

"Lanterns, not pirates," Mayor Tom whispers to me like it's a vow, then into the mic like it's a brand. The room laughs; the room agrees.

I take the stage, ink on my fingers, my heart learning tidy, even beats. "Welcome to the Books & Hearts Gala," I say. "If you see glitter, it's intentional. If you see pirates, tell Tom no."

Laughter softens us into community. I pull the sheet from the library endcap. Noah's crosswalk design, open books pouring into each other, a fox tail hidden at page twenty-seven so drivers slow for wonder, makes a fourth-grader gasp there and a grown man wipe his eyes like allergies and dignity are synonyms. Noah's ears go red; his mouth can't quite strangle a smile. Ethan stands exactly three feet away, close enough to catch, far enough not to steal. Pride lives soft in his face.

Kelsey from Cove Chatter hovers at the press line in a lemon cardigan and a pencil sharp enough to cut. "A quote about the redemption arc?" she tries.

"Poetry, donor wall, therapy dogs," I say, cheerful as the weather. "No minors. No prying. If you want a story, buy a heart."

She blinks. Writes Luz on gold. Presses it to the glass like she's pinning a bravery to a lapel. Touches it twice. The angle wobbles; the human stays.

The lights flicker once, twice, as if jealousy is a circuit. Before panic can rehearse, Ethan vanishes toward the breaker closet with his pocket screwdriver, and I press the mic smile my town trusts. "Intermission. Pet Ace. Whisper a poem to the window so it'll remember you." The quartet slants into something soft. Electricity decides to mind its manners.

Backstage by the staff door, where the quartet can't see and the donor wall can, he finds me with a heart in his palm. Blank. Silver. Cool. "For when you want to write the name you've been saving," he says.

A cafeteria blooms behind my eyes, linoleum black-and-white, lemon meringue, a concession-stand napkin in a boy's wallet. I fingerprint the silver heart once before hiding it in my pocket, next to my phone, next to the breath I owe a younger version of myself.

"After the program," I say. "After…" I bite the last word back because forever is heavy, and tonight wants to float.

"After," he agrees, and that, somehow, is enough.

ETHAN

If small towns had vital signs, tonight I can feel Willow Cove's under my palm: systolic laughter, diastolic hush when she speaks.

I reset the last breaker and lean against the cool of the utility door long enough to remember I am no longer running codes beneath fluorescent bulbs that turn men into ghosts. Across the room, Clara turns a sweater into crisis management, a mic into mercy. The donor wall glows behind her, names in neat hand, a red paper book like a coal at the center, and I think, not for the first time, that this is a kind of medicine I never learned in school.

Tom nearly decapitates a rubber plant. "Lanterns, not pirates!" he crows, which the town rewards with applause it didn't know it was saving since summer. Then he tapes down a loose cord like a man redeeming himself in miniature. Lila reads a poem about bridges that makes a teenager pretend not to cry. Ace poses for selfies like a dignitary. Midnight prowls the poetry display with sovereign contempt and, somehow, benevolence.

Kelsey hovers, pencil, cardigan, curiosity, and buys a heart without a question. That, more than any article she'll write, is her confession. Boundaries can be kindness when you use them to keep the weather off other people, too.

The auction table is a ridiculous miracle: ribboned baskets, gift certificates, one that reads PRIVATE BOOKSTORE BROWSING + AFTER-HOURS TEA as if the universe decided to give me an excuse.

"Twenty," I say, raising my paddle.

"Thirty," Tom, performing generosity with other people's money.

"Fifty," I answer without looking away from Clara. Napkin rules whisper in my head: Tell the truth even when timing hates it.

"Sold," she says too fast, cheeks warmer than her cardigan, and the room pretends not to clap for two specific people.

I meant to keep my declaration small tonight, surgical, neat, no unnecessary drama. But when Kelsey circles back with "Is it true you're entertaining an out-of-town offer?" and the teenagers nearby hold their breath like they're practicing for some future emergency, I hear myself say it the way I wish I'd said it at eighteen when we wrote rules on a napkin under the bleachers.

"I'm staying," I tell the room. "I turned it down. My life is here." The mic hums faintly; the room smells like beeswax and damp wool.

Silence finds its posture. Then applause, not the rowdy kind, something older. Relief, maybe. Rose says "Amen," and the word sounds like forgiveness, not spectacle. Henry promises me a sestina about epinephrine. Tom slaps my back so hard I might need the AED.

Backstage, by the staff door, Clara's hands find my lapel like she's steadying herself against a wind only we can feel. Breath meets breath. We don't kiss because timing has manners tonight, and so do we. She tucks my shirt button back into its hole like that's a vow. It is.

My phone buzzes once in my pocket with the area code that used to own my attention and now feels like a stray I'm done feeding. I flip it over, face down. Lila's text is the only one I read: Wear the blue shirt for the teardown. I sent a fox emoji and the word always.

The quartet returns. The lights hold. The town, improbably, becomes lovelier by the minute, as if gratitude is flattering.

CLARA

We stack chairs. We roll up extension cords. We fish one last crayon from beneath a folding table. The donor wall still breathes faint gold in the window, the red book at the center like a heartbeat. Its edges are crisp, paper heavy with intention.

"Walk me outside?" I ask, tasting the risk and deciding I like the flavor.

Under the awning, Harbor Street looks like a movie set that remembers restraint. Lanterns sway. The lake wears our lights and forgives us for calling it names when it storms. I touch the frame with my knuckles, threshold respect, and face the man who made public proof look like a love letter.

"Thank you," I say.

"For?" He steps close enough for heat to be a fact.

"For staying." Two words that feel like a door unlocking.

He kisses my temple once, my mouth once, the second longer, heat braided with laughter, and we stop on purpose. We put our foreheads together like conspirators. We choose not to embarrass the town that finally learned how to mind its business.

"Tomorrow," he says into my hair.

"Tomorrow," I answer, and my ribcage decides to trust the verb.

Then my phone hums. A voicemail preview tries to climb onto my day with its commas and its doorframes, and I tuck it into my pocket like the rude guest it is. Later, I tell myself. After lanterns. After soup. After the fox on page twenty-seven finishes its patrol.

We part before anyone has to have an opinion.

At home, Ocelot Friday smells like browned butter and the kind of patience that makes onions taste like the future. Noah pretends not to watch us in the kitchen and then grades Ethan's grilled cheese with a solemn nod, the House Seal of Approval. Midnight audits everyone's conduct from the back of a chair and begrudgingly head-butts Ethan's shin.

After, Noah drifts to the couch, sketchbook tucked lazy at his side. Rope bridges on TV sway and hold. Ethan and I stand too close at the sink with suds up to our wrists and the kind of quiet that feels like a newly discovered room in a house we already live in.

"Tell me something real," I say, because I promised the girl with the ink-stained napkin I'd keep that rule.

"I used to think urgency was a personality trait," he says. "Now it feels like a door salesmen wedge open with their foot." He rinses a plate, hands it to me. "I want to be bored next to you sometimes."

"Bold goal." I swipe flour from his jaw with my thumb. "Okay: I'll stop punishing you for silence with my own."

He kisses me like a toast, to boredom and bravery and dishes. We stop where we promised, because restraint is intimacy when you choose it.

Noah looks up and says, "You both make less noise than the bridge, and the bridge creaks less when it's happy." Which I choose to interpret as a son's blessing. He smothers a grin and wanders off to brush his teeth.

When the house hums with bedtime, I take the phone from my pocket, press play, and listen to a voice I'm done letting narrate my life: Final package. We can make the timing work. The hospital name used to smell like ambition. Now it smells like a door that slams.

I slide the message into a folder labeled NOT OUR STORY, cut a fresh red book, and write what I've been saving where the light will catch it: For the kid who needs the fox on page 27. I press it to the glass until the tape warms beneath my palm. Hush. Stick. Promise.

ETHAN

Sirens sound different in small towns. In the city, they tuck you inside their urgency until you taste copper. Here, they braid with gull cries and church bells and teenagers shouting at geese.

"Kid on the lighthouse steps," Tom blurts at the clinic door, tie already sideways. We go, Joan with the med bag, me with my hands, and the practice of moving fast without scaring anybody. Halfway up the stairs, I meet Clara, painter's tape still looped around her wrist, the particular fury of a woman who refuses to let the world learn the wrong lesson.

"You good?" I ask.

"Give me a minute and a wall," she says, and I become the wall.

We do the small heroics: exam, gauze, a grin for a boy who needs permission to cry. Ace does the heavy lifting without moving much at all. We walk the kid down while Tom holds the railing like it owes him rent. At the bottom, Rose pours FORTITUDE. Henry complains about the lack of imagination in a town where all our jokes are actually prayers.

And then, because timing also likes poetry, the wind drops, the lake tucks its hunger back under its skin, and the sky blinks with the kind of blue you earn. The day opens a door.

"Coffee?" I ask because grand gestures got us into this mess thirteen years ago, and small ones are what get people out.

"Later," she says, but her mouth tips like she might mean sooner. "Clinic at nine?"

"I'll be there."

She nods like we invented the calendar and walks back toward the bookstore with the gait of someone who has decided to stop flinching.

At noon, I write the email and make it behave like my mouth: Thanks for the generous offer. I'm declining. The timing isn't the issue; the choice is. My work, and my life, are here in Willow Cove. Please remove me from future outreach. I press send. Joan claps once, like a bell. Lila texts me a fox and a knife, and I assume it's a love letter.

At seven, I raise my paddle and buy exactly one hour of a life that will never be for sale. At eight, I say I'm staying into a microphone and the room believes me. At nine, under an awning that finally knows when to mind its business, I kiss the woman I still love and stop when we promised we would. At ten, in my quiet kitchen, I tape Noah's fox above the AED to make wonder and medicine shake hands.

And somewhere between midnight and the softest minutes just after, the rope bell across from her shop rings once, twice, three times, the odd little cadence that's been following us since the day a rumor walked into a bookstore wearing sensible shoes, and it sounds like permission. Then Noah turns a page upstairs, and Midnight thumps her tail against the chair leg, as if to sign her name on the moment.

CHAPTER THIRTY-FIVE

Lantern Light

CLARA

The fairy lights above the donor wall spit sparks, hiss once, and die. The room inhales. My back is pressed against the ladder, palms sliding on damp wood, and Ethan's hands find my waist instinctively to steady me. His grip is hot, grounding, scandalous for three seconds too long before the bulbs go dark. The entire town gasps in unison.

"Power strip," Maya says, already diving.

But Ethan is faster, coat off, hands sure, eyes on me like he knows I'm about to break into a sprint I can't afford. The big front pane pings, bright and thin at the top seam, and my stomach drops. Not my window. Not tonight.

We move in the same breath. He steadies the ladder; I climb. Tape, press, smooth. The rain nosing in at the corner fattens, thinks better of it, and slides away. Applause flutters from the aisle where Ace the Dalmatian has taken up his position in a teal bow tie, accepting tributes in the form of pats. Midnight the cat, unimpressed with mortals, sits on the cash drawer like a velvet judge.

"Doors, open," Maya orders, fogging the glass with a philanthropic sigh. "Cross breeze. Panic is banned."

I laugh, airless. Then I climb down and turn, and turn right into Ethan.

It happens like the weather: not forecast, inevitable. Warm palm at my hip. The clean cedar of him in the storm. That eyes-open catch we've been avoiding for thirteen years.

He waits until I nod, small, deliberate. Then he kisses me.

Not wildfire, current.

Heat curls low and patient, steady as a heartbeat; permission meets permission. His mouth tastes like peppermint and rain and promises; mine answers yes in a language we invented under bleachers and forgot how to speak until tonight. My fingers slide into the damp curl at his nape; his thumb grazes the place my pulse shows, and my knees forget what stairs are for.

"Terms," I breathe against his mouth, because I vowed never to drown, even for him.

"Still signed," he murmurs, voice frayed silk, and kisses me deeper.

Someone strums the unplugged guitar out front. Ace offers a single, polite woof, as if to remind us the town is watching. I break first, forehead to his, breathing like I've been running, and maybe I have.

"Breaker closet," I whisper, not moving, not ready to let go. "I'll sell hope. You tame physics."

"Deal." A grin. The dimple I pretend I don't remember.

He peels away; the room exhales; the fairy lights decide to behave. I cross to the mic while my mouth is still tingling and my ribcage is trying to decide whether to ring or riot.

"Intermission," I announce, voice steady because it has to be. "Meet Ace. Buy a heart. Whisper a poem to the window so it remembers you."

"Yes, Jackson, metaphors are half price tonight," I add, making the teen poet blush and the crowd laugh.

The town obeys, because Willow Cove believes in collective magic, and I press a fresh silver heart to the glass. The hush stick sound comes first, like a ribbon of luck, and then the words gleam: For anyone who needs today to be kind.

And then the weather outside clears its throat and tries one more trick, wind shouldering Harbor Street, the big pane singing a high, thin note like a held breath.

"Left edge, top seam," Ethan says at my shoulder again, exactly where I need him and will not admit I do.

We fix the corner in three heartbeats. And because adrenaline is a loan I refuse to owe, I pay it back with something true: I find his hand under the wing of the curtain, lace our fingers once, quick, like a promise, then go out to finish saving my own night.

We made it. The gala glows. Laughter at reasonable volume hums in the square; cinnamon steam drifts; lantern reflections jitter across the donor wall. Noah's crosswalk sketch gets unveiled to gasps and applause, kids hunting the hidden fox by page twenty-seven, while the Lakewalk Moms tear up like a weather system. Kelsey from Cove Chatter buys a heart without asking me for a quote and writes Luz in careful block letters; she touches it twice, surprised at her own softness. Rose dabs at her eyes and declares, "Lanterns, not pirates," like a benediction. Tom waves a round sticker that actually says it. Henry proposes a poetry kiosk for Town Hall and, for once, no one argues.

When the last paddle goes down, when the Harbor Street Strings tuck their bows, when the last cinnamon knot is forgiven for its sugar, I find Ethan at the staff door and do the reckless, careful thing a second time: I kiss him where only the donor wall can see.

"I said tomorrow," I whisper against his laugh.

"Count on it," he answers, grin like a vow.

We lock up under the awning while lanterns sway like they approve of us. The square smells like rain, rosemary, and applause. Ethan kisses my temple and starts toward the clinic end of Harbor with that shoulders set walk that says useful. I watch him go until the chime in my chest rings three clean notes and then, because I am brave in small, practical ways first; I send Maya home, count the till, feed Midnight two extra crunchies, and write three more names in my neatest hand.

The bell above the door jingles once.

"Not tonight," I tell fear. "I said tomorrow."

The door listens.

ETHAN

Oxygen tastes different after you tell the truth out loud.

I decline the back-to-the-city offer from my phone, with my thumb, not my mouth, before I can talk myself into a paragraph. Thank you for the package. I'm staying in Willow Cove. Send. The hydra (the out-of-town offer) hates fences; I adore them.

"Good boy," Nurse Joan says without looking up from triage, which is somehow both a blessing and a threat.

The clinic purrs like a machine with a soul. I hang Noah's fox sketch above the AED cabinet because people slow for wonder before they reach for panic; I've decided to build a life on that rule. I alphabetize the crash cart because it helps me avoid overthinking, and once, in a night I try not to remember, alphabetizing was the only way to prevent falling apart.

Lila blows in like music and lists. "Tell me you said no," she says, eyeliner sharp. I show her my sent folder. She exhales like the town uses her as a weather vane. "Good. Blue shirt for the gala, screwdriver for Tom's breaker, and when you kiss her tonight, use sincerity instead of sentences."

"Not tonight," I say, surprised at my own voice. "Tomorrow."

Her smile goes soft and proud. "Stay is a verb," she says, and smacks my shoulder with the paper fan program.

Flashback: senior fall, diner booth three, lemon meringue like a cloud with a sharp tongue. The scent of lemon zest made the whole booth sharp and alive. "Tell me something true," I asked. She said, "Books fixed me before I knew I was broken." I admitted the surgery language already lived in my hands. We wrote rules on a concession stand napkin with a pen that kept skipping, like even ink knew promises were heavy. No running without a goodbye. No turning silence into punishment. Tell the truth even when timing hates it. I folded it into my wallet like a relic.

Tonight it's in my ribs instead.

The siren at midmorning turns the sky into a blade. Lighthouse steps, kid with a twisted ankle, Tom attempting a heroic cartwheel, it's Willow Cove theater with real stakes. I reach the landing as Clara does, breath matched, a first-aid kit in her fist and a grudge against gravity in her eyes. We do the work, efficient as a duet: assess, wrap, coach the hop, laugh where it breaks the panic. Ace supervises like a saint with a punctuation tail; Midnight passes judgment from a distance, then headbutts my calf once as if granting approval.

At the base, Clara looks at me, and the weather inside my chest stops lying.

"You ran toward it," I tell her.

"Timing was rude," she answers. "Someone needed me."

So do I. But I keep the confession for tomorrow and use the only language we share when the town is watching: I touch her cheek with two fingers, ask a question with my mouth, and retreat before greed thinks it's invited. She tastes like rain and citrus sugar, with restraint that hurts in all the right places.

"Tomorrow," she says first.

"Count on it," I breathe, and for the first time in thirteen years, tomorrow feels like a place I know how to reach on foot.

CLARA

Dream: The dock is noon warm for once instead of storm wild. I walk the boards without slipping. At the end, the dented first-aid tin waits, the one from every dream since eighteen. Inside: the napkin with our teenage rules, ink darker than it should be, a new line in my hand; Make the timing worthy of the truth. The church rope drops three clean notes through my chest; when I look up, he's there, not to claim, to ask. I open my palm expecting the paper heart to dissolve.

It shines.

I wake smiling and, for once, the smile holds.

"Spill it," Maya says, dropping two lattes and a stare onto my counter. "You're glowing like a lighthouse with boundaries."

"He said tomorrow," I admit, and my heartbeat tries to vault the counter and go find him on its own. "I said it first."

"Good. We will not punish this delicate, necessary honesty by sprint-ing." She leans in. "Also, if Tom says pirate hats one more time, I will stage a coup."

"Lanterns," I agree, writing it at the bottom of the volunteer signup in curly letters that look like breath.

Kelsey from Cove Chatter appears in a lemon cardigan, holding a gold paper heart and an apology in a bakery bag. "Candied contrition," she says, setting it down. "I'm writing about lanterns, not gossip." She sighs. "Turns out some stories belong to the people inside them. Poetry, donor wall, therapy dogs, no prying."

"Imagine," I say, soft on purpose.

She prints Luz again, this time for someone else, and presses it to the glass. I watch the name take the light and decide forgiveness isn't performative when it's this small.

That night, the square strings itself in warm stars. The gala becomes the picture the town wanted to be, laughter at a reasonable volume, cinnamon in the air, Noah's fox hiding where drivers will have to slow down to find it. Lila reads a poem about bridges that makes even the goose pause his patrol. The donor wall gleams. And when the last chair stacks, Ethan finds me under the awning and does the most romantic thing I can imagine: he doesn't ask me for anything. He waits.

"Yes," I say anyway, surprising us both.

We kiss like people who learned the hard way how to stop at the edge of a cliff and enjoy the view. His hand slides into my hair; my fingers hook his jacket; heat rises, and laughter cuts it sweet before it burns. His palm cups my jaw; my fingers find the curl at his nape; the rest stays our own.

"Tomorrow," he says.

"Tomorrow," I promise, and feel the word take up residence behind my ribs like a tenant with good references.

The Harbor bell rings once, twice, once again, sealing the vow in odd cadence.

ETHAN

I don't sleep. Not the way I used to, punched out, fluorescent haunted, adrenaline's aftertaste in my teeth. I sleep like a person who plans to wake up and do the same good thing again.

Lila texts at dawn: Blue shirt. Fox napkin in your pocket. Read the short poem if Tom panics.

I reply: Staying. Full stop.

Nurse Joan hands me the clinic keys and raises both brows at the unasked question. "Be useful," she says. "Then be brave."

By noon, the town has decided to be beautiful on purpose. The lake wears the sky without apology. The rope bell rings one… two… three, and I take it as a sign I'm allowed to feel as happy as I look.

I find Clara in the bookstore doorway holding two things: a roll of painter's tape and a blank silver heart. Both are forms of courage. She presses the heart into my palm.

"For when you're ready," she says.

I print CLARA • NOAH in my worst, neat hand, because this is our donor wall and I intend to be worthy of its glass, and ask, "Window?"

She nods. We step into the frame together. Tape, press, smooth. Hush stick. The red book gleams at the center. The lanterns hum. Ace patrols with parliamentary gravity, then steals a bookmark and refuses to return it until bribed with a biscuit. Midnight slits his eyes and allows the scene to proceed, granting one imperious headbutt as approval.

"Tell me something true," she whispers, like we're seventeen again and the world just turned its head so we could speak.

"I sent the email," I say. "No thanks. No commas. No qualifiers. I'm staying."

Her mouth trembles, then steadies into something I don't have a word for yet. "Tell me something else."

"I want ordinary with you," I say simply. "Laundry folded while we argue about spice jars. Soup nights with Noah's sketches on the fridge. A house that smells like paper. I want to be bored next to you and call it peace."

She laughs and then does a thing that steals the floor: she reaches for me in the bright, public doorway and pulls me into the kind of kiss that ends arguments I didn't know I was still having with myself.

The bell above us rings once, then twice, then once again, our odd Harbor cadence.

"Tomorrow," she says into my mouth.

"Tomorrow," I answer, and finally, finally, it feels like a promise I've already started keeping.

Foreshadow: After we close, I'll bring a paper bag of peonies that smell like decisions, not apologies. I'll read Lila's borrowed lines and not faint. Noah will hide a fox in a sketch of three hands linked across a book spine and slip it under the register like a secret he wants us to find. And when the house goes quiet, we'll sit on the living room floor with soup spoons and vows we haven't named yet and choose the version of our lives we both keep dreaming.

For now, I kiss the corner of her smile and help her turn the sign to OPEN, because this is the kind of chapter you hold with both hands before you write the next one.

The window holds. So do we.

CHAPTER THIRTY-SIX

Stay Is A Verb

CLARA

The pane sings a warning, one sharp, glassy note, with the metallic tang of heated dust, and the whole morning tilts.

Wind shoves Harbor Street sideways. Fog skims the lake like silk being tugged too hard. The fairy lights over my donor window spit two irritated sparks, then go dark. A thin flame flares curious along the cord and leans toward gold paper hearts that hold this town together with tape and hope.

"Not today," I tell the storm, vaulting the counter. My fingers find the fire blanket, the painter's tape, the breath I save for emergencies and geese. The bell over the door jitter-rings like a startled bird, once, twice, right as the gust shoulders in a second time.

"Left edge. Top seam."

His voice finds me before I look. And then Ethan is there, rain in his hair, jacket half on, scrubs beneath like he sprinted straight from the clinic, hands braced on the ladder the way steady looks when it stops pretending. A beat of me resists, instinctive, before I comply.

"I make the plans in this store," I say out of habit, already climbing.

"Make this one with me."

The tiny flame flares curious. I drop the blanket, smother, press, hold. Heat nips my knuckles through the fabric. The cord gives a sulky hiss, the light strand dies, the danger shrinks to a ribbon of smoke.

"Doors. Open. Cross-breeze," Maya commands, hip-checking the vestibule like a benevolent witch with flour on her cheek and sugar knots balanced like an offering. "No panic. Panic is banned."

I obey.

Ace appears in the doorway with Mr. Pierce, a teal bow tie, therapy accreditation, and the dignity of a small-town celebrity. "Morale, reporting for duty," his look seems to say. He sits prim and offers a paw to a trembling seventh-grader who came to tape Alma Ruiz to the window and nearly watched her name burn. Midnight stalks to the sill, sits on my tape roll with papal disdain, and stares at physics. Mortals, his eyes say. Such drama.

"Good," Ethan murmurs from below. "Hold the seam."

I press a fresh strip across the hairline crack at the pane's top corner. The bead of water nosing in from the morning's mist hesitates, fattens, slides away. The window decides to be brave.

When I climb down, we turn toward each other at the same time, and the inches between us turn into math I don't want to show my work for. My breath remembers him first; my body, second, my fingertips brushing the damp fabric of his shoulder as if to steady myself.

"You're shaking," he says softly, not as an accusation, but as data. His palm hovers at my hip, a question mark I know how to read. I tip forward, just enough, and answer it.

The kiss lands like a match and settles like embers, a glow, a banked heat, a quiet burn. Warm mouth, careful hands, a steady voltage that lights me from sternum to fingertips without burning the room down. He tastes like mint and rain and the promise of a morning that won't apologize for wanting to be a day.

"Terms," I whisper against his smile, the word that keeps me from drowning.

"Still signed." His breath slides over my mouth and shivers right down my spine.

Ace gives one perfectly timed woof. We break with shared laughter, oxygen that doesn't cost anything, and then go back to being useful. Ethan resets the breaker with the gentleness of a man who knows better than to bully old wiring; I re-string a short run of lights and press two new hearts to the glass: Luz in careful block letters; For anyone who needs today to be kind in my neatest script.

The room absorbs calm like a good story. Somewhere outside, the rope bell at the church drops three bright notes down Harbor Street as if to say: permission.

"Clinic?" Ethan asks under his breath, glancing at the seventh-grader's scraped knuckle and then at my hands, as if choosing which to worry about first.

"I'm fine," I lie.

"You say 'fine' when you mean 'give me ninety seconds and a wall to lean on.'" He becomes the wall. My forehead rests on his shoulder for exactly one long inhale. The cedar soap on his collarbones smells like a remembered summer.

"Thank you," I say, which is too small and not at all small.

"Soup tonight?" he asks, still low. "Ocelot rules?" (Family-only night, no phones, just soup and truth.)

"Ocelot rules," I answer. The smile I'm holding slides into my voice. "Bring onions."

He leaves to be useful elsewhere, palm tapping the doorframe like a blessing, while Willow Cove decides to be itself again. I write two more names and count out change, and watch Ace collect three more shy hugs. Midnight jumps onto the poetry shelf to supervise the rest of my day as if he owns the lease. He does.

DREAM SEQUENCE — THE DOCK AT NOON

Not storm-dark this time. Noon. The boards are warm under my feet, as if they remember me. The lake wears the sky without asking permission. At the end of the dock sits the dented first-aid tin that keeps showing up in my head like a punchline the universe refuses to retire. Inside: our napkin of rules, ink darker than it has any right to be.

No running without a goodbye. No turning silence into punishment. Tell the truth even when timing hates it.

Someone, me, has written a new line beneath the old.

Make the timing worthy of the truth.

The church bell sends three clean notes across the water. A figure lifts a hand at the shoreline, not to claim. To ask. I open my palm expecting the paper heart to dissolve like it did when I was nineteen and building rafts out of wishes. This time it shines.

I wake smiling. It holds.

Maya doesn't bother with hello when she brings the second coffee. "Timing is just fear wearing lipstick," she says, reading my face like a page she marked for later. "Write the sentence you're going to say out loud tonight."

I write: After the fundraiser, I chose us.

The bell clears its throat and remembers its job. The morning softens. Rose and Henry deliver an aspirationally red scarf for the silent auction and a sermon I didn't ask for about shelves and hearts both needing dusting. The Lakewalk Moms affix QR codes to posters with NASA-level precision. Kelsey from Cove Chatter buys a gold heart without asking for mine. She writes Luz and presses it to the glass; her eyes get shine she didn't plan on. Mr. Pierce confirms Ace will wear teal because brand consistency is important to dignitaries.

At noon, Noah drifts out from the back with graphite on his thumb and old-soul focus stitched into his shoulders. "The library wants the crosswalk sketch for the end cap," he says, pretending not to hope. "Mayor Tom said he almost cried, but he didn't. Leadership."

"Leadership cries in supply closets," I remind him. "With the label maker running."

He tries to smother the smile and fails spectacularly. My heart does the thing where it turns into light.

We hang the sketch after lunch. Children slow down because wonder commands it. A second-grader in galaxy leggings breathes there when she finds the fox tail tucked into the gutter at page twenty-seven. Noah's ears go red; Ethan stands exactly three feet away, near enough to catch, far enough not to steal, and the look on his face is the one I have been trying not to need for thirteen years. Pride, quiet and enormous.

Back at the bookstore, an envelope waits under the till with a city return address and a subject line full of commas: Final package, timing consideration, relocation logistics. I filed it in the folder I labeled NOT OUR STORY and cut a new red book for the center of the window. For the kid who needs the fox on page 27, I write, at Noah's suggestion, and press it to the glass until the tape warms beneath my hand.

ETHAN

People used to say I was married to the work. It wasn't love. It was adrenaline.

Now my body knows the difference. Adrenaline is the sprint to Clara's door when the pane pings. Love is how my breath slows when her forehead rests against my shoulder, and the bell on the church counts to three like a metronome we share.

I have an email with too many commas and a voicemail with a voice like glass. Timing, it says, like it owns the word. My thumb hovers over the icon for half a heartbeat and then slides to the folder Clara named for both of us: NOT OUR STORY.

"Let the man alphabetize, Carol," Nurse Joan tells the walls when she catches me reorganizing the crash cart. "If it keeps him from emailing venture capitalists, I'll print him label tape myself."

"I'm not emailing anyone," I tell the epinephrine. "I'm staying." Saying it out loud lands in my ribs like a lantern finding its hook. Joan nods as if she's been waiting months for me to use a verb instead of a metaphor.

Lila blows into my office with eyeliner sharp enough to file motions and two coffees she swears are identical. "I need you to tell me the part you didn't put in your text."

"They sweetened the package," I admit. "Teeth-aching."

She raises one brow. The you-already-know look. "And?"

"And the door they're selling doesn't open to anything I want anymore." I swallow. "I told Noah I'm staying. I told Clara with my mouth and then with my feet."

My sister points the lid of her coffee at me like a sermon nugget. "Good. Buy peonies. Roses say sorry; peonies say decision."

We split the day. She bullies a vendor into loaning a second bundle of fairy lights; I bully a sulking J-bend into obeying. Between patients, I tape Noah's fox sketch above the AED cabinet because people slow down to wonder before they reach panic. I write the sentence on a sticky note and stick it above the sink, where I will see it while brushing my teeth: 'Stay' is a verb.

On my way to the square, my phone buzzes. Sloane again, a number I used to salute. I forward the voicemail to the same folder as the email and add a filter. Hydras hate fences. I adore them.

I pass the bookstore and don't go in, because I promised myself I would survive an afternoon without the reassurance of Clara's mouth. The bell inside my chest rings anyway.

CLARA

Gala night arrives dressed like a spell. Fairy lights turn the library room into a galaxy you can touch. Origami boats float in bowls at each table; lanterns shaped like books line the windowsills. The donor wall glows, gold, silver, and one red paper book burning at the center like a coal of intention. Ace shakes hands with children as if they voted him into office. Midnight pretends to disapprove of everything and then sits where he will be most admired.

"Lanterns, not pirates," Mayor Tom says into the mic, and for once, the room agrees with him on purpose.

I hand the night back to its owners, poems, bids, laughter, and it hands me a moment I did not plan. Between lots, a donation box coughs up a paperback and a folded square. When I open it, seventeen-year-old ink looks me in the eye.

If the stars are listening, I told them I'm going to fall so hard I'll break a new verb for it.

I press the napkin into the glass case where Willow Cove keeps its tenderness, ticket stubs, a prom photo that belongs to Rose and Henry's bones, a map of the lake that insists on being a heart from above. I label it the way I label everything when I can see the shape of it: Teenage nonsense that turned into a life.

The quartet pauses to drink water. The lights blink like a cat being difficult. Tom hovers near the breaker like a man auditioning for a cautionary tale. Ethan appears with a pocket screwdriver and a quiet that settles rooms. I step to the mic and turn intermission into permission: "Meet Ace. Buy a heart. Whisper a poem to the window so it remembers you."

Kelsey, wearing a lemon cardigan, sharpens pencils, buys a gold heart, and writes "Luz" again, then presses it to the glass with both hands. Her eyes water, a secret unspooling she didn't mean to show. I watch her touch it twice, as if to seal the name to more than paper.

Backstage by the staff door, Ethan presses a blank heart into my palm. "For when you want to write the name you've been saving," he says. The napkin in the case. The new line in my dream. The way my body didn't flinch when he said staying like it was a word people get to choose.

"After the fundraiser," I hear myself promise. "I choose us."

He smiles like the word fits.

The auction ends. The town glows. We stand under my awning and behave like a good ending, one careful kiss, then another, heat with a leash we chose together. "Tomorrow," he says into my hair.

"Tomorrow," I answer, and the bell in my throat rings three clean notes.

When my phone hums in my pocket, the preview renders itself whether I look or not: Final package. We can make the timing work. The old fear knocks.

I don't open the door.

NOAH

The lake smells like metal and salt and somebody else's decisions. Rope slaps the dock. Flags snap above the bait shop. The lighthouse blinks like it's trying to spell out a warning. The goose who keeps a file on me struts into the crosswalk, and I slam my brake just in time to avoid committing a misdemeanor involving feathers.

Across the street, Ethan's on the clinic steps with the world in his ear. He says something I've never heard a grown-up say to a call with commas: "Not tonight. Tomorrow at nine, if you need a no in person." He hangs up. Full stop. No sorry. No later. Full stop.

"Hey," he says when he sees me, voice careful, the way you hold a glass thing you want to keep.

"Is that the hospital?" I ask because I'm twelve, not stupid. "The one that thinks numbers are candy?"

He almost smiles. Doesn't. "It is."

"Are you leaving?" My stomach does the rollercoaster thing; I hate that it does. "Because you can't do this to us. You can't fix things and make soup and then, " I can't say the rest, so I draw it with my hands, poof, and hope he reads it.

"Walk with me?" he asks.

We walk. The boardwalk is slick; the rope bell throws three quick notes at the fog like it's rooting for me; the wind has opinions about everything.

"They offered me a door I used to think meant I'd made it," he says. "Turns out, it just opens into a room where I'm alone." He looks at me like the answer is between my eyebrows. "I'm staying."

"What if they offer more?" I push, because someone has to be the skeptic.

"Then I'll say a bigger no," he says, like it's obvious. "I want to be the kind of person you roll your eyes at in the car because my jokes are terrible."

"They are," I say, because mercy is a future skill.

He bumps my shoulder. "You can ask me every day if I'm staying."

"I will," I say, and because I'm me, I hand him the fox I drew on a napkin when I thought I couldn't sleep. "For the clinic AED cabinet. So people slow down for wonder before they panic."

He looks at the fox like it's a map. "Perfect."

We don't hug. We also don't. When Ace appears out of the fog and leans his head into my knee like a vow you can pet, I don't cry. But it's close.

CLARA

I set three bowls on the table and pretended I didn't choose the blue ones on purpose. Midnight pretends not to beg. Accepts tribute anyway. Onion goes sweet in the pan like patience; bread goes golden like a small victory you can taste.

We eat like people who learned to breathe again. Noah passes the texture test down the table with a solemn nod that would make any chef weep. Ethan doesn't crow. He doesn't have to. The grin that gets away with itself is enough.

After, Noah sprawls on the couch with a pencil and a movie where rope bridges behave exactly as rope bridges do in movies. Ethan and I stand at my sink with our shoulders touching, practicing the marriage I'm not saying out loud yet: rinse, stack, breathe.

"Tell me something real," I say, because napkin rules are real rules.

"I used to think urgency was a personality trait," he says. "It's a door salesman's prop open with their foot. I'd rather build a house."

"Here's mine," I offer. "I'm done punishing you for silence."

He kisses me like that sentence was water and he was the plant. Warm, careful, human. We stop before wanting turns into sprinting, because we invented the leash and we like it.

When he leaves, he touches the frame with his knuckle like he respects thresholds. "Tomorrow," he says.

"Tomorrow," I answer, the bell in my throat ringing three bright notes of yes.

I pick up my phone and listen to the voicemail I've been refusing. Final package. We can make the timing work. The words try to coil around me, but my hand is steady. My heart is steady. I press delete.

The window glows. The red paper book at the center looks like a future with our names already inside.

I cut another heart and left it blank for now. I tape it beside the red book and let it be the shape of the word I'm not saying yet.

Make the timing worthy of the truth.

It is.

CHAPTER THIRTY-SEVEN

The House That Listens

UNBOXED

CLARA

The bookcase tilts with a crack of screws and a groan of wood, the way a decision does, slow at first, then suddenly sure of itself. I'm on my toes with a stack of poetry hardcovers, promising the shelf we will not be the tragic couple who crushes themselves during move-in day, when the whole thing lurches toward me like a drunk elk.

"Ethan!"

He is there before the exclamation point lands, one palm on the side panel, the other under the sagging middle like he's catching a patient who forgot how to stand. The bookcase shudders, thinks twice, settles.

"Minimalist heroism," he says, breathing a little hard, cedar scrub soap and morning on his skin. "Also, you were about to be flattened by the collected works of everyone who ever made me cry."

"Better than pirates," I say, because Willow Cove almost got pirate crosswalks and we're all still recovering.

"Lanterns, not pirates," he intones, and grins the grin that made me a fool at seventeen and a believer last week.

Boxes rise like small apartment buildings across the living room—Ethan's labeled in a med student's block letters (KITCHEN — POTS; BOOKS — MED; CLOSET — SWEATERS; ANATOMY FLASH-CARDS / DO NOT OPEN AT DINNER) and mine in my loopy bookstore script (COZY THINGS, CAREFUL THINGS, HISTO-RY). Noah's contribution is a stack of sketchpads with a fox sticker marching across the spines like a parade.

"Where does the napkin go?" he asks, nodding to the shadow box on the coffee table. Inside it, the concession-stand napkin, creased and precious, rests above three lines we wrote as kids: No running without a goodbye. No turning silence into punishment. Tell the truth even when timing hates it. For a blink, I see the bleachers again, rain hissing on metal, cocoa steam curling around our frozen fingers.

"Here," I say, tapping the wall above the couch. "Center of the room. Center of everything."

He hangs it with surgeon precision while I thread fairy lights along the curtain rod and try not to watch his shoulders move under his t-shirt. The fairy lights wink like conspirators of cottage magic.

A soft thud from the hallway; Noah, ferrying a crate of paper hearts from the store. He nudges the door open with his hip and pretends he doesn't notice how we both look at him, as if we're still stunned that we get to keep this.

"You'll want the hearts for the window," he says, setting the crate by the sill. "Minimalist glitter."

"Trademark pending," I answer.

We work, joke, and argue gently about whether the mugs should live near the tea or the sugar. (Tea wins; Ethan has learned the secret of my moods.) For a second, the disagreement tilts sharp, old habits flaring, but then he grins, I roll my eyes, and we both laugh, the tension dis-solving like sugar in hot tea. In the lull after a laugh, I feel him cross the small distance between us, feel his breath catch, his fingers curl lightly at my hip, his mouth find mine. It's a familiar heat, we've been practicing patience so long it feels like a prayer, and the kiss lands like a promise we've already kept.

"Terms," I whisper against his smile.

He pulls back just enough to search my face. "You sure?"

The question isn't casual, it's reverent, like he's asking me for more than permission. He's asking me for forever.

"Yes," I breathe. "Ethan, yes."

The house was quiet, the kind of quiet that feels earned. Rain tapped the windows, gentle now, no longer a storm but a lullaby. Ethan brushed his thumb over my cheek as if I were porcelain. "I'm not going anywhere," he whispered. "Stay isn't a promise, it's a choice. And I choose you. Every day."

My chest ached with love, with relief. "Then don't stop choosing."

His lips found mine again, slower this time, lingering, no rush, no fear of running out of time. He kissed me like a vow, like a man who knew he had forever and wanted to savor every second of it.

Clothes slipped away piece by piece, as if the house itself conspired to strip us down to nothing but truth. Each button undone, each zipper lowered felt like laying down old armor, until there was nothing between us but skin and the air charged with wanting. I trembled, not from nerves but from the rightness of it, his hands mapping me with care, his body fitting against mine like it always belonged.

"Beautiful," he murmured against my collarbone, his breath scorching my skin. When he moved inside me, it was with a tenderness that undid me more than any hunger ever had.

I arched into him, desperate and certain, wrapping my legs around his hips. His rhythm was steady, unhurried, worshipful. He held me close, our foreheads pressed together as if he needed to see every flicker of emotion cross my face. My tears mixed with laughter when he whispered, "Home. You're my home."

The world narrowed to that rhythm, slow, steady, forever. Each thrust felt like a vow etched deeper into both of us, a brand of belonging neither of us would ever erase.

When release came, it wasn't shattering but a soft unraveling, like a knot finally loosed. We broke together, held together, whole at last. His weight pressed me into the mattress, grounding me, but his arms kept me wrapped safe, as if even in surrender, he wanted to protect me.

For long minutes, neither of us moved. Our breaths tangled, his chest rising and falling against mine. The rain whispered its lullaby outside, and the fairy lights blinked above like conspirators who'd just seen their spell succeed.

"Forever," he said simply, his voice wrecked and raw against my hair. And for the first time, the word didn't scare me. It set me free.

I touched his cheek, tracing the stubble there, memorizing the man who had been my mistake, my heartbreak, my second chance, and now, my home. "Forever," I echoed, and meant it.

We lay there, cocooned under the quilt, the scent of cedar soap and us thick in the air. My body hummed with him still inside me, the echo of his tenderness still alive in my bones. Every brush of his thumb, every exhale against my temple, felt like proof that we weren't just surviving, we were choosing, over and over, even when it hurt, even when it was hard.

"I want all of it," I whispered. "The mess, the mornings, the storms, the fights over tea versus sugar. Every part of you. Every part of this."

He kissed me again, softer now, the urgency gone, replaced with something steadier. "Then you've got me," he murmured. "All of me. Every day."

Later, when sleep tugged at the edges of my mind, I listened to the steady beat of his heart under my ear and thought: this is what it means to be chosen, to be stayed for, to be loved without condition.

The fairy lights still winked in their gentle rhythm, casting the room in a glow that made the boxes, the napkin on the wall, even the crate of paper hearts by the sill look less like clutter and more like roots, like the beginning of something that could last.

I reached for his hand under the quilt, laced my fingers with his. "This house listens," I murmured, half-dreaming. "It hears us."

Ethan pressed a kiss to my hair. "Then let it listen forever."

And I let the thought carry me down into sleep, the storm outside finally gone, replaced by the quiet certainty of a home we built not with walls, but with each other.

The morning after the storm, Willow Cove smelled of wet cedar and possibility. Mist clung to the eaves, softening the corners of the neighborhood, and the sea beyond the houses was a sheet of steel-gray calm. Our house, the house that listened, wasn't finished yet. Not the kind of finished that meant paint chips and curtain rods. Finished in the way that meant we had settled into it with our stories, our arguments, our laughter woven into the walls. But beginnings always wear a bit of dust and tape.

Ethan made coffee like a ritual, grinding beans with the same precision he used to memorize anatomy flashcards. I perched on the counter, wearing one of his old med-school sweatshirts, sleeves hanging past my hands, and watched him move through the kitchen as if it already belonged to him, to us.

"Do you think houses remember?" I asked, tracing the rim of a mug with my finger.

He looked up, amused, pouring steaming water into the French press. "Remember what?"

"The people who live inside them. The arguments, the love, the way a chair squeaks when someone leans too far back."

Ethan's smile curved like he was considering a hypothesis. "If they don't, then you're going to make them. You can't not leave echoes, Clara."

I liked that answer more than I wanted to admit. "Echoes," I repeated softly. "Better than ghosts."

We sipped coffee in companionable quiet until Noah shuffled in, hair sticking up in tufts that made him look like he'd been struck by creative lightning. He carried his sketchbook under one arm and offered a wordless wave before collapsing into the chair with the squeak Ethan had just predicted. The chair creaked like an old friend.

"Dream again?" I asked him.

He blinked sleep-heavy eyes. "Not a dream. More like the house talking back. Pages turning themselves. Walls that hum."

Ethan raised a brow at me over his mug. "And you say *I'm* the dramatic one."

Noah flipped the sketchbook open, showing us a charcoal drawing of the living room, fairy lights glowing like tiny galaxies. In the corner, he'd drawn three figures, us, but in the lines of the walls, faint shapes lurked, as if the house itself had ears.

I shivered, not from fear but from recognition. "It does listen," I murmured.

The day became a parade of unpacking. Every box we opened was a time capsule. Ethan's medical textbooks, with his tidy notes in the margins. My collection of secondhand editions, worn spines cracked by dozens of anonymous readers before me. Noah's paper hearts, folded with more care than origami deserved, slipped into unexpected places: inside my history books, tucked among Ethan's flashcards, waiting like gentle surprises.

By afternoon, the house looked less like a warehouse and more like a home, though every corner still hummed with possibility. We broke for lunch, grilled cheese that stuck to our fingers, tomato soup that fogged up the windows, and argued about who was worse at folding laundry. (Consensus: Ethan, though he insisted doctors had better things to do than fold socks.)

When the doorbell rang, all three of us froze. The sound cut through the warmth like a bell in a cathedral. Visitors had not yet become part of our story.

It was Willow, standing on the porch with a basket of muffins wrapped in a checkered cloth. "Housewarming," she announced, as though she'd been rehearsing the word.

Behind her, the drizzle had started again, faint as breath. She pressed the basket into my hands, her eyes darting past me to the flicker of fairy lights. "I wanted to see it," she admitted, softer now. "The house that finally kept you."

I pulled her inside, and for a while, the house listened to four voices instead of three. Laughter braided itself into the beams, crumbs gathered on the table, and the fairy lights glowed brighter as if pleased.

Later, after Willow left and Noah disappeared into his sketches again, Ethan tugged me toward the couch. He stretched out, head in my lap, my fingers automatically finding his hair. The simple intimacy of it nearly undid me more than any kiss.

"We're writing something here," he said quietly. "Not just living it. Writing it."

"And the house is the paper?" I asked.

He closed his eyes, lips brushing my wrist when he spoke. "The house is the witness."

Outside, rain pattered again, steady, endless. Inside, we breathed, we loved, we chose. And the house listened, the way it always would.

The night brought different music. Wind rattled the shutters, and somewhere a loose shingle knocked like a persistent hand. Noah's door was closed, the glow of his lamp seeping under the frame. I lay in bed with Ethan, our limbs tangled, our breaths uneven as if we were still learning how to sleep beside each other.

"Clara?" His voice was rough with drowsiness.

"Yes?"

"Tomorrow, let's paint. I don't want beige walls to be the only history this place carries."

I smiled into the dark. "What color?"

"Not beige." He chuckled, pressing closer, his chest warm against my back. "Something alive. Something that doesn't forget."

And as I drifted toward dreams, I thought of Noah's sketch, of fairy lights, of promises whispered into the beams. The house that listened was already alive. We only had to keep giving it something worth re-membering.

The next morning broke bright, a rare jewel of sunshine after days of gray. The light caught the fairy lights in the window, scattering rain-bows across the boxes still waiting to be emptied. It felt like the house itself was stretching, yawning awake in the newness of us.

I padded barefoot into the kitchen, hair a wild halo around my head. Ethan was already there, sleeves rolled up, painting supplies spread across the table like a feast. Color cards fanned out beside him, mugs of half-drunk coffee ringed with circles on the wood.

"Morning," he said, looking up with the grin that always tugged something inside me loose. "Choose your weapon."

I picked up a brush, twirled it like a baton. "What are we painting first?"

"The wall behind the couch. The one with the napkin."

My throat caught. That napkin, our code from years ago, deserved a background that sang. I sifted through the cards, landed on a shade of deep blue, storm, and sky mixed together. "This," I said.

"Brave choice."

We taped edges, we laid drop cloths, we laughed when Noah wandered in, blinking at the explosion of paint. "If you get blue in my hair," he warned, "I'll retaliate with glitter."

It became a battlefield of brushes. Streaks of blue across the wall, smears on our arms and cheeks, one bold slash across Ethan's jaw that made him look like a warrior out of some myth. The wall transformed slowly, patch by patch, into something alive, a backdrop for every story we would tell here.

By afternoon, we were spattered and exhausted, lying on the floor to admire our work. The blue glowed rich and steady, framing the napkin in the center like an artifact. I felt rooted, as if the house had finally exhaled with us.

"This," Noah said softly, "is what belonging looks like."

The days blurred after that, busy with the ordinary magic of settling. Curtains hemmed too short. A bookshelf that refused to stand straight. The discovery of a loose board in the hallway that groaned whenever someone stepped on it, as if complaining about being forgotten.

At night, Ethan and I unraveled in each other. Not always with fire, but sometimes with a gentleness that left me trembling. He kissed me like he was still memorizing, still finding new constellations on skin he had already mapped. Every touch whispered that we had time, that forever wasn't a prison but a gift.

One evening, curled in the living room with tea and fairy lights, Noah looked up from his sketchbook. "Do you ever feel like the house is... keeping score?"

Ethan frowned. "Score of what?"

"The balance of things. Laughter and fights. Secrets and truths." His pencil stilled. "Like it wants us to stay honest."

I thought of the napkin, the rules inked by our younger hands. No running without a goodbye. No turning silence into punishment. Tell the truth even when timing hates it. "Maybe it does," I said. "Maybe we built it that way."

Ethan's hand found mine, his thumb brushing circles into my palm. "Then let's keep our promises."

The first fight came a week later. Not the playful kind about mugs and sugar, but a sharp edge of something deeper. Ethan's hours at the clinic stretched longer, his phone buzzing with messages he didn't always answer in front of me. I accused without meaning to, words spilling fast and hot. He snapped back, tired and raw, and for a moment the room crackled with something dangerous.

Silence followed, heavy as wet wool. I could almost feel the house lean in, listening harder.

I wanted to run the way I always had before. Slam doors, disappear into busywork, pretend nothing mattered. But the napkin rules hung on the wall, a witness. No running without a goodbye. No turning silence into punishment.

So instead, I took a breath. "I don't want to fight like this anymore."

Ethan's shoulders slumped, his face breaking open with regret. "I don't either." He crossed the distance, cupped my cheek with paint-stained fingers. "Clara, I'm scared sometimes. Scared I can't be enough for you and for medicine both. But I don't want to hide it."

Tears stung my eyes, but relief surged stronger. "Then don't. Just tell me. Even when timing hates it."

The words from the napkin breathed back into us. The tension unraveled. His forehead pressed to mine, his breath shaking. "Thank you for staying."

"Always," I whispered.

The house seemed to sigh around us, a soft creak of wood settling. Listening. Approving.

That night, when we made love, it was different. Not desperate, not worshipful, but raw. Every kiss was an apology, every touch a plea to be understood. We clung to each other as if the house needed proof; we meant what we said. And maybe it did.

After, wrapped in the quilt with rain tapping the windows again, I whispered, "We're giving it stories."

Ethan kissed the top of my head. "Then let's give it good ones."

And for the first time, I believed we truly could.

The season turned slowly, as if even time was reluctant to rush what we were building. Autumn crept into Willow Cove with gold leaves and crisp mornings, and the house grew warmer with each passing day, layers of us accumulating like quilts.

Noah's sketches filled the walls now, framed in mismatched thrift-store finds. Ethan's textbooks lived alongside my novels, medical diagrams, and poetry volumes, their spines rubbing together like uneasy but necessary neighbors. The house smelled of cinnamon, coffee, and sometimes burnt toast, because Ethan insisted he could multitask while cooking and memorizing muscle groups (he couldn't).

One evening, Willow returned, her laughter filling the kitchen as she brought jars of homemade jam. We spread them on bread still warm from the oven, and the house seemed to swell with the sound of us together. "It listens," she said suddenly, echoing my words from weeks ago. "You can feel it."

I nodded, the truth of it thrumming in my bones. "It remembers, too."

But the house didn't only listen to joy. It heard the nights Ethan came home too late, eyes shadowed with exhaustion, body tense with burdens he couldn't always name. It heard the mornings when I doubted myself, when my hands shook while shelving books at the shop, when the ache of old heartbreaks lingered. It heard Noah's restless pacing, the scratch of his pencil through paper after paper until he collapsed in a heap of frustration.

And yet—it held us. The walls never judged, only carried our echoes until we were ready to hear them ourselves.

The night before Ethan's first big exam rotation, I found him at the table, notes scattered, head in his hands. His breath came uneven, as if the weight of every expectation was pressing down at once.

I slipped behind him, wrapped my arms around his shoulders. "You don't have to prove anything to me."

He leaned back into me, eyes closed. "Sometimes I feel like I have to prove it to myself."

"Then let the house remind you," I whispered. "It's already keeping score. And you're more than enough."

He turned, kissed me with a desperation that softened quickly into gratitude. "You're my anchor, Clara."

"And you're my choice," I answered. "Every day."

Winter brought storms, fierce and howling. The power flickered out one night, plunging us into darkness save for the fairy lights still glowing faintly on their battery pack. We huddled together under blankets, telling stories by candlelight. Noah drew by flame, his sketches wilder, freer, as if the house whispered in the scratch of graphite.

When the storm raged at its loudest, rattling the shutters, Ethan kissed me slow and steady, grounding us both. "The house will hold," he murmured. "It always does."

And it did. Morning came with calm skies, our little world still intact, the echoes of our laughter lingering in the rafters.

The first spring in the house was a revelation. Flowers spilled over the garden wall. Windows opened wide to salt air and birdsong. We painted the hallway a warm yellow, bright as hope. Noah covered the stairwell with a mural of paper hearts and foxes that seemed to dance when the light hit them.

It wasn't perfect, no home ever is. We argued about bills, about chores, about who forgot to buy milk. There were slammed doors and stubborn silences. But always, always, we returned. To the napkin on the wall. To the rules that had guided us since childhood. To the house that reminded us to choose each other again.

One evening, when the fight had been sharp and the reconciliation sharper still, I lay in bed beside Ethan, my fingers tracing patterns on his skin. "Do you think the house will outlast us?" I asked.

He caught my hand, kissed my palm. "It doesn't have to. We outlast ourselves by choosing every day. The house just… witnesses."

I thought of that, of echoes and roots, of walls that remembered. "Then let it remember forever."

On the anniversary of moving in, we gathered in the living room: me, Ethan, Noah, Willow, and a handful of others who had become part of our circle. The fairy lights glowed, the blue wall behind the napkin shining like a beacon. We raised glasses of cider, laughter spilling into the beams.

"To the house that listens," Noah toasted.

"To the love that built it," Willow added.

Ethan looked at me then, eyes fierce and tender. "To forever, not as a promise, but a choice."

My heart ached, full and steady. I lifted my glass. "To choose. Every day."

The house seemed to hum in response, a gentle creak, a whisper of approval. And I knew, as sure as breath, that it would hold us. Through storms and seasons, through fights and forgiveness, through every echo of our lives.

Because this house didn't just listen.

It loved us back.

CHAPTER THIRTY-EIGHT

Running Toward It

CLARA

The lake always warns me; today it doesn't.

The siren hits first, one long wail that irons the morning flat, then the lighthouse throws a blade of white through lake fog like someone drew a line between now and what-ifs. Wind shoves Harbor Street sideways. Gulls scatter like dropped letters. I'm already running, painter's tape looped around my wrist from rehanging donor hearts, breath tasting like copper and cinnamon from Maya's kitchen.

"Kid on the lighthouse steps, twisted ankle; Tom tried to carry him and nearly cartwheeled leadership into the bay!" Maya yells, flour on her cheek.

I don't ask questions. The bell above my shop gets into a nervous jingle as I bolt past; the window of gold and silver hearts watches me go like a congregation. Rain needles. The lighthouse stairs climb, slick and stubborn.

At the first landing, a shadow breaks from the mist and matches my pace. Cedar soap. Rain dark scrubs under a half-buttoned jacket.

"You okay?" Ethan asks, scanning me with that ER clarity that makes chaos behave.

"I'm not porcelain," I rasp. "I've got a first-aid kit and a grudge against gravity."

He huffs a breath that's almost a laugh. We round the last turn together.

The boy, with spiky hair and scraped knee, sits braced against the rail, both hands clamped on an ankle that's swelling like bad gossip. Ace is already there, teal bow tie damp, chin heavy on the kid's calf like a sandbag, radiating wetdog warmth. Mr. Pierce hovers with a towel and calm eyes that have put out more fires than I ever will.

"You scared the stairs," I tell the kid, kneeling.

He gives me a shaky half-laugh, which is exactly what I wanted.

Ethan crouches opposite me, voice gone quiet and precise. "I'm Ethan. Can I look? We'll go slow." He tests, supports. The boy's breath hitches, then evens out to Ethan's count. I wrap, he stabilizes, and Ace sighs, as if he approves of our teamwork.

We make a chair of our hands and ferry the kid down, step by careful step. One, two, three, the rhythm matters. Halfway, Mayor Tom appears, tie at halfmast, posture like resolving to be useful. He takes one look at his untied shoelace and wisely retreats to crowd control.

At the bottom, Rose and Henry materialize with a thermos labeled FORTITUDE. Rose presses a cup into the boy's hand; Henry makes a pun about "stepping up" so terrible the kid snorts and stops trying not to cry.

"Clinic?" Ethan asks me, low.

"Ride with Pierce," I say. "I'll lock up and meet you."

He nods. For one breath, we're just… us, wet, alive, a little out of breath. Lightning skitters somewhere that has nothing to do with the sky.

"You ran toward it," he says, like a diagnosis he admires.

"Timing was rude," I answer. "Someone needed me."

His mouth tilts; the look he gives me could steady a room. He leans in without rushing, palm warm at my jaw. The kiss is neither a rescue nor a test. It's the steady voltage we've been building for months, peppermint warm, rain salted, consenting, present. I make a sound I've never made for anyone else; he swallows it like gratitude.

Ace gives a single, pointed woof. Ace's union approves.

We laugh against each other's mouths, break before any line goes blurry, and go do the ordinary hero work, paperwork, ice, appointment card, and a sticker Ace earns by existing. By the time I jog back down Harbor, the wind has remembered manners. The bell above my door rings once, twice, three times like a private benediction.

Inside, the window of hearts glows; Daniel Ortiz in careful ink, Luz in block letters, Anonymous with a doodled goose, because of course. In the center, the red paper book we cut last week waits like an ember you don't leave unattended.

I press my palm to the glass. Hush. Stick. Promise.

Dream finds me in the sound of the heater and the soft clatter of quarters in the till: noon on the dock, boards warm under my bare feet, the dented first-aid tin at the end like a joke the universe refuses to retire. Inside: our napkin of rules, no running without a goodbye, no turning silence into punishment, tell the truth even when timing hates it, and a new line in my hand: make the timing worthy of the truth. The church rope drops three clean notes through my sternum. When I look up, he's there, not to claim, to ask. I open my palm, and for once, the paper heart doesn't dissolve. It shines.

I open the bookstore.

The morning shifts from emergency to ordinary. Tourists drip on the mat and apologize to Midnight, who glares like water is a personal insult. Mrs. Donnelly buys a mystery "with a repentant doctor who learns to knit," then winks so broadly I nearly trip over the romance spinner. The town hums back into itself.

At eleven, my phone buzzes with a city number I refuse to hear yet. If I said yes, it would cost Noah's stability, Ethan's clinic, the bookshop's heartbeat. I turn it face down and write another name on a silver heart: For anyone who needs today to be kind. Hush. Stick. Promise.

ETHAN

Across town, a fox pointed me to the right lever.

I used to think urgency was a virtue. Today, I'm learning to tell it apart from the only thing that ever kept a human being alive: cadence.

At the clinic, Noah's fox sketch grins over the AED cabinet, tail up, nose pointed, a private arrow at the handle that says in his voice: pull when it matters. I set the boy from the lighthouse up with ice and a plan, texted Tom three bullet points of what not to do, and dropped into my office, where Lila has taken possession of my chair and my better judgment.

"Tell me the part you haven't said out loud," she says, eyeliner sharp enough to file paperwork.

"They sweetened the package," I admit. "Commas that could buy a yacht and name it Regret."

"And?"

"And I told Noah I'm staying. I told Clara with my mouth and then with my feet." I open my laptop before old instinct can change the subject. "Watch me write an email that isn't a poem about self-sabotage."

I type: Thank you for the generous offer. I'm declining. The timing isn't the issue; the choice is. My work, and my life, are here in Willow Cove. Please remove me from future outreach.

Lila reads, nods once, and steals a donut hole. "I'll bring flats to the gala in case I have to body block a reporter from asking your girlfriend about forgiveness like it's a spectator sport."

"Boundaries are beautiful," I say, which is a sentence I only learned because Clara taught it to me with her window and a roll of painter's tape.

We split the day the way grown people do: she bullies a vendor into loaning us a second bin of lanterns; I bully a leak into minding its manners. Between patients, I alphabetize the crash cart, because order in drawers is medicine. Joan finds me labeling and shakes her head like a patient storm. "If alphabetizing keeps you from emailing venture people, alphabetize away."

On my lunch loop, I pass the bookstore without going in because I said I'd survive one afternoon without her mouth. The bell inside my ribs rings three times anyway, which is ridiculous and also true.

I imagine telling my eighteen-year-old self: the best part isn't adrenaline. It's soup. It's the way a boy shoves a sketch across a stoop like a treaty and pretends not to care. It's a cat's single, reluctant headbutt. It's a woman's hand warm at your jaw as she chooses now without punishing then.

I sent the email. I don't look at my phone when it buzzes. Hydras hate fences. Families love them.

At five, the square puts on its necklace of lights. I carry a box of lantern hooks down Harbor. Clara is under her awning, ink on her fingers, hair pinned like she negotiated terms with gravity and won. The red paper book in her window glows like a coal.

"Hydras?" she asks.

"Politely dismissed. In writing." He shows her the screen for proof.

Her breath catches like the first note of a song. She doesn't throw her arms around my neck. I don't sweep her into the stacks. We do the more dangerous thing: we let the quiet say what it says. She nods once and passes me a length of twine like a benediction.

"Dinner?" I ask. "Ocelot?"

"Six," she says, a smile breaking like weather. "Bring onions."

Noah meets me at the door with a chopping board and the solemnity of a judge. "Texture test," he declares. "No cheating with extra butter."

"Blasphemy. Butter is science," I reply.

"Then hypothesize sparingly," he deadpans. His side smile remakes my chest.

We cook. We eat like we believe in tomorrow. We triage algebra and donor calls, and whether Tom can be trusted with a microphone if someone else is in the room. After, on the couch, we do the holiest thing I know: nothing fancy and all of it together. At the sink later, Clara runs a cloth along the edge where the counter meets the tile, as if she's erasing the day's roughness with care.

"Tell me something real," she says.

"I used to mistake urgency for love," I answer. "Now it feels like a door salesman propping open with their foot." I touch her hip by accident on purpose; her breath forgets itself and then returns. "I want to be bored with you in ways that feel like home."

She laughs, quiet, grateful, a little stunned. "Me, too."

I kiss her slow; I stop first, because leaving room for tomorrow is a kind of reverence.

Later, when the house has settled and Midnight has done a patrol that was mostly theater, I walk home under lanterns and write three words on my bathroom mirror with a sticky note: Stay is a verb. I put my phone face down. The email is sent. The hydra can chew air.

CLARA

Lanterns, lists, and learning to want without apologizing.

Maya can read a weather pattern off my face the way other people read menus. She slides a latte across the counter and doesn't pretend she isn't eavesdropping on my silence.

"You pulled back last night," she says, velvet over steel.

"I kissed him on a staircase that wanted me gone," I mutter, wiping a nonexistent crumb. "That's forward."

"Retreat is just rehearsal for regret," she counters. "Use sparingly." She taps the red paper book with a fingernail. "Write the name you're saving when you're ready. Not because fear made you."

"I have a son," I say. "And a shop. And a town that will name a crosswalk after a creature that bit Mrs. Donnelly's skirt."

"All true." She softens. "You also have a life you're allowed to want."

The bell jangles; Kelsey, in her lemon cardigan, steps in, still wearing her grief gently, with candied orange peels and a look that says she's practicing being the kind of person who asks better questions. She buys another gold heart without prying and writes a name I don't know. When she presses it to the glass, her hand shakes, and I tape it with my steady one. We nod like women who have both learned how to carry what they can.

At noon, Noah and I hang his crosswalk sketch on the library end-cap. Kids gasp in a way that makes me believe the earth is going to be okay. A girl in star leggings finds the fox on page twenty-seven and whispers, "There." Noah pretends not to glow and fails spectacularly. Ethan stands exactly three feet away, near enough to catch, far enough not to steal. It is a distance I did not know I could love.

Ocelot at six is soup and grilled cheese, and Noah's adjudication of texture. Midnight countersigns with a single headbutt like he's granting parole. After, we stack plates and do nothing fancy on the couch, which is my new favorite kind of miracle.

Maya once said, "When did you stop switching your phone off at nine because you were punishing yourself for wanting?" Tonight, I try. I leave the phone face up on the counter like it's a pet I'm training. When the city number flashes, my palms sweat, a hollow opens in my ribs. But I don't flinch. I file the voicemail under NOT OUR STORY and write a new name instead: For the kid who needs the fox on page 27. Hush. Stick. Promise.

Later, in the doorway, Ethan kisses me like he means the world. I kiss him back like I believe it. We are both better at this than we were when we were children playing forever under the bleachers. Thank God.

He touches the frame with his knuckle, respects thresholds, and leaves. Behind him, the rope bell across Harbor tosses three clean notes down the street like a dare we've already accepted.

The house hums safe. I find the soft place in the couch where Noah left his sketchbook and tuck his pencil under it for later. In my notebook, I write three lines I should've written years ago:

Stay is a verb.

Patience isn't delay.

It sounds like a door unlocking.

ETHAN

Evening.

The town is strung in lanterns and prone to superstition. I am, inconveniently, the same.

In the afternoon lull before the gala, I walk the square like I can absorb steadiness through my shoes. Tom has hung a banner that reads LANTERNS, NOT PIRATES with the pride of a man who thinks he invented restraint. The donor wall in Clara's window reflects me back with my edges softened. I put my palm to the glass and feel the faint living warmth of tape under paper. Hush. Stick. Promise.

Inside, Clara is all ink and lists and the kind of competence that makes men like me want to be better citizens. "Hydras?" she asks without looking up.

"Deleted." I hold up my phone. "Proof."

She doesn't cry. She does inhale like the world just shifted one inch to the right. She hands me a spool of twine. "Let's make Harbor look like a wish."

We do. Lanterns lift like bright punctuation. Kelsey hovers at the edge with a reporter's notebook and a citizen's face. Ace preens in teal. Midnight performs disdain.

The quartet has just tuned when a breaker hiccups; the lights do a theatrical flutter; Tom clutches his chest like drama pays overtime. I'm already in the utility closet with a pocket screwdriver. Ten seconds, a click, and the ceiling remembers how to behave. When I reappear, the room exhales like I've done something impressive when all I did was show up at the right second with a tool.

Clara catches my eye by the staff door and presses a blank silver heart into my hand. "For when you're ready to write the obvious name," she says.

I close my fist over it like a vow.

We work. We listen. Lila reads a poem about bridges that makes Henry clap on the wrong beat and Rose dab her eyes with a napkin older than the town. Noah's endcap drawing gets the hush it deserves. The auctioneer says, "Private Bookstore Browsing + after-hours Tea," and I raise my paddle like a man willing to compete with Tom in public if that's what love requires. It does not. I win at fifty. Clara flushes, palm at her throat, heat in her ears.

Between lots, a donation box coughs up an old paperback and a folded napkin with my seventeen-year-old handwriting; If the stars are listening. I slide it into the glass case of town treasures. Teenage nonsense that turned into a life, the label will say tomorrow. Tonight it says: try again, better worded.

After the last chair stacks and Ace has posed for his final selfie, and Midnight has audited the cash drawer, I walk Clara to her awning. We kiss twice, the second deeper but still careful, still ours, thumb brushing her pulse, nose tucked at her temple, and we stop before we make a promise the porch deserves to hear. "Tomorrow," I say. She says it back like we invented it.

My phone buzzes when I'm halfway to the clinic. The city number glows like it thinks it owns my nervous system. I don't answer. I forward the voicemail to a folder labeled NOT OUR STORY. Clara, across town, hears the faint echo of the bell and doesn't ask.

At home, I write five words on a clean page and tack it above my desk: We'll see each other brave. Then I tape the blank heart to the edge of the page, empty on purpose. The right name will feel obvious when I've earned it.

Before sleep, I stand at the window and look down Harbor. Clara's shop is a lantern. The lake rehearses its hush. Somewhere, the rope bell rings one… two… three, permission, promise, prayer.

I have never been more certain of anything than this: the future sounds like that. And when I close my eyes, I don't dream of the city or its hydras; I dream of a red paper book in a glowing window, a boy laughing at a fox on page twenty-seven, and the warmth of a woman's hand at my jaw. Tomorrow is waiting, and this time, I'm ready to meet it.

CHAPTER THIRTY-NINE

Lanterns Against The Dark

CLARA

The first spark kisses the fairy lights above my donor window, and the whole room inhales.

"Power strip," I shout, vaulting the counter. The bell above the door trembles, fluttering like a trapped bird, and the lake outside slicks itself silver as wind shoulders Harbor Street. One thin flame licks toward the gold paper hearts I taped this morning, the constellation of names that has kept me brave.

Not my window.

The fire blanket smothers the cord with a muffled thump. Heat flirts with my knuckles through the fabric, daring me. "Doors, open," Maya orders, hip-checking both to make a cross-breeze as cinnamon steam rolls through with teeth and comfort. The lights stutter. Midnight springs to the sill, sits squarely on my roll of painter's tape, and glares at physics. Across the room, a seventh-grader gasps and then laughs when Ace the Dalmatian places a calm paw on her knee like a gentle-man escorting panic offstage.

"Left edge, top seam," Ethan's voice cuts through, familiar, steady. Cedar soap, rain, jacket half on. He braces the ladder like an oath as I slap a fresh strip across the pane that pinged last week. The bead testing us hesitates, fattens, slides away.

"We're okay," I tell the room in my librarian-meets-lighthouse voice. My hands are shaking. My mouth is not. I peel the blanket back. Only a signed kiss on the cord. The donor hearts glow with relief.

When I turn, he turns, and for a breath, the inches between us are the only math I understand. A paper heart slips from the glass, drifts down between us. Together, we catch it and tape it back. The bell clicks in a draft like permission.

We kiss.

Not reckless. Not a dare. Warm mouth. Honeyed patience. Heat like a steady current under skin, not wildfire. His palm cups my jaw like a map he never forgot; my fingers find the damp curl at his nape; the room brightens at the edges as if the town decided to dim the world everywhere but here. His breath skates my cheek; my ribs unlock.

"Terms," I whisper against his smile.

"Still signed," he says, rough silk. Ace offers a dignified woof: That will do.

Minutes later, the window is a vow again, not a hazard. Music hums beneath chatter. I press a fresh silver heart to the glass; For anyone who needs today to be kind, and the tape makes a hush-stick sound I could live on.

"Boathouse after clean-up?" Ethan asks, eyes on my mouth like the future is a language he's relearning. "Lipstick expected. I'll behave."

"Behaving is optional," I say, pulse scandalous.

Outside, the rope bell at the church drops three notes through the gray, our private semaphore. Lanterns wait in boxes. The town is ready to glow.

Dock dream, quick as a blink: noon-warm boards; napkin rules, tell the truth even when timing hates it, and a new line in my hand: make the timing worthy of the truth. The bell rings once, twice, three times. I open my palm. The paper heart doesn't dissolve. It shines.

"Okay," I tell the window, the lake, and myself. "Let's go be brave."

ETHAN

Urgency used to be my drug. Tonight I choose cadence.

The breaker yields to a pocket screwdriver and patience. The quartet tunes back into itself. Tom practices his Lanterns, Not Pirates smile in a dark window and almost believes it. I find Clara by the staff door, where only the donor wall can see, and press a blank silver heart into her palm.

"For the name you've been saving."

Her throat works. "After tonight."

"After tonight," I echo, filing forever where it won't burn us.

We carry the room between us like an instrument we've practiced, her warmth, my steadiness. When the auctioneer calls Private Bookstore Browsing + After-Hours Tea, I lift my paddle. I want one hour of a life that will never be for sale. Her cheeks are pink. Maya whispers finally. Midnight thumps his tail once on the counter like a magistrate approving the record.

Lila reads Bridges Don't Happen Alone, a poem that makes teenagers pretend not to cry, and Mr. Dawes holds his hat in reverence. Ace escorts a nervous donor to the wall, tail wagging reassurance. Kelsey from Cove Chatter stays behind the press sheet we printed: Poetry. Donor Wall. Therapy Dogs. No Minors. No Prying. When she writes Luz on a gold heart, her hands shake. I look away.

Later, under the awning, Harbor Street glows like a set the Good Witch would bless. Clara and I don't sprint for heat; we bank it. One kiss, then deeper, still careful, still ours. When we pause, foreheads touching, the future stops being a cliff and becomes a road.

"Tomorrow," I say into her hair.

"Tomorrow," she answers, and the bell in my ribs rings back, one, two, three.

Then my pocket lights with a number I used to mistake for oxygen. I don't answer. I have fences now. Hydras hate fences.

The voicemail transcribes anyway: Final package. Let's talk timing. I close my eyes, count four beats, and choose cadence again.

I text Lila: *Ocelot, still sacred.* She replies with a fox emoji and *is proud of you.* The lake breathes. So do I.

CLARA

Morning ambush.

The siren cuts the square; the lighthouse blinks late. "Kid on the steps," Maya pants, flour on her cheek, pointing uphill. I run before fear ties her apron.

By the landing, Ace rests his chin on a spiky-haired ankle, Mr. Pierce wielding a towel like chivalry. "I chased my hat," the boy admits, ferocious with embarrassment.

"You're okay," I tell him. "The stairs were rude." Ethan appears with gauze and a voice that reorganizes chaos. We duet, his hands, my words; my tape, his calm, until the kid is hobbling gamely down, a hero for surviving himself.

At the bottom, Rose presses a thermos labeled FORTITUDE into his hands. Henry quips, "You've stepped up today." No apology. The town resumes its pulse.

"Boathouse raincheck," Ethan says, eyes asking more. I nod first. "After tonight." We kiss anyway, restraint coexisting with relief. Heat hums for an hour.

Back at the shop, I straighten the hearts, touch the red book at the center, whisper: this is winding down, intense, then tender. Lanterns wait in boxes. Paper, hope, tape, breath.

Noon: a fox doodle from Noah; Ace says hi. Moms marshal QR codes like crusaders. Kelsey buys another gold heart without drawing blood. Midnight patrols the poetry shelf for apostrophes. I text Ethan: *Ocelot. Six. Bring onions.* He replies with a fox and a check mark.

Ocelot turns our kitchen sanctuary. Noah, sober, passes Ethan's grilled-cheese "structure test." He grins so hard he hides behind soup. We triage algebra, donor calls, and Tom's pirate hats. (He will; we'll intercept; Ace will confiscate.)

"Tell me something real," I whisper in sink-warm hush.

"I thought urgency was character," he says, bumping my hip. "Now it feels like a door salesman's prop. I want a life with you that knows how to be bored on purpose."

Bold. "I'll stop turning off my phone at nine like punishment." It lands as soft as a sweater. He breathes like I handed him a map.

We kiss like people who trust tomorrow, unhurried, heat steady, respect intact. When he leaves, he brushes the doorframe with his knuckle like a benediction. The bell inside me rings three notes.

Then the voicemail clears its throat: Final package. We can make the timing work. A hospital name is like a smooth stone.

"Not tonight," I tell the kitchen. Midnight bumps my shin: agreement.

A peppermint sachet waits on the knob, protection, town-style.

ETHAN

Fluorescent rooms taught me: right choices rarely shout. They ask quietly, Are you coming home?

Lila brings coffee and cinnamon-hard truths. "Say it to me the way you'll need to when it's loud again."

"I'm staying," I tell her, my chest, the fox taped above the AED. "No to the offer. Yes to this life."

"Good." She kisses my cheek, relief years deep. "Now tell the people who matter, and alphabetize something for Joan before she combusts."

I sent Sloane an email with nowhere for regret to hide: Thank you. I'm declining. Please remove me from future outreach. Hydras hate fences. I love them.

At the bookstore, Clara stands in the door light with ink on her fingers, eyes telling me she fought the same dragon. We string the last lanterns in silence. The donor wall throws our names back at us in gold and silver. The red book burns like a sun.

Noah wanders in with a sketch: Ace on crosswalk duty, bow tie perfect. Midnight is drawn as a celestial event. A fox doodle tucked at the corner.

"Texture test?" I ask, brandishing brownies.

He squints. "That's structure." Bites, judges, approves. Triumph tastes like cocoa.

Tom pops in, buttoning: "Lanterns, Not Pirates, always." Rose and Henry leave a scarf with a wink. Kelsey hovers, but doesn't pry. The town holds.

When the last lantern glows, Clara presses her palm to the window, over the red book. I press mine beside hers. Paper. Tape. Skin. The math of staying.

"Tomorrow," she says, welcome, not stall.

"Tomorrow," I promise, kissing her long enough to be remembered, short enough for neighbors. We parted laughing, tender and undone in the best way.

The doorbell answers, one, two, three.

We're almost home.

CHAPTER FORTY

Stormlight, Tape, And Yes

CLARA

The first pop sounds like a cork, bright, wrong, right before the fairy lights over the donor window spit sparks. The wire hisses; the air tastes like sugar going bitter; a thin ping flares high in the big pane, the kind of note glass makes when it's deciding whether to be brave. For a heartbeat, the whole town feels like it's watching through that pane, daring me to fail.

"Power strip," I say, already vaulting the counter. Too late to be careful. The bell above the door jitterrings, a nervous bird in a belfry. Outside, the lake is hammered tin; wind shoulders Harbor like it paid taxes. Painter's tape is looped around my wrist because in Willow Cove, hope is a craft project you do daily, taped to windows and stitched to breath.

Maya barrels through with flour on her cheek and the moral clarity of a general. "Doors open, cross breeze, panic is banned. Also, anyone who faints does cleanup duty." She wedges both doors with her hips and sets a tray of cinnamon knots down like communion.

A skinny flame licks toward the gold paper hearts I taped to the window this morning. Not my hearts. Not today. The air stinks of ozone and hot plastic; the fire blanket scratches like coarse wool as I rip it down, smothering, pressing, holding. Heat nips my knuckles through fabric. The flame sulks and folds into smoke.

"Left edge, top seam," a voice says, my bones recognize. Ethan slips in with cedar soap on his skin and rain in his hair, shrugging out of his jacket even as he braces the ladder. "I'll spot you."

"My store, my plan," I tell him, but my hands have opinions. I climb. Tape down. Smooth. Hushstick. A bead of water testing the seam hesitates, fattens, slides away like a rumor that didn't find traction.

Ace trots in at Mr. Pierce's heel, teal bow tie damp from fog. He sets his chin on a seventh grader's knee until the boy's breathing steadies. Midnight stalks to the sill, sits on my roll of tape with papal disdain, and stares at physics. Mortals, his eyes say. Such drama.

I climb down and turn at the same time Ethan does. For a breath, the inches between us are the only math I know. His palm hovers at my hip like a question. I give the smallest nod, and then heat finds home, warm mouth, thumb brushing my jaw, breath slow against mine. Steady voltage instead of wildfire. He tastes like peppermint and rain and a life I'm finally brave enough to look at.

"Terms," I whisper against his smile, because that word keeps me from drowning.

"Still signed," he says, voice low, and my bones approve.

A teen out front strums a test chord. The light decides to behave. The pane holds. So do I.

ETHAN

I've sutured in a moving ambulance and threaded a chest tube with a 14-gauge catheter while a med student tried not to faint into a biohazard bin. None of that taught me how steady painter's tape can make a man feel when the woman he never stopped loving presses hope to glass with her whole palm.

"Minimalist heroism," Maya declares, thrusting a cinnamon knot into my hand and one into Clara's. "Science says carbs prevent poor decisions. I'm basically medicine."

Clara laughs, breath still jagged at the edges in a way that makes my own lungs remember good uses for air. The laugh catches on the corner of her mouth when the pane pings again, and my body moves before my mind does, steady the ladder, spot her hand, shoulder to shoulder with the person who built a galaxy out of paper hearts.

When the room stops auditioning for catastrophe, I tip my chin toward the stockroom. She nods. Door. Quiet. The emergency light makes everything moon-blue. "Breathe with me?" I ask. Four in. Hold. Four out. Pause. Her shoulders drop. The world does, too.

"Dinner?" I try, because a man can want candlelight and still respect the workday. "Not the diner. A table where you don't have to translate the specials."

"After," she says. "Tonight's for the window."

"Then let me carry the ladder," I answer, because love is a verb, and sometimes that verb is logistics.

CLARA

Storm over; humanity resumed. The town files in to run its errands and its opinions. Rose arrives with a thermos labeled "FORTITUDE" and a red scarf that refuses to be undramatized by the weather. Henry follows with a pun that would get most people banned from history. The Lakewalk Moms tape QR codes to gala flyers with the zeal of NASA. The Crossword Crew whispers that they've hidden a message in the program visible only under blue light and swear me to theatrically feigned surprise.

Noah slips out from the back, graphite on his thumb, old soul eyes on my seam. "Held?" he asks.

"Held," I say, and the word lands in the window and in my chest the same way.

He produces the crosswalk sketch we've been quietly living with, open books becoming safe passage, foxes tucked where drivers will only see if they slow down to wonder. He doesn't let his mouth smile, but his eyes do. "Mayor Tom promised to behave."

"Lanterns, not pirates," I tell him. "Even Tom can learn."

He snorts; Ace thumps his tail; Midnight pretends he didn't.

LANTERN REHEARSAL, DREAM GRAMMAR
ETHAN

Town hall is a brick shoebox with opinions and a rubber plant that has seen things. "Imagine café chairs, tiny stage, poetry kiosks," Tom says, nearly decapitating the plant. Mr. Dawes warns that the goose union will sue. Rose requests tea "for repentant cardiologists." Henry proposes a sestina dispenser. I write AED in the chamber hall on my agenda and underline it twice. "And maybe a glitter budget," Tom adds, undeterred.

Kelsey from Cove Chatter stands in a lemon cardigan, pencil aimed like an angle. "Is the doctor who left this town now poised to profit from improvements?" she asks, all sugar over steel.

I stand. "I fix closets on Tuesdays and alphabetize the crash cart when Nurse Joan lets me," I say, careful and plain. "If you see me 'profit,' it'll be because I convinced more neighbors to buy paper hearts." A beat. "Cover the lanterns. Leave minors and gossip out of it. Boundaries are beautiful."

"Amen," Rose says in her Sunday voice. Henry adds, "Install the kiosk anyway," and laughter breaks the room's sharp edges without breaking its furniture.

After, by the bulletin board, Kelsey asks Clara for a forgiveness quote. Clara hands her a gold heart and a Sharpie. "Write the name of someone who made you brave." Kelsey blinks, writes Luz, presses it to the glass, and surprises herself by crying. Sometimes, angles remember they're human.

CLARA

Dream: noon on the dock at last, not storm-dark. Boards warm against my feet. The dented first-aid tin waits at the end. Inside, our napkin of teenage rules, ink darker than it has any right to be. No running without a goodbye. No turning silence into punishment. Tell the truth even when timing hates it. A new line in my hand: Make the timing worthy of the truth.

The rope bell drops three clean notes through my chest. A figure lifts a hand onshore, not to claim, to ask. I open my palm, expecting the paper heart to dissolve the way it always does right before I wake. This time it shines.

I wake smiling, mistaking it for bravery until it holds.

ETHAN

Lila blows into my office like a weather system with lipstick. "Tell me you emailed the hydra no," she says, sliding a coffee and a fox sticker across the desk.

"I did," I answer, because the sentence tastes like clean water when you've been living on adrenaline too long. "Staying is the job."

She smirks. "Good. Buy peonies, not roses. Decisions, not apologies."

"Noted," I say, pinning her advice to the soft board in my head next to Clara's laugh and Noah's fox and the way this town breathes when the bell rings thrice.

THE GALA, THE WINDOW, THE WORD WE EARN

CLARA

Hold the room, I tell myself before stepping onstage.

"Welcome to the Books & Hearts Gala," I tell a room strung in fairy lights and expectation. "Lanterns, not pirates." Tom fist pumps like restraint was his idea. The Harbor Street Strings make the air remember how to be gentle. Our donor window gleams, gold and silver names in my neat ink: Daniel Ortiz, Luz, Maya herself, and at its center the red paper book burning like an ember with good manners.

We unveil Noah's crosswalk design for the library corner. Gasps. Applause. A fourth grader in galaxy leggings whispers there when she spots the fox on page twenty-seven. Mrs. Donnelly's goose honks as if in approval, closing a loop none of us expected. Noah tries to swallow a grin too big for his face and fails spectacularly. Ethan stands three feet away, near enough to catch, far enough not to steal. Pride looks better on him than any magazine cover ever did.

The lights flirt with trouble; Ethan peels off to the breaker with a pocket screwdriver like a man answering his calling. "Intermission," I say into the mic. "Meet Ace. Buy a heart. Whisper a poem to the window so it remembers you."

Back by the staff door, the nook where only the donor wall can see, our liminal place since the first storm, he presses a blank silver heart into my palm. "For when you want to write the name you've been saving." My throat does the thing it does when a storm breaks without raining. I tuck the heart against the red book with my fingers and a promise.

The last paddle goes down. The last receipt prints. Ethan raises his hand for the Private Browsing + after-hours Tea certificate, and Tom surrenders at thirty. "Sold," I say too fast, cheeks too warm; the room reports that I'm glowing. Rude. Correct.

Cleanup. Lanterns do their gentle clink. Neighbors lean into each other like porch swings. Kelsey photographs the window and, bless her, only the window. When we step under the awning, Harbor looks like a movie set that remembered restraint. Ethan kisses my mouth once, then again, the second longer, careful, a promise that ends on breath instead of a door slam.

ETHAN

The alley beside the café carries sounds like gossip. My phone lights up with a number I used to salute. I should ignore it. I don't.

"Not tonight," I tell the voice made of glass. "No, not tomorrow at nine either. I sent my answer in writing. Please remove me from your list." I delete the contact, thumb steady, a small exorcism.

When I step back into the lantern light, Clara is at the edge of it, keys in hand, expression a careful plainness I've earned both ways. I hold up my empty hands. "I told them no."

"I know," she says softly. "I'm learning how to let that be enough while it's still new."

"Then let me make it old," I answer.

"Tomorrow," she says again, and this time it sounds like a plan.

LATE LIGHT, QUIET VOW

CLARA

Morning tries to pull a stunt at the lighthouse. A kid goes sideways on the steps; Ace plants therapy where pain was thinking about rooting; Ethan does gentle triage while I bully the weather with tape and tone. By the time we get the boy into Mr. Pierce's truck, I've remembered who I am when storms audition for the part of fate.

We stand under the lighthouse eave with salt on our lips and restraint burning pleasantly. He kisses me like we earned it, slow, warm, patient as a vow. "Okay?" he asks my breath.

I cup his jaw, thumb smoothing the day's stubble, and whisper back, "Yes." We laugh when Ace barks once like a chaperone with excellent timing.

Back at the store, I press the blank heart beside the red book in the window. Not naming a thing is not the same as hiding it; sometimes you put the frame up before you hang the picture. Lanterns blink their approval. The lake pretends to be glass. Midnight, tyrant of 12 Maple Street, allows me to live.

This is how we keep a town: lantern by lantern.

ETHAN

After lunch, I asked Noah to walk with me. The lake is practicing calm; the rope bell drops three notes like it's rooting for us. I tell him the truth plain: I was asked to leave; I said no; I'm staying. He tests the sentence for weak spots like a boy who learned the hard way to check the footings. Then he nods once and hands me a napkin sketch of a fox trotting along a book spine, tail pointing to the red lever. "For the AED," he says. "So people slow down for wonder before panic."

I add it above the cabinet where it belongs and pretend I'm not a man who needs a minute in a hallway about a napkin.

At dusk, I bring peonies to the bookstore, decisions, not apologies, Lila's words still pinned to my head, and ask Clara if she'll close early. She does, with a look that makes my knees reconsider their career paths. I unroll a string of fairy lights in her history aisle, and we read each other our favorite sentences from the books that started us. After, beneath paper constellations, I take the little velvet box that's been living in my pocket since the day I moved back and put it where it belongs: open, between her hands.

"I can't give you a different past," I say, voice steadier than I feel. "But I can stack tomorrow after tomorrow until the math loves us. Will you marry me, Clara Monroe?"

The ring is a simple band, bezel-set with a sapphire that gleams like a piece of the lake itself. She looks at it, at me, at the window where a red paper book waits like a lantern with our names in it. She laughs in that way that turns my spine into a home and says, "Yes. On one condition."

"Name it."

"Lanterns, not pirates," she says, eyes wet, mouth brave. "Always."

"Always," I answer, and the bell in my ribs rings three times like it's been waiting to be asked.

CLARA

We keep it small and ours a week later in the square because Willow Cove knows how to make ordinary holy. Rose and Henry read vows that sound like recipes; Lila makes Tom rehearse "by the power vested in me" six times and confiscates every pirate hat in a five-block radius. The Lakewalk Moms string the lanterns and pretend not to cry. Ace wears a boutonnière and takes his job as flower escort with dignity. Midnight claims the velvet ring box as a throne and has to be bribed off it with deli turkey.

Noah gives a speech he pretends is a joke. "Thanks for picking us on purpose," he says, voice wobbling once, and I feel the whole town shift closer to keep us warm.

When Ethan slides the ring onto my finger, I hear the old dock bell in my head, one, two, three, and then, below it, new music we wrote by hand: tape and breath and soup and foxes and a red paper book shining in a window that is finally, blessedly, ours.

We kiss like the beginning and the middle and the end of a thing that knows what it is. The lake applauds with light; the lanterns copy.

Somewhere in the noise, the future clears its throat to speak, and for once it sounds exactly like home.

ETHAN

Later, after the toasts and the dancing and the way the wind carries laughter toward water like it was made for it, Clara tugs me into her bookstore, our bookstore now, where fairy lights are still strung like a sky we get to keep. She pulls me into the history aisle and kisses me slow, the kind of slow that says stay, and I do, and I will.

"Okay?" she asks, the last of the nervous habits that made us.

"Yes," I say, the first of the quiet ones that will keep us.

On the front window, the red paper book holds steady, the blank heart beside it waiting for a name we'll choose together when the time is right. Outside, Willow Cove goes on being itself, soft, stubborn, vivid. Inside, we go.

DEAR READER — THANK YOU FOR LOVING WILLOW COVE. THIS BONUS IS WHERE WE KEEP OUR PROMISES: SMALL-TOWN MISCHIEF, FOUND FAMILY, FOXES IN THE MARGINS, AND A LOVE THAT CHOOSES ITSELF ON PURPOSE. SETTLE IN. LANTERNS, NOT PIRATES.

CLARA

The lake throws itself against the sky like it's got feelings about our vows. Wind shoulders Harbor Street, lantern strings lean hard, and the bell above the shop jitter-rings a warning. I am holding roses that still smell like morning and hot glue that still smells like a plan when the sky tears open.

"Power strip!" Maya shouts from the doorway of the café, curls wild, apron dusted in sugar. "Panic is banned!"

A crackle sizzles across the fairy lights framing our donor window. One spark leaps, hungry for paper hearts.

Not my window. The seam we swore would hold.

I vault the display, fire blanket in one hand, painter's tape looped on my wrist. The first kiss of heat is rude; the second is daring. I smother, press, hold. The flame sulks and folds in on itself as the wind goes greedy at my veil.

"Left edge, top seam," Ethan says, already steady at my shoulder like he was born to make weather behave. He leans in so only I can hear. "I've got the ladder." He catches the ladder, bracing it while I slap a new strip across the pane that sings its glass-thin warning. The bead of rain testing us hesitates, fattens… slides away.

I climb down into him, and for a breath we forget we're on the sidewalk, forget the rumor mill, forget the timeline that got us here. Breath finds breath; everything else quiets. He tastes like peppermint and patience. His palm cups my jaw like he remembers the map.

"Terms," I whisper against the corner of his mouth. This is how yes sounds, grown.

"Still signed," he says, then grins at the exact moment the bell decides to cheer. We both laugh. The town exhales.

Behind us, Mr. Pierce guides Ace up the steps in a teal bow tie. Ace sits and places his chin on a shaky kid's knee like it's the holiest job on earth. Midnight stalks along the sill, sits on my tape, and blinks at physics with papal disdain.

"Do we move this thing inside?" Mayor Tom asks, tie already at half-mast, eyes wide to match the sky.

"Lanterns, not pirates," I tell him, and he brightens like the slogan is a spell. (Willow Cove, remember this.)

Noah appears at my elbow, dressed like trouble learned manners: dark suit, graphite ghost on his thumb. (He'll have to scrub twice to lose it; he won't.) He tips his chin toward the boardwalk. "Give it ten minutes. The lake's just being dramatic, so it can be in the story."

He's right. It is.

ETHAN

We've sutured in ambulances. We've held breath in rooms that wouldn't. Today asks for something trickier: staying still while a town watches you be happy.

The sky calms, as if it has remembered itself. Lanterns lift their chins. Lila barrels down Harbor with a bouquet and a threat for anyone who tries to make my tie behave. "Blue suits you," she says, flicking my lapel. "Also, I'm retiring these flats tonight before they sue me." "So does staying."

I look across the square at the red paper book glowing from the heart of the donor window: deckled edges, the weight of a paperweight, the kind you can feel through your palm, and think about the hands that taped it there: ink-stained, steady, stubborn. My hands ache with the relief of finally holding a life I want.

"Ready?" Tom asks, as if readiness is something people can carry in their pockets.

"Ready," I say, and then Clara is walking toward me on the boardwalk we re-sanded last Sunday, veil tamed by three bobby pins and a dare. Rose and Henry walk ahead, as if they had invented tenderness. The Lakewalk Moms hold lanterns like stars we rented by the hour. The goose cuts through the aisle as if he paid for the honor. "He's on the list," Tom whispers, devastatingly earnest. Ace ignores him on purpose. Midnight inspects the ring box, yawns, and allows it to remain in our timeline. The lighthouse blinks its one-eyed blessing.

Noah takes his place between us. His voice is low and sure when he says, "Welcome. Thank you for choosing kindness on purpose. Also, if anyone sees the goose again, please inform him that the open bar does not apply across species." The whole town hushes.

"I have a speech," he says, and my heart leaves my body and sits on the dock to listen. "It's not long. People think stories are about big moments, but mostly they're about little choices adding up. Like foxes hidden in page margins, so drivers slow down and look." He cuts a look at Clara. She's crying, neat and furious about it. "I'm glad we slowed down. I'm glad we looked." He swallows. "Ethan, you showed up and kept showing up. Mom, you taught me that staying is a verb. I'm proud of both of you. Also, Ace will sign paws at the photo booth."

The town laughs the good kind of laugh, the kind that turns a day into a promise.

CLARA

There are a hundred versions of the first time we promised forever. Under the bleachers, breath tasting like hot chocolate and brass. On the dock, wind steals half our words and gives them back as vows. The night we wrote rules on a napkin with a pen that kept skipping, like it was warning us about storms.

Today's version is bright as wet wood. I take his hands. They're warm, a little nicked (a man of sockets and sinks, of stitches and taped windows). I breathe, and the tape on the pane hums its hush-stick sound inside my bones.

"Hi," I say.

"Hi," he says.

I tuck a paper heart into my vows and keep my voice level. "I loved you like weather when we were kids. It was big and loud, and sometimes it knocked things over. I love you like seasons now. It's a thousand small days where we choose each other on purpose. It's Nora Ephron's quotes on sticky notes and soup at midnight, movie lines scribbled on receipts when the pen's gone missing, and not turning silence into punishment and telling the truth even when timing hates it."

Laughter ripples. Lila dabs at her eyes like she lost a bet.

Ethan's smile goes dangerous and human. "I wrote you a sonnet that didn't work," he says, and the town groans happily. "So I wrote you this: I will stay when the lake is handsome and when it throws a tantrum. I will learn every aisle in your shop by Braille. I will never use our history as a weapon. I will alphabetize our crash cart, spices, and story arcs. I will choose you on the loud days and on the quiet ones, and if the weather breaks the window, I will catch the ladder while you tape our names back onto the glass."

No one is fine. Rose declares it a sacrament.

Maya clears her throat and produces the rings like she baked them. Noah opens the box with a flourish that could run a country. Midnight inspects, approves, and flicks a tail.

"By the lazy authority vested in me by the Commonwealth and the café," Tom says, beaming, "I now pronounce you husband and wife. You may, " he makes a small circular motion like he's directing traffic, "you know."

We do. The kiss is warm and steady and exactly as soft as the life we want. His jaw grazes my cheek; my thumb finds the hinge of his nape. We breathe each other back to the surface. The town applauds in lantern light. The goose honks in objection. Ace yawns in joy. The lighthouse blinks amen.

FLASHBACK — ETHAN

We are seventeen under the bleachers. She tastes like meringue and sky. I tell her the stars are listening; she tells me they're on our side if we are on ours. We write three rules with a pen that ask us if we're sure:

No running without a goodbye. No turning silence into punishment. Tell the truth even when timing hates it.

We fold the napkin, but fail to understand how much ink it will cost us. We leave it tucked where we can find it when it's time to pay.

NOAH

People think kids can't tell when adults mean it. We can. We see it in shoulders, in mouths. Who shows up when the cake collapses?

When the vows are done and the goose has been escorted off the boardwalk with dignity (Ace) and opinions (Tom), I slip around the back of the donor window. The red paper book glows like a dragon egg. My fox, hidden in the gutter of the chalk sign, looks smug in a way only foxes and small victories can.

Lila finds me and bumps my shoulder. "Good speech," she says.

"Good brothering," I say back.

Clara, my mother, who did this with superglue and breath, looks like a person who learned the word ease. Ethan, my father, who showed up and kept showing up, looks like a person who has learned the word 'stay'. I take a photo because someone needs to remember the exact shape of their mouth when the wind stops blowing against them. Graphite ghosts my thumb again when I caption it: We chose us.

Maya rings a bell with the gusto of a benevolent witch. "Dinner!" she announces. "And by dinner I mean joy with sides."

CLARA

The Boathouse smells like butter and vows. We eat food that tastes like the lake learned to be kind. Lila roasts Ethan in a speech that makes everyone cry in public. Rose and Henry dance like the clock owes them a favor. Tom starts the wrong song and calls it democracy.

"Photo booth!" Maya commands, herding us into a corner with props that are decidedly not pirate hats. Quick-cuts: frosting on Ethan's nose, Ace's solemn paw on a toddler's knee, Midnight's tail searing a confetti comet through the frame. Ace sits like a celebrity who remembers his first name; Midnight photobombs like a monarch who does not.

Then Noah clears his throat, and the room hushes with the speed of respect.

He doesn't like microphones. My fingers find Ethan's under the table; a squeeze, small and unseen, steadies the room. He does better without one. He stands on the low step by the window where the lanterns catch his profile and says, "I already said a thing earlier, but I want to say a different one. It's this: thank you for choosing us. Not just me and Mom. All of us. The town. The window. The foxes in the margins. I'm not afraid of the lake anymore." He looks at Ethan. "Or of believing you."

Somewhere, a rope bell rings even though no one can prove it.

ETHAN

Later, after the dancing and the cake and the part where Tom tries to stage manage fireworks with a whisk, we slip outside. Lantern light slicks the boardwalk. The lighthouse blinks its metronome blessing. My hand finds hers like it's got a map.

"Walk?" I ask.

"Always," she says.

We don't go far. We don't need to.

We take our time. The lake smells like cedar and a future that forgives. The crosswalk by the library grins in fox. The donor window throws our names back at us, gold and silver, and the red book burning like a small star.

"I have a surprise," she says, and pulls a folded square from her bouquet. It is soft around the edges, the way bags of flour and napkins and promises get after years. Our rules stare up at me in the handwriting of kids who didn't know anything and meant all of it.

"We made it worthy," she says.

"We did," I say. "And we will."

She steps into me, and the kiss that finds us is not for public consumption. It is slow and sure, made of breath, and the exact right kind of heat. When she breaks away, her smile is the kind that makes clocks charitable.

"Home?" she asks.

"Home," I say, and we mean different rooms in the same house and the same porch and the same couch and the same bookstore and the same clinic and the same town and the same life. We mean the same word.

MIDNIGHT (if a cat could annotate)

Approved. Tail flick. Don't be weird about it.

EPILOGUE LIGHT (A GLIMPSE)

(A tiny bell is stamped in the corner of the programs; Tom insists it was his idea.) A week later, we tape one more name to the donor window in the center where the red book lives. It reads: For the kid who needs the fox on page twenty-seven. People slow down to look. They always do when wonder is involved. They point at the red book's deckled edge; they touch the glass like a chapel, two fingers, then a smile.

Ace does rounds at the clinic and collects three new best friends. Ethan adds a low hook by the front desk for his therapy bow ties; we pretend they organized themselves by color and mood. A girl leaves with fewer knots in her chest and a sticker that says Brave counts.

The goose negotiates a truce with Tom around crosswalk etiquette. (No running. Yield for bells. Honk only once.) Tom chalks a tiny fox in the corner of the sign as a witness.

Lila texts me a picture of a pair of flats she can finally retire. Ten minutes later, she brings me the shoes; we pin them from the rafters of the Boathouse like a charm against blisters and against giving up too soon. She cries, then claims it's just the varnish.

Rose and Henry start planning a poetry kiosk. They commandeer an abandoned lifeguard stand, sand it, paint it robin's-egg, and stencil a quote: Borrow a poem, leave a story. By sunset, there are seventeen folded papers inside. One is a grocery list with a sonnet at the bottom.

Noah sketches our front porch with lanterns in the eaves and a cat ruling from the railing. He hides a fox in the stair shadow for anyone paying attention. He also adds a coffee ring to the corner on purpose, "authenticity," he says, smirking like a man who's met deadlines and won.

Maya pilots a new menu at the café: Joy with Sides becomes a real thing you can order. It's a flight of small comforts, cinnamon toast points, a ramekin of pesto eggs, orange slices, and a miniature slice of wedding cake wrapped in wax paper stamped with the bell. When she delivers two to our table, she clucks at us to sit closer. We do.

We host our first Lanterns, Not Pirates night at the shop, paper-folding and story-sharing until the bell rings nine. Kids write letters to their future selves and seal them with star stickers. Grownups confess the funniest lie they ever told to avoid a bake sale. Someone reads a paragraph about grief that makes all of us breathe in unison for a minute that feels holy.

On Friday, we will try a soft launch of longer clinic hours. The waiting room fills with work boots, macaroni necklaces, and a violin case. A man who hasn't let anyone check his blood pressure since he quit the mill lets Ethan do it because "your kid said you're staying." He leaves with a referral and an appointment he promises to keep.

That night, we had a local dinner date that we had kept promising ourselves during the chaos. The Boathouse saves the corner table by the window; candles reflect off the lake like a string of commas. We ordered the trout we split the first time we said "maybe" out loud. He brings me a bouquet that smells like peonies and new pages. I bring him two tickets to a gallery show where Noah hung three pieces under a pseudonym. We negotiate dessert like diplomats and end up splitting both.

After dinner, we walk the Lakewalk. Lanterns tilt; teenagers practice a waltz; the lighthouse blinks the world into measures. We talk about the next stubborn seam we'll learn to tape: how to be available without disappearing into everyone else's need. We make a rule: one hour on the porch most nights, with phones facedown, and the bell within reach.

Home is a verb. We practice it on the couch, on the porch, in the hallway when the cat decides the staircase belongs to her. We practice it when Ethan's pager rattles and he kisses my temple on his way to be useful. We practice it when I'm counting down the till and a tourist asks if the red book is for sale, and I say no, but the story is.

Sunday morning, a storm muscles the sky and fails to scare us. We brew coffee in the big French press that makes the kitchen smell like applause. Noah shuffles in, hair unparalleled, graphited thumb contradicting his claim that he washed. We make pancakes shaped like bells that look, frankly, like amoebas. Midnight pretends to be bored and then licks syrup off a saucer when she thinks we aren't looking.

On the second Saturday, we hold a community build day for the poetry kiosk. Fifty people come. Three bring power tools, ten bring muffins, and one brings a toolbox that turns out to be full of buttons that say Stay is a verb. We hand them out. People press them to their coats like they've been waiting.

At twilight, Kelsey from the newspaper arrives with a camera and a new hire trailing her, a travel writer on sabbatical who swears he's only in town to help his uncle fix a dock. He and Kelsey try to move the same sawhorse at once. There is spilled paint. There is eye contact that could power a lighthouse. Someone coughs, meet-cute. (We pretend we didn't hear. We did.)

We closed the shop early that night. We string one more line of lanterns across the porch. Ethan reads me two pages of a how-to manual in the voice he uses when he's trying not to laugh; I read him a paragraph from a romance where the bruise is replaced by a promise and the chase is replaced by the choice to stay. We fall asleep on the couch, our knees touching, the bell on the hook by the door catching the breath of the room.

A letter arrives on Monday, addressed in an unfamiliar hand. Inside: A Polaroid of the donor window from the 90s, my mother young, tape between her teeth, eyes fierce. On the back, a note: Found this in a box at the library. Thought you should have it. The bell rang for me, too. E. We don't know which E. We decide it means Enough.

On market day, Tom tries to outlaw flimsy paper plates after a brisk wind creates what he calls a Festive Cyclone. He drafts a resolution on napkins; we pass it unanimously. The goose abstains.

Before bed, we add one more name to the donor window: For the person who thinks they are late. Ethan writes it; his letters are sturdy and a little shy. When we step back, we can see our reflections layered with the names, how we are made of the people who slowed down to look, and the ones we have yet to meet.

And on a morning when the lake wears the sky like a compliment, I unlock the door of Monroe Books & More as my husband kisses me in the doorway and our son pretends not to see. He walks ahead to flip the sign to Open. The bell rings once, twice, three times. Permission. Promise. Home.

Two weeks later, we open the back garden of the shop for the first time. String lights swing between the birch trees, and the ground smells of lemon balm and damp soil. Children dart between chairs holding firefly jars, and someone tunes a guitar softly by the fence. We call it the Bell Garden. Everyone insists it feels like it's been there forever.

Mrs. Alvarez brings a basket of tomatoes, red as punctuation. She insists we slice them with salt on napkins, and for a while, the whole crowd eats like a family, juice on our wrists, laughter spilling into the grass. Ethan pretends not to have dirt on his collar from setting up tables, but I see it; I love it.

We begin to host Saturday Garden Hours, where people come to drink coffee, read aloud, share recipes, or simply sit where the air feels forgiving. The goose tries to claim the herb patch until Tom negotiates yet another treaty: rosemary is for everyone; bells still take priority.

Ethan and I start taking slow walks around the block at night. We pass windows lit like chapters, strangers laughing inside. He says he's learning to believe that choosing quiet isn't the same as vanishing. I squeeze his hand and say I'm learning that hope is allowed to stay, too.

At the café, Maya experiments with a bell-shaped teacake drizzled with honey. She brings one over still warm, winks, and tells us joy has a recipe. We split it three ways, even though Noah swears he only wanted a bite. He sketches the crumbs anyway, later turning them into a print that hangs by the register.

One afternoon, Lila drops off a stack of postcards. Each one has a fox in the corner and a line at the top: Tell someone why they matter. By evening, the basket is empty. The next morning, one comes back, addressed to us. It says only: Because you stayed.

The poetry kiosk fills faster now. Haiku folded into triangles, limericks tucked behind sonnets, recipes with verses at the bottom. One child contributes a knock-knock joke labeled as free verse. Rose and

Henry leave each evening with their pockets stuffed with borrowed words.

We keep adding names to the donor window. Each one feels like a rung on a ladder to somewhere kinder. We read them aloud sometimes after closing, our voices threading with the hum of the lake. And always, the bell listens.

The story isn't finished, but maybe it doesn't need to be. Maybe the point is that home, once chosen, keeps writing itself in pancakes, in painted kiosks, in chalk foxes, in late-night lanterns. In us.

And when the bell rings again, whether once, twice, or three times, we answer. Always.

They were home, not in secrets or storms alone, but in every stubborn choice that brought them back to Willow Cove.

Clara once thought survival meant keeping her walls high and her truths hidden. Ethan once thought ambition was the only compass worth following. But when he steadied her on the boardwalk, when she pressed another paper heart to the glass, the truth landed in both their chests: family is not built from perfect timing, but from the people who show up anyway.

This wasn't just forgiveness. It wasn't even redemption. It was a re-write, the girl with ink-stained hands and the boy who left learning how to be a man who stays. A second chance threaded through fox sketches, donor hearts, and a town nosy enough to cheer them into braver love.

The lighthouse blinked across the water, the donor wall glowed with names, and inside the bookstore, a mother, a son, and the man who claimed them with patience finally breathed the same rhythm. Not because the world bent easy. But because they chose to.

Fierce Reader, thank you. For following every whispered rumor, every storm-lit kiss, every fox hidden on a crosswalk page, every vow that asked you to slow down for wonder. You carried Clara and Ethan through gossip, heartbreak, and the messy, beautiful courage of saying yes to love again.

The window may be taped with paper hearts, but the life inside it? That's theirs.

And they're only just beginning, new bridges, new battles, new dawns destined to glow brighter than the lanterns over Willow Cove. This time, the story isn't written by fear or timing. It's written by them.

Want More Small-Town, Second-Chance Heat?

Join the VIP Reader List for sneak peeks, bonus epilogues, behind-the-scenes extras, and giveaways you won't find anywhere else! Click here to sign up: https://www.bjsteelebooks.com/

ACKNOWLEDGEMENTS

Every book begins as a whisper—an idea tugging at your heart until you finally sit down and listen. *The Secrets We Keep* is no exception, and it would never have come to life without the people who walked beside me through every page.

To my readers, you are the reason I keep writing. Every late-night message, every review, every time you fall in love with a broken hero or a fierce heroine, you remind me that stories matter. Thank you for letting Clara and Ethan's journey find its way into your hearts.

To my family and friends—thank you for believing in me even on the days when the words refused to come. Your patience, love, and encouragement are the backbone of every chapter I write.

To my writing tribe—the critique partners, beta readers, and fellow authors who remind me that creativity thrives in community. You catch the flaws I can't see, celebrate the victories I almost overlook, and remind me to keep going when self-doubt whispers too loudly.

To the indie romance community—you prove daily that love stories are worth fighting for. Your passion fuels mine, and I'm endlessly grateful to be part of such a fierce, supportive, and fire-hearted group.

And finally, to every reader who has carried one of my couples through betrayal, heartbreak, neon vows, or storm-lit kisses, this story, like all the others, is also yours. Thank you for reminding me that love, no matter how messy, is always worth writing about.

1. Knocked Up by the Billionaire Boss

A grumpy enemies-to-lovers romance

Ava Hart thrives under pressure, even when dealing with infuriating boss Liam Blackwood. Cold. Commanding. Billionaire CEO in a suit. One reckless, forbidden night flips their dynamic, leaving her with a growing secret. Secrets don't stay buried in Manhattan Tower, where ambition is cutthroat and trust is a rare commodity. As loyalties shift and careers are threatened, Ava must choose: protect her future or risk everything for the man who drives her crazy... and might own her heart.

2. Knocked Up by the Billionaire Boss: Germany

Enemies in the office. Lovers in the clouds.

Ruth Meyer never meant to fall for Klaus Schmidt, her arrogant, insanely hot German billionaire boss with a dangerous past and even more dangerous enemies. One night in a luxury Miami penthouse changed everything. Now she's pregnant and caught in a web of global sabotage, corporate betrayal, and a vengeful ex who will stop at nothing. When a private jet explodes and Ruth vanishes, Klaus will risk everything, even his empire, to bring her home and protect the family he never thought he'd have.

3. Knocked Up by the Billionaire Boss: Manhattan

An enemies-to-lovers grumpy romance

Nate Sterling is ruthless, rich, and emotionally untouchable, until Evelyn Harper storms in: bold, brilliant, and impossible to ignore. She's the only one who dares challenge him in boardrooms and behind closed doors. One elevator ride, one forbidden night, and a pregnancy secret that could ruin their reputations, or ignite a love neither of them saw coming.

4. **Knocked Up by the Billionaire Bodyguard NY**

Her bodyguard. Her mistake. Her baby.

Sloane Carter, billionaire CEO, is a target in a world where power equals danger. Enter Ronan Stone, ex–special forces, her brooding, grumpy bodyguard assigned to protect her. He moves into her life and her bed. As passion blurs the lines between duty and desire, a surprise pregnancy raises the stakes. With enemies circling, they'll fight not just for survival, but for love, legacy, and the future they never planned.

5. **Knocked Up by the Billionaire Boss – LA**

A grumpy enemies-to-lovers office romance

Damien Wolfe built his billion-dollar empire from the ground up, but secrets hide behind Wolfe Tower's sleek glass walls. Lila Monroe, his new assistant, is curvy, sharp, and completely off-limits. Except she pushes every one of his buttons. One heated night leads to a surprise pregnancy neither of them can ignore. As emotions flare and rivals close in, Damien may lose more than his company; he might just lose the one woman who was never part of the plan but is everything he needs.

6. **Knocked Up by the Billionaire's Best Friend – LA**

A best friend's brother, surprise baby, grumpy/sunshine romance

He's my best friend's older brother, brooding, off-limits, billionaire next door. One towel mishap turns into one night of toe-curling, rule-breaking passion. Now I'm pregnant, and Rhett Wolfe is about to find out the curvy girl he swore he'd never touch is the only one he can't stop thinking about. As secrets spill and family ties are tested, our baby might be the second chance we never expected.

7. **Knocked Up by the Billionaire Boss Oil Tycoon – Dallas**

A Billionaire Legacy Romance of Power, Passion, and Scandal

Debbie Bennett is smart, driven, and in no mood for drama. Taking a temp job at Stone Energy was supposed to be a quick paycheck, not a collision course with Dallas Stone, the dangerously sexy heir to Texas's most powerful oil dynasty. With a sharp tongue and a past full of secrets, Debbie has no intention of playing nice with the arrogant billionaire fighting to control his father's empire. But one stormy night of explosive chemistry changes everything. Now, Debbie's carrying more than just a grudge; she's carrying Dallas's baby. As boardroom battles turn dirty and family secrets come to light, Debbie and Dallas must face the ultimate challenge: trusting each other in a world where betrayal is currency. Because in the ruthless world of Texas oil, love might be the biggest power move of all. If you love billionaire drama, steamy chemistry, Surprise babies, and high-stakes legacy feuds, *Knocked Up by the Billionaire Oil Tycoon – Dallas* is a sizzling must-read. Perfect for fans of legacy romance, alpha billionaires, and heroines who never back down.

8. **Knocked Up by the Billionaire Boss – Vegas**

She's my intern. My enemy. My addiction.

Now she's pregnant, and doesn't know I'd burn Vegas to protect her. Aria Tate is fire in heels and trouble with curves. I tried to stay away, but failed. She crashed my empire, smart-mouthed her way into my bed, and ruined my rules.

Now every glance is a war. Every touch, a surrender. And after one unforgettable night… She's carrying my legacy. But danger's circling. Enemies want her gone. And I'll kill before I lose her. She thinks I'm heartless. She's about to learn how far a billionaire will go for what's his.

9. **The Secrets We Keep (Book 1 of 7) New Series Release! Coming soon, Book 2.** Join the VIP list today, just click the link below and drop your email: https://www.bjsteelebooks.com/

In Willow Cove, gossip spreads faster than a summer storm, and Clara Monroe is about to be the headline.

Twelve years ago, Ethan Hale was the boy who stole her heart, then broke it.

Now he's back, no longer the small-town golden boy, but a billionaire doctor burned out from city life. He returns with swagger, charm, and the same devastating smile… only this time, he has no idea he's the father of Clara's twelve-year-old son.

As the town's newest physician, Ethan is determined to rebuild his life in the very place he once left behind. But between small-town gossip, meddling neighbors, and a fundraiser that throws him into forced proximity with Clara, he quickly learns two things:

Willow Cove never forgets.

Neither does Clara.

Every stolen glance reignites old passion. Every brush of his hand tempts Clara to trust again. But secrets this big don't stay buried, and Ethan is about to discover that fatherhood is messier, and more rewarding, than he ever imagined.

With a protective single mom guarding her heart, a secret son with a sketchbook full of surprises, and a town that thrives on second chances, Ethan must prove he's not the boy who left… but the man who's here to stay.

A swoony, slow-burning small-town, second-chance romance with a secret baby twist, perfect for fans of steamy love stories, meddling townsfolk, and happily-ever-afters that are worth the wait.

10. **Next book: Coming Soon: Join our VIP list today. Make sure you get on the Pre-Order list. Want to name a Character or be listed in the Book 2 of the Series, "The Secrets we Keep?" We will send you an email if you are on our exclusive list.**

Willow Cove's gossip mill has nothing on Mr. Pierce. With his eyes on the mayor's seat and his grip tightening on the town's future, one wrong secret could burn everything down.

Maya Monroe has always been the town's fixer, best friend, event planner, and keeper of smiles. But when Pierce's schemes force her to choose between protecting Clara or saving Willow Cove itself, Maya finds herself tangled in lies, loyalties, and the one man she swore she'd never fall for.

As the town braces for its biggest fight yet, love and loyalty collide. Friendships will be tested, hearts will be risked, and some secrets will prove too dangerous to keep.

Full of meddling neighbors, political heat, and slow-burn romance with a twist, Book 2 takes Willow Cove and other Small town destinations deeper into love, betrayal, and second chances.

Willow Cove never forgets.
And neither does Clara Monroe.

She built her life on secrets, twelve years of raising her son, guarding her heart, and keeping her past locked away. But when Ethan Hale, the boy who once broke her, comes back as the town's new doctor, every hidden truth is suddenly at risk.

Ethan left chasing ambition, but he's back, burned out, with more swagger than sense, and no idea he has a twelve-year-old son waiting for him. Between small-town gossip, meddling neighbors, and a fund-raiser that throws them into forced proximity, Clara and Ethan find themselves face-to-face with everything they ran from.

Every glance reignites what they lost. Every touch tempts Clara to trust again. But secrets this big don't stay buried, and Willow Cove is ready to collect the cost.

The question isn't just whether Clara can forgive Ethan. It's whether Ethan can prove he's not the boy who left, but the man who's here to stay.

Get ready, Fierce Reader. This small town is about to set the stage for love, redemption, and second chances worth fighting for.

Tropes You'll Devour:

✦ Small-Town Romance

✦ Second Chance at Love

✦ Secret Baby / Surprise Son

✦ Protective Single Mom

✦ Billionaire Doctor Hero

- ✦ Meddling Neighbors & Gossip
- ✦ Forced Proximity (Fundraiser Chaos)
- ✦ Family, Forgiveness & Healing
- ✦ Swoony Slow Burn with High Heat
- ✦ Happily-Ever-After Worth the Wait
- ✦ Enjoyed the Story? Let's Keep the Love Going!
- ✦ If this book touched your heart, thrilled your senses, or made you believe in love all over again, please consider leaving a review on Amazon Kindle.

Your words help other readers discover new stories, and they mean the world to authors like me.

💌 Spread the Word

While Amazon doesn't require referrals, your personal recommendation is one of the most powerful gifts you can give.

Please share B. J. Steele's books with your friends, family, co-workers, blog readers, and social media followers. Every share, shoutout, and retweet helps us reach new readers and takes us one step closer to making B. J. Steele a #1 Bestselling Author!

https://www.bjsteelebooks.com/ Visit our website to see what's coming! See you soon.

✨ Join the VIP List

Want to be the first to know about new releases, sneak peeks, and exclusive content?

Join the VIP list today—just click the link below and drop your email:

https://www.bjsteelebooks.com/